CROSSINGS

CROSSINGS

SARAH JOHNSON

SWEETWATER
BOOKS

An imprint of Cedar Fort, Inc.
Springville, Utah

This is a work of fiction. The characters, names, incidents, places, and dialogue are products of the author's imagination and are not to be construed as real. The views expressed within this work are the sole responsibility of the author and do not necessarily reflect the position of Cedar Fort, Inc., or any other entity.

ISBN 13: 978-1-4621-1957-8

Published by Sweetwater Books, an imprint of Cedar Fort, Inc.
2373 W. 700 S., Springville, UT 84663
Distributed by Cedar Fort, Inc., www.cedarfort.com

LIBRARY OF CONGRESS CATALOGING-IN-PUBLICATION DATA

Names: Johnson, Sarah Blake, 1966- author.
Title: Crossings / Sarah Blake Johnson.
Description: Springville, Utah : Sweetwater Books, an imprint of Cedar Fort, Inc., [2016]
Identifiers: LCCN 2016042429 (print) | LCCN 2016043847 (ebook) | ISBN 9781462119578 (perfect bound : alk. paper) | ISBN 9781462127306 (epub, pdf, mobi)
Subjects: LCSH: Magic--Fiction. | Harpists--Fiction. | Orphans--Fiction. | LCGFT: Fantasy fiction. | Novels.
Classification: LCC PS3610.O3766 C76 2016 (print) | LCC PS3610.O3766 (ebook) | DDC 813/.6--dc23
LC record available at https://lccn.loc.gov/2016042429

Cover design by Priscilla Chaves
Cover design © 2017 by Cedar Fort, Inc.
Edited and typeset by Erica Myers and Jessica Romrell

Printed in the United States of America

10 9 8 7 6 5 4 3 2 1

Printed on acid-free paper

For Rick,
my fellow adventurer,
and for my friends

Praise for *Crossings*

"Crossings is a haunting, beautiful book that never leaves you. Gorgeously written, with characters who stay with you long after you read."
 —Kimberly Loth, author of The Thorn Chronicles series and The Dragon Kings series

"Moving and dangerous, this book will keep you turning the pages late into the night."
 —Kimberley Griffiths Little, award-winning author of the Forbidden trilogy

I have found taste reconciling itself to habits, customs, and fashions which at first disgusted me.
—Abigail Adams

First Crossing

Chapter One

~ A TOKEN ~

Eliinka danced her fingers across the harp strings. She hoped she would gain enough coin so she could leave soon. Then it would be less likely that someone she knew, like Rakel or another friend, would see her.

The smell of fresh bread filled the early morning breeze. Most of the market was still in the shade, but soon sunlight would flood the square, along with thick crowds. Maybe someone would enjoy her music so much that they would hire her for an evening or two.

A coin clanked in the small copper bowl, and she murmured a quiet "thank you" as she dropped her head down. A section of her long hair loosened from its braided twist. She moved several brown strands away from the strings. Her chest tightened. She had thought she would get more work. The last man who had hired her had promised to tell his rich friend about her. He was sure that his friend would consider hiring her on a regular basis.

She didn't belong here, not as a street musician hoping to earn enough coin for dinner. She had sold almost all of her possessions after her parents had died last year, except this harp, her mother's harp. Playing this harp brought back memories of her mother, so she refused to sell it. Also, it allowed her to make a living as a musician. She never made enough from performing, so she also taught.

Screams of a woman's voice rose from across the market square. "I'm innocent. He lied. I didn't—I don't have a gift!"

Eliinka plucked louder, faster, pulling the strings so hard they struck each other, trying to drown out the future as market-goers stopped to watch a young woman stumble on the cobblestone street. Tones piled upon tones and notes ran into each other, tumbling out of place.

Two city guards yanked the woman to her feet and dragged her past the overflowing vegetable stands, past the squawking chickens, past the trinkets, past the stacks of bread, and through the upper corner of market, stopping before they reached the fountain. They yanked off her cloak, ripped the back of her dress, and the larger guard cracked his whip. The woman fell. He struck again and again. Blood droplets splattered his washed-out gray uniform. Then the thin guard dumped a bucket of water over her back.

No. With a slap of her palm, Eliinka dampened the harp strings, squeezing them tight until they cut into her skin. Not saltwater. They'd execute the woman in a few minutes. It was what they always did if someone used their gift, their powers.

It wasn't right. Even if one had broken the law, the punishment was too severe. It seemed to happen too often—usually to women too.

The whip snapped again and the woman screamed. The stilled stories from Eliinka's childhood spiraled back into her mind, stories she had forgotten, stories about bravery and sacrifice. Over fifty years ago, soldiers had killed her great-grandparents along with all the others who believed in the faith of Eleman Puusta. All were killed who tried to convince the parliament of Pelto to not go to war against Viru, the country to the south. It was not talked about often, but Eliinka had been able to glean from the whispered conversations that her great-grandmother had used her gift of singing to alter emotions and others had used their gifts of speaking, of persuasion, even after the use of gifts had been made illegal. They had only delayed the onset of war.

The whip cracked again, and Eliinka closed her eyes, released the strings, and plucked a simple folk song. Years ago, when she was seven, she had played in such a way that her thoughts flowed through her arms and out her fingers; commands sang out from her harp. She had told her mother to make sweetbread. Immediately, her mother had removed her hands from the harp. "Never use your gift again," she said.

Eliinka wasn't even sure what she had done. She wasn't sure if she really had a gift or if it would be possible for her to use her gift again. How did people know if someone used their gift? Anyway, she wouldn't interfere. She wouldn't take the risk. The penalty was death.

At the next scream, Eliinka opened her eyes. The woman looked in her direction. "Someone help me," she cried.

Eliinka stopped mid-tune. The bile in her throat sank to her gut. It didn't matter that she wouldn't have enough money to buy food today. She couldn't watch. She scooped up the copper bowl and backed between a metalworker's shop and a meat stall that smelled of fresh blood and wet feathers. She stepped over the innards of chickens and continued up through the market. She paused near the open sacks of a grain stall and dropped the coin into a pouch tucked into her long skirt.

Eliinka turned a corner into an empty alley and rushed away, gripping her harp, ducking under hanging baskets and drooping fabric shade covers. She slowed to keep the harp from hitting the copper bowl and considered the possibility that she had a gift, like her mother thought. Since her parents' deaths, she had avoided thinking about the possibility that she may have a gift. But if she did and knew how to use it, would she have risked using it today?

She zigzagged through side streets and back alleyways, taking the quickest way home. She felt relieved that she hadn't seen anyone she knew in the market. If she had, they would have known that she couldn't make it on her own and they would have felt sorry for her.

That woman was probably dead by now. Eliinka's heart beat so hard it tried to break out of her ribs. Her hands shook, and she dropped her key as she tried to open her door. As she leaned down to pick it up from the dirt, she scanned the empty street. She was glad she lived in a quiet area far from the noisy market.

Eliinka stepped inside and slammed her door. She set the copper bowl down and embraced her harp. Her stomach rumbled, but it wasn't because she had skipped her morning meal.

She set her harp on the table next to a cracked wooden plate. The afternoon sun entered her one small window and dusted her harp with diffused light. She tried to ignore the smells of steaming beef stew and freshly baked sweetbread that sifted through the walls from her neighbors' homes. The door of her narrow cupboard creaked when she opened it. She shoved aside a tin cup, grabbed a plain round of stale bread, and shifted a loose board in the back, finding two hidden coins, which she added to her pouch. Three coins were worth almost nothing.

After dropping the bread onto the plate, she leaned against the table, reached for her harp, and plucked all nineteen strings, from high to low, pulling so hard that the strings struck each other. With most of her possessions sold, she had moved into this one-room home two months ago to save money. Hopefully she could find more students soon. She didn't want to play in that market again.

A silent footstep whispered and Eliinka spun around as her door shut. A woman glided across the center of the room. Eliinka stepped sideways, bumping into her table.

The woman froze.

"Hello," Eliinka said as she released her breath. It was rude to enter without knocking, but this woman must have come to hire her.

This woman stood tall and surveyed Eliinka. Her dress, made of the finest silk, was embroidered near the wrists, waist, and bottom of the floor-length skirt. Fabric ribbons, braided into the light brown hair twisted on top of her head, cascaded down her back. Embroidered blue diamonds covered her handbag. She was tall, more than a hand taller than Eliinka. She looked no more than eighteen, only a year or two older than Eliinka. Her intense deep-blue eyes flicked to the harp. Her blue eyes were very unusual. Most had brown eyes, like Eliinka did.

"I'm Eliinka, the harper. I'm available to play this evening." And every evening, Eliinka added in her mind as she stretched out her hand.

The woman brushed Eliinka's fingers, not giving the normal handclasp.

"Vibrations of your music echo throughout the land," she said in a lilting, soft voice. "It is said that when you stroke harp strings, trees and flowers bend toward you. It is said birds stop singing to hear your voice, and that when you play a song, the sun delays his setting so he will not miss a note. It is said your music creates wonderful dreams for those who slumber."

An honor of a formal spoken greeting! This was the first time Eliinka had been spoken to in such a way, but her heart stopped as the words repeated in her mind. Who said such things about her music? Perhaps someone who had heard her perform had exaggerated her skills or, more likely, this woman embellished Eliinka's skills so as to make the greeting more impressive. She scuffed her feet on the rough, wooden-planked floor.

"I know of no one who tells such tales of my music. It's not possible to do those things. Delay the sun?" A shaking tremor entered Eliinka's voice. No one knew she had a musical gift, and even if it could be that powerful, she would not use her music, not in the ways this woman suggested.

The woman raised one eyebrow, glanced at the harp and back to Eliinka. Then she moved closer, and Eliinka realized she had let the silence go on too long, leaving the woman waiting. "I play for private events, and I teach several students." She didn't say she didn't have many students, now just two. Or that she had less work during the winter: no celebrations, no weddings, and little need for a harp player.

"It is said your music can bring peace." The woman shifted closer, and now stood less than an arm's length away.

"If you wish, I will play for you right now. Would you like to sit?" Eliinka chose the nicer wooden chair, the one with fewer gouges in the seat, and moved it next to the woman.

The woman made a small motion with her hand and Eliinka turned to see if she was going to request a song. The woman settled into the chair just as the door cracked open and two sturdy men slipped into the shadows of the room. Their beards were trimmed very short, more like several days' growth, rather than the beards all men had. They did not wear uniforms, but were obviously her personal guards.

She must be very wealthy to have private bodyguards, Eliinka thought. Maybe she'll hire me and pay so well that I'll never need to play in the marketplace again.

When Eliinka sat on her chair, it rocked back and forth on its uneven legs. She rested her harp on her left thigh and pulled its back against her left shoulder. Her stomach rumbled as the cooking smells intensified from her neighbor's oven. After she played a short song for this woman, Eliinka would ask when she wanted her services.

The woman had mentioned peace. Eliinka placed her fingers on the strings as she chose the song she would play: a peaceful lullaby, the lullaby every mother sang to help her baby fall asleep. Her long, narrow fingers coaxed the enchanting melody to life, and the open chords followed like a waterfall, the separate notes falling one after another. She hummed the melody while she played. The strings responded like a smile to her touch. After she finished, she leaned back in her chair, listening as the overtones faded into silence.

"For a moment peace entered my heart. Could you—" The lady waved back the guard who approached her. "Your music has power. Come with me. You will be my musician."

"Your musician? Typically my patrons hire me only for an evening or a full day." Eliinka did not want to sound too desperate for a job, even though her stomach grumbled. Who was this woman who could afford a full-time musician? It was common for the wealthy to hire guards and maids and cooks. She had heard that the singer, Ainola, had been given a contract by Governor Tuli and now only worked for him. It was so rare for a musician that she had never considered the possibility for herself.

"Your housing—a private room, food, clothing, and anything else you desire will be given to you. You will be able to immerse yourself in your music, and you will have the finest harps to play."

Eliinka studied the back of her hands, turned them over to examine her palms. This was an incredible opportunity. She needed to be careful with her words: she did not want this woman to change her mind.

"Who are you?"

"Jereni." The lady narrowed her lips.

Eliinka did not recognize the name, but this lady surely had friends, the friends who must have told her about Eliinka. Many people had heard her play when she had performed during the summer festival during the past two summers. It may have been one of them or perhaps someone who had hired her to play background music for a dinner.

"Do you live here in RitVa?" Eliinka asked.

"No, but you may return to visit when you wish."

Eliinka ran a finger up and down a string. She had always lived in the city. She couldn't imagine living in another town.

"We will make a contract." Jereni pulled out a sheet of vellum, an ink container, and a curious, gold-inlaid quill from her handbag. Ink decorated the parchment like a melody swirling and dancing. Jereni's ornamented handwriting was beautiful, but it was oddly slanted, and unlike any handwriting Eliinka had seen.

A written agreement was a great honor, and it put them on equal footing. Eliinka stroked the smooth wood of her harp as she placed it on the table. Even if Jereni did not live in RitVa, her house would give her a place to live, perhaps a home. She would not have to keep struggling for survival. This was the first contract she had seen, so she read the words carefully.

Eliinka will serve Jereni with her talented hands, her bright mind, her clear voice, and her pure heart.

Jereni will supply a comfortable room, nourishment, quality clothing, the finest instruments, opportunities to perform, and an excellent education.

Eliinka ran her fingertips down the harp strings as she thought about how her life used to be before her parents' deaths last year. What might change if she signed this contract? She would not be hungry, she'd have a place she belonged, and she'd be able to play her harp all day.

Jereni's lyrical voice sang like a lullaby. "Eliinka, your music will grow. You will play most evenings and for special events. The rest of the time you may practice the harp and participate in other activities. Our contract is a privilege."

Leave RitVa, her home? The only place Eliinka knew? She tensed a string. Could she leave the place her parents were buried? She needed to plant the flowering huuttaa tree on their graves at the year mark and perform the last ritual of Eleman Puusta. It was her responsibility, and she was the only one left in her family to do it, but she could always return for a few days to fulfill her obligation.

Also, what about her friends and students? Her students might not miss her, but her friends . . . she would miss them, even though she hadn't seen them much since her parents died. She hadn't even seen Rakel for a month. Plus, how could she tell Mikali, Rakel's older brother, that she had left? He dropped by to see how she was doing whenever he was in town. The last time he had come, he had brought her food that lasted a week.

"What salary do you require?" Jereni asked.

Eliinka stared down at her hands . . . if Jereni was going to supply everything . . . she wasn't sure what would be fair.

Jereni dipped the quill into the ink. "Three talir per month should be acceptable." She added another sentence to the contract.

She must love music to be willing to pay so much. That was more than four times what Eliinka made every month on good months, and she would have no expenses. The contract would protect her; if Jereni broke it or treated her poorly, Eliinka could return to RitVa.

"Can I use your quill?" As Eliinka signed her name, a thrill rushed through her. Real employment and perhaps a place she could belong. Life would be better, easier.

Jereni interwove delicate loops and curls throughout her signature, which was even more elaborate than the ornamented words she had spiraled on their agreement. Next, she removed a ring from her right hand. Eliinka leaned forward, wondering why. Jereni blotted blue ink onto a gray-blue gemstone and marked an unfamiliar seal—a diamond around a narrow tree with hanging branches—next to her name. She wiped off the stone, slid the ring back onto her index finger, and, after the ink dried, rolled up the parchment and tucked it into her bag.

"Here is my token." Jereni removed her necklace, a chain of engraved gold bars. "I'll abide by our agreement."

"That's too valuable." A token! This was more serious than Eliinka had assumed. Tokens were only used in rare, unbreakable pacts made in older times. She couldn't wear such a necklace.

"The token is given," Jereni said. "Tokens seal our contract."

Eliinka's hands trembled as she accepted the necklace. She had signed the contract and now could not refuse the token. Heavier than she expected, she fingered a link. Every golden link was engraved with a diamond pattern. The gleaming gold glittered in stark contrast to her woven, light brown dress. Who was Jereni, this woman who could give such valuable jewelry as a token to a mere musician? Eliinka wished she could hand the necklace back, but knowing that was not allowed, she fastened it around her neck. The cold metal shocked her skin.

One of the guards opened the door, and a harsh breeze swirled past Eliinka's feet and burned out the embers of her tiny fire. Outside, horses' hooves scuffed the dirt.

"Your token?" Jereni asked in a soft voice.

Eliinka had nothing to give. Every uneven ridge in the worn floor pressed into the leather soles of her thin shoes. There was nothing of worth here, not on the shelves or in the cabinet or in her chest.

Jereni tapped her fingers on the table.

"I have nothing that has enough value to be a token," Eliinka said. She scanned her room again, then looked down at the agreement. This was the opportunity she needed.

"A token is required."

Eliinka looked up at Jereni. "I know. But what could I give?"

"You do have one possession." Jereni's eyes flicked to the harp.

An internal staccato, Eliinka's heart beat so hard it tried to break out of her ribs as she realized the inevitable. If she gave her mother's harp as a token, she could lead a life as a musician, but it would mean giving away her strongest connection to her mother.

The other guard crossed the room. His boots clacked loudly against the wood.

"Your harp could be your token," Jereni said. "According to tradition, the token should have personal value to you. The necklace you now have is my mother's." She stood up and glanced at the door, like she was impatient. "Tokens are required to seal our contract. Eliinka, the harp would always be available for you to play."

Nothing in the world had more value to Eliinka than what she must give. Her breath stopped. The lack of air hurt like a slicing knife. The tradition of a token elevated their agreement and should put her on equal ground with Jereni. It made their agreement stronger. How could an honor of a token be so complicated?

Eliinka choked on her words. "My . . . my harp will be my token." Her ribs collapsed. This was like losing her right hand. Her mother's harp was the last thing she had ever thought to give away, and now it could never be hers again.

Even if it was no longer in her possession, she would never leave her harp. How could she play her music without her harp? She now wished she had not signed the agreement. The necklace, her life—they were not worth this price.

But Eliinka raised her eyes to Jereni and whispered the pledge. "I'll abide by our agreement."

Chapter Two

The river hurtled downstream over rocks and around sharp bends, sending up white spray as it strained to leap up onto the banks and drag trees into its current. Eliinka jerked hard on the reins and stared at the crashing water.

They surely would not cross: it was too deep—too wide. The violent current would sweep them away. A cool breeze slapped her face, and Eliinka pulled her scarf up to the top of her cheeks.

"Where are we?" she whispered, but she did not raise her voice. Jereni had rarely spoken to Eliinka since they had left her home, so she kept her thoughts to herself.

Why was she scared to ask Jereni where she lived? She bit her lips, frustrated with herself. Perhaps it was because of Jereni's coolness, or the long ride and the realization that she would be stuck in a back corner of Pelto. Or perhaps it was the guards and their total silence. Perhaps it was her anger that the harp was no longer hers.

Uncertainty churned up hidden fears. She had assumed Jereni lived within a day's ride of RitVa. Six guards had joined them outside RitVa, making eight guards. Eight guards! They had continued riding southwest. Now they were three days away.

Eliinka shifted in the saddle, ignoring as best as she could her sore muscles. After they had passed a small farm yesterday morning, they had climbed steadily through low hills and scattered trees. When they entered a forest, their path had dwindled into a winding, narrow trail. It would not be easy to return to visit RitVa—definitely not as easy as Jereni had implied.

Jereni's horse lunged forward at a gallop and splashed into the water. When she reached the center of the river, Jereni turned in her saddle easily,

12

as if her horse was not fighting the current. Her eyes locked on Eliinka's, and she yelled over the roar of the water, "Trust your horse! Follow me!"

It was dangerous to cross. Eliinka held tight on the reins, hesitating.

Still, Eliinka would not break their agreement. Whatever the penalty was for breaking a contract, it had to be harsh. Plus, her token harp was in Jereni's waxed saddlebags. It did not matter where they were going, staying with her mother's harp was even more important than the contract.

Eliinka gripped her horse's neck, the horse Jereni had given her, and urged him forward. The water roared like thunder. The icy river splashed at her legs and sloshed into her boots. She shuddered. Urging her horse forward, she focused on the towering trees and dry rocky bank on the other side of the crossing.

After her horse climbed up the bank, she relaxed. Her wet skirt clung to her legs. Shivering, she pulled her traveling cloak tighter around herself, wishing for a warming fire. Thankfully, Jereni had given her both a warm cloak and new boots. Her worn shoes, which she had repaired more than once, would have fallen apart by now.

Jereni dismounted. Her skirt was dry: she had raised the hem to her thighs. Her dress, in the latest fashion, showed no signs of their long ride. She pulled on dry boots.

"I should have removed my boots." Eliinka's words sounded lonely as they dissipated into the forest. She pulled off her boots and dumped the water from them. Now they smelled like wet leather. After she squeezed her feet back into them, she wrung out the fabric of her skirt, trying to stop herself from shivering.

A guard handed Jereni and Eliinka their flasks. Eliinka sipped and then drank quickly, enjoying the fresh spring water.

Jereni drank deeply, her flaming blue eyes never leaving the river crossing. She was stunningly beautiful. Her light brown hair was tinged with blond, high cheekbones accented her oval face, and all her dresses were cut perfectly for her figure. Yet her men did not seem to notice.

Questions and doubts hummed in Eliinka's mind about the contract. How could she begin a conversation with this woman who had more wealth than she had ever imagined and who was obviously deeply private and proud? She sensed, by watching the guards, that Jereni was not someone to cross.

They remounted their horses. The trees, noticeably taller on this side of the river, sprouted between large, broken rocks that spilled across the landscape. Here in the mountains it was late winter with almost no signs of the spring that was everywhere in RitVa. Only a few tight buds swelled on sheltered branches.

Eliinka trailed behind Jereni. Once, she glanced back at the landscape on the other side of the river, and a mix of homesickness and disorientation swept over her. The path had taken so many turns that even with the setting sun, she wasn't sure which direction Pelto was in. It would not be possible to find her way back home on her own.

When they stopped riding at dusk, the guards set up their camp, just like they had previous nights. They pitched one enormous tent for Jereni, which included an outer room where Eliinka slept. One guard piled several logs onto the fire, and four others positioned themselves where darkness met the firelight.

While the quarter moon crested the trees, Eliinka and Jereni ate their meal. Eliinka had never gone so many days without touching her harp, so she played her harp in her mind: rhythms, chords, and melodies piled on top of each other, growing stronger and stronger until words burst out. "Would you like me to play for you?"

"Not tonight. You will play after you arrive at my home."

"It's been three days. I should be doing something, but I've done nothing yet."

"You crossed the river with me." Jereni turned toward the tent while Eliinka searched for words, anxious to learn more about Jereni, stumbling in her mind to find a way into conversation, while wondering why she needed to wait to play the harp. Not playing it left her empty, as if part of her were missing.

"You're the best rider I've ever seen. And . . . and thank you for the horse."

Jereni shrugged and entered the tent, a tent so tall she easily stood upright inside of it.

Eliinka followed, and as she passed through the entrance, the fabric fell across the opening between the entrance room, the small sitting area where she slept, and Jereni's room. She would ask Jereni more questions tomorrow.

Flutes shrieked. Branches snapped. Yells and sounds of fighting crashed into Eliinka's dreams, waking her, and she rolled over, covering her ears. *Why are flutes screaming in this wilderness?* she wondered. Jereni dashed through the divider, throwing off her nightdress, shoving her arms into the sleeves of her dress, and yanking the hem down past her knees. Eliinka threw off her blanket, blinking herself awake.

"Do you know how to use any weapons?" Jereni asked.

"The bow, but I don't—"

Jereni dashed back into her room. Returning with a spear and a woman's sword in her right hand, and her cloak around her shoulders, she thrust a bow and a handful of arrows at Eliinka. "Protect yourself." She sprang outside.

"I don't fight!" Eliinka yanked on her damp boots. Harming others went against her faith, against all that Eleman Puusta taught. Anyway, how could she be expected to fight? Only men fought. She only knew how to use the bow because target shooting had been a favorite pastime of her father. Clangs and yells grew closer. She didn't want to get trapped inside the tent, so she stepped just outside the entrance, looking for a good place to hide. Maybe in the trees.

Wiry bandits, waving clubs and knives, poured into the clearing from all directions. They were barefoot, and their tattered, coarse-woven shirts hung on their bony frames. Jereni's bodyguards fought, their swords slashing through the air, glinting in the firelight.

Eliinka gripped the bow firmly to stop her hand from shaking. Her feet were cold and wet. One bandit ran at her. His arm rose. Eliinka let loose an arrow, aiming at his thigh. He fell before he could strike. She fisted her shaking hands and stepped forward. It was hard to see through the darkness. There was nowhere to hide and men kept running toward her. She cursed under her breath as she shot three more arrows, careful to aim at the bandits' legs, dropping them to the ground.

Eliinka glanced toward Jereni to see if she was still alive. Jereni looked at Eliinka and heaved her spear right at her. She froze, unable to close her eyes as the spinning metal tip approached. It flew over her left shoulder, just missing.

A yell came from behind. She spun. A bandit fell right next to her, a knife still gripped tight in his hand. Her heart jumped into her throat. He had been going to kill her. A guard rushed by. Eliinka held an arrow ready, on the bowstring, and ran toward Jereni, who stood near the fire in the center of the camp. If she could get there, surrounded by guards, she would be better protected. A bandit broke through the guards, dodging them, swinging a club.

Jereni swung her sword down, killing him as another large bandit dove at her back.

As he thrust with his long knife, Eliinka released her arrow. It spiraled forward through the smoke and flames and entered the bandit's upper chest, under his arm, just as he reached striking distance. He fell.

A high-pitched flute screeched. The sounds of fighting turned into running feet pounding on the earth. The remaining bandits fled.

Nodding to Eliinka, Jereni picked up her fallen cloak. She pulled it around her shoulders while stepping over the man she had just killed with her sword.

Unable to move, Eliinka stared at the bow in her hands, the next arrow already nocked and ready. She had shot arrows at men and hurt them. *It was in self-defense*, she argued to herself. It was allowed by her faith to protect one's own life. Still, she felt unclean. Smoke filled her lungs. Her eyes watered.

All eight of Jereni's bodyguards circled the camp, searching the forest. They dragged four men across the ground and silently dropped them at Jereni's feet. One guard bandaged another's arm.

"Who injured these men?" Jereni frowned.

After a long, drawn out breath, Eliinka said, "I did."

Jereni raised an eyebrow. "Eliinka, how many arrows did you shoot?"

"Five."

"Did you *aim* at their thighs?"

"Yes." Her father had taught her to never aim toward any living creature, and tonight she had, tonight she . . . she had shot . . .

"It is more merciful to kill." Jereni's eyes reflected the embers of the dying fire. "We cannot travel with them." She motioned toward the large bandit. "Yet, you managed to kill their leader."

Eliinka dropped the bow, collapsed to the hard ground, and looked at her hands, expecting to see blood dripping from them. "I didn't try to kill him." She held back her tears, refusing to let them cascade down her cheeks. Was her future, her eternities at risk? Killing was forbidden. She picked up one of the remaining arrows. She broke it in half, broke the halves in half, and threw them into the fire.

Jereni spoke in a hushed voice to her guard leader. He motioned, and the other guards dragged the wounded men away, into the trees. "Take care of them. Dispose of the dead."

Eliinka broke a second arrow.

"Stop! Those are my good arrows." Jereni heaved Eliinka up by her wrist. She ordered a nearby guard, "Bring water to my tent. We will leave at first light."

Nothing seemed real. As Eliinka passed the fallen men, her whole body shook. Blood still flowed from wounds, from slashes across faces, from holes in chests. There were so many, she couldn't count the dead bodies. Her legs wobbled as Jereni dragged her to the tent.

"You must calm down!" Jereni opened the divider to her room. "Come in!"

Eliinka stumbled into a room of sorts: bright silks draped the walls and elaborate carpets covered the ground. Her harp sat in a corner.

"Examine my back! What do you see?" Jereni removed her cloak and spun around, exposing her back to Eliinka.

"You're bleeding." Eliinka's stomach flipped upside down. Blood dripped from Jereni's torn dress.

"Promise you will never tell anyone of my injury." Jereni still clenched her sword.

"But you need help!"

Jereni turned, and with her other hand she gripped Eliinka's shoulder so hard that her fingernails cut into Eliinka's skin, almost puncturing her flesh. "You must promise me. Immediately!" Her eyes flashed, and she lifted the sword. Its tip was still red with blood.

Eliinka pulled away and tripped backward into the tent wall.

"I . . . I promise that I'll never tell anyone of your injury," Eliinka said, hoping that giving this odd promise would calm Jereni down.

"Bring in the pan of water. You will tend my wound." Jereni placed her sword on top of the chest.

Eliinka rushed into the outer room and returned with the pan from where the guard had left it just inside the entrance.

"Cut away the fabric. Clean the wound with water." Jereni handed Eliinka a knife and a cloth. She lay face down on her mattress. "Then press the cloth to my back until the bleeding stops."

Blood seeped through the dress's fabric. Eliinka took a deep breath and sliced the dress from the neck to the waist. She pressed firmly on Jereni's skin, hoping to stop the blood flow.

"How is it?" Jereni tensed, but did not show any sign of pain.

"It's still bleeding. It's a hand in length. Deep too. This is the worst cut I've ever seen."

"Bring my mirror."

Eliinka found the silver mirror sitting near a candle.

Jereni took it, twisted her body, and examined her back. "The cut is to the bone and should have stitches. Can you use a needle?"

"Not well."

"Your face is pale. If you are not experienced with a needle, you will not sew my flesh. Pull the skin tightly together and bind it as tight as you can with the bandages."

The ground moved upward at a funny angle. Eliinka shifted her weight evenly between her feet.

"Will you faint?"

"Just tell me what to do." Eliinka spoke through gritted teeth, and after steadying her hands, she again held the cloth firm against Jereni's back.

"You fought well. This was your first time." Jereni tried to look at her wound again.

"Yes." Eliinka's voice sounded strange, like it wasn't her own, like she was not herself. She had shot men.

The light flickered, bringing her attention back to Jereni. The wound was no longer gushing blood, so Eliinka held the skin together and wrapped it tight, looping cloth around Jereni's lower ribs.

"Your hands are still shaking."

Eliinka curled her fingernails into her palms. She couldn't stop thinking about her arrows plunging into their targets, the man crumpling to the ground, and Jereni's cold attitude. Fear rushed through her. She had almost been killed. She had taken a life. Everything fogged in front of her.

"You protected me. You will be rewarded beyond our contract." Jereni picked up her nightdress from the carpet. "Did you get injured? Any cuts or bruises?"

"No. Well, I don't think so." Pain shot through Eliinka's head, but it was not from injuries. It was not her own blood on her hands and clothing. "Are we safe now? We must be near the borders to be attacked by bandits."

"The attackers—they call themselves People of the Flute—know my guards are trained fighters. None that hate me are that bold. They did not realize who they were attacking. But they do now. They are frightened and will not return. We are safe. Go rest."

None of what Jereni said made any sense. Eliinka rinsed her hands in the pan of water, cleansing the blood from them as a way to stay a moment longer. She could not tell if the water was hot or cold.

"Jereni, I have a question." The contract was written as if between equals, and Eliinka reminded herself she needed to treat it that way.

"You may ask." Jereni's voice came out terse, irritated.

"Where are we? I thought all of Pelto was within a two or three days' ride. Which town are we near?"

Jereni pulled her nightdress over her head, letting it drop over her body. She pursed her lips. "Did our agreement state we would stay within Pelto?"

"No."

"The climate to the south is very enjoyable."

"But that's where the Kingdom of Viru is! We can't be in Viru."

"We crossed the border when we crossed the Urho River."

"We . . . we've always been at war with Viru," Eliinka said. "We can't go there. Their men kidnap our youth." This was only one of the many stories that were told. "Their clothing doesn't cover all their skin, and it's even said that some mark their bodies with colorful designs. They're savage barbarians. The king rules with violence. You don't have enough men to protect us!" Her breath ran out.

"Viruns are not what you think," Jereni snapped. "Jalolinna, the capital, is my home." She raised her chin as if daring Eliinka to say more.

Why would Jereni want to live in Viru? Pelto was safer. Eliinka stepped backward until her shoulders touched the wall of the tent. How could she return to RitVa? And what about her harp?

"No harm will come to you. You are under my protection."

Eliinka's shoulder muscles tightened and her hands clenched each other. She should not have signed the contract. Would she be able to practice her faith, her meditations?

In a silvery lilt, Jereni said, "Do not be afraid. Viru is good."

Eliinka picked up the harp from the open bag and sat on Jereni's bedding. Not caring that Jereni had told her to wait until they arrived at her home, she struck wrong, harsh notes as she played a folk song. Irritated at the discord she created, she played the song slower, in tune, thinking. Jereni had saved her life, so she would have to trust her—a little. They had a contract neither could break. She would find a way to reclaim her harp and a way to fulfill the contract, perhaps find a way to alter it, so she could return to Pelto. As she played, she relaxed and the ache, the emptiness dissolved. When she finished the song, she hugged the harp.

"You must sleep now." Jereni uncurled Eliinka's fingers from the harp frame. She grabbed Eliinka's wrist, pulled her to the other chamber, and returned to her room without a backward glance.

Eliinka lay down and wrapped herself in a blanket. She shivered as she tried to remember what else was said about Viru. But no one had ever visited Viru.

Not peacefully, at least.

Chapter Three

The clinking of the hooves on the cobblestones counterpointed Eliinka's heartbeat. Sweat beaded on her skin, and the sun beat down on her head.

Jereni was Virun! The clothes she had put on this morning were obviously not Pelten. Her arms and neck and lower legs were bare; her dress was elaborate, the brightest blue, and she wore gold necklaces, bracelets, and anklets. No Pelten woman would ever consider dressing like that!

Early yesterday morning, before breaking camp, Jereni's guards had shaved off their beards. None of the men had a trace of a beard today.

It should have been obvious. As she rode, Eliinka thought about what had been abnormal when they had first met: Jereni not knocking on the door, her formal greeting, her slanted handwriting, the guards never speaking, and Jereni giving the token.

The city was huge and the roads were cobbled, a big change from the previous two and a half days of riding: the morning after the attack it had been such challenging terrain that Eliinka wondered how her horse could keep its footing, and she had struggled to stay on its back. Jereni had ridden as if she did not have an injury and had not shown any pain when Eliinka had changed her bandage in the evenings. As yesterday morning passed into afternoon, the riding had become easier. The faint trail looped into rolling hills and descended to flatter land. The trail grew into a small lane that widened when they entered a region filled with prosperous farmlands. Today, the sixth day of their travels, it became a wide road that led to the outer quarter of the city.

They had been riding in this never-ending city for almost an hour. Eliinka's muscles ached, and she hoped they'd arrive at Jereni's house soon. This was all so different from Pelto. The wide streets, lined by low wooden buildings, were crowded with people milling about. The crowds of people wore bright, colorful clothing that was tightly woven, and all the women's arms and legs were bare, like Jereni's. How could they wear clothing like that? Their hair was loose, falling down their backs. None of the men had beards, unlike Pelten men, and they wore short-sleeved shirts.

Eliinka tried to block out the cheers and chatters of an unfamiliar language, but couldn't. She kept her focus forward, on Jereni's back, and moved so close behind that the tail of Jereni's horse flicked the nose of Eliinka's horse.

They climbed a hill toward an immense stone building topped by steep wooden roofs. Bright blue, red, yellow, and green paint colored every wall. A sudden unison of low and high horns blew, and Eliinka was swept past gleaming gates into a large courtyard.

A guard grabbed her horse's halter. "Lapne avt." It was the first time a guard had spoken out loud that she had heard. He spoke slowly and clearly as he motioned toward a tall building to the right.

What was she supposed to do? Eliinka looked at Jereni.

Jereni, who was already off her horse, gave her only the slightest glance. As she walked across the courtyard, everyone bowed.

The token gold necklace slid against Eliinka's neck as if it would slice into her skin. It suddenly occurred to her that the necklace was far too valuable for a typical wealthy person to give away or even own.

This wasn't a normal building or house. It was a palace.

Two men greeted Jereni. The older one, with gray hair, was slightly shorter than Jereni, sturdy, and thick. The younger man was tall and slender, with short, dark brown hair. They walked together through towering doors.

Eliinka slid off her horse on the side opposite the guard and pounded her head against the saddle. How could she have been so blind? She was trapped, a hostage, maybe a slave, to Viru's princess.

There were other stories told, legends about Viru's princess. Beautiful and cruel, she was strong and fearless. She couldn't be killed and she strikes down men with only a glance. This explained why Jereni was so skilled with the sword. Why she was so powerful and killed without remorse. Why she would plunge fearlessly into battle. It would be easy to be fearless if one knew they couldn't be killed.

She remembered their conversation the other night, when she had called Viruns bloodthirsty barbarians. Jereni's response—she should have seen it then. Eliinka ran the words of their agreement through her mind.

She had forgotten about time—it was possible the agreement would not end until her death.

The guard led her horse away. Eliinka stood there, alone in the courtyard, curling her fingernails into her palms. Viru was ruled by a king. It was so different than Pelto, where the people had a say and parliament ran the affairs of the land. The gates clanked shut. Jereni was gone, out of sight, and though many glanced Eliinka's way, none approached her. Servants, men, and women filled the courtyard, intent on their tasks; some were hurrying, one was running, and all were moving with purpose. They spoke with a quick clip and tripping rhythm. The language: no wonder Jereni's guards had remained silent. It was part of her disguise. Eliinka took a tentative step toward the building the guard had pointed to.

What was she supposed to do? Dare she break the contract and find a way home? Escape past all these guards and through the wilderness and the forests by herself? There was no way. She turned a full circle, taking in the busyness and the bright-colored buildings and the full, heavy, dropping sun.

A young, slender girl of twelve or thirteen with waist-length hair and a broad face beckoned from the tall building. Eliinka followed her through massive doors that were twice as tall as she was. Her footsteps echoed on polished stone floors inlaid with pictures, and as they walked through one hall and another and another, they passed relief-carved wooden paneling, towering windows, and colorful tapestries. They wound down narrow stairs into the kitchen, a long room with many fires and cooking hearths. Everyone turned and stared as they entered. Eliinka interlocked her fingers, squeezing them tight. The girl motioned to a narrow bench with her small, callused hands, and placed a plate of food on the table in front of Eliinka.

Eliinka sat on the bench, realizing she was starving. She had not eaten in hours. But she choked on her first bite. The flavor was sharp and hot. She pulled her seared tongue to the roof of her mouth and, sealing her lips to keep from yelling out, she swallowed without chewing. Quick, she grabbed the cup and gulped down juice, which soothed her tongue only while the juice passed over it. Poking at her food, trying to choose something that would not burn, she listened to the chatter of the cooks talking with the girl. It was all a blur of sounds; she could not understand any of the words or sentences. She chewed a piece of bread, and, under the stares of the girl, gulped down the spicy food, drinking juice and eating bread between every single bite.

Their food. Their language. Their clothing. All so different, so strange beyond what she could have imagined.

After Eliinka finished eating, the girl led her up several flights of stairs, through a series of halls, and opened a carved door. The girl pointed, but didn't enter, so Eliinka stepped inside and the girl closed the door behind her. Her first step echoed on a dark hardwood floor, her next sunk into a thick carpet.

In one corner, on a small table, sat the harp. Her harp. If she could play it and close her eyes, she would pretend to not be here, pretend she had never signed the contract.

A small fire flamed in the corner hearth and cool evening air flowed through the open windows, carrying the spicy scent of an unfamiliar flower. Fabulous tapestries hanging on the walls told unfamiliar stories of battles and hunts, weddings and celebrations, and individual portraits of men and women were hung along the wall between the fireplace and the outer wall, which was lined with three windows. Cushioned chairs faced the fire and were arranged around a large, low table upon which lay several books.

She did not belong here; not with such wealth, not in a palace. Not in Viru.

Eliinka fingered the cold necklace that bit at the back of her neck and considered removing it and flinging it onto the table, into the fire, out the window into the black night, somewhere . . . anywhere.

The door opened and Princess Jereni swept into the room wearing a narrow golden crown decorated with jewels. She had changed her dress. It was cut in a Virun style and was a dark, deep red. The cloth itself was patterned with raised threads. She wore the same gold necklaces, bracelets, and anklets that Eliinka had seen before. Still standing near the door, Eliinka nodded to her. She did not bow.

"Change my bandage." Jereni motioned toward the fireplace. A basin of water rested on the hearth and clean cloths lay on a footstool.

No servants entered the room. They were alone.

Was it trust? It was not, Eliinka realized, but it showed Jereni's confidence that she could control Eliinka if needed.

Eliinka glanced at the harp. She found the courage to speak.

"Am I here as your prisoner?" Clenching her fists, trying to keep her hands from shaking, Eliinka hoped her question would not anger Jereni.

"You are my musician." Jereni sounded insulted. "You will not be treated as a servant, but as my guest. You will be given the best room, very near mine." She touched Eliinka's upper arm. Eliinka wanted to jerk away, but feared Jereni would be insulted and strike her.

In a silvery lilt, Jereni added, "Do not be afraid. Viru is good. You would not have willingly come if you had known my identity."

"You are the princess of the legends." Eliinka's words spilled out before she could stop them, but she did not add the rest of her thoughts: *you are the princess who kills anyone who crosses her.*

"The legends about the princess of Viru are not all true."

Eliinka wondered which legends were true and which were not, but Jereni did not elaborate.

"My bandage must be changed." Jereni shoved the books aside and sat on the table. Even though her dress covered much less than a Pelten dress, it still covered the entire bandage. She pulled down the top of her dress, exposing her back.

After hesitating for a moment, Eliinka removed the outer bandage. She grimaced at the fresh blood seeping through the inner bandages. "You're still bleeding." She bit her lip. "You need stitches. You need a healer, some-one besides me."

"It's too late for stitches. The inner bandage must be changed, but be gentle. Apply this cream." Jereni pointed to a small jar near the bandages. "Then bind it tight. Perhaps the scarring will be minimal." She showed no sign of any pain as Eliinka touched her back, carefully peeling away the bandage from the skin.

As Eliinka worked, Jereni spoke. "The girl who guided you earlier is your maid, Milla. She will tend your fire, clean your room, wash your clothes, and take you where you need to go until you know your way around my palace. After we are done tonight, she will take you to your room. Every evening, you will play for me here in my study. You can bring me the peace I seek."

How could Jereni want peace? She was a barbaric princess, one who didn't mind killing. She acted like the princess of the legends, just like all the stories told.

Eliinka carefully and firmly secured the bandages.

"I'm finished," Eliinka said.

Princess Jereni pulled her dress up and over her back and shoulders. She turned and looked right at Eliinka. "We fought for each other's lives." She paused as if in thought. Her eyes passed across the wall of portraits.

"As my musician, you will receive the blue diamond on your hands."

"A blue diamond?" Eliinka outlined one of the diamond patterns on a link in her necklace with her fingernail. Diamond patterns accented the dress Jereni wore tonight. Diamonds decorated the carpet, the ceiling, and the picture frames. It must be a symbol of the royal family.

"It is traditional to mark the lower arms and hands of a musician with the blue diamond."

Eliinka had assumed that this particular story about Viru was false. Not one person they had passed in the streets this morning had a marking, not on their arms, faces, or legs, and Jereni had none either. Eliinka did not want her skin marked.

"My symbol will be placed tomorrow morning. You will find it beautiful." Jereni steadied Eliinka's shaking hand and touched the back of Eliinka's forearm, drawing a line to the center of the back of Eliinka's hand. "It is a great honor."

Eliinka's skin tingled. People in Pelto never marked their skin. It was a primitive, barbaric practice. How could Jereni call it an honor? She had never seen such markings, and now she would have them all over her hands. Was there a way to refuse?

"The harp is waiting for you." Princess Jereni reclined in a thick leather chair.

Eliinka rushed to the harp and collapsed into the soft chair sitting beside the small table. Playing it would clear her mind and make her stronger; it would make the aches and pains in her muscles from the long ride go away. Her stomach knotted. She couldn't allow her skin to be marked. It would most certainly hurt, but more than that, she would be forever marked and when she returned home, everyone in Pelto would know she had been to Viru.

Yet the contract was clear: she had promised to serve, to obey. Jereni had the power to take everything away, even her music, if she broke their contract.

Eliinka plucked each string sharply, one at a time, making biting sounds. The harp was in tune. While playing an active dancing song, a song that moved as quickly as her thoughts that leaped from one idea to another, she considered how to escape her situation. The fire flamed brighter, and Jereni placed her feet up on the table and leaned her head back, staring at the row of portraits hanging on the wall closest to Eliinka.

Perhaps the only time Jereni could feel peace was when music was played. Jereni's eyes closed, so Eliinka glanced around the room, looking from Jereni to the door to the fire, which still flamed too bright. She played a string of notes as she modulated into a new song, the lullaby that Jereni had enjoyed before, the lullaby her mother had first taught her. It was her mother's favorite song.

Eliinka wished that the token harp that had been her mother's could somehow be hers again. She wished her contract void. She wished that Jereni would forget about the markings she planned to put on Eliinka's arms, and she wished she could find a way back to Pelto, to a simple, peaceful life, where in a few years she could marry a man she loved and who loved her. Cool night air filled her lungs as she took a deep breath and focused on what she wanted: a place where she belonged, a home—filled with family and friends like she had before her parents had died.

Memories of Eliinka's mother tugged, and when she repeated the song, she played with all her heart, dreaming, wishing. The tempo increased and the song fused with her emotions. It was no longer the calming lullaby, but a fast-paced, urgent song, where the melody and harmony flipped and raced. Higher notes flowed on top, higher than the strings normally sounded, and as Eliinka fully entered the music, subtle emotions and power flowed through her arms and fingers and she thought what she dared not express, telling Jereni to return her harp and release her from their contract. The music flowed, lulled her into relaxation as she blocked out the world around her.

A hand clamped on Eliinka's shoulder. She jumped. What was she doing? Playing like this? Her heart stalled. She stopped using her gift and nuanced the song back into the calm lullaby. How had she used it without any forethought, when she should keep it hidden? If her gift was allowed in Viru, Jereni might insist that Eliinka misuse her powers. Had Jereni sensed that she was using her gift? Was that why Jereni was gripping her shoulder with such force?

"The lullaby must be played much slower. It should create a relaxing atmosphere. You are anxious, and it enters your music." Jereni released her shoulder. "You don't trust me, do you? Do you think you will be treated poorly? That our contract can be broken by either of us?" The corners of Jereni's eyes wrinkled as a faint smile surfaced.

"No. No, I mean, yes, I believe you will keep our contract. That you will treat me fairly, as promised." Eliinka played while she spoke, plucking each string with too much force. The melody came out unevenly, and she could not find the heart of the song. She had broken her promise to her mother when she used her gift. She hit a wrong note.

Jereni winced. As she walked out of the room, she said, "Practice the songs you plan to play for me each evening."

Chapter Four

~ BLUE DIAMOND ~

Wrong note after wrong note crashed into each other and tumbled to the floor. Eliinka lost her place. She had never played so poorly. Someone tapped her on her shoulder. They must want her to stop playing.

"Eliinka," Milla said.

Morning? Her playing hadn't been real?

Eliinka opened her eyes. The sun glinted through the window. How did she sleep through her daily morning meditations? Perhaps because this bed was the nicest she had ever slept in. Tomorrow she would wake early, before Milla entered, and later today she would find a quiet place to meditate. She jumped out of bed, and her feet sank into a soft carpet.

Juice and steaming bread and fruits sat on a table in front of a fireplace. A small fire burned. The just-baked bread smell mingled with the sweetness of flowers blooming in a tall tree outside her open window.

The previous night Eliinka had been too tired to notice her new room. It was huge, with a sitting area in front of the fire. The tall ceiling was close to two stories high and large windows overlooked the colorful city. Another door was on the opposite side of the room, flanked by tall wooden cabinets. Inlaid wooden furniture sat about the room, and in the corner stood the painted screen that she had bathed behind last night when she could barely keep her eyes open. She moved to the nearest window to look outside. This room was up high, three floors or more above the ground level.

Milla said several sounds, sounds that must be words, and pointed at the food and at a dress draped on a chair.

This was not a dream or a nightmare, though in some senses it was both. *My new life*, Eliinka thought, and *I have to learn how to live here*. For now. She wished her harp were with her in her room. She always played before her morning meal; it was the best way to begin the day.

Milla spoke again, pointing to the dress. Eliinka's own dress was nowhere within sight, so Eliinka picked up the Virun dress, amazed at how little fabric it had and how light it was. She struggled to put it on, and Milla had to help her. She wanted to tell her to go away, that she could dress herself, but how, when they didn't speak the same language? The dress felt wrong. It was wrong. It was form-fitting and short; the hem fell above her knees. The neckline was lower and more open than she had ever before imagined someone would wear, and its sleeves barely covered the top of her shoulders. The air tickled the skin on her arms and legs. And her neck. The necklace now lay on bare skin below her collarbone.

Milla pointed to some dangling topaz earrings that lay on the table. Eliinka took out her own earrings, ones her grandmother had given her, and put them on. This was beyond what their contract required. The elaborate room and clothing. The jewelry.

Milla pulled out the chair near the table and stood near the fireplace. It appeared she would wait while Eliinka ate.

As Eliinka choked down her food, she thought about the day ahead. Was there a way to refuse? She could not find her way home on her own. So far, she was being treated well and she should have more freedom if she cooperated. She would always have plenty to eat. She left half the food on her plate and stood, nodding to Milla that she was done eating. If she refused the markings on her skin, Jereni would take away everything. She took a deep breath and followed Milla out the door.

The artist pricked Eliinka's arms and hands all morning. Sharp, cold metal inserted into her skin. But she did not jerk or pull away. She did not scream. Instead she closed her eyes, willed herself to another place and listened to harp music in her mind. Even so, she was unable to block out the occasional increase in pressure as the artist worked.

The pricks stopped and Eliinka opened her eyes. Milla said words Eliinka didn't understand and motioned for her to follow. She did not look down at her arms as she blinked back stinging tears. They walked through a maze of halls past staring guards. When they approached a group of chatting women, their blur of words stopped. Eliinka wanted to hide her skin. After continuing down the hall and up a wide staircase and into another long corridor, they reached a familiar ornate door, the entrance to the study where Eliinka had played the harp the previous night.

After knocking, Milla opened the door. Eliinka stood on the threshold, hesitating, but Milla pushed her into the room.

Her arms! She gasped as she saw them at last. Deep-blue diamonds and intricate designs decorated them. How could she ever go home now? Peltens would never accept her, not like this.

"Good morning," Jereni said, from where she sat in front of the fire.

Eliinka stumbled through the doorway. The door slapped shut.

"Show me your hands."

After a slight bow, Eliinka crossed the room and held out her hands. The narrow diamond on the back of each hand was placed so one point touched the bottom knuckle of the middle finger and the opposing point, in the long direction of the diamond, touched where her hand met her wrist. Narrow, intertwining lines led from the base of the diamond up to a small circle placed in the middle of Eliinka's forearm.

"This is beautifully done."

Eliinka flexed her fingers. It seemed Jereni waited for a response, so she spoke. "This is never done in my land. My hands, my arms, they are . . . " Jereni's face was impossible to read, but she seemed to grow more distant; her skill with the sword and sparks of anger that occasionally flared in her eyes came back to Eliinka. She didn't want to upset Jereni. Nothing in their contract stated she could play the token harp, and she wanted to keep playing it. Her mind fumbled for something to say that might ease the tension in the air. "Please, I'd like to know the meaning of the symbols I wear."

Jereni touched the circle on the back of Eliinka's arm. "The circle suggests unending and eternal." She ran a finger down to the wrist. "The intertwining lines signify how each of our lives influence the other, and how you will be interwoven into Viru." Jereni traced a blue diamond. "The diamond is the symbol of the royal family. At this time, you are the only living person in my kingdom with the mark of my family. You are given an honor to be my musician."

Eliinka turned her head away to hide the moisture in her eyes.

"Is there any pain?" Jereni asked.

"A little." Most was in Eliinka's mind, the shock that she was in Viru. The necklace slid against her bare skin, and she tugged her neckline up.

"Music can make you forget pain. When you leave the study in a few minutes, Milla will take you to the Dining Hall and show you the large harp that sits there. You can play it. You will have time every day to practice."

Eliinka nodded. She didn't get to practice on her token harp? She curled her fingernails into her palms.

"That is the harp you will play for official events. It will take time for you to become proficient, yet you will need to play soon. Also, today you will start your language lessons. Milla will show you the way."

Eliinka didn't want to speak their language! Yet the contract required that she serve Jereni. She thrust away the thoughts of breaking the contract or refusing. If she did, she wouldn't be allowed to play her music at all and would have no hope of ever returning to Pelto. If she could play her music, she could survive the challenges of living in Viru. Maybe if she did well, Jereni would return the harp.

"You may get sun and fresh air in the Garden Courtyard in the mornings, if you wish. This afternoon, after you practice, you will start your culture and language lessons. Lord Zerin will teach you of Virun culture and practice conversing with you in Virjalo. These lessons will be every day for an hour before dinner in the White Room, just off the Dining Hall. In one week you will speak only in Virjalo with me."

Impossible! The language sounded like a mixture of sounds without words. There was no way she would be able to carry on a conversation for even one minute.

"Tonight you will play at a formal dinner in front of my guests. You must prepare. You can't make mistakes like you did last evening. Also, you will come to this room, my study, every evening and play for me." Jereni opened a book that was in her lap.

Eliinka lightly touched the swollen skin on the back of her left hand. She moved her fingers. Her skin didn't hurt. She'd still be able to play the harp. She glanced at her token harp. This evening, and the harp, seemed very far away.

"Eliinka." Jereni's voice cut through her thoughts.

"Yes." She stood up straighter, hiding her fear.

"You will never be asked to do anything that you are not capable of doing. Eventually you will love Viru in the same way you love your music."

Chapter Five

Milla led Eliinka into the Dining Hall, a towering room that was big enough to hold a large house. A massive table stretched the length of the room. It would seat over a hundred people. Milla moved her hands like she was plucking harp strings and pointed to a corner where a large harp sat with other instruments.

Eliinka barely glanced at the horns, bells, drums, and some odd, unfamiliar stringed instruments that sat on a slightly raised platform near the harp. This harp was huge, almost as tall as Eliinka, and had at least fifty strings, many more than her token harp. It was too large to hold in her lap, so she sat in the chair behind it, leaned forward, and plucked a string. The wood was not only carved but also inlaid with precious jewels and gold. First, she played using the strings she was familiar with, then she slowly added strings, in upper and lower octaves, listening to the new pitches. Each note vibrated, pulsing into her skin and soaring up to the high ceiling. The harp was in tune.

The music soaked into Eliinka's flesh and surged through every nerve. This harp had amazing tone and responded to her touch better than she could have imagined. While she played, she forgot about the markings on her arms, that is until she glanced down and saw the colors, the patterns.

Suddenly, she stopped mid-song. The strings continued to vibrate.

Eliinka plucked one string, over and over, louder and louder, telling herself that her arms didn't hurt, telling herself she wasn't really sitting in a palace in a hostile, foreign country, telling herself she was lucky to be alive. One string became two strings, dissonant, then three strings, striking against each other. The sound was too harsh, so she sank back into the song.

After a couple hours, Milla returned. Losing her concentration, Eliinka dragged her fingers high to low across the strings. She still was not fully prepared to play for the dinner this evening, but if she only played simple songs she would make no mistakes.

After they exited the hall and crossed the corridor, Milla cracked open a door. Eliinka leaned inside. The walls were various shades of white in floral patterns. Perhaps that is why it was called the White Room. It was a good-sized room, one that she would have thought large before she had been in the other rooms of the palace. Most of it was open space and four large windows let in light. A seating area with chairs was in one corner near a cabinet and a table with four chairs sat in front of the nearest window.

"Jervi." Lord Zerin was standing next to the table. He was the younger man who had spoken with Jereni when they had arrived. His voice was deep and melodic. Though slender, he was more muscular than he had appeared at a distance.

"Hello. Jervi." Eliinka said.

Zerin appeared to be a year or two older than Jereni, about twenty. He set down several papers, folded his arms, and stayed silent while she sat in the chair on the close side of the table. His sea-gray eyes, circled by the lightest touch of green, contained a constant hint of a smile, or maybe it was impatience. Then he sat down facing her.

He spoke slowly and clearly, but Eliinka didn't recognize any words, except his name, Zerin. The next hour would be painful. She wanted to play the harp, not be here. But she sat up straight. Didn't anyone besides Jereni speak Pelten?

Zerin pointed at the table. "Poyta." Eliinka repeated the word. He stood up and pointed at the chair. "Tuoli."

"Tuoli," Eliinka said.

Zerin sat back down. "Istu." But he didn't point at anything.

She said, "istu." He motioned for her to stand up. He said, "istu." Then he stood and when sitting down said, "istu."

"This is ridiculous," she mumbled. *Was the word sit or did it mean something else?* It would take forever to learn to speak a single sentence. He pointed at the table again and said something too quick for Eliinka to catch.

"Poyta," she said, assuming that this was a review.

"Ya." Zerin nodded. He pointed at the chair again. After she said "tuoli," he pointed at the wall and said "Valkea."

"Valkea." So did this word mean wall? She wondered. Or was it the color white? He wouldn't understand if she asked him.

They continued the lesson, Zerin pointing at various objects, saying a word each time. His eyes looked blank, like he was bored, and occasionally he glanced at the door. He probably also wanted this lesson to end. Eliinka's head started to ache and she hoped the lesson would end soon.

"I'm never going to learn their language," she muttered. "I'm not sure if I want to." Still, she had learned the words "chair" and "table" and "sit," at least she *thought* the word might be "sit." Eliinka wanted to give up, but told herself it would take time, just like when her mother had started teaching her to play the harp.

After several more minutes, Eliinka rubbed her eyes and sighed out loud. "This is hard."

"Struggling to speak and understand will help you learn faster." Zerin suddenly spoke in Pelten with a light, exotic accent.

He had known Pelten the entire time! thought Eliinka, feeling suddenly irritated. She gritted her teeth. "I could've understood more if you had translated words for me, told me what the word was instead of making me guess! Maybe I would have learned something!" He was so irritating, pretending he didn't know what she had said when she had angrily been complaining.

"Princess Jereni prefers that we speak in Virjalo. I'll only speak in Pelten to explain difficult concepts." Zerin knit his eyebrows together. "I don't understand why Princess Jereni gives you lessons."

"What do you mean?"

"My time is highly valued by the princess, yet she commands me to teach you of Virun culture in our language." He stood and shook his head. He spoke slowly, with less inflection than when he spoke in his native tongue. "You are her musician, which in itself is a privilege. But you are treated as a noble. You wear the finest clothing and have been given valuable jewelry. And you are from Pelto!"

"We have an agreement." Eliinka's skin prickled.

There was no king here. Jereni ruled Viru! She was powerful. Eliinka had heard that Viru was different than Pelto. But this? Pelto would never allow a woman to be involved in government. A woman would never be allowed to rule.

Why did Jereni want an agreement with her? Just for her music? She wanted to scratch away the blue diamonds on her hands.

"You don't have to teach me if you don't want to. I don't need to learn your language to play music."

"She already knows how I feel. You will learn Virjalo. From me," Zerin snapped. "She bends traditions to her own purposes." Zerin hurriedly gathered his papers from the table. He strode past Eliinka, but paused at the door. "I don't think she should allow anyone from Pelto to be so close to her."

The door slammed shut.

Chapter Six

~ NIGHTMILK ~

Eliinka paused before turning the brass handle. With only one week in Viru, she couldn't even attempt a real conversation. She slipped through the door, shutting it lightly behind her.

"Jervi. How are you tonight?" Jereni spoke slowly and clearly in Virjalo. She sat in her chair, her feet on the table. No fire crackled.

"Jervi." Eliinka gave a slight bow and stood just off the big rug, the one that framed the sitting area. She closed her eyes, running over possible phrases she could say. Nothing would make sense. A light rain pattered on the closed window and she wished for a light sweater. Small goose bumps chilled her, and she wrapped her arms around herself. She wanted to play the harp, not pretend to have a conversation in a language she didn't know.

Silence filled the room. Jereni took her legs off the table and turned to fully face Eliinka. "What words do you know?" Her tone seemed to be either curious or frustrated, perhaps both.

Eliinka guessed at what Jereni said in Virjalo and pointed to items around the room—the harp, chair, carpet, and other objects as she said the words. She pointed to Jereni's back. Jereni said something that seemed to mean that it was fine. This was even worse than their short, superficial conversations that they held for a few moments during the evenings before she played for a few hours.

After she had named everything that she knew in the room, she pointed out colors. Then she shrugged her shoulders. There was nothing more to say. And she had said nothing tonight, just words.

"Tomorrow night, we'll try talking again." Jereni leaned back in her chair, opened a book, but didn't turn any pages.

Eliinka caught the words "tomorrow," "talk," and "again." She let loose her breath that she hadn't realized she was holding and sat at the harp. As soon as she finished one song, she began another.

The next two nights went the same: a brief conversation using only very basic phrases. She could only say that her day had been good. Even if she had wanted to, she couldn't say that she had had a bad day or that things were hard or even ask for help, because she didn't know the words.

Twang. The broken string whipped across Eliinka's wrist, leaving a light red welt. The ruined song died as it smacked other strings, scattering notes around the study. She grabbed the loose end and leaned her forehead against the top of the token harp.

They had skipped the exchange of meaningless words tonight because Eliinka had come earlier than normal. The previous four nights had been beyond frustrating. But now what could she do?

She slid her fingers up and down the other strings. She needed a replacement string. *When will I be able to play this harp again?* The warm breeze flowing through the windows brushed the bare skin on her legs and raised the hairs on her arms.

Back in Pelto the food and clothing were familiar, and she understood what people said. She had friends and could go wherever she wanted whenever she wanted. Their words here sounded like nonsense, with only an occasional word she could understand when she eavesdropped on conversations. She could not fit in, ever.

Here? She was in essence a prisoner.

Jereni touched her shoulder and Eliinka jumped. How did Jereni never make any noise when she walked?

"Why are you frightened of me?" Jereni spoke in Pelten, at a quick clip.

"The string. It broke. I'm sorry I disturbed your meditations." Eliinka remembered the stories she had heard about the princess, the legends written in Pelten books—what happened to those who angered her. She would not mention how frustrating it was to not understand anything anyone said, and how everything was strange and different: the food, the dress, the climate. Or how she didn't totally trust Jereni. How she would prefer to always play this harp instead of the big one in the afternoons.

"We still need to speak Virjalo as much as possible, so you learn it well, but I'll speak in both languages for the next few weeks. It will help you learn more quickly." Jereni took the harp into her arms and examined the break. "Maybe we can restring it with the broken string. It broke close to the end."

Jereni hummed as she removed the short piece of the string and tossed it aside.

"You play the harp." Eliinka could not keep the surprise from her voice. Why did Jereni need her to play?

"Yes." Jereni stretched out the longer piece, holding it next to the harp. "It is long enough. My harp maker will make an extra set of strings for this harp. It takes three weeks. But this string might do for now." She untied the bottom end of the string, unwound several wraps, and retied it at the bottom.

"My nobles talk of you, Eliinka. They are amazed at how well you play, even though it is Pelten music." She looped the top of the string, then turned the lever, listening, playing fifths and octaves, tuning the string quickly. Perfectly.

Jereni set down the harp, walked to the door, and cracked it open. Eliinka expected someone to enter, but Jereni said something in Virjalo to the guard and shut the door. When Jereni returned, she stood in front of the low fire and gazed at the wall of portraits. She did not sit back down in her chair.

Eliinka played a new song, a dancing song. But she stopped when Milla and Jereni's maid entered the study carrying the large harp between them. Jereni must have asked the guard to tell them to bring in this harp. They sat it on the floor near Eliinka. Jereni sat at the large harp, tipping it to her shoulder before the door closed. After checking the tuning, she played a couple arpeggios.

"Though my nobles are impressed with your playing during dinners, you must learn to play better, and you need to learn Virun songs. Pay attention to what I do. Watch how I pluck the strings," Jereni said. "Your tone will improve if you alter your approach." She played another arpeggio and then a series of chords, like she was loosening up her fingers.

"Think about the note, every individual note, each string, where and how you touch the string." Jereni plucked a single string. "Make the tone sound the way you intend." Jereni demonstrated a variety of sounds including a biting sharp-edged note, a dampened echo, a clink with a fingernail, an odd twang, and she somehow made the string sound sharp and then flat. She taught Eliinka how to play harmonics, so the string sounded an octave higher. Last, she somehow played a melody from one solitary string.

Eliinka touched her fingers to her harp strings, anxious to imitate what Jereni could do. It was amazing. Her mother had always wished Eliinka could have lessons from a master harper, and now she had that chance.

"Your abilities are far beyond mine," Eliinka said, "yet you chose me to be your musician."

"Only a musician truly appreciates another talented musician. But you need to learn about harmony and balance. Playing duets will help you."

"How can we play at the same time?" Eliinka had never heard two harps played at once. How could it be done?

"Begin with a simple tune." After Eliinka played the first phrase, Jereni joined in, interweaving arpeggios and chords throughout the melody that Eliinka played. Jereni created a countermelody that accented the melody at times and temporarily became the focal point. She also added different rhythms, Virun rhythms, to the music, and she was so talented that she covered Eliinka's hesitations and mistakes and blended their music so it sounded like they had played together for years.

When they finished the song, Jereni stopped playing and leaned the harp down to the floor.

"Life is more than music. Yet music can make life livable. Your music will sound better after you gain experience." Jereni moved back to her chair. Flames crackled in the fire.

Eliinka brushed her fingers across the strings. The tones merged and blended. The shadows of the darkening sky and the light of the fire created slight flashes that reflected in the moving harp strings. She thought about her past two weeks in Viru. Yes, there had been hard days—days when she became angry, days when she could not communicate, days when she became frustrated because she did not understand the culture and never wanted to understand it—but this evening she wanted to dance and jump and spin circles and play the harp all night long. Her emotions could hardly be contained inside her skin. The music she could play in the future beckoned in un-played undertones.

Jereni's maid entered from a side entrance and set two mugs on the large, low table, laden with Virun books.

"Drink nightmilk with me," Jereni said, lifting a steaming mug.

Standing, because she was not asked to sit, Eliinka picked up her mug. It was filled to the brim with white liquid. She sipped. The earthy sweet flavor reminded her of Jereni's music: natural and vibrant.

"Nightmilk?" Eliinka asked.

"The specially bred royal cow is milked at midnight; this milk bestows more strength and greater clarity of thought to those who drink."

Eliinka scuffed her feet on the lush carpet. "Princess Jereni, I had no idea you were not from Pelto. You have no accent and speak like a native. Where did you learn to speak—" Eliinka broke off, not sure if she should speak so boldly.

Jereni gazed at a portrait, a painting of a beautiful woman, the most beautiful woman Eliinka had ever seen. The woman appeared young, not much older than Jereni was now. Centered on her forehead was a small, blue diamond.

After a long hesitation, Jereni said, "My mother. My mother was from Pelto." Before Eliinka could ask anything else, she motioned to the harp. "Play the lullaby again."

Chapter Seven

~ NO WORD FOR PRAYER ~

So many new words to learn! Eliinka had been in Viru for more than a month and her head felt full, like no more words could fit. She had an actual physical ache above her temples after each lesson.

"Can we have our lesson somewhere else today?" Eliinka asked in Pelten as she settled at the table in the White Room.

Zerin spoke slowly, emphasizing each Virjalo word. "Can you ask in Virjalo?"

How to ask? Eliinka chose the most important words, even thought they didn't express exactly what she wanted. She pointed to him and then to herself. "Outside lesson?"

Zerin tipped his head up and looked at the ceiling as if in thought. "Where could we go? It would make it easier to teach you more words."

Thankfully, Eliinka understood more words than she could speak.

A few minutes later they entered the Garden Courtyard. This garden was very different than anything she had ever seen in Pelto. It was very large, filled with wandering paths and nooks with benches. Near the center was a pond, and off to the far edge near the palace kitchen was a small herb garden.

Zerin pointed, and she learned the words "tree," "flower," "grass," "rock," "dirt," "bush," "vine," "path," "butterfly," and "insect." After they reviewed each word, they walked along a garden path. Zerin again pointed to the vine and said, "lehti vine." He pointed to a yellow flower on the vine and said "lehti flower."

There were many flowers in the garden and though the lehti flower was beautiful, other flowers were more eye-catching, Eliinka thought. But the scent! She did not have to lean close to a flower to enjoy the sweet, fruity fragrance. She wanted to pick one and bring it back to her room.

"My mother grows these in her garden at her home," Zerin said. "The flowers are long-lasting when cut and the plant blooms for months, from spring until when winter begins."

They took another path, walked past the pond, and rounded a corner. Eliinka stopped, even though Zerin continued forward.

"The tree," Eliinka said. The narrow limbs bent over, giving the tree the appearance of a fountain. It was a mature tree, twice her height, with a slender trunk. She reached out and brushed a soft, narrow leaf. Until now, none of the plants or trees she had seen were the same as in Pelto. But this was a huuttaa tree!

"What is this called?" Eliinka asked as Zerin returned and stood at her side.

"That's the huuttaa tree."

"The name is the same as in Pelto. Why?"

Zerin shrugged his shoulders. "I don't know."

Eliinka wanted to express how the tree had special meaning in Pelto, how she needed to return and plant one on her parents' grave on the first anniversary. But she didn't know the words, so she just stared at the tree, thinking about home.

Toward the end of a culture lesson about the various industries of Viru, Eliinka realized that Zerin had never mentioned one topic. She'd been in Viru for three months and had never seen even the smallest hint of religion, not in a tapestry or picture. There was no place of worship in the palace. Religion was widely practiced in Pelto. Though her own faith had relatively few followers, everyone believed in God.

As Zerin finished talking about the weaving guild—they had the highest expertise—and began to talk about the construction guild, Eliinka wondered what the word was for religion. She glanced around the room. How could she ask about it?

"Eliinka, are you listening?"

"Sorry. I was thinking about a topic we've not covered."

"What is it?"

"It would take a whole lesson." Or a week of lessons, she thought. "Do you have special ceremonies . . . or do you meet regularly as a group to talk about . . ." She had no idea what the words were for religion or God or prayer in Virjalo. Eliinka stood and moved to the side of the table where she knelt for a moment. Zerin raised one eyebrow and looked confused. "Or some in Pelto do this." She raised her arms above her head and looked upward. "And they say special words. Or others do this." She sat cross-legged, her fingertips touching in front of her. Ah, she did know something that might help.

"I practice daily meditations," Eliinka said.

"You are asking about . . ." Zerin paused and switched to Pelten, "prayer or religion. We'll need to discuss this topic in your language."

"Yes, what are the words?" Eliinka asked in Pelten as she again sat down. "I've not seen any signs of religion."

"We have no word for prayer."

What? Eliinka thought. *Viruns are even more uncivilized than what is told.*

"The word for religion is *lupaus*. There's not much to explain. A priest performs ceremonies when there is a marriage or a funeral. He also does a ritual at harvest time." Zerin shifted in his chair. "Is it the same in Pelto?"

"Yes," Eliinka said. *And much, much more.* "Also, most people meet in small groups to learn and to pray. The major religion has a special meeting at the beginning of each month." There must be more about religion in Viru than he was saying. "What are your beliefs?"

Zerin wrinkled his forehead. After a pause he said, "I want to live a good life."

A loud knock hit the door and it cracked open.

"We are past time." Zerin jumped to his feet, his chair scraping the marble floor. "I have another meeting. Tomorrow we will discuss agriculture."

He ran through the door and Eliinka slowly walked back to her room. Zerin didn't have any religious beliefs. But he was a good man.

Eliinka felt a tug of homesickness in her heart. So many aspects of life were similar here, or close enough. But they had no belief system. Their religion was just a couple ceremonies, not a way of life.

The next afternoon, Eliinka finished her practice time in the Dining Hall by running through the lullaby. She always ended her practice with this Pelten song. The only time her fears fully faded was when she played the harp. In all her time here she had never left the palace. Once she had tried to see how much freedom she had and attempted to walk outside the palace grounds. The guards had stopped her from passing through the double gate. Still, she was allowed to go anywhere inside the palace and its courtyards and gardens.

She repeated the lullaby, thinking again how she might return to Pelto and how she could get her harp back. Her gift was surely not strong enough, and she did not understand this people or the culture well enough to use it, even if it was strong. And she wasn't quite sure how to wield her gift or use it unnoticed. Though she had thought through so many possibilities, there was no way to get home. Not by herself. If she broke the contract and slipped away, there was no way she could cross through the wilderness without assistance. Breaking the contract? She should not even consider making that choice. Perhaps if she pleased Jereni, she would alter the contract and allow her to return.

Eliinka stopped playing suddenly in the middle of the song, breaking the lullaby. She had lost track of time.

Chapter Eight

~ WHAT ELSE IS THERE TO DESIRE? ~

Zerin always arrived on time. Eliinka jumped to her feet, ran from the Dining Hall, and skidded to a halt on the marble floor of the long corridor as she reached the door. The lessons had become more interesting once she understood some words. And the one time she had been late, Zerin had scolded her and it seemed he purposely made the lesson that day more boring. She stepped into the White Room as he rounded the corner and sat quickly before he entered.

"Is there anything you need? Anything you want?" Zerin spoke in Pelten as he shut the door and turned to face her.

"Why are you speaking in my language?" Eliinka asked.

"It will make our conversation easier. You don't know enough words."

"That's true. I don't like to have to guess what you are saying." Like yesterday. It had taken too long to figure out the word "wood," even though he had pointed at all the objects made of wood in the room.

"Is there anything you need?" Zerin repeated

"Princess Jereni supplies me with all that I need," Eliinka said as she pulled her eyes away from his. Light-gray clouds blew by the window, and the room flooded with shadow then sunlight then shadow. But Jereni didn't give Eliinka all she needed. Not her harp. Yes, she played it at times, but it wasn't the same as owning it again. Jereni gave her a place to live, but not a home, not a place she belonged. Only on the surface did she have all she needed.

Zerin was one of Jereni's close advisors, and he would not help Eliinka return to Pelto or get back her token harp. It was best he did not know what she truly wanted. He would probably tell Jereni, and she did not want to lose the privileges she had, such as playing her token harp every evening.

Zerin crossed the room, his footsteps whispering against the stone floor. He folded his arms and stared at her.

Eliinka drummed her fingertips on the table and thought of the harp, wishing she could escape the beating silence. His eyes lingered too long, and her face heated up, so she added, "What else is there to desire? I'm allowed to stay here and serve her for my entire life with my music." Eliinka traced the pattern down her left arm and outlined the diamond on her hand. Her entire life! Or until she figured out another option. "Princess Jereni gives me her protection."

"And you willingly give her your life."

"I give her my music."

"She trusts few people, Eliinka, very few. Yet she trusts you." Zerin placed his hands on the table and continued to stare.

Eliinka was not sure that was true. They only conversed for three or four minutes some evenings before she played for Jereni. She had given her a little more instruction a couple times on the harp. Though Jereni was friendly inside her study, it was as if they had reached an uneasy truce, and Eliinka believed that neither of them fully trusted the other. The only other time she saw Jereni was when she played for the evening meals as requested.

"Do you miss Pelto?"

Eliinka rubbed the back of her hands. Her skin didn't hurt anymore, except when she looked at her diamond pattern. "Lord Zerin, I live in Viru now . . . "

"Will anyone miss you?"

"Yes." Was there someone, anyone, who really missed her? A distance had grown between her and her friends after her parents' deaths. "Rakel, a friend, will wonder where I am. She may ask her older brother, Mikali, to look for me. He is always traveling. And my students surely noticed I'm gone, but none of them were serious about music. The parents that cared will find another teacher."

Who would be waiting for her when she returned? She had no living relatives. Where would she go?

Zerin sat down, waiting for Eliinka to say more, it seemed.

"What about your family?"

"It's been one year since my parents died." Everything had changed after her parents' deaths. So many others had died at that time too with the illness. "Next week marks the commemoration of their death. I should . . ." How could she not visit her parents' graves and finish the rites of faith by planting the flowering huuttaa tree after the year of mourning was up? There was no one else who could do it for them.

"Should?" Zerin asked.

"Visit their graves."

"Do you ever want to return?" Zerin leaned forward on his elbows. His eyes reminded Eliinka of the sky at sunset.

"I've made promises to Jereni."

"So is there nothing you wish for?" Zerin emptied a leather pouch onto the table. Tumbling coins clattered, interrupting her thoughts.

Eliinka picked up a large coin. Jereni's face was on the front. As she examined the likeness, she realized that though she feared Jereni, she also respected her. That her reasons for living here had grown to more than their contract and hoping to get her harp back. Her musical talent had grown, and she played the harp better than before, better than if she had not come.

"I agreed to serve Princess Jereni." It was the safe answer, the correct answer. But Zerin waited as if expecting her to say more. Eliinka flipped the silver coin over. It was quite different from the coins that appeared each month in her room, her salary in Pelten coins that were worthless here. "I've never seen Virun money before."

Zerin sorted the oval coins, organizing them into stacks by their size and switched to Virjalo. "We'll visit the city market tomorrow morning. Today you will learn about money and the phrases for buying and bartering."

"Is this written in Virjalo?" Eliinka pointed to the symbols on the smallest, thinnest coin. It was shiny and new, with a picture of a building on the front. Small symbols were impressed on the edges of the coin. Another symbol inside a diamond was on the back.

"Yes, and this is the number one." Zerin touched the back of the coin.

"This explains why Princess Jereni's writing is so beautiful. Will I learn to read and write in Virjalo?"

Zerin clinked the coins against each other. "Today you will learn the names and values of these coins. Princess Jereni will decide if you'll learn to read."

After Eliinka learned all the names and values of the coins, Zerin replaced them in the pouch. He handed Eliinka a woven handbag with a long strap that was embroidered with flowers. "This is for you, from Princess Jereni."

The bag weighed more than Eliinka expected, so she opened it. "This is too much money."

"Princess Jereni wants you to have sufficient coin for anything you want to buy in the market. Meet me here an hour after the morning meal."

Eliinka followed two steps behind Zerin as they walked through the halls, down the stairs, and into the outer courtyard. The day was already warm. It would be hot by midday. Zerin spoke with the palace guard, who opened the gate.

As they reached the bottom of the hill, the streets became more crowded, yet a path opened for their passage, and people turned and stared. Although market-goers rushed about, balancing their goods, jostling and bumping each other, no one touched Eliinka.

"Zerin, everyone looks at me. They step away as I pass."

"Everyone recognizes you," Zerin said. "You are from Pelto."

"Everyone? But I'm wearing Virun clothes. I don't look that different."

"Your hands wear the blue diamonds."

Sellers called out loudly from their market stalls. Buyers shoved forward. Small children dashed underfoot while their mothers bartered for a better price. Smells of ripe fruit, baking breads, and crackling meat filled the air.

Small booths and large booths sold everything: food, jewelry, cookware, clothing and shoes, even musical instruments. Eliinka stopped to look at the instruments. Shiny horns hung from the rafters, drums rested on the ground, and the most fragile instruments rested on the table. But there was not a single harp, not even a small one. She tried to convince herself it did not matter. She didn't have enough money, and even if she did, she wouldn't buy a harp. It would not be the same as her harp she had given as a token.

A lively tumble of a tune came from a flute up the street. When they reached the young man, Eliinka paused, remembering her desperation to earn enough for a round of bread when she had played in the central market in Pelto. She pulled a coin from her bag and tossed it onto a brightly woven flute case laid out in front of his feet. Zerin tossed one next to hers, and they continued up the street.

"We came here for you to practice speaking," Zerin said. "Choose a booth and buy something." When Eliinka stopped at a fruit and vegetable stand, a woman cut a fruit and handed a piece to her.

"Do they offer tastes to everyone?" Eliinka asked Zerin.

"They offer to everyone. If people taste, they often buy." Zerin pointed to an enormous fruit, half the size of Eliinka. "That fruit, the lakka, grows on a tree. I prefer it in juice because it has many huge seeds—try a piece."

Eliinka bit off a small piece so she would not get a seed, just enough to taste.

"This fruit stand has the largest selection. What do you want to buy?"

Eliinka hesitated. She glanced at Zerin.

"Remember what you learned."

Eliinka pointed to a fruit she recognized from the palace kitchens.

"I would like to buy two—" Eliinka turned to Zerin and asked, "What are they called?"

"Valinta."

The woman's eyes strayed to Eliinka's hands.

"I would like two valinta." Eliinka held up two fingers. The woman handed her the fruit, and Eliinka paid her.

"You spoke clearly. Well done." Zerin placed her purchases into a net that he pulled from his clothing.

They continued forward, moving through the always-opening passage in the crowded market. A breeze filled with the smell of fresh bread, and Eliinka's stomach rumbled.

"Do you see anything you wish to buy?"

"I've never had extra money and—"

"Princess Jereni expects that you will buy something more than food. You are looking without intending to buy."

"My head hurts from thinking in Virjalo." Eliinka's head always hurt after a tough lesson, and this was going to be a long one.

"You're here to practice speaking. That's what today is for."

"Would you suggest a booth for me to visit? I'm not used to having so many choices." They walked through another section of the never-ending market, and Zerin finally stopped near a medium-sized jewelry booth. "You should be able to find something here."

Eliinka stepped forward, holding her hands behind herself while she surveyed the wares.

The woman at the booth eyed Eliinka's necklace and handbag. Eliinka did not look at the necklaces displayed. She did not dare remove her token necklace, so would not buy one. She ignored the bracelets. A bracelet would get in the way of playing the harp. More people loitered near the booth than earlier, and Eliinka sensed them watching her.

"How much are the earrings?" Eliinka said, just like she had practiced.

The woman spoke too rapidly. Before Eliinka could ask her to repeat her words and speak slowly, Zerin leaned into the booth. His eyes flashed as he showed the woman his ring, an intense blue aquamarine set in gold. He spoke so quickly that Eliinka had no idea what he said. Paler than parchment, the woman bowed her head and apologized.

Zerin held onto Eliinka's upper arm as he hurried her away from the booth, and a pleasant shiver tingled on her skin. He said, "She was trying to take advantage of you. The price was six times what it should be."

"But why?"

"You are not what she thought," Zerin said. "She believed you would pay a high price. She did not see me." *Or my arms*, Eliinka thought as Zerin guided her through the market. "People might not recognize me from a distance. But when they see my ring they realize I am close to Princess Jereni," he continued.

Zerin slowed his pace, and Eliinka pointed to another jewelry stand. "What about that one?" It was a small booth, less than a booth actually, just a blanket laid out on the cobblestone that displayed only earrings. A girl about her age sat cross-legged, crafting an earring.

Eliinka stooped over her jewelry. "Good afternoon."

The girl stood up and smiled. Her eyes flitted from Eliinka's hands to her face, then to Zerin, where they stayed.

"Your earrings are beautiful. How much are they?"

"All the same price. Fazvish a pair," the girl said.

Zerin nodded his approval.

Eliinka pointed to a pair of earrings made with flat, azure-blue stones, the same color that marked her skin. The blue stone mounted in brass would cover much of the earlobe, and the multiple brass twisted strands that cascaded far below the stone would reach her shoulder. They were similar in style to what many of the women were wearing. "I would like to buy these, please." Eliinka handed the girl a coin.

The girl placed the coin in a simple pouch she wore at her side. "Thank you." She stared at Eliinka's hands and bowed.

"I'm only a musician." Eliinka touched her hands and wondered if the markings were why the girl would bow.

They walked up one busy street and down another. Zerin didn't seem in a rush and pointed out landmarks of the city: a fountain, an ancient gate that was still connected to what used to be a wall around the oldest section of the city, and a fabric museum that he said Jereni's mom had founded. He stopped once to point out a unique metalworking shop, and they watched a man and woman hammer and shape metal for several minutes. Last, they paused at a café. "This has the best food in all of Viru. Next time we come to the market, we'll eat here. But we do have time for a drink."

They sat at a small table. "Two marja juices, please," Zerin told a server.

Soon, two tall, thin glasses of black-red juice were brought to them.

Eliinka took a sip of the cool juice. It had a deep, rich, almost nutty flavor. It tasted better than any juice she had drunk before. They drank in silence, watching the market-goers. Right after they finished drinking, Zerin paid and they rejoined the crowds.

As they headed up the hill toward the palace, Eliinka said, "Thanks for showing me the market."

"It's where I go when I need to experience a bit of everyday life." Zerin grinned, and for the first time he seemed relaxed near her. "It's good for you to see things outside the palace, and it will help you understand more of our culture."

The outing had been more enjoyable than she had anticipated. After Eliinka found a way to regain her harp, maybe he could be someone she could ask to help her return home. If he was someone she could trust.

Chapter Nine

~ SO MUCH BLOOD ~

Eliinka's door handle rattled, waking her.

A man cursed, and her door creaked open.

Holding in her urge to scream—not wanting the intruder to know where she was—Eliinka rolled out of her bed onto her carpet, ducking low. Two silhouettes paused in her open doorway. The door snapped shut. Why would they come into her room?

It was a moonless night, and the clouds blocked any glimmer of stars. If she couldn't see the men, they couldn't see her, so she crawled her way through the darkness to the edge of her room, listening. She would slip out and call for the guards.

As Eliinka's sight adjusted to the darkness she could barely make out the men's shadowy figures. She shrank into the wall. A smell of crumbling leaves blew through the open window with a fall breeze.

"The princess's door is in the opposite wall," one whispered.

"Good. Should we take care of the foreigner?"

"She's not worth it."

Eliinka slid toward her fireplace, glad she had learned enough from Zerin to understand their words. She grasped the handle of the fire iron and rushed through the darkness toward the closest man. She swung downward with all her force and screamed. The man fell with a thud.

A gleam of metal flashed. Eliinka swung the fire iron wildly, back and forth, between her and the second man, yelling so loud that her lungs hurt. She stumbled when she backed into a chair. A flash of metal sliced toward her just as she caught her balance, and sharp pain speared her left side, in front, where her arm met her chest. She screamed again. Dampness trickled down her chest.

Guards spilled through both doors, from opposite sides of the room. One seized the attacker from behind. As the room filled with torches, the shadows disappeared, and the room became visible, illuminated as midday. Her two chairs lay on the floor, tipped over. One of her small tables was broken in half. A short staff, with a long knife attached to the end, clattered on the floor as a guard ripped it from the muscular man's hands.

The other man lay unmoving on the floor. His crushed temple bled. Dizzy, Eliinka slumped against the wall. She tightened her grip on the fire iron. Her chest throbbed.

Within moments, Jereni strode in. The attacker struggled between two guards.

"You are a fool!" A knife was in her hand, and she slashed him twice across his face. "Take him. Extract answers." She pointed to the dead man. "Remove the body—immediately."

Blood flowed down Eliinka's chest and arm. She turned her head away.

"Call a healer." Jereni pried the fire iron from Eliinka's hand and laid her on the carpet. "Milla, revive the fire. Heat some water." After ripping a strip off a sheet, she pulled Eliinka's split flesh together. She knelt on the ground at Eliinka's side, pressing harder and harder until it felt like her shoulder would split in two.

"Hold on, Eliinka. The healer is coming."

Milla added wood to the fire and blew, coaxing flames from the blackened coals.

"It hurts. The pain—please, my pain." Eliinka balled her right fist. She bit her lips to keep from screaming.

The healer pulled back the cloth. *When did he arrive?* Eliinka thought.

Warm blood dripped down her shoulder, and Eliinka shook as a cool breeze hit her skin. Jereni rinsed her hands in a basin that Milla held. She wiped them on her stained robes and left the room, returning in a moment with a flask in her hand. She leaned over Eliinka, and held it to her lips. "Drink this wine. It will dull your pain."

"I can't drink it." Eliinka turned her head aside.

"You must drink something."

Eliinka shook her head.

"You will recover," Jereni said in her gentlest voice, but even so, she sounded uncertain.

The healer pulled out his tools: needle, thread, knife.

Eliinka flinched. "Please play the harp for me? Please. Take away my pain."

"Milla, bring a harp. Now."

Within moments, Milla returned with the token harp in her arms. The healer stitched while Jereni played a soothing song.

Eliinka sucked in a deep breath and turned her head away, then took another deep breath. She fought to ignore her flaring nerves, the biting insertion of the needle, the pull of the thread, and the tug of tightening stitches as her skin pulled together. She focused on the music, the sounds that created images of tumbling streams and majestic forests. After the healer tied off the last stitch, Jereni completed the song.

"I hurt," Eliinka said.

Jereni filled a mug with hot water, poured in a bluish brown powder and stirred while the healer cut off the bloodstained portion of Eliinka's nightgown and applied bandages, securing them in place.

"Drink this," Jereni said as Milla helped Eliinka to a sitting position. The floor fell away from Eliinka and seemed to spin to the side. Milla held on as the room continued to twist.

"This tea will help with your pain. You need to sleep." Jereni held the mug to Eliinka's mouth and tipped it so the tea trickled down her throat. "Milla, help Eliinka into her bed."

Pain pierced deeper into Eliinka's upper chest as Milla and the healer carried her to her bed. Milla fussed over Eliinka, tucking blankets around her, while the healer gathered his supplies and left. After a minute, Milla dropped to the floor and scrubbed where blood had fallen.

How could she lose that much blood and still be alive? Was her hair damp from sweat or blood? Each shallow breath sent sheets of flames through her chest.

"Eliinka." Her bed shifted as Jereni leaned forward and switched to speaking Pelten. "You fought well with a makeshift weapon." In barely audible words, Jereni whispered, "Eliinka, reach deep inside yourself and find the power to recover. Please live. I need you to bring me peace. I need a friend."

Could Eliinka give her friendship to Jereni? If she lived?

Zerin burst through the door, bowing as he ran across the room.

She fought the heaviness of her eyes, but could not hold them open. So she listened while she fought sleep.

"Sit with Eliinka tonight and tomorrow, Zerin," Jereni said. "Milla will assist you. Give Eliinka more of the sininen tea when her pain becomes unbearable."

"Where was the guard outside her room?" Zerin asked. "Why did those men attack her?"

How did Zerin know? Is he concerned about me? Eliinka wondered.

"That guard is dead. Ilari believes they were coming for me and that Eliinka woke and stopped them."

"Your kingdom is still at risk until, until . . . If you would listen to your council—"

"The year of mourning is not yet up for my father. Do not press me, Zerin."

"Will she live?" Zerin asked.

Eliinka held her breath, hoping for a positive answer. If it were negative, she would give in to the agony and not fight death.

"She lost a lot of blood."

"What are her chances?"

Loud stomping steps echoed through Eliinka's room, then Jereni—it must be Jereni, Eliinka thought—threw open a door. "As long as she breathes there is a chance. That's why you are here, day and night. You are responsible for Eliinka's well-being. Zerin, keep her alive, and you will be rewarded."

Chapter Ten

~ DEEP FRIENDSHIP ~

An odd, yellow light glimmered from Eliinka's left. The brightness hurt. She tightened her eyes and turned her head away from the glare. She wished she could return to the sleep that eased the pain.

"Would you like the curtains closed?" Zerin asked.

Eliinka's eyes flew open. Why did Zerin sit in her room? "I like the morning light." She shifted her weight. "Ouch."

"How's the pain?"

"My shoulder, my chest . . ." Eliinka took a deep breath, not knowing how to describe the piercing throb. She gazed at the ceiling. "I took a man's life last night, again, my second time, to protect Jereni. The first time, on our journey here, it was accidental. But last night—Zerin—I feel horrible."

Last night Jereni had spoken in Pelten again for the first time in months. Did she really ask Eliinka to be a friend?

Milla entered with a platter of food—the morning meal—and set it on the table nearest the bed. She pushed the table closer to Eliinka.

"Eliinka, what are you hungry for?" Zerin asked.

As she tried to sit, sharp, jagged pain speared her arm, shoulder, and chest. She plopped her head back down against her pillow. She couldn't even sit up.

"I'm not hungry."

Milla draped a small blanket around Eliinka's shoulders and helped her to a sitting position. Eliinka peeked between the blankets at the large bandage on her shoulder and chest, and she forced a smile. "So this is why I hurt so much. It even hurts to breathe."

Zerin poured hot water into a mug and, after measuring the bluish brown powder, sprinkled it into the water and stirred. He placed the steaming tea into Eliinka's hand.

"What's this?"

"Drink. It's more sininen tea. It eases the pain."

Eliinka didn't think anything could stop the pain. She blew at the surface of the foamy, cloudy liquid and wrinkled her nose at the pungent smell.

"Drink."

Eliinka took a deep breath that ripped at her chest and poured the tea down her throat. She drew her mouth tight. "That tasted horrid. The juice, quick."

Milla handed Eliinka the glass of marja juice, her favorite. She gulped it down.

Dizziness slid into Eliinka's head, and she tried to blink it away. With every small movement, the furniture and Zerin spun. The door opened. Jereni and the healer blurred as they crossed the room.

She should bow. Eliinka struggled again to get out of bed.

"Stay down, Eliinka. Milla, get her a new nightdress." Jereni turned to Zerin, a laugh in her voice. "It appears that you gave her more sininen tea."

The healer removed the bandage, and, for the first time, Eliinka saw her wound. She focused her eyes, pushing the dizziness away. The stitches ran from the top of her left shoulder, where it connected to the arm, down into the flesh of the upper breast. When the healer wiped her skin clean with a wet, warm cloth, Eliinka sucked in her breath. She reached out grabbed what was closest, a hand, and squeezed tight. The pain. The pain.

Zerin? Was she crushing his fingers? She relaxed her grip. Should she let go? Yes. Even though she wanted to hold tight.

The healer applied a cream, and her whole body stiffened, though she tried to relax.

"You are doing well." Jereni swept Eliinka's hair away from her face. "You will live."

"The cream stings."

"Yes, but it fights infection," Jereni said.

As the healer applied a fresh bandage, Eliinka clenched her teeth. At least she was lying down and wouldn't faint.

"Zerin, gather everything you need," Jereni said. "You'll work from Eliinka's room today." He bowed to Jereni, and after a quick glance at Eliinka, he left with the healer. "Eliinka, sit up. You need to change into a clean nightdress."

Even though Eliinka sat up slowly, the room spun again. She fell back down to the bed. Milla, who had returned with the nightdress in her arms, helped her up and removed the torn remnants of cloth hanging from her body.

"Thank you, Eliinka, for fighting off the attackers last night," Jereni said. "Rest as much as possible today. You must eat, even if you aren't hungry."

"Who were those men?" Eliinka asked.

"Assassins. A few are unhappy with my rule."

Milla helped Eliinka put her left arm through the sleeveless, loose nightdress, and Eliinka pulled her right arm and head through the other openings.

"It shouldn't be this hard. I'm so dizzy." As the hem tumbled against her thighs, Eliinka leaned against the bed, tired from such a small effort. Milla helped her into bed. Eliinka remained sitting and Milla pulled a sheet over her legs.

"You stopped my bleeding last night," Eliinka said to Jereni. "You saved me. Thank you for playing the harp. It made the pain bearable."

"You've killed men, twice, to protect me." Jereni shifted her weight, and as she looked away, she blinked, hard.

It was the first time Eliinka had seen Jereni express emotion. She wondered how much Jereni understood of Pelten culture, if she knew of their rituals. She could offer Jereni what she had said she really wanted, a formal Pelten friendship, even though it would make it harder for Eliinka to leave Viru. Without hesitation, Eliinka held out her right hand to Jereni, palm up, middle three fingers touching, thumb and fifth finger stretched wide.

Jereni stared at Eliinka's outstretched hand and whispered, "Thank you." She extended her right hand out, palm down. They interlocked their thumbs and little fingers, placing the three middle fingers on each other's wrist.

"Forever," Eliinka said, in Pelten.

Jereni echoed, "Forever."

As they disentangled their hands, Eliinka wondered what the Pelten ritual of vowing deep friendship would mean in Viru. If Jereni would value it like a Pelten would, and if they could really be friends. A wave of pain overtook Eliinka's thoughts, and she collapsed onto her bed as she also wondered if she was truly willing to give all it required, to do all she could to understand Jereni and to help her reach her dreams.

Chapter Eleven

~ A CHALLENGING TASK ~

No, you can't go." Zerin frowned. "Today is the first day you've been able to even sit up without help."

"Help me to Princess Jereni's study. Please, Lord Zerin. I've not played the harp for four days."

"Six days, actually," Zerin said. "You were hardly conscious for the first two days."

"I need to play for her, like always."

"Drink the tea. It will help you."

"Later. After I've played." Eliinka pushed the cup away. The tea made her dizzy, took away part of her senses. Even if it hurt to play, she needed to feel the vibrations of the strings and enter the world of her music, the place where she could block out everything, even the pain in her chest. "It's evening, when I always play. Please, help me to her study."

"Princess Jereni has not requested you to play. She visited again this morning—"

"When I was sleeping." Eliinka dropped her feet over the side of the bed and put all her weight on her legs. Milla had come earlier and helped her get dressed. She had fallen asleep after she had eaten. "I'll go by myself."

"You can't make it. You're too weak."

"I'm fine." Eliinka took a step. After one step, she reached out to a chair and steadied herself. "I'll call for Milla. She'll help me."

"You must rest."

"I'm tired of lying in bed." Eliinka took another tottering step toward the door. And another. At least there were no stairs on the way to the study. "I'll drink the tea when I get back."

"You will hurt yourself."

"I can make it."

Zerin sighed and shook his head. "If you insist on going, only stay for a few minutes. Milla will wait for you outside the door, and I'll warm the tea for when you return." Zerin held her around the waist and walked her through the door and down the hall.

Eliinka tripped as they turned a corner, and he tightened his hold on her. Sneaking a glance up to his face, she slowed her walk. Short stubble grew on his cheeks and chin, and she wondered what he'd look like if he grew a beard like a Pelten man.

When they reached the end of the hall, he opened the door to the study.

Glowing firelight spilled across the table. Eliinka leaned against the doorframe, resting for a moment, while finding enough energy to cross the room. Jereni leaned over several loose parchments, and the light played on her face, accenting her high cheekbones. The door clicked shut behind Eliinka. Jereni pushed aside the parchments and jumped to her feet as if she had been expecting Eliinka. "Please, come sit with me."

Out of habit, Eliinka bowed. Her shoulder throbbed. She walked slowly across the room.

"Eliinka, you need not bow to me in this room. You are to greet me as a friend within my study." Jereni reached out and grasped Eliinka's hand and greeted Eliinka in the manner women greeted in Viru. It was Eliinka's first time, but she had seen it done. With their left hands they clasped each other's right shoulder, their right hands cupped each other's left elbow, and they kissed each other's cheeks, first the left, then the right.

Eliinka had never seen Jereni greet any woman in this manner.

"You may call me Jereni within these walls. It is best if you use my title at other times."

As Jereni lowered her hands, Eliinka nodded her head. It made sense that their friendship would use Virun customs. But what would their friendship really mean?

Jereni motioned to the chair at her right.

Eliinka lowered herself onto a comfortable cushion, sitting so she could see the harp. The fire warmed the air, and the scent of sweet lehti flowers flowed through the open window.

"Our friendship, our lives, our music connects us." Jereni motioned to their steaming mugs.

She must have expected me, Eliinka thought. *Or hoped I would come.* She sipped the nightmilk. It warmed her on the inside.

Jereni sipped from her mug and then sank back into her chair and placed her feet on the table. "The Festival of Light is next month, on the shortest day of the year. You will attend as my guest and friend. There will be celebrations, performances, feasting, and dancing." A glimmer of a smile splashed across her face. "It is the biggest celebration of the year. For two days my entire kingdom celebrates."

Jereni spoke for several more minutes without pause, the most she had ever said in an evening. Eliinka listened, wondering if she would also perform at the festival, wondering how much their friendship would change her life, wondering if she would still get to play the harp each evening. Or maybe she could now play it whenever she pleased.

"One year, my fourteenth year, I disguised myself and snuck out of the palace to celebrate with the city, to interact with my people. The festival looked so alluring from my window, so colorful and exciting, the sounds so inviting." Jereni laughed. "The people were quite delighted when they realized that their princess had mingled with them for hours. My father had one hundred guards searching for me that day. He was not happy."

Jereni glanced again at her parents' portraits and downed her nightmilk.

"You cannot misunderstand my words because we will speak in Pelten now. You will leave this room with a task, a confidential, important task. You will speak of this to no one." The blue intensified in Jereni's eyes and reflected the flames.

A secret task? Eliinka tightened her grip on the mug.

"You now speak Virjalo fairly well. You are in a unique position and can converse with all classes of people, from the cooks and maids to the noblemen and women."

Speak to others? To accomplish her task? Eliinka adjusted her fingers around her mug. The blue diamond on her skin tightened. How? In all her time, even though she had learned quite a bit of Virjalo, she had only held conversations with Jereni and Zerin and Milla. The nobles looked at her as a servant and ignored her, never glancing at her, like she was invisible. The cooks and guards all knew she was privileged and were deferential, only speaking when she spoke to them.

Fine worry lines creased across Jereni's forehead. "My advisors continue to remind me that I must marry, that a husband is needed to give me heirs to my throne, heirs for my kingdom. It was a surprise when my father died last year. We expected him to live for many years, live to see his grandchildren and great-grandchildren. It is possible I never would have taken the throne, and many believed it should skip me and pass directly to my oldest son. Because I have no living relatives, they have argued over who will choose my husband.

"Zerin believes my council can choose the man, yet they dare not until I give them permission. But they will not choose."

Eliinka did not know what to say, so she sipped the milk. Somehow it relaxed her.

"There is no need of a marriage for the purpose of a political or military alliance, or my father would have chosen a husband for me before he died." Jereni shrugged her shoulders in an unconvincing attempt to appear disinterested.

"It would have been simpler if he had chosen. Perhaps he waited for me to show interest in a man. Or maybe he did not see a match. The men . . ." Jereni shook her head, ". . . the men of my kingdom respect me, but they do not speak with ease when near me. Yet my advisors demand that I marry soon. The choice and announcement needs to be made shortly after the year of mourning is over." Jereni leaned forward.

"Eliinka, your task is to choose the best man for me."

Eliinka clunked the mug back onto the table. How could Jereni expect her to do that?

Jereni, in a serious, intense voice said, "You will choose my husband."

"Why don't you choose?"

"That isn't possible. It is tradition for a woman's husband to be chosen for her. For me to break this tradition would create dissent in my kingdom. No one would support me. My kingdom would be overthrown within a week, and a civil war would break out. I've followed tradition and taken the steps of rulership. All that remains is for me to marry, receive the crown, be declared queen, and take my vows to serve my people. I wish to serve as well as my parents. You are healing quickly. You will start your search as soon as you feel you are able to walk on your own."

"You want me to choose?"

"According to tradition, at least according to what is written in the old books, a friend is allowed to select the husband if there is no living family member."

A friend.

Eliinka forced her teeth together, clenching them tight to keep her jaw from dropping open. She grabbed control of the loose thoughts that flew around her head. It appeared that Jereni did understand their vow, their promise of friendship, and completely trusted her. This was their first true conversation after extending hands of friendship, and now Jereni . . .

Friends gave advice, listened, helped, but to select a husband? This decision would affect all of Jereni's life, her kingdom, her happiness.

"Is there any man that you prefer? Have you noticed any glance of interest?"

"Hidden fear is in their eyes when they are near me," Jereni said. Flames crackled in the fireplace and sparks leaped into the air. "The reputation of my swift justice is well deserved. You have not seen my unleashed anger." Eliinka started at Jereni's audible huff and saw a brief, unattainable longing fizzle into an inevitable glare that seemed to diminish the fire. "Even so, any man would become my husband, walk in my shadow, and share my bed for the honor to join the royal family. No man would dare refuse."

"Jereni, you deserve a husband who loves you." Eliinka hoped Jereni would give her a clue of a man she preferred.

"Is true love possible in the royal family?" Jereni scanned the portrait wall of previous kings and queens. Pain crept into her words as her voice lowered in pitch. "Love cannot happen for me." Her attention returned to Eliinka. "A man who does not fear me will be sufficient."

"Zerin is the only man I know."

"Zerin is pleasant, almost a brother in some ways to me, but he is for another woman." Jereni picked up her empty mug and moved it from one hand to the other.

Eliinka swallowed. Zerin was already claimed by someone. How could this upend her emotions? Why did she feel a loss? She realized she did enjoy their daily time together.

"My husband should come from the noble class."

"How can I meet potential husbands?"

"Watch my lords, observe how they treat others. Most of them visit the palace every week or so. They will all attend the festival. You will not play or perform so you can meet them all. They will not hide their real character from you. Speak with them, and at the festival dance with them. Listen to the servants' views of these men. Eliminate each man who is inadequate. The morning after the festival you will give me the name of the chosen man. After that, you must be present with both of us when the betrothal is announced by me."

This was real. Jereni's future happiness depended on her. "So the man gets no choice? The woman no choice, either? In Pelto, both the woman and the man choose each other, though in some cases, the man chooses."

"The woman's family selects the man, unless she has no close living relatives. They usually talk to his parents before the woman announces the choice to the man."

Eliinka glanced to the harp. Her energy was fading, and she would not be able to play today. She bent her fingers until her fingernails cut into her palms. She wished she had more strength.

Jereni finally set down her mug. "Tomorrow you will be presented at the evening meal as the person who thwarted the assassins and killed one of them."

"Those men? Were they Flute People?"

"No. The Flute People stay in the wilderness and only prey on travelers. They pose no threat. This attack was planned in advance, planned by other men. Do not worry. You are safe."

Eliinka traced the back of her hands. It seemed an impossible assignment to choose Jereni's husband.

"Until you've selected my husband, our relationship will appear the same to everyone outside this room. That will allow you to mingle, and they will more openly express their thoughts."

"Is there any man who will treat you the way you want?"

Jereni gazed at her mother's portrait. She leaned forward, placing her chin on her hands. Her mother was beautiful, and though she smiled, her eyes held a mix of longing and sadness. After a long moment, Jereni suddenly sat up.

"Actually, Eliinka, you need to learn our dances." Jereni tapped her toe. "Zerin will teach you during your afternoon lessons. A musician will be assigned."

Eliinka pursed her lips. What would Zerin think? Would he pretend she was the other woman, whoever she was? Would they hold hands while dancing? She hoped she could pretend she wasn't interested in him.

"You must rest. Your shoulder pains you. Remember, it is wise to not let others know of your injury. It will give them an advantage in battle or disagreements. Go and drink a mug of sininen tea. Get some sleep. Does Milla wait near the door to help you to your room?"

"Yes, she waits." Eliinka stood. She had not played the harp, the reason she had come to the study. Weakness flooded her body. She grabbed the chair with her right hand until her lightheadedness cleared. She'd play tomorrow. The distance across the room seemed much farther than normal.

Halfway to the door, she paused to rest, glancing back at the princess. Jereni sat deep in thought, firelight reflecting on her face.

A trace of fear flickered in Jereni's eyes as she spoke in a faint, but clear whisper, "Please choose my husband well."

Chapter Twelve

Eliinka danced with yet another man, the tenth—or was it the eleventh?—in a long line of men she'd danced with this evening. Deep-crimson folds of fabric swished about her thighs as she swirled to the music. Normally the Great Hall was used for formal events and for when Jereni met with her people. But tonight the celebrations were held here and it was filled with what seemed like all the nobles in the kingdom.

Who was the best man? Every man fell short of what Jereni deserved. Not one was intelligent, good, strong, or brave enough to be the choice. She had not yet met a man who would make Jereni happy, not one who Jereni would fall in love with. The lively music, or maybe it was her stress, made Eliinka's heart beat faster than it should. The dance finished and she stepped to the side of the floor to catch her breath and observe.

There would be time to dance or talk with everyone during the festival, or so she hoped. The morning after the festival ended, she must give Jereni a name.

Jereni had avoided mentioning the task throughout the previous month, but Eliinka often saw distant, worried expressions on Jereni's face, and once had caught her staring out a staircase window with a discouraged expression while she watched the men at their weapons' practice. The days had become cooler, but never cold like winter in Pelto. Eliinka had spent time in the kitchens and other places where servants congregated and heard about the men who mistreated servants. She had found the enormous library and spent time in that room, browsing, meeting nobles and visiting with them. She had done all she could to find the best man.

Every evening, when they talked before she played the harp, she had listened to clues from Jereni. There was not one man whom Jereni thought would make a good husband, no man she preferred. Jereni had no hope that a man could love her.

There must be one.

"Would you like to dance?" Someone tapped Eliinka's shoulder from behind.

Zerin!

"I'd enjoy dancing with you." Yet he wasn't whom she needed to dance with. If only she had already found the right man, she could enjoy this evening.

He took her hands and her skin pulsed at his touch. They sidestepped across the floor, and it was different, better than when he had taught her in the afternoons.

"You are distracted. You are not acting like yourself, dancing with everyone. What is your purpose?" Zerin asked as he danced her into a private corner.

Needles prickled deep in Eliinka's recovering muscle. "All that I do is for Princess Jereni."

"Princess Jereni said you are not capable of lying, and I want to believe her." Zerin leaned over Eliinka. His voice rose as steam. His breath hit her forehead. "Until recently, you just played music. You are now talking with everyone, even though you don't enjoy it." He motioned at the dancers.

Eliinka took a breath, choosing a response. Zerin was probably the only one who could tell that she wasn't enjoying the socializing. But her deadline loomed and he was interfering. How could she choose if he kept her from meeting all the men?

"Princess Jereni wishes that I improve my language skills by speaking with many people."

"She's using you as a spy in her own palace."

"No." Eliinka stared at Zerin, but when he returned her gaze and his jaw tightened, she looked away.

His words came out short, low. "She should have told me. She trusts me, or did until you arrived."

Eliinka could hear the bitterness in Zerin's voice and it made her angry. He was accusing her of being a spy. She wished she could tell him of her task and get his thoughts. It was true that she was dancing with everyone. She glanced back into his eyes. She would rather be dancing with only Zerin tonight.

"She has not asked me to spy. You can ask her." Eliinka pushed lightly on Zerin's chest, shoving him away. "She seems sad tonight. Why don't you ask her to dance? She has greeted almost everybody, but no one dances with her."

"How can I dance with my princess?" Zerin folded his arms and shook his head. "I dare not touch her."

"You know Princess Jereni better than any other man. If you danced with her, then others also would."

"You don't understand. Princess Jereni will choose who she dances with."

Eliinka turned her back on Zerin and walked back onto the dance floor, where she struck up yet another conversation. She wished she could dance more with him, that she could explain herself. But she would not, not even if he dragged her to Jereni.

Zerin did not dance with any other women, but only stood at the side of the room and watched her. Eliinka wondered about Jereni's words. Which woman was the one for him?

She was careful to not flirt with the men she met, and she managed to dance with almost every unmarried nobleman. Some avoided her, but most were willing to have a short conversation. Jereni appeared to avoid watching what Eliinka was doing, and after Jereni left the room late in the evening, the crowd quickly dwindled.

Eliinka worked her way back to Zerin and stood at his side. They both stood silent, neither looking at the other.

"Believe me, Zerin. I'm not a spy." Eliinka turned to face him.

"You don't seem to be the type to dance with every single man."

That's true, she thought. She would have preferred dancing the whole evening with one man; she would have *especially* preferred for that particular man to fall in love with her.

A crooked smile drew Zerin's lips apart, showing his white teeth. He folded his arms and continued to stare out at the dancers. "You have danced every dance this evening, more than any other woman in the room. Many see a beautiful woman having a good evening."

Eliinka's heart jumped at the word "beautiful."

"I'm not sure what I see," Zerin added.

Her shoulders sagged.

"There is no reason for you to stay now that Princess Jereni has left."

"You are staying until the end?" Eliinka asked.

"Always."

"As you said, there is no reason for me to be here. Good night." Eliinka slipped through a side door and stopped where Zerin could not see her. She watched him survey the room as the last dancers faded away and the music dissipated into silence. Had he said she was beautiful and meant it? They had spent so many hours together, her learning to express herself in Virjalo, and still, they could not communicate. She rushed upstairs to her room before he stepped out of the Great Hall. She didn't have time, not to think of Zerin or dream for herself.

Which man was worthy of Jereni?

Not one.

Eliinka leaned into her windowsill and gazed at the distant stars, seeing nothing.

It was the final night of the festival and diners settled into their seats for the feast. Jereni sat at the head of the table, Zerin and Shimlon at her sides. Eliinka sat in her assigned seat, on the far side of the table, at least thirty chairs away from Jereni. Before the cold chair warmed up, two lords near Eliinka leaped to their feet. "We won't eat at the same table as a woman from Pelto," one said. The other raised his voice even louder so it echoed up to the roof. "We refuse to sit near her."

A loud scrape of wood on marble blasted through the room. Jereni's serving man caught the chair before it struck the floor.

Eliinka sunk into her chair.

"Guards!" Jereni pointed to the two lords.

Her voice roared like an approaching thunderstorm while her guards dragged the two lords to the front of the room. "Eliinka is here by my personal invitation because of her service to me. Do you dare interfere with my commands? Do you dare interrupt my banquet?" Jereni stalked close to them, her eyes flaming. Her voice echoed in the corners of the Dining Hall.

The heavy-handed guards forced them into awkward bows.

Jereni raised her hand, her body leaned forward, and she narrowed her lips. Eliinka tightened all her muscles, shifting in her chair. Jereni glanced Eliinka's way, met her eyes, and turned away from the men. "Guards, hold them at the side of the room."

All in the room released a collective breath.

"Eliinka, come here."

Eliinka walked up the length of the table, wondering what Jereni planned. Would she now publicly announce her as a friend? Zerin's face whitened. She knelt before Jereni.

"Trust me," Jereni mouthed. She motioned Eliinka to stand as she pulled an empty basin across the table. A fine dagger appeared in her hand.

Eliinka stood up straight, ignoring her instinct to step away.

Or run.

Jereni, with a smooth motion, grabbed Eliinka's left wrist, stretched out her arm, and lifted the knife.

"Please, no." Eliinka whispered. All her muscles tightened. Her veins vibrated. *No!* As the knife approached her skin, she tried to tug her arm away, but Jereni held her wrist tight. *No!* This was barbaric. It brought back to her mind the Pelten stories of Viru. Their tortures. Their bizarre customs.

Jereni slashed Eliinka's inner forearm with the finely honed edge.

The cold, quick sensation of skin purposefully sliced. Beading of blood. Nerves screaming. The fingernails of Eliinka's right hand pierced the skin of her palm. How could Jereni do this to her? She held in her scream.

Jereni flipped the knife into her left hand, the gold and jeweled inlays sparkling in its rotation as she stretched out her right arm and slashed her own inner forearm in a similar manner. She placed their forearms together, interlocked their fingers, and held their arms above the basin.

Eliinka forced herself to look away from the blood dripping down her skin and focused instead on the people's rapt faces filled with a combination of admiration and fear. She did not dare move; she hoped she would not faint. *Courage, courage*, she repeated in her mind.

For a long minute, their blood mingled and dripped into the basin. Jereni examined her people with piercing scorn.

"Eliinka becomes Virun," she announced.

"No!" Eliinka gasped under her breath, so quietly that Jereni did not hear. She clamped her teeth tight. What did this mean? Even though life was good here and she had all she needed, she didn't want to be Virun. She missed Pelto, and she still wanted to go home.

"Take my cloth and bind up my arm," whispered Jereni as she relaxed her fingers and shook loose her hand from Eliinka's.

Eliinka picked up a large, white dining cloth and wrapped Jereni's forearm. She reached for a cloth for her own arm, but Jereni took it from her and bound up Eliinka's arm in a similar manner. Eliinka glanced at Zerin, whose eyes were wider than she had ever seen.

"I declare Eliinka to be Vala. She is now Virun. You will now address her as Lady Eliinka." Jereni glared at her subjects. The people rose and bowed. Eliinka stepped away to return to her seat, but Jereni grabbed her elbow. "No. You stand at my side."

"You are no longer lords." Jereni glared at the men. "You will never again see my face. Guards, take them to the dungeon."

Eliinka wondered what Jereni would do to them. She would not ask. She did not want to know.

The serving man returned with another chair, placing it next to Jereni's at the head of the table.

"Now we will eat."

With effort, Eliinka was able to spear the meat and bring it to her mouth. The spices burned her tongue and throat. She did not drink the wine that Zerin pushed toward her, but drank the marja juice. Her arm still pulsed. How deep was the cut? Would she need stitches? Would she be able to play the harp this evening?

How could Jereni make her Virun with her words? What did "Vala" mean? Would everyone here accept her because of that? Would Zerin? Would it be possible to return to Pelto now? Did this mean she would stay in Viru forever? Even if it did, she still would not belong here. A few words and a ritual would not change that.

This was the quietest meal ever heard in the palace—even the music seemed subdued. Eliinka ate, aware that everyone was watching her, but each time she looked up, the people shifted their attention away. As Eliinka completed the final course, Jereni leaned over and her lilting voice whispered into Eliinka's ear, "Come. Leave with me through my door."

They left through the ornate door in the rear, the door only Jereni used, and entered a small, elaborate sitting room. Jereni relaxed in a chair. "We'll wait here for the dance to start."

"Why?" Eliinka held out her arm as she shifted her weight from one foot to another. "I don't understand." A drop of blood seeped through the cloth near her wrist. She wished for a numbing cream, like they had in Pelto.

"My people will never treat you that way again! If they do, they'll be killed immediately!" Jereni frowned.

Eliinka cradled her aching arm in her other hand. Now her head hurt.

"Your presence, your stare contained my anger." Jereni crinkled her eyes. "Somehow." She leaned forward and stared at Eliinka as if she were searching for an answer.

"My arm . . ."

"The Vala ceremony has not been performed for over a hundred years."

"What does Vala mean?"

"Vala means . . . " The dance music began and Jereni stood up. "It is a title. You are now of Viru. It is as if you were born in the palace."

Eliinka followed Jereni into the Great Hall. Jereni said nothing more as she scanned all her subjects who were either dancing or talking. She kept straightening her skirt and touching the bandage on her arm. Maybe her arm also hurt.

Unsure what she was supposed to do, Eliinka stood at Jereni's side, listened to the musicians, and watched the dancers. She tapped her foot to the rhythm. Which man was the right one for Jereni? How would she know?

"Eliinka," Jereni said as the second song began. She grabbed Eliinka's shoulder and searched her face. "You will attend the dance tonight for me."

"For you?" Eliinka asked. The dance had just started.

"Come to my study early in the morning, and we will talk more." Jereni left the room without a glance at any of the nobles.

Now standing alone at the front of the room, Eliinka caught Zerin's attention and motioned with her head to the corner. Everyone watched as she walked across the floor to meet him.

Zerin hurried to her side.

"I need your help tonight, Lord Zerin. Princess Jereni asked me to stay at the dance, but I don't know what I'm supposed to do."

He lowered his head. "Forgive me for my accusations against you yesterday, my lady. I had not realized you were held in such high esteem." His lips quivered and his shoulders slumped. "Princess Jereni will be very angry with me."

"She doesn't know and doesn't need to know."

Zerin shifted his weight, still keeping his head bowed. "I will advise you to set the mood for the evening because Princess Jereni left early tonight."

Eliinka forced a smile through the growing pressure that grew inside her heart. She moved through the crowd, greeting people by name, speaking with the men she thought might be the best prospects for Jereni. But lords who before had spoken freely with her now hesitated in their words. No man asked for a dance. If a man treated her this way, how would he treat Jereni?

She returned to Zerin, frustrated, wondering how to proceed.

"You are not dancing tonight." Zerin stood farther away than normal and kept his chin down.

"I danced with almost everyone last night. Tonight is different." Eliinka choked on her words. "They think I am different. No one will touch me." She knew she did not belong here, no more now than when she had first arrived. The only change was now everyone stared. And now that no one would even speak to her, she would have a harder time choosing Jereni's husband.

Zerin brought her a glass of marja juice and pulled up a chair for her. It was apparent he would not ask her to dance either.

"Feel free to go dance with others." Eliinka turned to Zerin, forcing a half smile.

Zerin obeyed and danced with three women who were probably twenty years older than him. He returned to her side after a few dances.

"You need not stay until the end," Zerin said.

So he would not dance with her either. Eliinka wished he would. It would distract her and she could pretend that this dance was only for enjoyment. She folded her arms and stared out at the dance.

Were there any men she had not met? As she watched, she realized she had met them all.

As Jereni had said, any man would want to marry her. She was the princess. A beautiful woman. A strong woman who needed a man who would respect her, a man who was strong-willed and could be her equal. Most important, which man would love Jereni, love her deeply, and not just marry her because she was the princess? The few men that would have been the best choices were married and unavailable. Still, there were two or three who might not be poor choices, though they were not ideal.

The last song ended. The remaining dancers cheered the musicians, and everyone exited, their chattering voices leaving the now quiet hall. Eliinka thought about the type of man that Jereni deserved, a man who was strong, intelligent, and loving. He must exist. She leaned toward Zerin, wishing she could ask him for advice. But she was unable to find any words.

"It's late." Zerin said. "You must be tired. I'll walk you to your room."

Eliinka dropped her face into her open hands. She could not fail Jereni.

"Are you well?"

"I'm afraid to speak with Princess Jereni." Eliinka clenched her hands. She avoided sitting up, fearful she might confide in Zerin.

"Your words don't make sense. Anyway, you won't speak with Princess Jereni tonight. You need to go to bed."

"I can't sleep." Eliinka walked the length of the Great Hall, walked up a wide corridor, and entered the Dining Hall. Zerin followed. She sat down, pulled the large floor harp against her shoulder, and ran her hands across the strings. Zerin stood as a sentinel, waiting.

Eliinka paused, fingers frozen to the strings. "I may play all night. You need not wait for me."

Harsh, dissonant intervals played out into a confusing array of melodies, and it sounded as if she could not decide which song to play. Tension resounded round the room.

Zerin sat in the nearest chair.

Servants passed in and out, cleaning up from the earlier banquet, moving quietly, but Eliinka ignored them as she played song after song. The hall emptied of all movement within half an hour. Zerin snored lightly, slumped forward in his chair. He wasn't going to leave before she did.

She stopped playing. Zerin showed no interest in anyone. Who was the woman Jereni had referred to? An urge to reach out and touch his hand almost overcame her logic. She was not in Pelto where a woman and man could clasp hands. There it was a friendly gesture. Here? She had not seen physical contact between men and women unless they were dancing.

She swallowed her desires, desires she shouldn't have, and stared at the harp, which blurred in her eyes.

What man? She tapped the harp frame. She had not experimented with her gift since she had tried to use it on Jereni that first night, but perhaps she could use it to find the answer. Also, she would only use it for a good purpose, not for amusement or to force people against their will. She would not be going against what her faith taught.

There was no other option. She had no name.

Eliinka was not sure what her gift could do or if it could help her choose the man, but the room was now empty of servants, and Zerin slept. She had never heard of gifts while in Viru, so she assumed that it was not forbidden. Anyways, since no one would hear her, no one would sense her gift.

She clutched the strings, tightened them, ready to release a strong, quiet tone. She gazed at the blue diamonds on her hands. It was so strange to not choose and perhaps even marry a stranger. No wonder Jereni didn't believe love was possible in her marriage.

Love would be possible for Jereni, Eliinka thought, if she chose the right man. In Pelto, people fell in love and got married. Her own parents had been deeply in love and happy. That's what she had always planned for herself: a marriage of love and friendship, but that was not possible now, not unless she could get back to Pelto.

Her gift wouldn't be able to give her a name, but she could use it to help her relax and consider all the possibilities. Perhaps it would allow her to go deeper and hear the answer.

As she began, she carefully played an occasional note that soared above, adding sounds that would be hard to discern to the untrained ear. She experimented with layering them into the song, similar to when she had used her gift in the room with Jereni when she had first arrived. Once she was confident with this new technique, she played a new song, a song of longing, a song of questioning. As she used her gift, the music grew light and airy, and celestial voicings sprang from the strings. Her mind cleared and the stress of the past month lifted. The song was like a quiet summer brook tumbling under still, shady trees. She enjoyed the power of shaping the song, and the music grew into a never-ending flow that wanted to move faster and overflow its banks, yet it was deeper and calmer and more alive than she had ever played before. As faces of men passed through her memory, she knew deep inside that they were not a match, and eliminated them. Then one more face entered her mind.

Her fingers slipped and she hit a wrong note, breaking her dream-like state, and she stopped playing.

Zerin woke to the silence and sat upright, rubbing his eyes.

Eliinka stretched and stifled a yawn. She leaned her forehead onto the harp. The man was not who she expected, but she had no doubts. One man would please Jereni.

"Lord Zerin, I'll go to my room now."

Zerin walked Eliinka through the halls to her room. They passed the towering windows, and in the distance, hints of the faint light of sunrise edged the horizon. She hurried. She needed at least a couple hours of sleep. He bowed low as she stepped into her room. "Sleep well, my lady."

Eliinka left the door cracked open to watch him walk away.

But he stood there watching. He motioned to the bandage on her arm. "Do you feel all right?"

"I'm fine. Don't even think about making me more of that tea. Good night, Lord Zerin."

"Good night."

"Thanks for waiting with me tonight."

"I'm always the last to leave." His face flushed, and he bowed again before rushing away.

She shut the door, wondering if he perhaps had feelings for her.

Chapter Thirteen
~ THE COMPLICATIONS OF THIS CHOICE ~

"My lady." Milla placed the tray on the table, and the smell of just-baked bread swirled in the brisk morning air.

"Thank you." Eliinka blinked her sleep away as she sipped her juice. Milla bowed.

Eliinka spilled the entire glass of juice. Zerin had also bowed to her last night. Why? Milla refilled the glass and wiped up the juice. Eliinka grabbed a piece of fresh bread. She would eat quickly and hurry to the study where she would give Jereni the name.

"After your meal, my lady, I'll change your bandage." Milla pointed to a blue rectangular strip of fabric resting on the table.

Beads of sharpness ran up Eliinka's arm. Last night flashed back before her, the knife, the silence in the room, the slashing cut.

Why?

Why had Jereni, in her anger, sliced Eliinka's arm? She hated to think what Jereni would do to those she did not like. If she was back home in Pelto, she might go to bed hungry occasionally, but at least she wouldn't have all these scars or the blue diamonds on her arms, and she would not have men trying to kill her again and again. She would not have to protect herself and deal with her nightmares and the guilt that came during restless nights because she had killed men. *In self-defense,* she reminded herself.

She gulped down her juice. Yes, she had everything she needed here, but it could never be home.

"My lady." Milla interrupted her thoughts. "Is there any other food you wish to request from the kitchen?"

Sharp rays of sunlight hit Eliinka's face. Milla was calling her "my lady." "Why do you call me 'my lady,' Milla?"

"You are a lady, my lady." Milla began to make Eliinka's bed.

One short moment had changed so much. One slash of a knife. Now even Milla acted as if she were Virun nobility.

"Please, Milla, tell the cook and her assistants that the morning meal was wonderful." The tray included all of Eliinka's favorite foods. She refilled her glass with fresh marja juice sprinkled with mint, doing it quickly before Milla could insist on pouring it for her.

After Eliinka finished eating, she unwrapped the bandage and examined the cut, a reddish brown line—the width of a thick thread—that contrasted against her skin. It was longer than she had remembered, extending much of the length of her forearm. It still stung, but there was no real pain unless she moved her arm. Milla gazed at Eliinka's cut with fascination, almost reverence.

Milla gathered the swath of blue fabric and snugly wrapped Eliinka's arm. The patterns on the fabric caught the morning light, reflecting patches of blue onto the ceiling.

"Anything else, my lady?" Milla placed the dishes back onto the tray.

"No, not this morning."

After putting on a dress, Eliinka hurried out into the hall, rethinking her choice. What if she chose the wrong man? But who else was there for her to choose?

The study was empty.

Eliinka studied each portrait, ending with the one at the far end nearest the window: Jereni's mother. She was beautiful, even with the blue diamond and lines on her forehead. Her mother looked into the distance, past the painter, as if her heart were in another place. How many of these women had enjoyed their marriages?

Her own mother had never had her portrait painted. The memories, memories she thought she'd never forget, were fading, and it was harder to recall her mother's dark brown eyes, curly black hair, and the light scent of lavender in the oils and the soaps she used every day on her skin.

The air was stagnant, so Eliinka opened the windows and gazed at the pale, hazy horizon and the shadowed forest. These windows faced north, the direction of Pelto, the direction of home.

The quiet gave her too much space to think about the pain of her parents' deaths, so she ran her fingers along the wood of her token harp, running her fingernails into the notches where her mother had carved her name underneath the base. This harp was all she had left that connected her to her mother. Within a minute she began to play and her fingers moved nimbly over the strings. As she played music of Viru, touches of Pelto entered. She upped the tempo of the song, pushing herself, focusing on both technique and the emotions she teased from the strings as she wondered why Virun music made her feel more alive.

The door swung wide open, and Jereni entered, not smiling, not frowning, her expression not curious, but resigned.

Eliinka greeted Jereni in their usual manner of a clasp and kisses to each other's cheeks. She touched Jereni's bandage as they released their embrace: their bandages were cut from the same cloth. "You have given me great honor. What role will I play?"

"Do not worry, our contract remains valid."

Eliinka nodded her head. It appeared there was no way to alter or eliminate their agreement.

"When you first arrived, you were my musician. You risked your life and killed men to protect me. We vowed friendship, and after last night you are now my trusted confidant and advisor. You will sit at my side during the evening meal. Our time in this room will continue as before."

This was more than Jereni had said the previous night. Yet what did it really mean? An advisor? Like Zerin?

Jereni sat in her chair, leaned forward, and interlocked her fingers. Eliinka did not sit, but turned to the hearth, watching a light breeze play with the ashes and wondered that so little air could create sparks on the coals.

"Now, your report, your decision." Jereni waited through a long pause, and when Eliinka turned around, she asked, "Who will be my husband?"

"The name of the man is Mikali."

"Who?" Jereni blinked slowly.

"There are few men worthy of you. But he is a perfect match. Mikali will love you and please you."

"Who is Mikali?"

"Does your husband have to be Virun?"

"It is much simpler if he is from Viru, but it is not required." Jereni sank into her chair, tapping her fingertips together, creating a slow beat, the most serious expression settling on her face. "No princess in our history has ever married a man that was not from Viru."

The weight that Eliinka thought would lift from her shoulders when she announced the name did not leave. She had assumed any man would want this marriage, but Mikali? He had his own dreams. What if he did not want to marry Jereni? He was the only man who might not. But the name had come so strong that he had to be the right choice.

"Who is Mikali?"

"Mikali is the older brother of Rakel, a friend from my childhood." Eliinka breathed out in explanation. "He is handsome, intelligent, and has a good, pure heart. He showed little interest in girls, so I'd tease him. One day, when I was about ten, he said that he would only consider the girl he'd seen in his dreams. She was his true love. This girl was tall and beautiful, intelligent and powerful. You match the girl he described." Eliinka partly relaxed as a small smile grew on Jereni's face.

"His father, Aalto, was a government leader before his death. Their family is respected and well-known throughout Pelto. Mikali is two hands taller than you and sturdily built. He is twenty-four or twenty-five years old. His green eyes are so . . ."

"Who is his grandfather?"

"Aalto's father's name? Hyokata."

"Hyokata? Did he command Pelto's armies when you were a little girl?"

Eliinka covered her mouth. Muffled words emerged. "I'd forgotten. He attacked Viru. He wanted to take Viru's border lands and convince Viru to leave Pelto alone forever."

"He attacked. We did not provoke Pelto."

"Mikali never fought against Viru. He—"

"Viru's armies chased Hyokata. They didn't stop until he was captured. My father ordered his death." Jereni paused. "I hated that war. My father had left Pelto alone for many years, at least until Pelto attacked. But he withdrew his armies after Pelto was weakened."

"I'm sorry." Eliinka wanted to take back her choice. She wished Jereni could choose her own husband. This was a peculiar tradition, one she should have refused to participate in. "I thought Mikali was the best match. I can choose another man if I have more time."

"Mikali's name is announced. You chose a Pelten! Why?"

"He—"

"My husband will hate me."

"No. That war was twelve years ago. He doesn't hate anyone. I will take back his name. Tell me a man you prefer here in Viru and I will select him."

"That is impossible. You chose the best man, one you describe as strong, handsome, intelligent, one you mistakenly believe could love me." Jereni stared at the fire and whispered. "Mikali has been chosen. The ramifications, the logistics, the complications of this choice—it is too late to recant his name. It is as if you poured water into the source of a mountain stream—the water will flow to the sea and can never be removed. Eliinka, the man is chosen. There is no turning back."

"Mikali will love you."

"He will not come willingly."

"He might." Eliinka hoped he would, though now that she thought about it, she could not see how it was possible.

"Come to my council meeting, in ten minutes. You will announce Mikali's name to my advisors. We'll make plans, and Ilari will send men to observe him. A man will shadow him at all times. In two weeks we will have sufficient intelligence and a raiding party will bring him here."

A raiding party? Eliinka shook her head. *No!* She could not let that happen.

Jereni squeezed Eliinka's hand. "We will speak more of this tonight."

In a dazed stupor, Eliinka meandered upstairs to the Council Room. She would rather play the harp, practice shooting her bow and arrows, meditate in the garden—do anything to forget Jereni's words, anything to take away her poor choice.

Eliinka regarded the carved door of the Council Room. The intricate, deep-relief carvings in the diamond-shaped panels depicted scenes from Virun landscapes and history: treed mountains, the river, animals, and weapons. She clicked the long, carved brass handle and peered through the narrow crack. A sturdy wooden table was centered in a richly furnished room. She stepped inside. Zerin and two other men rose from their chairs and bowed to her.

Not more bows. Eliinka shifted her weight from one foot to the other, uncertain of where she should sit or if she should remain standing. The room was stifling hot, even though a light, cool breeze gusted through the open window. Zerin gave a slight, distant nod of his head. The door opened wide, and the men bowed to Jereni.

"You may sit in this chair, at my right." Jereni pointed to a chair next to Zerin.

She waved her arm at a tall, sturdy man on her left, who appeared about forty years old. "Lord Ilari is in charge of the military and guards." She pointed to the older, gray-haired man seated across from Zerin. Eliinka recognized him. "This is Lord Shimlon. He's in charge of all my affairs within Viru, including all the royal industries and enterprises."

Though Eliinka did not understand all the Virjalo words as the meeting progressed, she understood the general meaning of what was said: the meeting covered a variety of topics ranging from the weaving industry to taxes to guard training. The advisors answered Jereni's questions and discussed potential solutions. Jereni was efficient and fair and listened to her advisors' counsel as she made decisions.

"There is one more item." Jereni glanced at Eliinka, speaking slower. *So I can't misunderstand her Virjalo*, Eliinka thought. "The traditions of Viru are valued in my heart and soul. They are important to our strong culture and keep order in our society." Her advisors shifted in their seats and stopped shuffling papers.

"The ancient tradition and long-standing custom of either a family member or close friend selecting each woman's husband will be honored by me. Eliinka is here to announce the name of the man who will become my husband."

Zerin nodded and smiled half a smile as if he now understood all Eliinka had been doing this past month.

She swallowed. He might not be happy about her words, but she turned to Jereni, and after bowing her head, gave the announcement.

"Princess Jereni, Mikali, son of Aalto, is chosen to be your husband."

Jereni's eyes laughed.

After a long, breathless pause, Shimlon asked, "Lady Eliinka, could you tell us about Mikali?"

"Mikali is a brave, intelligent, and well-respected man. He is honest and owns a large trading firm. His father was a government leader." The men glanced at each other. Zerin bent his elbow and rested his jaw on his fist. He stared at Eliinka, almost like he wanted to ask her a question. Perhaps he remembered that she had spoken of him months earlier.

"Go on, I want to know more about this Mikali," Jereni said.

"Mikali is quite tall, taller than Jereni by two or more hands, and is sturdily built."

Ilari picked up a quill and frantically scrawled notes on a parchment. Jereni leaned forward and motioned for Eliinka to continue.

"He has dark brown hair, green eyes, and is considered handsome by every girl I know," Eliinka said. "He is as comfortable at a formal dance or theater performance as he is riding or hunting. But most important, he has a pure heart, is kind, and loves to interact with people—" Eliinka stopped speaking when Ilari whispered in Shimlon's ear.

Zerin frowned, shaking his head, mumbling, "He can't be . . ."

"Eliinka, tell my advisors where Mikali lives."

"Last I heard, he lived in RitVa, in Pelto."

Ilari gasped.

Shimlon hit the table with his fist.

"But," Zerin started to say more. Instead, he shook his head.

"Eliinka," Jereni said. "You are excused."

As soon as the door shut behind her, the men's voices erupted into an argument, the loudest was Ilari, saying this would instigate another war.

Eliinka knew she had made a poor choice by choosing a man who was not Virun. Why had Jereni accepted Mikali's name? She must really be willing to marry him, even with all the issues she had brought up. No one would have known if she had asked Eliinka to choose another this morning. Maybe there was no man she wanted to marry in Viru and Jereni was willing to take this risk. It was no use trying to understand Jereni or her culture. Eliinka had given Mikali's name, and now Jereni planned to have her men kidnap him. Just like what the legends said: Viruns snuck into Pelto and kidnapped young men.

Wishing that everything were different, Eliinka hurried back to her room. She lay on her bed, staring at the ceiling as she considered what she had done. She wished she had considered the consequences first. Since she had not slept much last night, she allowed herself to drift off, but instead of resting for an hour, she slept through the midday meal and all afternoon and missed her lesson with Zerin.

When Eliinka woke, her temples and forehead hurt, a minor headache. She rushed to the study. Jereni wasn't there. Without giving a glance toward the token harp, she walked to the hearth and watched the flames eat away at the edges of the logs. She would not have announced Mikali if she had known Jereni would kidnap him and force him to come to Viru. What was she thinking? She had been too excited to find a good match and had not thought it through.

She lowered herself to the carpet, relaxed, and positioned herself into a meditative attitude of crossed legs, hands in front with fingertips touching. She murmured the words of her meditations, just like her mother had taught her, "Elavaksi. Give me peace and understanding." She forced herself to breathe slow and deep, and as she did, she cleared her mind and closed her eyes.

Half an hour later the door opened. Jereni entered with silent footsteps. Eliinka ignored her. Several minutes later she heard a maid enter and set what were probably mugs of nightmilk on the table. A book dropped on the floor. Still, neither spoke.

Eliinka sensed that Jereni waited for her.

"I am so naïve." Eliinka opened her eyes. "I wish I better understood the culture of Viru."

Jereni sat on the floor next to Eliinka and clutched Eliinka's knee. "It takes years to learn a culture. But you will learn. You will accept that we do what is necessary, even when it is not easy."

She pulled Eliinka's sleeve down from her shoulder. She pressed the scar and flesh at several points.

Eliinka did not flinch. She rotated her shoulder and moved it forward and back, up and down. "There is still some tenderness, but no pain." She pulled her sleeve back up.

"You will begin learning the knife and staff tomorrow. Now that you are healed, you will train with the noblewomen," Jereni said.

Eliinka traced the blue diamond on her right hand. Women never trained to fight, at least not in Pelto. *It might be useful to learn to protect myself,* she thought.

"There are repercussions and unanticipated consequences to our choices. Your coming here was a good choice and has made life better for everyone."

Jereni continued, "The blossoms that spring breezes blow off a tree cannot be gathered any easier than you can change the consequences of a choice." They sat quietly for a few moments, watching the flames turn the pieces of wood to ash.

"Let's drink our nightmilk while it is still warm." Jereni returned to her chair.

Eliinka sat in the chair next to Jereni. She picked up her mug and swirled the milk. As she sipped, her headache faded.

Jereni took a slow drink and held the mug between her hands. "Your description of Mikali fascinates me. But is he brave?"

"Mikali is brave. He . . ." Eliinka set her mug down and swallowed her uncertainty as she considered the fabric wrapped around her arm. After yesterday, she could perhaps express her opinion. She paused, then placed her hands on an arm of Jereni's chair and knelt at Jereni's feet. "Consider that perhaps Mikali would make a better husband if he chooses to come with you. Please . . . please give Mikali a choice."

"He won't want to come to Viru." Jereni frowned. "Would he consider harming me, if brought here?"

"No."

"What if no guards are at my side?"

"He would never hurt a woman," Eliinka said. "Every man pales in comparison to Mikali. Will you force him to marry you?"

"My mother married my father. Mikali will marry me. He is chosen."

"I think he'll choose you if given the chance." Eliinka did not think she could face Mikali, not if he was captured. She remembered the stories of how Viruns mistreated their captives. They were kept in dungeons and used when soldiers needed practice. Her thoughts caught on themselves.

Maybe the stories were false. The legends about the Princess of Viru seemed untrue. The other stories might be untrue as well.

"Your request will make a dangerous mission more risky. It could make the mission fail." Jereni contemplated the portraits of her mother and father. "Eliinka, failure is not an option. But the decision won't be made until after Ilari reports back to me."

"Thank you." Eliinka's shoulders relaxed. This was better than she had hoped for. After she swallowed the last of her nightmilk, she sat at the harp and played a slow, contemplative song. After she finished the song, Jereni joined in with the large harp, and their song grew and expanded and swelled until Eliinka forgot her worries.

When they reached the end of their duet, Eliinka trailed with a few more notes. Jereni paced back and forth in front of the fireplace, and when Eliinka finished the next song, said, "Have you considered a man for your husband, Eliinka? Has any man caught your attention?" A silvery edge rang in Jereni's voice.

A husband? Eliinka gripped the harp strings so tight her fingers hurt. For her? She would not admit she was interested in Zerin. He did not follow Eleman Puusta, and Jereni had said he was taken.

"It is not my place to choose," Eliinka said. "Not in Viru." A faint fear rose inside her. In Pelto she would have a choice, but here . . . she had no say. Not if Jereni believed she was now Virun. If she married a man from Viru, she would never be able to go home.

Chapter Fourteen

~ A GOOD MATCH ~

My men returned late last night."

The juice felt dry as Eliinka swallowed it. She sat across from Jereni at a round table in a small dining chamber situated across the hall from Jereni's room. Except when there was a banquet, they now ate every meal together in this room. Although not as private as the study, with servants constantly moving in and out with plates of food, it allowed time to visit.

"The men returned late last night." Jereni curved her lips into a smile as she repeated her words. "Mikali will be here within two weeks."

Eliinka pushed her plate aside, checking that no servants were in the room. "Please, Jereni. Don't kidnap Mikali. You want him to love you."

"He won't choose to come here. We killed his grandfather. Peltens hate us!" Jereni took another bite. "The report matches everything you said. Except he is stronger than you told me. He has never lost in either training or competition, even when matched against two opponents.

"Did you know that? Still, we will take him even though some of my men will die. Mikali will marry me. It is a better choice for him than sitting in my dungeon. He'll be convinced when he hears my words."

"He is very stubborn. Please, Jereni. He will refuse you if you force him. Do you want to meet him in bonds, trussed up like a captured boar?"

Jereni raised her chin.

"You convinced me to come to Viru. Please try the same with Mikali. He is like a brother to me. He visited me and helped me when I was living on my own. I'm sure he noticed I disappeared." Eliinka would never admit to Jereni that when she was small, she dreamed of marrying him. She did not want any men killed on account of her choice, not Mikali or any of Jereni's guards. "We could travel to Pelto, meet him there. I could convince him to come to a remote town that you choose or to a village close to the border. I'll write a letter. I can cover my symbols, and you can travel in disguise as a wealthy woman traveling on business. Please try this first."

"Do you think he would choose to come to Viru, even if he finds out my identity?"

"Can we try? It will be easier to capture him if needed, if he is by himself." Eliinka could hardly believe her own words. She squeezed her fingernails into her palms.

Jereni shifted her food around her plate.

"Give him a chance to fall in love with you," Eliinka said. She could imagine Mikali falling in love with Jereni. With each passing day, she had realized what a perfect couple they would make. If they could overlook their different cultures, they would be very happy together.

"Are you willing to do this, trick him to meet us, even if it means we may use force to bring him here when he refuses?"

Eliinka swallowed hard. At least this way Mikali would not be forced, at least not at first. "I will. You need a chance of a marriage with love."

"He will know who I am before we reach the crossing. You will wear Pelten clothing, at first, until he is convinced to come with me. The seamstresses will sew dresses for you."

Eliinka nodded and tightened her hands until her knuckles turned white. She would return to Pelto, but not in the way she wished.

Jereni reached into a fold of her dress and unveiled a delicate, narrow dagger whose blade was almost as long as her middle finger. The stub handle, with intricate inlaid designs of interweaving gold and silver wire, was designed to be held between the thumb and the first two fingers.

"This dagger is for you. You will hide it in your dress." Jereni handed Eliinka the dagger. "This afternoon, you will go to the seamstresses and three of your dresses will be altered for it."

Eliinka wondered if their conversation had been manipulated by Jereni. Had she wanted Eliinka to volunteer to go to Pelto? And what was the dagger for? It would be useless against Mikali. Realizing she was too silent, she said, "Thank you. Do your dresses have hidden pockets?"

"Yes, all of them." Jereni palmed her own dagger, slightly larger than Eliinka's and even more ornate, with a sapphire placed in the butt. She flipped it around her hand with lightning speed. "No one except the seamstresses realize I carry a knife." She laughed as she secreted it back into her dress, "But I suppose Zerin suspects I do, especially after I pulled it out that evening you became Vala."

Eliinka wished that she were surprised that Jereni kept a weapon on her, but she was not. She balanced her dagger in her hands: it was beautiful, a piece of art. "Where do I keep it?"

"After your dresses are altered, you will keep your knife in its sheath, in your dress." Jereni patted her own hidden pocket. "You will need to practice removing it quickly."

"Are we carrying weapons with us for protection?" Eliinka hoped she wouldn't need to carry a bow. "We won't be attacked again this time, will we?"

"Those people—the Flute People who attacked us last time after we crossed the borders into Viru—did not know at first who they attacked. They took advantage of the situation, of what appeared to be normal travelers. This time my men will wear their uniforms."

"The Flute People live in Viru, but—"

"They have not bowed to the crown for over a hundred years, closer to two hundred. They refuse to meet with me. They attack my farmers and harass travelers at times, but they dare not attack my guards and soldiers. Perhaps someday that edge of my kingdom will be a safe place, but the Flute People are a wild people who do not wish to obey my laws or become civilized."

"This knife?"

"Only for close combat. You will probably never use it to fight."

"*Probably?*" *I'm being trained to use a knife in the weapons training*, Eliinka thought.

"It is unlikely. We leave tomorrow morning." Jereni secreted her knife into her dress. "Now it is time for you to learn the signals I use with my guards so you will understand my messages."

Eliinka had noticed that Jereni used signals. She wondered why she would also need to learn to communicate with the guards in this way.

They sat in front of the fire, and Jereni taught her one signal after another, insisting that Eliinka practice and memorize each one. More than once she said, "Knowing these signals can make a difference between life and death."

Second Crossing

Chapter Fifteen

~ WHAT YOU REALLY WANT ~

Eliinka and Jereni sat in the dim shadows created by the moon's light filtering through the trees, in the flickering of the smoky fire that smelled of wet, green wood. The knife sheath hidden in Eliinka's dress scraped against her hip, and she adjusted its position to make it more comfortable. Next, she pulled her cloak tighter around her shoulders and wrapped a fur blanket around herself. Her breath misted in the evening air.

The bright stars hung like the flowers in the sky above the Syrjassa Mountains. A distant music floated high and sweet above the treetops.

They traveled light and carried no harp with them, so Eliinka dreamed of her token harp, imagined playing a song, imagined touching the strings. She realized how much she missed playing her music. Even a day without the harp left her with an aching hunger.

Shouts from her right broke the stillness, and a guard yanked a teenage boy by his long hair into the light of the fire, shoving him into a bow until dust licked the boy's face, his hair falling dangerously close to the fire.

"What is this?" Jereni leaped to her feet.

"We found him in the woods, spying," the guard replied.

"Search for others! If you find them, bring them here. No one will sleep tonight."

Huoli, the guard leader, yanked a knife from strips of cloth wound around the boy's calf. He handed it to Jereni.

"Double the watch!" Jereni spun his knife around her hand. The blade traced circles in the air.

The boy moved his bare feet, blue with cold, toward the fire. Rags, not even patched clothing, hung from his boney frame.

"Did your people not understand my mercy last time?" Jereni asked. "No gift arrived, no emissary."

He dropped his head.

"Look at me!"

He tipped his head even lower. Jereni flipped his knife in her hand so the blade rested on her inner forearm, and struck the side of his head with the hilt and the inner edge of her hand. His body pitched to the side, and he fell to the ground.

"Answer me!"

"They fear the princess," he said in a clipped, tonal accent as he clambered to his knees, keeping his head low, his forehead in the dirt.

"Your people will no longer hide inside my kingdom. They will stop attacking travelers. More soldiers than you can imagine will come and scour the wilderness." Jereni circled the fire, while playing with his knife in her left hand. She picked up a long stick and stirred the fire, and when the flames had roared up to her waist, she threw the stick into the burning wood.

The boy did not move, though he knelt in an uncomfortable position.

"You won't travel with us." She heaved him to his feet, and pressed his knife against his neck.

He leaned away and, losing his balance, fell backward, almost into the flames. A guard leaped forward and held him upright. The boy's jaw shook, and he rubbed his throat.

"Please, give me his life." Eliinka moved between Jereni and the boy. It was times like this that she remembered how barbaric Viruns could be.

"We don't keep slaves." Jereni narrowed her eyes. Her breath misted in the cold air. "But that is not what you're asking for."

"Please, don't hurt him. He's just a boy. Maybe he is a chance for—"

"Drop him." Jereni frowned as the boy fell, throwing dust onto her boots. He shifted away from them, toward the warmth of the fire.

"Huoli, don't let him escape," Jereni said. "Find out why he was watching us and if any other Flute People are nearby. And take his flute away. He might use it to call others."

Huoli leaned down and patted the boy's shirt, where it bulged on the side. He pulled it up, baring the boy's bony ribs as he removed the flute.

"He's starving," Eliinka said as she leaned down and handed him a large chunk of bread from dinner.

As the boy shifted away from her, he tore off a piece of it with his mouth.

Jereni grabbed Eliinka's elbow and pulled her across their campsite and into their tent, almost ripping off the flap. As soon as the flap dropped, Jereni brought her face close to Eliinka's. "Why do you interfere?"

"I'm sorry."

"Eliinka, you are cruel!" Jereni tossed the boy's knife onto the ground. "You give him hope."

"If we feed him he would have a full stomach, probably for the first time in his life." Eliinka picked up the knife and examined the rusted blade. A dull edge. The only reason he was not bleeding. "If you give him a chance, you can use him to send a message."

"He will refuse to obey me! And you encourage him to . . . to think he can spy with no consequences."

Eliinka knelt and held out her arm, twisting it so the shiny line they shared faced upward. "Forgive me. I wish to do your will. He may be a way for you to make contact with the Flute People." She pulled her arms to her chest and sank onto her bedding.

"You do not yet fully understand our culture. These people have avoided contact with the rulers of Viru for centuries. They are fiercely independent. It has been over a generation since the army has reminded them of their place." Jereni removed her crown from its case and placed it on her head. She stalked outside, saying, "It is time to remind them again."

Eliinka paused at the tent door. It felt like just when she believed she was accepted, their friendship rocked precariously, sliding out of balance. Yet there were moments when Jereni was the friend she had always wanted. At other times Eliinka was reminded, too vividly, that she was still finding her place in a foreign land.

Jereni stood near her chair, her arms folded, silhouetted by small flames licking half-charred logs. Her guards paced the perimeter, their weapons held ready. The boy lay perfectly still on bare dirt that sparkled with ice crystals. His eyes moved back and forth from Jereni to the sky. Jereni was correct. No one would sleep tonight.

Stepping back out into the frigid night air that snapped at Eliinka's bare skin, hands, and face, she bowed to Jereni and moved to her side. As she held her arms over the fire, the boy stared at the markings on her hands and forearms.

Jereni frowned and placed her hands on her hips. Huoli stepped to her side and whispered into her ear.

"What is your name?" Jereni asked the boy.

The boy scrambled backward, but his gaze did not leave Jereni's face or the crown on her head. Huoli lowered his sword toward the boy.

"This is your chance, boy," Jereni said. "My mercy has been shown twice: tonight and last winter when my camp was attacked. Those four men returned to you, did they not? The men Lady Eliinka spared." She motioned to Eliinka.

Nodding slowly, the boy stared at Eliinka.

"Give me your name and your obedience, and you will go free."

"Answer Princess Jereni," Huoli said.

Eliinka nodded encouragingly. "She keeps her promises. I gave her my loyalty."

"Ahds," the boy answered. He did not look at Jereni, but kept staring at Eliinka.

"Ahds, if you promise to take a message to your people and return to me with their answer in three weeks, you will go free," Jereni said.

He stole a glance at the forest as he clambered to his knees and said, "You are the princess!"

"There will be no more attacks, no more stealing from my farmers, no more frightening my people who travel. If there are any more attacks, my armies will come." Jereni slipped off a gold bracelet and handed it to him. "Give this to your leader. Tell him of my desire for prosperity for all my people, including the Flute People."

The boy held the bracelet tightly and rubbed it between his fingers.

"Tell your leader to come with you and talk with me. His safety is guaranteed."

"Jereni," Eliinka whispered. She held up Ahds's flute and knife. Jereni gave a slight nod of her head.

"Do you remember all this?" Jereni asked. "Will you deliver my message?"

"I will." Ahds stood up straight, and when Eliinka handed him his flute and knife, his eyes lit up.

"You may leave now or in the morning." Jereni turned away. "Huoli, feed him as much as he can eat and give him food for his journey."

Before Jereni entered the tent, Ahds knelt toward her and bowed his head. "The princess," he whispered.

After Eliinka secured the tent flap in an attempt to block the cold draft, she dropped her cloak to the floor. "The boy seems harmless. Will he keep his promise?"

"It is a low risk to release him," Jereni said. "Yet there is potential for him to give the Flute People my message. If their leader comes, we will have achieved peace inside my kingdom's borders."

Eliinka held her hands above the brazier. After she was warm, she changed into her nightdress and dropped into her bedding, pulling the fur blankets up to her chin. Tomorrow she would wear a Pelten dress and enter Pelto. She would speak Pelten again and enjoy familiar food instead of the spicy dishes that sometimes still burned down her throat. How would it feel to step onto Pelten soil? If it were for another reason, she would be excited, instead of worried.

"Peace is rarely found, real peace is . . ." The silvery edge slipped into Jereni's voice. "Have you found what you want in Viru? Do you *know* what you really want?"

Eliinka traced the diamonds on her hands. Did she dare express her desires in words? She visualized the token harp, the harp given her by her mother, the harp that would never again be hers. She shook that loss away.

Her parents: the memories surged back. Her mother teaching her to play the harp, and then, while she practiced every day in the late afternoon, her mother baking sweetbread for their dinner. Her father singing along while she played. But they were only entering the borders of Pelto, not going to RitVa. It would not be possible, not to regain her harp, or to visit her parents' graves and pay her respects like she was required to.

Eliinka looked up at Jereni, who was waiting with a raised eyebrow, knowing she was delaying her response. She looked for words, wondering what she could say that was truth.

"Do you wish to return to Pelto?"

Eliinka shook her head. "I value your friendship in the same way I value my music and my life. I will stay at your side." It was a near-truth. She did value their friendship. In many ways Jereni was a better friend than any she had ever had before, but at the same time she wished they had brought the harp with them and that she could annul the contract and erase the markings on her arms. In so many ways she wanted to return and slip away into a life in Pelto.

Chapter Sixteen

~ PIECES DO NOT FIT ~

"What will we do if Mikali doesn't come?" Eliinka asked. The cold winter sun had reached its low peak in the sky. She'd been hopeful, but now she was not so sure he would come.

Their horses' hooves crunched in the snow as they rode through a forest of bare trees and dormant shrubs toward the entrance of the Satu Inn in Kaikula, a tiny village on the southwest edge of Pelto.

"There are options—options more dangerous than what we are now doing. Your letter will draw him here. Mikali will come."

"I hope so." In the letter Eliinka had told him that Jereni reminded her of the woman he had described from his dreams. She had also invited him to dinner the evening they would be at the inn.

Jereni ran her hand along a branch as they passed, gathering a small bit of snow. She smiled as she tossed a handful in the air.

A guard took their horses to the stable, and they entered the near empty inn. The only two men inside played a game of dice at a table. Guards from Viru! Eliinka recognized them even though they had grown short beards and now looked like Peltens. She adjusted her sleeves, designed to cover the back of her hands, making sure her marks did not show. The sleeves were designed slightly longer than a normal Pelten style, but not so different so as to bring attention to her. The long skirt of the Pelten dress, which had kept her warm during the ride, now felt heavy and awkward. It also felt odd to have her hair twisted again on top of her head. She realized that she had become accustomed to the dresses of Viru.

The innkeeper welcomed them. He hovered close by, eyeing Jereni. After a minute, his wife came out from the kitchen and dragged him away, and a half smile appeared on Jereni's face. They settled at a table at the rear of the main room, and the wife served their midday meal. The guard who had entered the inn with them sat nearby, with one empty table between them.

Within an hour, the guard who had carried the message to Mikali arrived. He reported to Jereni and said, "He's within an hour's ride. A woman rides with him." He joined the other guard at the table.

"His sister, Rakel," Eliinka guessed. She wished Rakel had not come, though they had been close friends. "She might complicate things."

"We can handle her. Yet Mikali has ridden quickly." Jereni shifted her chair so it faced the door. She played with a Pelten ribbon woven in her hair that she wore down, not pulled up in the Pelten style.

Eliinka stood and leaned against a large window that faced south. The sun had fallen halfway to the trees in the west, and the full moon was rising, pale and large in the eastern sky. She played a harp tune in her head, but the tension, the possibilities of all that could go wrong, kept disrupting the music; the worst possibility included several dead guards, an injured Mikali, and a screaming Rakel.

Would it be possible for Mikali to come to Viru and fall in love with Jereni?

If she had her harp, maybe, for both Mikali's and Jereni's sake, she would risk using her gift, hoping that neither of them would sense it. Or, as she thought about it, it was not the proper use of the gift, was it, to create love? Using a gift for good was allowed in Eleman Puusta, but one shouldn't force others or interfere with their choices, unless they were harming someone.

At last, two horses trotted toward the inn. Eliinka rushed out through the door. Mikali! He was like she remembered: tall, muscular, and athletic, with a rugged, bearded face.

Mikali leapt off his horse and helped Rakel dismount. They disappeared from view as they led their horses into the stable, and Eliinka winced at the cold, wishing she had thought to throw on her cloak.

"Hello," Eliinka called when they reappeared. Rakel trailed Mikali as they crossed the yard, picking her way through the snow.

"It's been a long time." Mikali grasped Eliinka's hand. "You moved away, and you didn't tell me."

"I made the decision rather suddenly. I should have sent a letter sooner." Eliinka turned and greeted Rakel with a quick hug. "It's such a surprise to see you today."

"It's cold outside." Rakel leaned against Mikali. "We can visit over drinks."

"I'm so glad you came. We weren't able to travel all the way to RitVa," Eliinka said as Mikali opened the door. She led them to the back of the room where Jereni stood to greet them. Her dress, although cut in the looser Pelten fashion, accentuated her figure, and her flowing hair framed her face, falling below her shoulders. She gave Mikali a warm smile.

"Jereni, I present Mikali and his sister, Rakel."

Jereni stretched out her hand to Mikali. As their hands grasped, Mikali's left hand lingered on her elbow. He released her hand slowly. Jereni said, "It's a pleasure to meet you, Mikali. Would you join us for our early evening meal?" She shook Rakel's hand and motioned them to join her at the table. Jereni shifted her chair toward Mikali as she sat down.

Rakel narrowed her eyes at Jereni and placed a hand on Mikali's shoulder.

Jereni waved at the innkeeper who rushed out and placed bread and a water jug on the table.

"Your meal will be served as soon as it is prepared." He poured wine into their goblets.

"You have traveled far today." Jereni leaned toward Mikali.

Mikali shifted his chair closer to Jereni. "Eliinka's letter surprised me. I changed my plans after receiving it. It's been so long since we have seen Eliinka that Rakel came with me."

"Your dress is beautiful, Eliinka. It's in the newest style," Rakel said. Her glance at Jereni's dress became an open-eyed stare.

"Thank you." Eliinka placed her hands in her lap. It was good the necklace was hidden by the higher-necked Pelten dress. Rakel would have too many questions if she saw it. "Are you still designing clothing?"

"Yes," she said, jerking her head back to Eliinka. "I've been experimenting with colors and new styles."

"I'm glad to see you're doing well, Eliinka," Mikali said, "and that you have found your place in the world."

Eliinka glanced at Jereni, who was studying Mikali closely.

"What have you been doing?" he asked.

"I still play my harp. I also help Jereni. How is your business going?"

"It's grown enormously. I travel even more. You're lucky I was in town so I could receive your message."

Eliinka nodded. It wasn't luck. His traveling had made it harder for them to time their trip. But Jereni's men had discovered his travel schedule.

"Tell me about where you travel and what you do." Jereni took a sip of wine.

Rakel started talking to Eliinka at the same time he answered Jereni. "Where did you meet Jereni? I've never heard of her."

"We met when she visited RitVa. It was her first time to visit the city. She liked my harp music so I decided to travel with her."

"Really?" Rakel asked. "Her clothes are the fanciest I've ever seen."

"She likes clothes." Eliinka searched quickly through her mind, trying to find any subject to distract Rakel from Jereni. "I've not been back for many months. How is everyone doing? Aino, did she get married?"

Within a minute, they were chatting, almost like when they were young, where Rakel did most of the talking. Rakel drank her wine, and Eliinka drank water, wishing for fresh juice. They talked about mutual friends and who else had married whom in the last year, with Rakel giving detailed descriptions and her thoughts on each man and on what their friends wore for the ceremonies. As they ran out of people to talk about, Rakel paused and glanced at Jereni again, so Eliinka asked Rakel about her weaving. For the next ten minutes, Rakel enthusiastically described her weaving and a new pattern she had created.

Eliinka was only half listening so she could overhear Mikali and Jereni. She wasn't sure that Mikali would choose to go to Viru; not even he would consider traveling there. No Pelten would. When Mikali asked Jereni where she lived, she sidestepped his questions.

After the meal was placed before them, Mikali discovered that Jereni was also involved in business, or as Jereni put it, she was involved in a variety of industries, but the running of her businesses was done by others.

The food made Eliinka homesick. The sweetbread tasted exactly like the recipe her mother used to make. She took a second piece and asked Rakel another question about the clothes she was designing but then tuned her out again.

"Can we establish business ties?" Mikali asked Jereni. "Find a way for us to work together?"

"A relationship would benefit both of us and would allow us many more enjoyable meals together. But you were not invited here to speak of business." Jereni tucked a strand of hair behind an ear, and shifted the conversation to the safer ground of Mikali's enjoyment of the outdoors. All the time an enchanting smile teased Jereni's lips.

Rakel paused her torrent of words as she squinted and closely examined Eliinka's dress. She reached out and fingered the skirt. "I've never seen such a fine weave and yet you've brought this dress on your travels. Where did you find it? Who made it?"

"Jereni gave it to me." Eliinka reached under the table and tapped Jereni's knee to get her attention.

"This dress is amazing," Rakel said. "Where did she find one made of such high-quality fabric?"

"One of my businesses specializes in weaving. The fabric was obtained from them." Jereni pushed her half-full plate to the side. "This was an excellent meal. The sweetbread was my favorite." Her and Mikali's chairs had moved so close to each other that their shoulders were almost touching.

"A dinner of this quality is far beyond what a country inn normally serves," Mikali said.

"My particular request for a special meal was made in anticipation of your coming." Jereni moved her head within inches of Mikali's and whispered. "Thank you. This has been most enjoyable." They gazed into each other's faces.

Rakel shifted in her chair.

"Will you share your music with us, Eliinka?" Mikali asked.

Jereni pulled away from Mikali and turned to Eliinka.

"We are traveling," Eliinka said, but the excuse was weak. "I didn't bring my harp."

"But you would never leave your harp!" Mikali pointed at Eliinka's dress. "Something is not right. The pieces do not fit together." He turned to Jereni. "Why have we never met before? This inn is not on a trading route, and you never answered my question of where you live. Yet, you claim to own many businesses."

"All I have said is truth."

"Yet I've never heard of you in my trading or travel. I have visited every city and almost every village in Pelto. I have traveled to neighboring lands. I saw your horses in the stable. They are of a fine breeding, but different than any horse I've ever seen. They are not Pelten horses. They are also not like the horses of Pohjola and Ulkomaani."

Mikali leaned toward Jereni. "Your necklace. Your gems are not from Pelto. That quality does not exist here." He reached out and took Jereni's right hand. Tension leaped through the air. The fingers of his right hand swept over the back of her hand and came to rest on her ring. "Your ring, the gem has an unusual emblem on it. I've never seen your seal on any document." He set her hand down on the table, yet he still held her hand in his. He whispered, "Why have we never met before? How can you be unknown to me? Please, who are you and where do you live?"

Eliinka placed a hand on Jereni's shoulder, softly, hoping it would nudge her desires and remind her of Eliinka's pleas.

Dice clattered from the table where the guards started their game up again. The kitchen door creaked open, and the innkeeper's wife came and poured more wine. She returned to the kitchen, and the door closed with a thud. Rakel picked up her glass, and took a sip while watching Mikali and Jereni.

"My vagueness is for my own protection," Jereni finally said. "You would never have come to visit me in my home, so we came here to meet you."

"Never? I would have traveled much farther than Kaikula to meet you after reading Eliinka's letter."

"The risk and hazard would have been too great." Jereni gave Mikali a half smile, a sad smile. "You would not have come. Mikali, thank you for the most enjoyable afternoon of my life." She slid her hand away from his and stood up. Jereni's two guards were suddenly at her side, standing at attention. The time that had stalled just a moment before careened forward, and Eliinka wished for her harp. If she could play something relaxing, moving, it would help ease everyone's emotions.

"I am Jereni, Princess of Viru."

Eliinka gasped. Jereni had told him who she was, here, in the inn. It was now hopeless. She hadn't tried to trick him or set him up so she could force him to come.

Rakel jerked her chair backward, bumping into Eliinka.

"You would not have come."

Mikali reached a hand out to Jereni. She brushed it away.

"We leave immediately." Jereni strode toward the door, her guards at her sides.

Chapter Seventeen

~ A SMALL PRIZE ~

Eliinka rushed after Jereni. She stopped at the door and said, "I'm glad you came, Mikali. It was nice to see you again. You too, Rakel."

"Traitor," Rakel said.

"Viru is not the place we were taught. You would be wise to give Princess Jereni a chance." Eliinka turned her back to them and stepped outside. A light snow was falling, and she pulled her hood over her head. Princess Jereni's and her horses were saddled and waiting for them in the front yard, almost like Jereni had anticipated a quick exit. The setting sun tipped the tops of the tallest trees, a numbing breeze blew, and Eliinka wrapped her fur-lined cloak around herself.

Mikali strode after Jereni, but her guards blocked him. When he stepped to the side to get around them, they grabbed him. He did not struggle, not like Eliinka expected.

"Jereni, may I ride with you?"

"No!" Rakel dashed to Mikali's side and yanked on his arm. "No, we need to return to RitVa. *Forget her*! Let's go home. She probably has an army close by, preparing to attack. We must leave. Now."

"I promise I won't disclose your identity. I won't compromise your safety." Mikali brushed Rakel's hand off his arm and took one step toward Jereni.

"No!" Rakel's voice echoed across the snow. The horses stomped their feet. Clouds of steam came from their mouths.

A second of silence seemed to last for eternity.

"Yes, you may come. Rakel may have my room for tonight. It is paid for, and two of my men will ensure she arrives safely home tomorrow."

It seemed that Jereni understood men better than Eliinka did. How could she have known he would follow her? Though if he hadn't, Jereni's men would have waylaid him. Now they could pull Mikali farther into the wilderness, perhaps even all the way to Viru as he traveled with them. She would have more time to convince him. If he refused, Jereni's guards could force Mikali to come.

Eliinka touched the diamonds on her hands. Mikali trusted her and based his decision on that trust. Had she changed so much that she would consider abusing old friendships and rip Mikali away from his homeland? Yet she hoped he would be happy, that he would love Jereni.

"I'll stay with Mikali," Rakel said.

Jereni gave Rakel a long, searching look.

Rakel folded her arms and lifted her chin. It was possible Rakel would convince him to not accept Jereni.

"If that is your wish," Jereni said. "Rakel, may our journey together be pleasurable and may our friendship blossom as flowers in the spring."

Now Rakel would be involved, and Eliinka wished once again that Rakel had not come with Mikali. Eliinka's horse trampled dead flower stalks under its hooves as she turned it around, ready to return to Viru.

Shadows of men blended behind distant trees in the untamed forest of Pelto. Eliinka caught an occasional glimpse of the guards, only because she knew many of Jereni's men were scattered, out of sight. They moved at a rapid pace, too fast to talk, which meant Eliinka could ignore Rakel and her muttered complaints. They had veered away from the road within an hour of leaving the inn, taking a different route than the one by which they had come. They hurried, though they would not enter Viru until the following day.

The sun was hunched low in the sky when Jereni pulled her horse to a halt. Below them, a trail ran across a small grassy valley.

"Mikali, your horse is swift." Jereni smiled mischievously. "Will you race me across this valley?"

"I've never lost a race."

"But you have never raced me." A competitive edge sliced through Jereni's voice.

Jereni called to her guards, and one returned to her side. She gave him instructions in Virjalo, and two guards rode ahead.

Mikali edged his horse nearer to Jereni, and she said, "My men will mark the finish line at the other side of the valley."

"I love a good race. But the winner deserves a small prize." Mikali rubbed his horse's neck. He glanced at Jereni.

Jereni raised an eyebrow. "What type of prize?"

"The winner will choose the destination of our journey."

"I choose the city of Jalolinna, my home." A broad smile parted Jereni's lips.

"And I choose Metsakauni, my hunting lodge, a half day's journey to the North. I will beat you, by two lengths."

Perfect, Eliinka thought. Jereni would win, and Mikali would come to Viru, and if by chance he won, she still might be able to convince him to return with her. His lodge was far enough away from any cities that Jereni's men could stay nearby.

"What about me?" Rakel muttered. "I only want to go home, not to Mikali's lodge."

Eliinka gave the word, and they took off, cloaks billowing in the wind. Both horses appeared evenly matched for the first minute. Jereni shifted her weight, leaned forward, and took a small lead.

Eliinka, Rakel, and the remaining six guards followed at a trot. She rode in front, but Rakel urged her horse up next to Eliinka.

"*Why* did Princess Jereni want to meet my brother? What did you write in your letter?"

Eliinka's hands tightened on the reins. She could hardly admit to herself, let alone Rakel, that they were, in essence, kidnapping Mikali.

"How did you meet her? Why would you go near *anyone* from Viru?" Rakel spit out the words, echoing the belief of all Peltens.

Eliinka ignored the questions about how she came to Viru. "I was speaking about Pelto and described Mikali. Princess Jereni wanted to see if such an amazing man existed."

"You're a traitor!" The orange, dying sun reflected on Rakel's face. She clicked her tongue and urged her horse into a gallop.

Eliinka flicked the reins and passed Rakel.

"Viruns are barbarians! Why should I believe anything you say?" Rakel's yelling faded as Eliinka's horse galloped forward.

Jereni's horse reached the finish line five lengths before Mikali. Eliinka urged her horse forward, and when she reached them, she jumped off her horse and gave Jereni a hug.

"Your horse!" Mikali was shaking his head. "Congratulations! I have never seen a horse run so fast. You are an expert rider."

Rakel dismounted and shot a dark look toward Eliinka.

Their breaths misted in the air. They sat on chairs covered with fur blankets in front of a flaming fire. Rakel pulled a fur blanket tight around her shoulders. The guards raised Jereni's tent and a second, smaller tent. Frying meat and baking sweetbread smells wafted toward them on a light breeze that passed by the cooking fire.

A guard handed them steaming mugs. A fragrant sour-sweet smell filled the air.

"What is this?" Eliinka asked after she took a sip. Though it had a floral flavor, there was also a tangy bitterness. "I've never tasted it before, have I?"

"No, you have not," Jereni answered. "This hot drink is made from dried rahfvi and drunk when traveling in the deepest cold."

After a short and pleasant conversation, Jereni folded her arms. "Mikali, tomorrow we will travel through wild lands over invisible trails. The journey will be difficult for Rakel."

"Mikali, don't go," said Rakel. "What about your trading?"

"Viru is the only neighboring land I have not visited. I'll write a letter of instructions to Karis. He already works with me and will watch over my affairs."

"The legends . . . remember? No one ever returns." Rakel gave Jereni a pointed glance. "Will you?"

"Of course," Mikali said.

A brief cloud passed through Jereni's eyes. As Rakel opened her mouth, Jereni exclaimed, "It's always been my dream to travel throughout the land of Pelto and experience its culture firsthand."

"When I return to Pelto, you can travel with me, and I'll show you my land," Mikali said. "Maybe we can even spend time at Metsakauni."

Rakel kicked the snow, scattering chunks into the flames. Steam sizzled into the air.

"The journey is difficult, Rakel," Jereni said. "We would enjoy your company, but you may return to RitVa."

"I'm going to stay and *protect* my brother, even though I'd prefer to go home."

Eliinka leaned over to Jereni and whispered, "Rakel might need a promise of safe return."

"Rakel, you have my word, my promise, that when you wish to return to Pelto, you will be given safe transport to your home. You need only inform me, and you will leave on your journey within one day."

Jereni called to a guard, and he brought a sheet of parchment to her. She handed it and a quill to Mikali. "For your letter. You said you needed to write instructions."

"What do I write? How do I explain this?" Mikali smoothed the blank parchment and turned the quill in his hand. Lines of worry furrowed his brow.

"Remember your promise. Do not make mention of me or Viru."

Mikali leaned down and in sharp-edged, bold handwriting struck the paper with ink.

Dear Karis,

I am entrusting my affairs to you for a period of time. I am traveling to see more of the world. A promising possibility of a profitable trade agreement arose. Rakel is with me.

Farewell for now,

Mikali

Mikali handed the parchment to Jereni.

"A guard will leave tomorrow morning to deliver it to Karis." Jereni rolled it up and handed it to a guard.

As the evening drew to a close, Jereni pulled a round of cheese from her bag. "This cheese is made from a prized distinctive milk that comes from my specially bred cows. It is my favorite cheese." She cut off four thick slices with her knife, then handed a slice to each of them. The flavor tasted familiar to Eliinka. She wished they were back in Viru with her mother's harp where she could play and let her music carry her away into a world she would create, where there was no conflict. No anger. No pretending.

"Sleep well," Jereni said. She stood, glanced once more at Mikali, and entered her tent.

"Good night, Mikali, Rakel." Eliinka followed Jereni, ducking through the tent flap to where Jereni waited.

"Go quietly. Listen outside their tent," Jereni whispered.

"What if they see me?"

"Be careful. We need to know what they say, what Mikali says. That will determine my actions."

Eliinka cracked open the flap and waited. Snow began to fall. How well did she know Mikali? Had he changed? Her feet shivered inside her boots.

"Mikali, there are so many guards." Rakel spoke clearly and loud as if she wished to be heard. She stood, letting the blanket fall onto the snow.

"Don't worry. A good night's sleep will do you good." Mikali guided Rakel by her elbow, but she hesitated outside their tent.

"I *never* sleep outdoors, *never* in a tent. This is winter."

He entered the tent and popped his head out. "Rakel, come in. This is more like a nice room than a tent. It is carpeted and there are beds. You'll stay warm: there is a brazier and more fur blankets. Come in!"

Mikali pulled Rakel into the tent.

Eliinka crept outside and approached the back of their tent wall, her footsteps padded by the soft snow. She listened through the fabric, not feeling the guilt she assumed she would have about eavesdropping.

"This is a bad idea. Why did you race? Your wager was foolish."

"I was sure I would win, like always. I wanted to spend a couple more days with Jereni to learn more about Viru. Her horse was faster than I realized. But I won't go back on my word."

Rakel muttered something under her breath before speaking clearly. "Did you see all the guards outside? More arrived this evening and they are well armed. I counted over twenty. You only have your sword. Princess Jereni is from Viru! You've heard the stories. The legends about their princess. Remember, Viruns killed our grandfather! It's a barbaric land. I don't trust her. If we go to Viru, she won't ever let us leave. Can't you see she is kidnapping us? No one knows where we are; no one even knows we've left RitVa."

"Eliinka trusts her. She wouldn't have introduced us if she thought we might be in any danger. Anyway, I've always wanted to meet a Virun. The stories about Viru have always interested me. What's real? What is exaggerated?" The tent fabric expanded outward. "Viru must be more advanced than we thought. Look at this tent fabric, for example. Maybe she'll trade with me."

"Mikali, listen! I *won't* go to Viru! We can sneak away tonight."

"I don't want to go to Viru either. But she won the race. We can visit and see what the country is really like."

"What is Eliinka doing with a Virun? She's hiding something."

He was quiet. Eliinka tightened her fists and held her breath, waiting to breathe until one of them spoke.

"Rakel, you don't have to come with me. But I will go. I want to know Jereni better."

"The first woman you notice in all your life has to be from Viru. A princess with enough guards to drag us away. A princess with armies. We aren't safe."

"Actually, I've never felt more protected in all my life." Mikali laughed. "I'll step out while you change. We'll sleep. Then we'll see what morning brings."

Eliinka darted back to the larger tent, glad for the falling snow that would cover her footprints. She breathlessly slipped inside as Mikali opened his tent door.

There was no sign of the Flute People, and their entire journey was without incident, except for the river crossing. Though the rain-swollen river ran fast and rough, ice ledges formed where water and bank touched. Eliinka halted her horse, and while waiting for the others, she removed her boots. She would wait as long as possible to enter the river, where the cold water would chill her to the bone.

When Rakel halted her horse, Eliinka said, "Rakel, you'll be more comfortable if you remove your boots so they stay dry."

"I can't do this!" Rakel shook her head. "I can't cross that river. Look at those ice chunks."

Jereni turned her horse until her knee almost touched Rakel's. "You may ride with me on my horse. You will be carried across in safety."

Again, Rakel shook her head.

"The water is cold, yet there will be a warm fire, and hot food and drink, on the other side," Eliinka said.

Jereni removed her boots, stuffed them inside a saddlebag and added, "Rakel, come up with me on my horse."

Rakel backed her horse away from Jereni.

"There is no other crossing, Mikali," Jereni said. "If she cannot cross on her own, encourage her to ride with me. Or will she ride with you?"

Mikali looked toward the towering forest on the other side of the raging waters. The sound of wind blowing through deep hollow pipes sounded faintly above the river.

He brought his horse next to Jereni's. "So this is the entrance to your kingdom?"

"The allure of the land of Viru is powerful and irresistible." Jereni smiled.

"Viru is very beautiful." But Mikali looked at Jereni, not across the river.

Rakel had ridden back toward the direction they had come and was stopped by the guards.

"Do you wish to return home accompanied by Princess Jereni's men?" Mikali called. "Or will you cross the river with me?"

"Neither!" pouted Rakel. Yet when he dismounted, stood at her side, and removed her hands from the reins, she allowed him to lift her from her horse.

Mikali helped her onto his own horse.

Jereni said, "Rakel, take off your boots so they don't get soaked. They will stay dry in my saddlebag. You can change into dry clothes on the other side."

"But men are watching. They'll see my legs," Rakel snapped. Despite her words, she yanked off her boots, shoved them into Jereni's hands, and hitched up her skirt, directing a spiteful glare at Jereni.

Jereni grabbed the reins of Rakel's horse and entered the river.

Mikali urged his horse forward.

Rakel swore as spray hit her skin.

Eliinka held tight and plunged her horse into the water. The violent ice-cold water hit her calves and she shivered. She focused on the welcoming campfire that flickered under the trees.

Chapter Eighteen

~ A FRIEND? ~

Eliinka pulled a gorgeous deep-red dress from the cabinet.

"I won't wear that," Rakel said. They were her first words to Eliinka since she had yelled at her, calling her a traitor when she had seen Eliinka's markings their first morning after crossing the river, when Eliinka had changed into a Virun dress. She challenged Eliinka with a glare.

Eliinka would rather have headed straight for the study and played the harp, or even played the big harp in the Dining Hall after arriving at the palace. Their travels had taken over a week, too long without plucking the strings. But she smiled at Rakel, hoping to get her settled quickly. This dress was Rakel's favorite color.

"What about this one? Princess Jereni sent ahead to have these ready for you." Several other dresses hung inside the cabinet. The seamstresses must have worked day and night to sew them all. This was one of the best rooms in the palace with its elaborately carved furniture, a thick bed, a screened washing area, decorated walls, thick carpets, and a window that overlooked a small courtyard garden.

"No. I won't wear it. They are all Virun dresses. And Eliinka, look at you—your hair, your dress. Your skin."

Eliinka's hair swept past her neck and shoulders, loose and free, unlike Rakel's, which was wrapped up tight on her head. She remembered how different it had felt wearing Virun dresses with their very short sleeves, short skirts, and low necklines when she had first arrived, how she had felt almost naked. But she was no longer shocked when she looked in a mirror. Now, she realized she preferred them and the increased freedom of movement.

"If you wish for different clothing, it will take a couple days. We can have dresses made in the colors and styles you wish, or if you prefer, you can sew your own clothing with fabrics of your choice." Eliinka clicked the cabinet door shut while biting her lips to keep herself from snapping at Rakel. She hoped she could be patient, especially now that Rakel was willing to have a conversation.

After a long, uncomfortable pause, Eliinka said, "I'll do all in my power to make your stay comfortable. I really will. What do you need?"

"Everything is so different here. And I'm tired. I just wish I were at home. My own clothes, jewelry, things, and friends are all there." Rakel slumped into a chair. Tears pooled in her eyes. "I can't understand what anyone says."

"I can interpret. I can help you."

Rakel shook her head. "Eliinka, you're *not* the friend I remember. I can't trust you."

"You—you didn't want to stay my friend. Not after my parents . . ." Eliinka clenched her fists. "Whenever we met, you acted uncomfortable and would leave as soon as you could."

"Of course. You didn't want to do anything fun, not anymore. You only wanted to play your harp. You didn't want to talk, walk the market and look for boys, go to dances, or have any fun. Now I'm here where there is nothing to do. No dances. No men to flirt with."

"There are many aspects of life here that I think you will enjoy."

"Will I ever be allowed to go back to Pelto?"

"Princess Jereni gave you her word. If you requested it tonight, you'd leave in the morning."

"You tricked us into meeting her. She deceived us so we would come with her."

"Don't criticize Princess Jereni!" Eliinka snapped. "Rest, freshen up if you wish. There is a bathing area behind the screen. The bath should have hot water in it. I'll return soon to escort you to the evening meal." She shut the door hard. She should be nicer to Rakel, but talking with her hurt. She did not want to remember the time in her life that Rakel mentioned: the time when she could not deal with her parents' death and cried for months and no one cared.

Rakel's sobs escaped through the door.

Eliinka climbed the flight of stairs to her room, taking two steps at a time. She bathed and changed into clean clothes. She knew she did not have much time before the evening meal, but she did not care. She needed to clear her thoughts. After sitting on the carpet, she took a deep breath and closed her eyes. Normally, she only meditated in the morning, but she needed to relax this afternoon. It would help her find her way.

"Elavaksi," she whispered. "Give me peace and understanding." Usually while meditating she would experience a quiet peace and comfort, but she did not. She was unable to empty her mind today.

After dinner, anxious to play again, Eliinka hurried to the study. She didn't even take time to check the harp's tuning, but jumped into a song, exercising her fingers. It took three songs for her to find the relaxation she had not been able to find with her earlier meditations. Rakel faded from her mind, and she continued to play, seeing how fast she could move her fingers across the strings. Jereni's maid entered the room and placed two mugs of nightmilk on the table. Warm nightmilk would be especially good tonight.

"You came early tonight." Jereni shut the door firmly behind her.

Eliinka stopped playing and greeted her with a clasp of arms and a kiss to each cheek. She picked up her warm mug and held her hands around it.

"A leader from the Flute People arrived this afternoon. No one expected they would come. Or that they would give their allegiance to me. Ever."

"They respect you," Eliinka said.

"Actually, it is you that he referred to and your actions and mercy toward them when we passed through the wilderness."

"And?"

"There is more to do. We will have more talks next month. We will send gifts: goats, sheep, fabric, other items that should be useful to them."

"So is it now safe to travel in the wilderness?"

"Yes. It is now safe everywhere in my kingdom. I wish prosperity for my people, for all my people, including the Flute People. My parents did much to improve conditions, and I will continue their work." Jereni stood and paced in front of the sparking fire, still holding her nightmilk. She took a sip.

"Mikali's sister hates me. That's obvious. What else should I know about Rakel?"

"Our friendship is now nonexistent. She said she doesn't trust me anymore." Eliinka gave a wry smile. "Rakel does not want to be here. She loves to socialize and go to parties at friends' homes. As you know, weaving is her passion."

"The weaving guild is in Ommella, not far from here." Jereni glanced up to her mother's portrait. "My parents built the weaving industry. The weavers are indebted to my mother for their knowledge and skill. She was a master weaver and taught them improved methods. If Rakel is interested, she can go visit them. Taina, the head weaver can teach her advanced techniques. Rakel should accompany you for the next several days so she becomes familiar with my palace. Language lessons will be moved to the morning."

Eliinka rubbed the blue diamonds on her hands. Rakel, her relentless chatter, her arrogant attitude—every day would be longer than long.

"Your announcement about my engagement was not made public outside of my council because of the most unusual circumstances." Jereni sat down in her chair and placed her mug on the table. She interlocked her fingers.

"You once said your parents loved each other and had a wonderful marriage. What does it take to create a marriage of love? How did they do this?"

Eliinka traced a large diamond inlayed in the wood of the table. The room's silence pressed in on her, an ache of missing her parents surged. "I'm not sure. They enjoyed doing activities together, like riding horses and picnicking, yet they also had their own interests. My father loved taking his bow and going hunting, and my mother loved playing the harp. Maybe they stayed in love because they were friends."

"And with Mikali?" Jereni murmured. "A friend? Could we be friends? Is there a way for him to learn to love Viru and want to live here?"

"There are many activities in Viru that Mikali would enjoy. Riding his horse, hunting, social events. Show him that Viru is now a place of peace. Do you believe Mikali is the man that I described?"

"Yes. But will he forgive me and Viru for his grandfather's death?"

The flames flickered, and they slowly sipped their mugs of nightmilk as they each thought in silence.

Jereni leaned back, tapping her finger on the edge of her chair. "Of course, choosing to visit here is different than choosing to stand at my side."

Chapter Nineteen

~ WITH AN OPPONENT ~

It only took until the end of her language lesson on the morning of the third day for Eliinka's patience to become as thin as late-spring lake ice. Cracking. Splitting. Unstable gray ice. It felt as if Rakel had not left her side since their arrival. She ran down the stairs, heading toward a practice field at the back of the palace, not caring if Rakel could keep up. More than ten women were already at the field. Some stretched, while others practiced with swords and knives. She left Rakel standing in the shade at the side of the field and began warming up in the brisk air, eager to release her frustrations during training.

Eliinka had not practiced even five minutes when Jereni entered the courtyard, near where Rakel stood. The clatter of weapons ceased, and all the women stopped exercising and bowed.

"Exercise is healthy for the mind and body, Rakel," Jereni said. "Will you join us today?" Rakel declined.

When Jereni stepped into the sunlight, all the women bowed again. "Continue on," she commanded. Although they returned to their activities, they continued to give their princess fleeting glances.

Jereni watched each woman in turn. She stopped pacing and watched when Eliinka swung a padded staff toward Lady Roosa in a two-person exercise. Lady Roosa paled and backed away after less than a minute of sparring, giving a fearful glance to Jereni, so Eliinka grabbed a bare staff to perform an individual exercise, a dance against unseen opponents. Jereni nodded her head in approval.

Next, Eliinka set down the staff and picked up the bow. She emptied a quiver of arrows, half into a swinging target and the other half into small fruit that Jyrina, the instructor, threw into the air. It was obvious Jereni had only watched the other women to be polite.

"Your skills have improved," Jereni said. "You are an excellent archer. Show me what you have learned with the knife." The other women drew farther back, to the edges of the field, halfheartedly practicing.

First, Eliinka reached into a basket of throwing knives, pulled out one knife and focused on her target: a narrow, short bushy sapling placed in front of a huge stump that was tipped on its side. She threw the knives, one after another, with both her left and right hands in turn, slicing the branches off the sapling half the time. Close, but not accurate enough. It was hard to master the spin so the blade angled perfectly forward when it met its target. She wiped the sweat from her forehead, then performed a solo exercise that demonstrated all the knife techniques she knew. She worked against her unseen opponent, the air, and moved fluidly until her moves metamorphosed into a dance.

"And with an opponent?" Jereni's blue eyes brightened.

Eliinka motioned to the other women, who suddenly became busy, avoiding her sweeping scan of their backs.

Jereni picked up two wooden practice knives. "We'll use these."

Eliinka's hands became as ice. *We.* She would rather collect honey from a hive of angry bees. She had seen Jereni's fighting abilities in actual combat.

"Your skills eclipse mine," said Eliinka.

"You need practice against a stronger opponent to continue to improve." Jereni tossed her a wooden knife in a wide, arcing loop.

Eliinka automatically reached out and caught it by the handle. The wood blade was sharpened. She was not sure how to proceed against Jereni, who was both faster and stronger. Jereni lunged, saying, "Pretend this is real."

The women set down their weapons to watch, and Jyrina stopped training a woman with a staff. Eliinka blocked, stepped back, thrust forward. Jereni was fast. Thank goodness this was only practice. Both controlled their knives so that when they struck each other, it was a light touch that would not do harm. She didn't want to slip and cut her, so Eliinka relied mostly on hand combat techniques.

Within two minutes of sparring, Eliinka was defeated twice.

"Eliinka, focus. Do not hold back."

She fought harder, attacking and blocking with greater speed, using more complicated footwork and body movement as she blocked all of Jereni's attacks. Though she tried to find an opening, it always closed before she could strike.

Jereni slipped in close, down low.

Suddenly, Eliinka's feet flipped into the air, and she fell backward. A loud ripping of fabric cut through the air.

Her scar was exposed to all on the practice field.

Eliinka dropped her knife. It scattered dust. The reddish-pink scar of her stitches contrasted against her skin. Rolling over, breathing hard, she bent her knees and dropped her forehead to the grass. Her right hand went to her left shoulder. Her hair fanned out on the ground. She should have blocked better.

After Jereni scanned the palace windows, she pointed to all the bowing women and said, "Each and every one of you will come and swear to me that you will tell no one of Lady Eliinka's injury or its location."

Eliinka remained on her knees and forearms, wishing to sink into the ground, pulling together the torn edges of her dress, trying to hide her scar, while each woman and Jyrina came in turn, and while kneeling before Princess Jereni, swore on their lives that they would not reveal Eliinka's wound. She still did not understand this belief that one should not divulge where one had been injured, but as woman after woman gave her oath, Eliinka knew it was more serious than she had understood.

Rakel watched with a blank face. Jereni flew to the shadows to where Rakel stood, and said, "Rakel, this is a serious matter. Will you also swear to me that you will not divulge Eliinka's wound?"

Rakel took a step back.

Jereni moved closer to her. She still held the wooden knife in her hand. Eliinka's muscles tightened. She never wished to be on the receiving end of Jereni's glare.

"You must swear! Give me your word!"

Rakel held her head up defiantly while forcing out the words, "I promise to not tell of Eliinka's injury."

"You should also learn to protect yourself." Jereni flipped the knife around her hand.

"I'll never learn to fight. *I'll* never harm anyone." Rakel pulled her bottom lip into a pout.

"Jyrina and Lady Roosa will escort you back to your room." Jereni turned her back on Rakel.

Flouncing from the practice field, Rakel left. Lady Roosa ran to catch up, and Jyrina followed.

"Cloak yourself, Eliinka, and come with me." Jereni spoke in a gentle, low voice that only Eliinka could hear.

Eliinka slowly stood, holding the shoulder seam together, failing to fully hide the scar. She retrieved her cloak, pulled it tight to her dry throat and followed Jereni up the stairs.

"I'm so sorry." Bruises from their sparring flared in Eliinka's arms and ribs and thighs.

"You have improved." Jereni waited for Eliinka to rise to the same step. "You have learned much."

Eliinka tightened her fists. Her whole body ached. What was she doing here, in a palace, learning to fight, in Viru—in a place she did not belong? All her choices, coming here, choosing Mikali, resulted with painful consequences that she had to live with.

They continued to walk up the stairs. Eliinka did not ask where they were heading or say anything else as she hurried to keep up with Jereni. When they reached the uppermost floor, Jereni stepped through a door onto a roof, into a garden Eliinka did not know existed.

"You fought well, but your skills need to improve beyond what is possible with the women. You will not practice again with them. From this moment on you will practice with my instructor and me. Eliinka, it is necessary to know how to fight, so when you see an opening you will recognize it and seize it, and if necessary, by coercion compel the peace."

"Is it possible to force peace?" Eliinka shook her head.

"Not force. Strongly encourage. Some will never act unless they become uncomfortable." Jereni walked on a path past an arch of lehti vines and stopped at a tree whose buds were swelling. She leaned on the wall, her back to the city. "It is time. My choice will please you." Jereni smiled.

What choice? Eliinka thought.

"Lord Zerin is chosen to be your husband."

Eliinka's heart swirled, and she wasn't sure if she was scared or thrilled. Perhaps both.

"He'll be a good match for you. You know him well."

"What if he rejects me?"

"Lord Zerin won't. His mother and I discussed this match yesterday, when she was visiting. She approves."

"Please, could you speak with him for me?"

"No. You must follow our traditions. Since you are so closely tied to the royal family, you are required to inform him in my presence, where your voice can be overheard by me."

"May I wait? I'll tell Lord Zerin after Mikali agrees to marry you." Eliinka hoped that if she waited a bit longer and expressed interest, Zerin would fall in love with her.

Chapter Twenty

~ BEING STUBBORN AGAIN ~

alfway down the stairway, Eliinka stopped at a tall, narrow window and gazed out at the tiled roofs, the tiny fields and farms, and in the far distance, dark green forests. Her thoughts returned to her and Jereni's conversation about her intended husband.

Zerin.

Her lesson with him was in ten minutes, and it was the first time she would be alone with Zerin since Jereni's announcement.

For a moment, Eliinka considered running away. She touched the blue diamonds on her hands. Running back to Pelto?

That would never work. How could she support herself without her harp, her mother's harp? What about her contract with Jereni? Their friendship?

Maybe someday she'd find a way to return to Pelto, but it would be less likely if she married Zerin. Would it make it impossible to return?

Would Zerin love her? Eliinka turned her back on the window and thumped down the stairs. Did she love him?

Was love something that could grow and develop in time? Jereni made flirting look so easy, even when she toned it down in her palace. Should Eliinka act differently today with Zerin? Could she hide her mixed emotions if she tried?

Last evening she had asked Jereni to find out more about marriage customs, and Jereni had finally said, "Zerin will never mention marriage. A decent Virun man would never consider doing so in the vicinity of a woman. He probably doesn't know that it's done differently in Pelto, that the marriages aren't arranged, and that a man asks the woman. Don't worry, Eliinka. He will be pleased with my choice. If there was a woman he had been interested in, I would have noticed, or he would have dropped a hint to his mother." When Eliinka had not responded, Jereni had added, "You'll be happy with him."

As with the beginning of every lesson since the Vala ceremony, Zerin sprang to his feet when Eliinka entered the White Room. After bowing, he rushed to hold her chair.

She dropped into it. He had never shown any sign that he wanted to be more than a friend, or even be a friend. She wanted Zerin to touch her hand, or maybe even ask for longer lessons so they could spend more time together.

Zerin bowed again, even lower.

Eliinka's chair scraped and skidded loudly against the floor as she jumped to her feet and shoved her chair back from the table. Not another bow. "I know everyone does it, but I'm tired of it. Do not bow to me!" She did not raise her voice, but the trembling, the intensity was in each word.

"This respect is required because of your position, my lady. Princess Jereni demands it."

Eliinka slapped the table. Then she struck her fingers on the wood, drumming one after another. Her fingertip smudges marred the polish. "Then don't bow to me in this room, or during our lessons."

"I dare not cross the will of my princess."

Why is he so stubborn? Eliinka thought. Swallowing her next words, so she wouldn't yell at him or start to cry, she nodded, keeping her mouth tightly shut. There was nothing she could say, command, or plead that would sway Zerin. He again held the back of the chair, moving it toward the table as she lowered herself down.

He circled the table and sat in the chair opposite her. "Your conversational skills are now very good. You know much about our culture and history. We don't need to meet anymore."

Flustered, Eliinka's tongued stumbled, and as she felt blood rise to her cheeks, she stammered, "I . . . I enjoy our conversations and our time together. I wish to continue my lessons."

"As you wish, my lady."

She dropped her eyes to her hands, laid out before her on the table. Zerin no longer called her by her name. She pulled her lips between her teeth. How could she marry a man who insisted on bowing to her *every* time she entered or exited a room? According to Jereni, they would maintain their separate rooms (an unusual arrangement, Eliinka thought), and Jereni had made it clear he was not to stay the night in Eliinka's room since it was attached to Jereni's. Virun marriages were so different. Also, whenever she brushed by him, Zerin almost recoiled at her touch as if she, like Jereni, had also become untouchable.

Feigning interest, Eliinka asked occasional questions as he explained the historic development of piping water inside the palace and how King Juusi had expanded water lines throughout the city. Water had been piped to the main rooms, including hers, generations earlier for washing purposes, and the king had wished that convenience for his people. Only the drinking water was now lugged around to ensure its purity.

The lesson drew to a close. Eliinka cleared her throat and took a calculated gamble.

"Let me make it clear, although I may not be able to stop your bows when I enter a room, I insist that you do not bow to me at the conclusion of our lessons. Jereni will not insist on that."

"You're being stubborn again, my lady." An amused smile crossed Zerin's lips, but his eyes did not meet hers.

"Only on issues I care about, Lord Zerin." Eliinka stood and moved toward the door. He followed. Using her most playful voice, Eliinka said, "Our afternoons together will not end anytime soon."

"As you wish, my lady."

Eliinka reached toward Zerin to touch his arm, but pulled back, not wanting another cold rejection. Not today.

"Everyone treats me differently. Who will accept me as Eliinka?"

He did not answer.

As she left the room, she glanced back with a sad smile. At least he did not bow. She would try harder tomorrow with Zerin; she would see if he would not draw back when she touched his arm. She would also insist he again call her by her name, and not say "my lady" during their lessons. There was no reason in private to be so formal.

At least she would not need to announce anything to Zerin, not until after Jereni's betrothal was official.

Chapter Twenty-One

~ DON'T KNOW WHAT TO SAY ~

Tonight Jereni did not enter the study by herself. Mikali entered with her, and Jereni signed "continue," so Eliinka did not stop playing. She played the strings by feel, without glancing at her hands. There would be a good reason for her to use a guard hand signal in the study. Perhaps she planned to discuss marriage tonight. Jereni would expect her to inform Zerin after Jereni's betrothal. Maybe she could explain to Jereni that she did not love him, try to find a way out. She switched to a Virun song that took all her concentration, hoping that would fill her mind so she would not think of him.

"What room is this?" Mikali asked.

"This is my study, where I relax in the evenings. On the wall are paintings of my ancestors, the rulers of Viru. My family has ruled for a thousand years, for as long as our recorded history." She stepped in front of the two most recent portraits and gestured. "This is my father, and this is my mother."

"Your mother is very beautiful, Jereni," Mikali said. "She has a light-blue line and diamond on her forehead, the same as the pattern on Eliinka's arms and hands." He scanned the other portraits. "She's the only one. Why?" He gazed again at Jereni's mother.

"My mother received the diamond on their wedding day because she was from Pelto. It is a great honor to receive the mark of the royal family."

Mikali whirled his body to face her. "Ah, that explains your mastery of the Pelten language. It truly is your mother tongue."

Jereni smiled and motioned to the chairs in front of the fire. "Please, come sit with me." Sensing Jereni's nervousness, Eliinka shifted the song into soft, calming music.

After he sat, Mikali slowly surveyed the room.

Jereni picked up a book from the low table between them and the fire and held it in her lap. She hesitated before speaking. "The princess of Viru is required to take a man to father heirs for the throne."

"And what will be the role of . . . this man?" Mikali ran his fingers through his short beard.

"On the wedding day, the princess is crowned queen. This man will become a prince. He will create heirs to the throne and have great influence on the land of Viru." Jereni tapped her fingers together. She continued to speak in her lyrical, captivating voice. "Traditionally, in Virun marriages, a family member or close friend selects the best man. Eliinka saw no one worthy in my kingdom and chose you."

"Eliinka?" Mikali glanced her way. Eliinka ducked her head and leaned it on the top of the harp. The pace of the song increased, and she took a breath, and slowed it to the speed it should be played.

"She tempted me with the idea that my marriage could be one of love and friendship. She wanted a husband who would actually love me, and believed, rightfully so, that you are my equal and could stand at my side, not behind me. She did not understand the ramifications of her selection, but once she did understand, she pleaded with me that you be given choice."

Mikali stood up. He kept his back to Jereni, but Eliinka could see his face, and he appeared surprised. He motioned to the portrait of Jereni's mother. "Did your mother have choice?"

"My grandmother was impressed with her and decided she would be the best woman for my father. She was given options and decided to join the royal family. My father treated her as if she had choice, but no," Jereni conceded, "she did not have choice. She was forced to marry him."

"And if I choose no . . . " said Mikali. His muscles flexed as he leaned close to Jereni. Eliinka sucked in her breath.

Jereni's face paled. She glanced at Eliinka, who nodded encouragingly. The stress in her oddly thinning voice was obvious. "My following of tradition is not as exact as many would prefer. One possibility is that tradition would be shattered and the selected man would not become my husband. This has the potential to cause widespread discontent, especially with the rumors spreading that you are the chosen man." She ran a finger across the bottom edge of her eyes. "Another man would be chosen and the heirs to the throne would not have the most outstanding father, and the marriage would only be for the purpose of creating an heir. The prince would be allowed absolutely no influence in my kingdom."

The moisture in Jereni's eyes was as morning dew on the grass. She blinked hard and took a deep breath, squared her shoulders, and murmured. "The other alternative is almost as distasteful to me."

"And what is this alternative?" He continued to gaze at Jereni.

Jereni answered in a forced whisper. "It is to do what my father did to my mother. He forced her to come here, and my grandmother forced her to announce their betrothal. She grew to love him, but she always missed Pelto and harbored a secret desire to return. Mikali, forcing you would be an unwise choice, for you would never love me."

"Are your men standing outside the door? Would you force me to stay?"

"No! Eliinka said that trust and honesty are critical foundations of a friendship and of a marriage. I hoped that you would . . . " She let the book fall open with a thump onto the table. "It's so hard to express my feelings. My thoughts should be like the pages of this book, open for your perusal."

Jereni shifted forward in her chair. "Our time together has been wonderful. The princess desires . . . " She lifted her head. "I desire a husband who is a companion and friend. My mother spoke of Pelto, often. We could visit there together. To spend time in Pelto, with you, would be pleasurable."

"I need to speak with Eliinka in private." Mikali folded his arms.

Eliinka stopped playing.

"If you wish, come meet me in the garden on the roof after your conversation," Jereni said as she walked to the door. "Eliinka will show you the way. Would you like nightmilk? I'll have it prepared for us."

"Nightmilk would taste good." Mikali's attention flitted again to the portrait of Jereni's mother. "Princess, what about the blue diamond?"

Jereni intertwined her fingers. "It is not a barbaric practice like foreigners believe. It is a privilege to wear the blue diamond."

As soon as the door shut, Mikali started pacing from the window to the fireplace and back. "Eliinka, what are you doing here in Viru? Can I trust her? Would she let me walk away? Why in the world did you think I could be a good husband to her? A princess!"

"She is—"

"She is Virun! We are Pelten!"

"We can trust her. Mikali, Princess Jereni is beautiful. Intelligent. Powerful. Isn't she all you want in a wife?"

"What about my home? My business?" Mikali leaned down and stirred the coals. Tiny sparks fell, and the coals crumbled into dust. "The more I think about it, the more I realize how impossible it is."

A cool breeze blew in through the window, scattering papers from the table. Eliinka knelt down to pick them up. "Your dreams?"

"That's the problem! I recognized her when I first saw her. Princess Jereni matches perfectly. I traveled everywhere, searching, and had lost hope that my dreams were real. But they are. She is the woman. How can I walk away from her? It is an ironic twist that she is Virun." As Mikali spoke, he stacked kindling in the fireplace.

"Viru is not the place I had thought it was," Eliinka said.

"Their history, their traditions, their brutality. They killed my grandfather."

"That was before her rule. She is different," Eliinka said. It wasn't right for him to judge Jereni on rumors and history.

"Do you plan to ever return to Pelto, Eliinka?"

"I might someday. Yet the climate is better here, and I love to play my music."

"Are you truly happy here in Viru?"

"Yes," Eliinka said faintly, in a barely audible voice. She thought about how she still missed Pelto, but also about how much her music had grown, about Zerin and her hopes and fears. She nodded her head and said louder, "Yes. Mikali, I'm happy." As she said this, she realized that, deep down in her heart, she was truly happy in Viru. "Jereni treats me well, like a friend." She shut the window, so the papers wouldn't blow away again. "Will you ride away or will you give Jereni a chance?"

Mikali knelt down and blew on the embers. The wood caught fire, burning slowly at the edges. He turned around and opened the book Jereni had dropped. "It's so different here." He flipped through several pages. "I can't read this. I can't understand their language either. But Jereni is perfect."

"Honestly, Mikali. She doesn't claim to be perfect." Eliinka glanced at the scar on the inside of her arm. "She sometimes rushes into things, makes quick decisions."

"Do you think we could be happy? Me and Jereni?"

"Would you ever be happy with another woman after meeting her?"

"No." Mikali pulled a box from his pocket, and after opening it, showed Eliinka a gold ring, circled by deep-blue sapphires and diamonds. "I've carried this with me for years, waiting, hoping, dreaming of meeting my future wife. Is it good enough for a princess?"

"She'll love the ring. It's beautiful. Blue is her favorite color."

"Love wasn't supposed to be this complicated." Mikali put the ring back into the box.

"Do you love her?" Eliinka asked. How could Mikali love Jereni so quickly? They'd spent so little time together. She thought of Zerin and wondered if love was possible between them.

Mikali nodded. "I fell in love with Jereni the first moment I saw her. I'll ask her to marry me, the Pelten way. We'll find a way to make our marriage work. But I'll stay Pelten."

Jereni was not within view when they first entered the garden, but Eliinka and Mikali walked along a path until they found her, leaning on the wall, looking down on her city. It was a clear night and the stars shimmered. Three mugs of nightmilk waited on a garden bench, steaming in the chilly air.

"The nightmilk will get cold." Jereni held out a mug to Mikali.

"Thank you." After Mikali took a sip, he set down the mug and shifted so close to Jereni that they almost touched.

"Jereni, will you marry me?" Mikali took her right hand. "In Pelto, it is traditional for the man to give his betrothed a ring as a token of his love and faithfulness." He slipped it on her middle finger and wrapped his arms around her.

"Mikali, is this how it feels to fall in love, to quiver at the touch of your hand?"

Eliinka grabbed her mug of nightmilk and slipped away as their heads leaned together into a deep kiss. Would Zerin ever want to kiss her that way?

No, not today. No, not today. The thought kept repeating itself through Eliinka's mind as she paced the courtyard where four saddled horses stood ready. Zerin hardly glanced her way. When Jereni smiled and winked, Eliinka cast back a glance of false confidence. She would at least pretend like she wasn't scared.

Early that morning, Jereni had told Eliinka that they would go riding, and that is when Eliinka would inform Zerin of their betrothal. If it were for any other reason, Eliinka would be thrilled to go riding out in the countryside.

How was she going to talk with him? About marriage?

Ten minutes outside the city, Jereni turned her horse and guided them onto a side path. Even though a light breeze softened the heat of the day, sweat trickled down the back of Eliinka's neck. After riding up a gentle slope, they passed through a forested area and continued riding until they reached a large meadow where a midday meal of fruit, cheeses, and bread waited on a blanket. Jereni kicked off her riding boots and dropped her feet into the meadow grass. She pulled the token harp out of her bag and played a short tune.

How would Zerin respond? Eliinka took a deep breath, trying to calm her nerves. Would he be happy? Was it possible for them to fall in love?

"Mikali, there is a nice view from that rise." Jereni placed the harp next to Eliinka and pulled her boots back on. Jereni gave Eliinka a nudge as Mikali took her hand. They walked up a small knoll, only thirty paces away, within hearing distance. Jereni acted almost—almost giddy.

"They're a perfect match," Eliinka said.

"You chose well, Lady Eliinka." Zerin sat with his back rigid, his arms folded.

"It's beautiful here." Eliinka plucked a long blade of grass. She played with it, wrapping it in a circle around her finger. She picked another blade of grass and looped it so it held a circular shape. She picked more grass blades and formed a chain. "You're a wonderful friend." Her voice trembled. "You've made my life easier. It's different here, and I'm still learning about the customs. I still can't say everything."

"Though you only arrived last spring and it's not even been a year, you speak well. It's like you've always been here. You're one of us."

Would their marriage give her strong ties and make her more comfortable in Viru? Would it truly make it her home?

Jereni and Mikali engulfed each other in a close embrace on the crest of the hill. *Will Zerin ever kiss me that way?* Eliinka wondered. *Would he want to?*

"They touch." Zerin frowned. "But it is her right to break tradition."

What could she say? The longer Eliinka waited to speak, the harder it was. Speaking in Virjalo was becoming more comfortable, but now that she was stressed, she thought the words in Pelto and then translated them into Virjalo, preparing what she would say. She reached out and tugged two harp strings so they touched each other. She was probably pulling them out of tune.

"You are very drenching."

Zerin tipped his head toward her as if he hadn't heard clearly. "Could you say that in Pelten?"

"You are very handsome."

"You said I was soaking wet in Virjalo, but the words are quite similar in our language." Zerin chuckled. "You so rarely make errors anymore, and that was not the compliment I expected."

It was frustrating to live in Viru, especially at moments like this. The language wasn't easy and even though Eliinka could speak it sufficiently for conversation, she didn't know all the words she needed. She pulled the harp into her lap and glanced toward Jereni who smiled and sent her a pointed, demanding glare.

Though her fingers were numb, Eliinka plucked a couple random harp strings. She took a deep breath. The words flowed out all at once, in one rush. "Lord Zerin, it is Princess Jereni's will that I marry two weeks after her wedding. She selected you and announced your name to me."

Inhaling, inhaling, but unable to breathe, Eliinka gasped for air.

Zerin rose and gave Jereni a deep, slow bow. Jereni acknowledged him with a wave of her hand.

Eliinka wanted to hide; she wanted to undo her words.

He did not want her. This was not what she had dreamed of as a little girl or had even imagined the previous year.

"This is a great honor." Zerin sat back down at her side.

"Honor?" Eliinka blinked her eyes, keeping the tears in them.

"Our expectations may be different, but I will protect you until the day I die."

Eliinka nodded. She moved a hand toward him and let it sit near his.

Just as she started to withdraw her hand, he reached out and awkwardly picked it up. A warm sensation ran up her arm.

Eliinka gripped his hand and slid closer to him, almost to where their knees touched.

"Lady Eliinka, just so you understand—we will keep our traditions and . . . and wait to show affection." Zerin shook her hand loose.

Jereni skipped across the grass to the blanket and gave Eliinka a hug and Zerin a big smile. "It's official. He will make you so happy."

Stopping herself from breaking into tears, Eliinka hugged Jereni again. "Thank you. And I want Zerin to stop bowing to me. He won't listen to me. Tell him to stop. Please."

"Zerin, don't bow to Eliinka. Make her happy."

Eliinka wondered if Zerin was unhappy. He showed no emotion. She traced the diamond on her hand as she asked, "What do I do now?"

"We will plan your wedding." Jereni's grin stretched wide across her face.

Eliinka tried to imagine Zerin holding her in his arms, pulling her close, and kissing her.

He did not look her way.

Chapter Twenty-Two

~ OUR DREAM ~

Rakel only exploded once, the evening when she walked into the small dining chamber where Mikali had enfolded Jereni in his arms, his lips pressed against her cheek, his hands tangled in her long hair.

"How can you touch her? Stop! Let's go home." Rakel grabbed Mikali from behind and tried to yank him away.

Mikali released Jereni, but kept her hand in his. "We're getting married. I'm going to live in Viru."

"You can't. You promised—" Rakel ran from the room.

Eliinka chased after Rakel and grabbed her shoulders, stopping her just outside the room. The door slammed behind them. "They love each other. Don't interfere."

"*You*." Rakel pulled away from Eliinka. "You stole his heart, not for yourself, but for her. It's an arranged marriage. You chose him. That's why you returned to Pelto and brought him back here."

"He loves her."

"It's wrong," Rakel said. "Everything here is wrong. I see it in your face. You are unsure. You can't hide it from me, even if no one else sees. Jereni expects you to marry Lord Zerin. Remember our *dreams*, our conversations when we were children? Our husbands would be different. They would really *love* us, love us for our whole lives. And don't tell me you'll accept an arranged marriage, a marriage to a man you don't love and who doesn't love you."

Eliinka stepped back as if she'd been hit. "Rakel, I like Zerin. A lot. I trust Jereni." She thought about how Zerin hardly paid attention to her and compared that to how Mikali looked at Jereni, and an ache to be loved resurfaced.

"Well maybe that is the problem. But you can't make me trust her, or obey her. I want to go home, but I can't leave Mikali."

Mikali stepped into the hall, shutting the door. "Rakel, please come back in."

"This is foolishness!" Rakel said. "Mikali, are you just marrying her because she's a princess and lives in a palace? You've only known her for two months. Will you fight against Pelto when she declares war? Will you kill Peltens? No Virun has ever wanted peace. Never."

Rakel spoke so loud that Eliinka was sure that Jereni could hear her through the door.

"Jereni wants peace," Eliinka said.

"You are Virun now, Eliinka. Of course you say that. Don't try to tell me your loyalties are with Pelto. Now you are trying to make Mikali Virun too."

"I still love Pelto," Eliinka said. Yet it was true her loyalty lay with Jereni. She had given her her word. But was she Virun? Just because she spoke the language and dressed like them didn't mean that she was.

"No," Mikali said. "I will remain Pelten. Jereni and I have spoken about this, and she accepts that. I love Jereni. We invited my friends from Pelto to our wedding."

"What about Mother? Did you invite her?"

"You know she can't make the journey. But I did send her my greetings and love."

"Jereni lures your friends here," Rakel said. "Will she slaughter them? Do you really think they'll trust her enough to come to your wedding? We are in Viru! She is Virun!"

"Jereni wants peace with Pelto. Can't you see that, Rakel?" Eliinka knew when she said the words that it was true. "She'll be your sister-in-law. Try to get along with her."

"She is Virun!"

The door swung open, and Jereni stood there, in the archway. Eliinka was sure she had heard every word—she saw it in Jereni's face.

"It's more comfortable to visit in here." Jereni smiled. "Our dream is that Mikali will take me to Pelto someday. We dream it can become our second home. Rakel, you can leave whenever you wish, but I hope you will stay for our wedding." Jereni reached out to give Rakel a hug and a kiss on her cheek as she passed through the door, but Rakel ducked away.

"You are right." Jereni caught Eliinka right outside the door. "I would love to have peace with Pelto, for all my lifetime and for my children's. But they have no good feelings toward me and my kingdom."

Chapter Twenty-Three

~ GIFT OF FRIENDSHIP ~

The Peltens had arrived at the palace, all men, either government leaders or Mikali's friends. Mikali had only been in Viru for three months, and now these Peltens had come for his wedding. As Zerin called out each guest's name, they moved to the front of the Great Hall where they greeted Rakel, Mikali, Jereni, and Eliinka. Eliinka would rather play the background music than stand here. But the Peltens only paid attention to Jereni, with her crown and shimmering blue dress, a dress that reflected the light and accented the silvery diamonds woven throughout the cloth.

The first man to come forward, Karis, presented a gift from the entire group: two beautiful, matching knives, whose blades were made from a swirling mix of two metals.

Karis greeted Eliinka with a quiet nod, hardly giving her a glance. But when the next guest reached Eliinka, he recoiled at her arms and walked on.

The third man approached and paused.

"I am Lady Eliinka." She grasped his hand in the manner of Pelto. "Thank you for coming."

"You learned our language for our visit. Thank you." He stepped away.

Eliinka felt she was acting, pretending to be a person she was not. With each man, each greeting, Eliinka struggled to reconcile within herself that all believed she was a native Virun.

He had come? Eliinka recognized the last man in line, Timo, a middle-aged, slightly heavy man with gray-streaked hair and trimmed beard. He bowed to Jereni, the first guest to bow to her, and introduced himself as a councilor to Pelto's governor. He was no taller than Jereni, perhaps a hair shorter. She had thought he would not come, though his name was on the guest list. He had been a friend of her father and a prominent man on

Pelto's leading council at that time. He was of their faith and had visited Eliinka's father several times in their home. He would surely recognize her. What would it mean to her if he did not?

Timo's attention passed by her face and flicked to her arms. He turned away.

"Eliinka, daughter of Kallela." She stammered as she took a half step forward and grasped his hand in the Pelten manner. "I extend my hand of hospitality. Timo, if any need arises, if there is anything I can do for you, please, don't hesitate to call on me." Eliinka released his hand and stepped back into her place.

His hazel eyes darted from her hands to her dress to her face. He looked again to Jereni, then back to Eliinka.

"Eliinka, I hope to hear your beautiful harp playing during my stay."

Jereni leaned between them. "Councilor Timo, Lord Zerin forwarded your request for a meeting. Lady Eliinka will meet you outside your room tomorrow morning and escort you to a private meal with me."

The next morning Eliinka spoke to the guard to find out which room was Timo's. She walked up the South Wing, thinking of the countless hours Zerin had spent supervising the preparation of these rooms for their guests, and the irony that they had had almost no time together. She adjusted her sun-yellow dress, and gave a slight knock on Timo's door.

Timo emerged, and they walked in silence until they entered the Garden Courtyard. She inhaled the early scent of spring, the new green growth, and bursting flowers smells, which happily arrived months earlier in Viru than in Pelto.

"How do you like Viru?" Timo gave Eliinka a sideways glance as he spoke.

As she guided him across her favorite garden path, she reached out and brushed the leaves and buds of the lehti vine with her fingers, releasing its sweet scent. Her gold lattice earrings brushed her neck and upper shoulders, reminding her of her bare skin that would be covered if she were in Pelto. "The weather is pleasant here. The food . . . well, I'm used to it now. My music has grown."

"Your parents would be surprised to find you living here in the land of our enemies. I didn't recognize you at first. You have matured into a beautiful woman from the little girl that I remembered."

"Few realized I left." Eliinka paused near the stream. What would her parents think about her choices if they were alive? She plucked an oval leaf from the nearest tree, a huuttaa tree, the only plant in the garden that was native to Pelto. Why was this tree planted here? "No one knew I came here. No one recognized me as one from Pelto yesterday, not even you." She examined the leaf with more interest than she had.

"Princess Jereni has treated you well."

She looked back to him and nodded.

Timo's gaze settled on the necklace that rested on the bare skin of her upper chest, and for the first time in months Eliinka wished she were more covered. "Eliinka, you seem unsure about your life here. You can return to Pelto with me. Stay in my home until you find a place of your own."

"I . . . " Was that what she really wanted? "I can't. I gave Princess Jereni promises I won't break." Eliinka creased the leaf in half. Her promises with Jereni. She had to accept the reality that she would never live in Pelto again because she wanted to play her token harp, and now, because of her commitment to Zerin.

"You will keep my confidences, won't you?" Eliinka asked. Timo had been one of her father's closest friends, one he had said he would trust with his life.

"Yes."

"I have an arranged marriage to a man." Her cheeks warmed. "We are friends. I think I love him. He doesn't love me. What more can I do?"

"If you are already friends with the man you will marry, you will have a good marriage and love will grow." Timo stepped closer to her and lowered his voice. "If you wish to live here your entire life, you must accept Viru as your native land."

They stood silent. Would he be able to answer her questions about her gift? He was of her faith. Eliinka scanned the courtyard and the pathways and glanced at the half-hidden benches, making sure no one had entered the empty garden. She gulped down her fear.

"Timo. You would never betray me? Would you?"

"Of course not." He looked confused. "But why would you need to ask? You must know I would do nothing that would bring you harm or pain."

"No one knows, but my parents. I have a musical gift."

Timo's eyebrows raised for a brief second and his eyes grew larger. He smiled.

"Use your music, your gift here in Viru. Only use it for good and when needed."

"I'm not sure, exactly, how to use my gift. If it will be noticed. If there are consequences for using it in Viru."

"I've never heard of a Virun with powers."

"Never?" Eliinka asked.

"You were never taught? Why do some have gifts and not others?"

Eliinka shrugged her shoulders.

"Some believe that one can only have a gift if their parents or grandparents have gifts. That is true. Also, I've never heard of anyone with a gift who doesn't follow Eleman Puusta."

"Never?" Eliinka guided Timo toward the North Wing.

"Not that I know of. Gifts are connected with our faith, which is one reason non-believers harassed and killed many of us years ago. They will not detect your gift, if you use it subtly. That was the problem a generation ago. People used their gifts forcefully, at times not for good, and others without gifts didn't like being forced or manipulated against their will. Within a couple days, they could shake off the effects and act how they had originally planned. If a gift is used lightly and isn't used to oppose what one wants, it is more difficult to detect."

"I don't fully understand my gift. I hardly know how to use it. How can others tell if I'm using it?"

"Since you are a talented musician and music is how you exercise your gift, they will believe that your music moves them, that your music affects their emotions and brings ideas to their minds. Music is a good shield and makes the gift less obvious. You will be safe if you are careful and only use your music to influence, not reverse a person's desired actions."

"I don't know if I should use my gift. If it would be wise. Also, I don't want to risk my new life here. Once I thought Princess Jereni suspected I have a gift."

"I was astonished to see you standing at her side yesterday where one would expect to find a family member. Your path to her side would be an amazing story. Perhaps you'll share it with me while I'm here." Timo wrinkled his forehead and paused, but only for a moment. "I am most impressed with Princess Jereni. She seems peaceful, and her beauty is far beyond the rumors. Only an exceptional woman would gain Mikali's attention. Also, I was surprised at her mastery of our language. She speaks with not a trace of an accent and with the fluency of an educated Pelten."

"She does." They didn't speak more as Eliinka led him out of the garden and up a flight of stairs. They passed through well-lit halls and climbed more stairs. Once, Timo paused to look out a window, but when Eliinka stopped to wait, he hurried and caught up.

"She'll meet with us here. It's a privilege to dine privately with Princess Jereni." Eliinka rested her hand on the elaborate door handle of the small, upstairs dining chamber. Realizing she still held the huuttaa leaf, she slid it into a pocket. She would put it away in her room tonight. It would remind her that she would find a way to plant the huuttaa tree on her parents' graves. Someday she would find a way to return to Pelto, or at least visit.

Timo remained standing as Eliinka greeted Jereni in their usual manner of a hug and kisses and waited while they took their seats. Eliinka was pleased to see her token harp sitting on a side table. She hoped Timo would like the music she would play.

Servants carried in large serving platters filled with meats, cheeses, and fruits as well as three pitchers of fresh juices. Timo filled his plate to overflowing and tried all three juices. Eliinka only drank marja, her favorite juice. They spoke little while they ate, but when they finished, Timo stood and bowed.

Jereni waved the servants from the room.

"Princess Jereni, thank you for your gracious hospitality, and thank you for meeting with me. There are two items I wish to address. First, I bring a personal gift from me and my family." Timo reached into a pocket. He pulled out a beautifully embroidered fabric hairpiece.

Jereni's eyelashes fluttered, and she twirled the hairpiece between her fingers.

"My daughter made it."

Jereni unfolded the hairpiece. She examined the embroidery and fingered the long, trailing ribbons. The colors were subdued, as always in Pelto. The style was similar to what Jereni had worn when Eliinka had first met her, but the embroidery pattern was original, a circle inside a square.

An ache, a longing for Pelto came on strong. There was so much that Eliinka loved and missed: the sweetbreads and subtle flavor of foods, snow and winter—

"Eliinka, could you put it in my hair?" Jereni spoke in Pelten. She expertly twisted her hair up on her head in the Pelten way. Eliinka fastened the hairpiece, arranged the attached fabric ribbons, and handed Jereni a mirror. Jereni's eyes danced.

For a moment, a distant look landed on Timo's face. He blinked, and then said, "Second, I bring you greetings from Tuli, the governor of Pelto, and the leading council. We are pleased with the opportunity I have to visit your kingdom. I hope our two lands can enjoy good relations, and I will try to so influence my government."

Jereni smiled.

"Some do not wish for any contact with your kingdom," Timo continued. "They do not trust you. But I believe your marriage with Mikali will open up opportunities for peace."

"Your words are appreciated." Jereni said. "I also dream of close ties. We can maintain our unique cultures while we learn of each others' lands and customs."

Eliinka wondered if close ties would be possible. Most Peltens would not be open to a treaty. Even all the visitors, Mikali's friends, came only out of respect for him and curiosity. They had the same attitude as Rakel.

Jereni spoke in a lyrical, almost song-like voice.

Two individuals touch and enjoy a dance.
Both benefit, both are refreshed.
Two trees in the garden are touched by the same breeze,
enjoy the same sun,
are visited by the same birds and bees
yet still produce unique fruits.
Individual notes sound,
yet together they
create beautiful harmony
that give joy to all who hear the music.

Silence echoed.

After a lengthy pause, Timo said, "You speak poetically in the language of Pelto. Your knowledge and intelligence are far superior to what has been rumored."

"You expressed a desire to hear Lady Eliinka play the harp. Now is your opportunity." Jereni motioned to Eliinka.

"What do you wish me to play?" Eliinka asked as she picked up the harp.

Jereni leaped out of her chair, a playful smile on her lips. The cascading fabric ribbons of the hairpiece swung around. She stepped to the door and spoke through it before turning back to them. "We will play together. Eliinka, you lead off. Let's play my favorite Pelten folk tune, the lullaby."

Faster than Eliinka thought possible, two servants carried in the large harp.

"Consider this private performance of our music as a gift of friendship to you, from my hands and heart." Jereni smiled at Timo as she sat at the larger harp and pulled it against her shoulder.

Eliinka plucked the strings and released a simple, unembellished melody. Music flowed throughout the room. By the third phrase she added lower notes. She repeated the melody, adding quiet arpeggios, while Jereni layered in deeper harmonies, complex Virun rhythms, and a counter-melody. The pure joy of creating music spread through Eliinka's muscles, flowed through her veins.

After two melodic variations, Jereni took over the melody and made it her own. Jereni's virtuoso rendition was so accomplished that even Eliinka marveled. Eliinka's notes became quieter and quieter and faded. Jereni completed the song herself, playing tenderly, with great longing, as the song circled back into the quiet, calming lullaby that Eliinka had played for her when they had first met. Jereni ended by playing the simple melody in the lower octave while she sang the words to the lullaby.

The last note hung in the air. *This music*, Eliinka thought, *perhaps this is what holds me in Viru.*

Timo clapped and said, "I thought such exquisite music and harmony could only be heard in the heavens. This interweaving of music with Eliinka not only demonstrates your unity, but also your ability to listen, communicate, and cooperate. Your music speaks to my heart and soul." Timo's brow wrinkled. "I hope we can work together for the good of both of our lands."

Jereni strolled to the window and gazed toward Pelto. The hairpiece ribbons lifted and twisted in the breeze. She spoke in a quiet whisper as she pivoted toward him. "Thank you, Councilor Timo. We will need to correspond after you have returned to your home. Perhaps we'll meet again in the future."

"That would be a pleasure. Congratulations on your marriage tomorrow." Timo bowed, and Eliinka led him from the room. He turned around before passing through the door. "Princess Jereni, thank you. I now understand Eliinka's choices."

Eliinka hummed the lullaby as they walked back through the corridors and gardens. They did not speak until they reached Timo's room. "Perhaps it would be best to let my music just be music and not use my gift."

"It is your choice. Do what you feel is best." Timo crinkled his eyes. "Eliinka, you are thriving here, in a foreign land. I can understand why you hesitate to return home."

"Viru is in my blood somehow, and Jereni believes I will love Viru someday."

"Perhaps you already do." Timo shook her hand before shutting his door.

How could he think that? Eliinka stood speechless in the corridor. Even though her music had changed by her coming here, she could not love Viru.

Chapter Twenty-Four

~ DO NOT BE AFRAID OF LOVE ~

Their betrothal had been announced two weeks ago, and Eliinka tried to distract herself and not think about Zerin, but he was all she thought about. His sea-gray eyes, which sparkled like fireflies on a warm summer evening; his laugh, a quiet deep chuckle; and now how much she wanted him to love her. Eliinka glided her fingers over the strings as she sat in the stagnant air of the empty study. Firelight fluttered in the room even though it was a warm evening.

Zerin always sat at her side when they were together. At times it seemed they both played the roles thrust on them. She believed, or maybe she just hoped, that the beginning of love crept along the edges of their friendship, sensed, but always out of sight, out of reach. She wondered if their deepening friendship and their concern for each other would spark into a romantic love. Perhaps . . .

Jereni's maid carried in a tray and placed four mugs of steaming night-milk on the low table. The earthy scent of the milk filled the air.

Eliinka continued to play as the maid stirred the fire and placed two logs on the coals. After she left, Eliinka considered the two unique chairs that had appeared near the low table. They were made of cushioned leather, but were wider than a normal chair, not long enough to lie down upon, but long enough, she supposed, for two people to sit side by side.

The door swung open, and laughter preceded Jereni and Mikali. Zerin ducked in behind them, out of breath. He had been busy all day preparing for their wedding tomorrow. Eliinka jumped up and hurried to greet him while he bowed to Jereni.

"These chairs were made special for us. We can now sit together." Jereni playfully grabbed Mikali's hand and they sat together on one of the new chairs, their shoulders and sides touching.

Zerin sidestepped Eliinka.

Our marriage will never work out, Eliinka thought, *not like I want. It would hurt less if I didn't like him.*

"Innovation can exist, Zerin. Don't be so bound to tradition." Jereni grasped Mikali's hand and held it high in the air. "Appropriate touching is allowed before marriage. We touch when dancing; we can touch at other times. The holding of a hand or an embrace is not disapproved. A kiss is allowed." After a quick kiss to Mikali's cheek, Jereni stood and put a hand on Eliinka's shoulder and faced Zerin. Mikali leaned back in the chair, opened a Pelten book his friends had brought him, and began to read.

Zerin's shoulders sagged. He scuffed his left boot on a wood plank.

"It has been three years since Anali died. To have such an accident on your wedding day was hard for all of us." Jereni spoke in Virjalo, in a whisper.

Eliinka shrugged off Jereni's hand and turned away. No one had ever mentioned Anali before. She blankly viewed the nearest tapestry, a wedding feast, on the wall. Her fingernails tightened into her palm. Zerin had loved another. She blinked hard.

"Do not be afraid to love." Jereni spoke in her calming, silvery voice. "Zerin, you need to find happiness again."

"I was chosen, yet I was never able to give Anali a kiss. I'm afraid Eliinka will also be taken from me."

Eliinka felt like the last tilted fencepost of a long forgotten, fallen fence. Why had Jereni never mentioned this? What had happened to Anali? Zerin would never love her. Never want her.

"Listen to me, Zerin," Jereni said. "We will do all we can to protect Eliinka. Remember, her life is as valuable as mine. Eliinka will remain in the palace until after your wedding. Do not be afraid of love, Lord Zerin."

Eliinka moved toward the door, not wishing to hear more. Maybe Zerin was also afraid, as Jereni said, but she would not stay in the study tonight. She wanted Zerin to touch her because he wanted to, not because Jereni commanded him.

Jereni guided Zerin toward Eliinka.

He caught Eliinka's hand as she reached for the doorknob. Numb, she barely felt his touch. Zerin led her to their large chair and, as they sat, let go of her hand.

"The nightmilk is still hot," Jereni said. She sat again, and when Mikali wrapped his arm around her, she leaned her head into his chest.

Zerin hesitated, but after Jereni nodded at him, he picked up his mug and drank.

After a moment, Eliinka picked up her nightmilk and sipped. Even though Zerin was next to her on the same chair, she did not move close and sat so their arms and legs did not touch.

Chapter Twenty-Five

~ PLACE IN MY HEART ~

The wedding celebrations had lasted most the night and Eliinka had retired at dawn. She had had an unsettled sleep, whether it was from the sunlight or nervousness about her own wedding she did not know, and when it was early afternoon she rose from her bed, shaking the fuzzy tiredness from her head. The Peltens would leave soon, right after the midday meal, and Jereni had asked her to see them off.

Guests mingled, waiting to begin their journey when she arrived at the outer courtyard. They were speaking with Zerin, and she joined the conversation, greeting each person by name and thanking them for coming. Rakel flounced up to the far side of the group, ignoring Eliinka.

"Karis, I'm coming with you. I'm going home to Pelto."

"Good afternoon, Rakel." With effort, Eliinka added a warm tone into her voice.

Rakel glared at Eliinka.

"I wish you a most pleasant journey. Would you like to take your looms and weaving supplies with you?"

"No!"

Eliinka was surprised. She had convinced Rakel to visit the weaving guild in Ommella for a few days. After she had returned, she had supplied her with everything for weaving and Rakel had spent most of her hours in her room at her loom, experimenting with the new techniques that Taina had taught her.

All now listened to their conversation in the dead-silent courtyard. Even the horses ceased moving.

"Do you have any requests?"

"I'm *finally* going home," Rakel said with a sour tone.

"I'll kindly remind you that from the first day of our . . . " Eliinka paused, searching for the right word, "day of our reunion that Queen Jereni promised you safe passage to Pelto at any time."

"She *stole* my brother."

"Prince Mikali married the woman of his dreams. It was his choice."

"He's no longer my brother. I refuse him place in my heart," Rakel yelled. "You've destroyed my life. I hate you!" Rakel shook her fist at Eliinka, then slapped her cheek. "Traitor! You should rot in a dungeon."

"I'm sorry our treasured friendship was unable to continue in Viru." Eliinka spoke with an evenness that belied her anger. "I give you safe passage to the borders. Your fellow travelers will surely escort you safely to your home." She spoke in rapid-fire Virjalo to a guard. Four guards mounted their horses and joined the group from Pelto.

Eliinka shook Timo's hand. "May you and your companions have a pleasant and safe journey."

"Thank you for your hospitality." Timo bowed to Eliinka and mounted his horse and joined the other guests from Pelto.

Eliinka stared at the palace gates, long after they loudly clanked shut behind them. Her thoughts and emotions were battered, she realized. A piece of her wanted to go back to Pelto, yet at the same time she was relieved they had all left and that she was still here.

"We don't need to stay out here anymore," Zerin finally said. He nudged her shoulder and they walked back toward the palace. When they passed Milla at the tall doors, he said, "Bring nightmilk for us, into the study."

It wasn't evening, the normal time to be in the study, but Eliinka did not mind. It would be private. Maybe she could play the harp.

Zerin left the door to the study wide open.

"I didn't expect her to yell at me," Eliinka said.

"Jereni will be angry."

"Furious. But she won't be back for several days and by then everyone will forget."

"I won't forget," Zerin said. "She will hear of her rudeness."

"Not from me or from you. Rakel lost her temper. She's homesick. Upset about Mikali marrying Jereni." Eliinka knew these weren't good excuses. Why was she justifying Rakel?

Milla brought in two mugs of heated nightmilk and set them on the table. She bowed and asked, "Is there anything else you wish for?"

"No," Eliinka said, and Milla shut the door behind her.

Zerin's jaw tightened, and he glanced at the shut door. He shifted away when Eliinka leaned toward him. He cupped his mug in both of his hands. Why did he show no interest in her at all?

Eliinka glanced at her untouched mug of nightmilk. Usually she would have drunk from it immediately. "You never mentioned Anali. I'm sorry she died."

He nodded.

"How long did you know her?"

"She lived next door to me in my village. My family moved here, to the palace, when I was seven, and after that we rarely saw each other."

"I'm sure she was beautiful."

"Anali was beautiful." Zerin turned his mug in his hands. "Her accident happened while she was riding a horse. I've often wondered why she died. Why so many people die when they have so much life ahead of them."

"Why does anything happen in our lives?" Eliinka shifted in the chair. "Zerin, I am here, in Viru. It doesn't make any sense that the last year of my life could happen. But I'm happy." *Mostly happy*, she thought. "Happy that . . . that I'm here with you."

"Did Jereni explain to you that marriage is a lifetime commitment? That is different from Pelto, where marriages can be broken."

"There are many beliefs about marriage in Pelto. My . . ." Eliinka hadn't yet mentioned her faith to Zerin. What would Zerin think if he knew of her beliefs? It probably wasn't the same here, but in Pelto those of her faith had been persecuted and killed, so they practiced their faith quietly. And he had seen her meditations and had never questioned her. "My parents had a wonderful marriage, the type of marriage I want. Their marriage was for their lifetime, and after." She picked up her mug, and it warmed her hands. She wished she could visit their graves, like she should.

"After?"

"Yes. For forever."

Zerin shifted his mug to his other hand and studied Eliinka. "Pelto does have many different beliefs about marriage."

"It's quite different here too, the arranged marriages." Eliinka finally sipped her nightmilk. She would have to ask Jereni how she was supposed to deal with having a room situated in a different wing than Zerin's, another odd palace tradition.

"Do you love Viru? Jereni said it would take time, but that you would eventually."

"Zerin, I want to spend my entire life with you. I enjoy being with you. I want a marriage of love and respect." Did he like spending time with her? She leaned closer to him, hoping that tonight, when no one was around, he would consider holding her hand or even kissing her. When she placed her hand on his knee, he choked and set down the mug, spilling drops of nightmilk on the table.

Zerin stood up and paced back and forth in front of the low fire.

Closing her eyes, Eliinka dreamed that Zerin would someday tell her that he loved her.

While standing in front of a tall mirror, Eliinka adjusted her wedding dress. It was simpler than Jereni's, but still heavily embroidered with white shimmering threads on white fabric. Her dress was loose and flowing. At least something was comfortable.

"The seamstresses did wonderful work," Jereni said. Jereni and Mikali had returned last night.

"Zerin doesn't love me," Eliinka said. The last week had passed too quickly, and Zerin had kept his distance, both emotionally and physically.

"He will. You are a perfect couple. You just can't see it."

Eliinka turned away from the mirror. She was not ready. But she never would be. If she thought she could run and hide, she would. Out of habit, she moved to her window to look outside, but it was a cold spring day and the window was shut. She flung it open, and a rush of coolness splashed her face and hands.

The wedding was held in the Great Hall in the afternoon. Many guests came, more than she expected, and the room was almost full. When Eliinka stood in front of the priest, Zerin at her right, she wished she could marry in her own faith and wished he was also of the faith of Eleman Puusta. The only time a trace of religion in Viru was seen was during festivals or ceremonies such as this. The same priest who had married Jereni and Mikali said the same words he had at their wedding, while Zerin and Eliinka faced each other, hand in hand. First, Zerin took the vow, promising to cherish and honor her.

The priest turned to Eliinka. "Eliinka, do you solemnly promise, under the eyes of God, to accept Zerin as your husband and that you will always be faithful and true, and that you will cherish and care for him always."

Zerin's hands tightened on hers, and his thumbs gently massaged her fingers.

He was as nervous as she was.

Eliinka whispered, "Yes." Louder, she said again, "Yes, I will."

Next the priest declared them man and wife. Unlike what Mikali did to Jereni after their marriage was official, Zerin did not embrace Eliinka and did not lean down to give her a kiss. He dropped her hands, and gave her a tiny nod.

A small group of musicians began to play background music: an ensemble of a flute, a drum, and a stringed instrument played with a bow. Servers placed platters of food on a table.

"Congratulations!" Jereni rushed forward and gave Eliinka a hug. She shook Zerin's hand. "You must take a week away. Arrangements have been made for you to stay at my château, in Rauhalinna."

"It is not needed," Zerin said, and at the same time, Eliinka asked, "Where?"

"This is my wedding gift for the two of you. Rauhalinna, my château, is three hours to the southwest in the mountains."

"Thank you," Zerin said, but he did not smile. He excused himself and after a moment, brought back two glasses, and handed the one filled with marja juice to Eliinka.

Zerin stayed at her side while they visited with all who had come to their wedding. It was Eliinka's first time to meet his mother, and as they visited and got to know each other, she felt happy and comfortable. But it was temporary, for when she glanced up again at Zerin, doubts came back. This was not how she should feel on her wedding day.

"I have a present for you, Zerin." Eliinka had not planned this, the song wasn't perfect yet, but today was the best day to play it. "I wrote a song for you. It's the first song where I have written the words."

After most of the guests had left, they went to the study. The room was quiet, except for the crackling of embers in the fireplace. Jereni and Mikali were already there, sitting in front of the low table since she was helping him to learn to read Virjalo. She looked surprised, but gave a welcoming kiss to Eliinka's cheek. "Congratulations. I didn't expect you here this afternoon."

"I'm going to play a song for Zerin." Eliinka nervously sat and pulled the harp onto her lap. She hoped Timo was correct and that no one would notice if she used a light touch of her gift, especially if she only encouraged what was already desired. Perhaps if anyone noticed and it was not allowed in Viru, her position would protect her. She would have love in her marriage.

Eliinka took a deep breath, steadied her shaking hands, and stroked the strings. A beautiful melody sounded above lush rolling chords; the rhythm of a heartbeat thumped a low pulse. Higher, faint notes duplicated the melody and she used her gift lightly, not letting herself be fully immersed in her music. As she sang about everlasting love and desire, friendship and romance, her thoughts about true love filled the space between her and Zerin, and with a light touch she encouraged the beginnings of love (if there were any) to grow stronger. *It was a good choice*, she told herself. She wasn't creating love, just bringing it to the surface, hurrying it along.

When Eliinka finished, Zerin lifted her up, and brushed his lips against the diamonds on the back of her hands. The notes she had played burst alive and fluttered inside her heart. He held her hand, and two logs burst into flame, illuminating the room.

Jereni's arms were wrapped around Mikali's shoulders. A half smile rippled across her face as her eyes flitted to Eliinka. "You're also a poet. That is the most fascinating song you've ever performed."

For a moment, Eliinka questioned her decision, but only for a moment. She joined Zerin in their chair, and leaning into him, relaxed into his arms. The same thrill ran through her like when she played her harp and made no mistakes.

He brushed his lips against hers, the lightest whisper.

Eliinka's heart swirled and jumped, bounced erratically. She reached around Zerin's neck, pulled him close, and their bodies met. His breath warmed her mouth as they moved together. Their lips met, but within a second Zerin pulled back, making space between them.

"They're watching," he whispered. But Zerin's hand encompassed hers.

Eliinka laid her head onto his chest, where she could listen to his heart beat. Rapidly.

Chapter Twenty-Six

~ AN OPPORTUNITY ~

"You could visit Pelto." Eliinka handed the parchment back to Jereni. "This invitation is brief, but it bears the governor's signature." Almost two months had passed since Jereni's marriage; he had not returned Jereni's greetings promptly.

"You should read it." Jereni slid the parchment to Mikali. She reached up to her hair, and after untangling her hairpiece that had shifted out of place, handed it to Eliinka. "It keeps slipping. Can you make it stay in?"

Eliinka fingered the embroidered hairpiece, the present from Timo; its long ribbons fluttered in the light breeze that passed through the window. She stood and ran her fingers through Jereni's long hair, twisting several strands together and looping the ties.

"Jereni, this is an opportunity for relations with Pelto." Eliinka sat again at the table in the spacious Council Room and grasped Zerin's hand.

Zerin sorted through several parchments with his free hand and passed two of them to Jereni.

"The letter does not ask for a treaty," Mikali said. "It doesn't even mention diplomatic talks. I hoped for at least that much. It congratulates us on our marriage. And it vaguely extends an offer for a meeting with the governor. It's only written so he appears friendly."

"Does he even read the documents he signs?" Eliinka scanned the letter again, more carefully. "It looks like a clerk wrote this. But Governor Tuli's signature is at the bottom and he extends an invitation."

"It is a courtesy letter, not a true invitation. They fear me," Jereni said as she took back the parchment. "My armies won't attack Pelto during my lifetime. We'll only fight if needed—to protect my kingdom."

Mikali leaned over and kissed Jereni on her cheek. "We could go to Pelto. You can meet my mother, and I'll show you all the places you've wanted to see."

"The governor does not really want a meeting." Jereni fiddled with the hairpiece, knocking it out of place, and narrowed her mouth. "The invitation is vague. It's not possible for me to leave my kingdom right now. It will take time to make proper arrangements and ensure my safety. Yet this letter requires a quick response; the messenger says he'll wait to escort us to the governor."

Jereni paced the room, circling the table, pausing at the window. The Council Room, situated on the top floor of the palace, faced north toward Pelto. The late afternoon sunrays danced on her face. An early summer breeze flowered the air with freshness and life.

Mikali circled the table the other way and snagged Jereni around her waist. He pulled her close, running his lips down her cheekbone. She pulled away before he reached her lips.

"You would enjoy seeing my land, my home," he said.

"We cannot go. Not yet. We must be certain we have a formal peace with Pelto before we travel there." Jereni picked up the letter and studied it.

Jereni is correct, Eliinka thought. It wasn't the right time for her to go.

"Yet someone should visit in my stead." She lifted up her head. "Eliinka, you will go as my representative."

"How?" Eliinka curled her fingernails into her free palm. "There are no women in parliament. They won't let me speak to them."

"You'll prepare the way for my visit to Pelto someday. You can find a way to make a treaty and bring me peace, a peace so we can trade and visit each other's lands. We need an agreement that we will not attack each other." Jereni shifted the parchment to her other hand.

Eliinka gripped Zerin's hand tight. Pelto and Viru had never tried to have any sort of agreement, formal or informal. Though her great-grandparents and others of her faith had worked against Pelto's plan to attack Viru, their efforts opposing the war was because of desire for peace, not because they wanted relations between the countries. The first time there had been any peaceful contact had been at Jereni's wedding, and Eliinka was sure most had only come so they could spy on Viru firsthand. Historically, Peltens and Viruns only fought each other.

"You will do well," Jereni said. "You are the best choice because you understand me and you understand Pelto, and you will act in accordance with my will. Four guards will be assigned to travel with you. This comes so soon after your marriage that Zerin will accompany you." A grin burst onto Zerin's face. "Sending two of my advisors will convince Pelto's government of my sincerity."

Jereni picked up the parchments that Zerin had prepared for her. As she left the room, she said, "You will leave tomorrow."

Zerin encircled Eliinka in his arms. Her heart beat much faster than normal. This was a chance for her to visit Pelto. She would show Zerin her land and where she had lived. She would visit her parents' graves, plant the huuttaa tree.

Eliinka would try to achieve Jereni's goals too. She would try to meet the governor. Peace might not be possible, but Jereni believed it was, so Eliinka would try to find a way to make the peace that Pelto and Viru had never enjoyed, a peace never experienced in the thousand years recorded in their histories.

Third Crossing

Chapter Twenty-Seven
~MUSIC OF THE WILDERNESS~

Several times as they traveled through the wilderness, Eliinka thought she heard the faint call of flutes. She looked, but even from the vantage point of her horse she never saw anything other than birds and foxes and squirrels, or their tracks in the dirt.

As the second evening turned to dusk, Eliinka and Zerin soaked in the warmth of the roaring campfire and finished eating a hot meal. Eliinka pulled a wrap around her shoulders, fighting the mountain chill, thinking about the impossibility of their task.

"Zerin," Eliinka said, "the governor of Pelto might not accept me as Jereni's representative."

"Why?"

"Women don't speak there."

"Why not?"

"I've never heard of it being done. Women are not allowed in government. Women in Pelto have almost no rights, no property, no position, and little respect."

"But you are the chosen voice. Your beauty will distract them. They will listen to you."

"Perhaps." Eliinka pulled a round of cheese from her bag and cut off two slices, releasing an earthy smell. "Jereni gave this to me for our trip. It's made from nightmilk."

Zerin tasted it. "The cheese does have a special flavor, like the nightmilk. This is from the first batch. It was made special for our trip." He took another bite.

"Why does Jereni limit who is allowed to drink nightmilk?" Eliinka asked. "Why is it special?"

"It's another royal tradition. They believe that certain foods are only for the royal family and their friends. I didn't drink until after our betrothal."

"It is flavorful, one of my favorite drinks." When Eliinka drank the milk, she always felt a hope that she might find her place in Viru and that she would no longer be torn between her future and past, between reality and dreams.

Zerin finished his cheese and stroked Eliinka's hand. The flames danced on his face. "I'm happy Queen Jereni chose me. I'm fortunate you are my wife." Zerin kissed each of her fingers in turn. She wanted to melt into his arms, but it was too early to retire.

Jereni had sent a small travel harp that Eliinka wished she had known about so she could have taken it with them on their previous journey; it had half as many strings as her token harp so Eliinka played a simple tune and thought about their travels. In only three or four days they would be in RitVa, and she would show Zerin where she grew up and introduce him to the foods and culture he had only studied. What would he think?

Suddenly, an otherworldly sound rose from the forest, joining her song. Although Eliinka realized that sounds carried far in the silence of the night, she peered into the darkness of the trees. With her elbow, she patted her knife, hidden in her dress. A hollow music came from all directions, not one. It must be the Flute People playing. They would be safe.

"Lady Eliinka, do you want us to investigate?" asked Huoli, the lead guard.

"No, stay at your posts and enjoy the music. Those who live in the wilderness play for us." Eliinka set down her harp.

Huoli nodded, spoke to the other guards, and they returned to their positions at the margins of the camp, just outside the campfire light. The messenger from Pelto moved closer to his small fire.

Eliinka leaned back against a log. Zerin wrapped an arm around her shoulders, and she leaned her head onto his chest.

The prelude lulled and a concert began in full. First, the simple five-note melody played in unison, then it divided and sounded in multiple octaves. The notes parted into multiple melodies, winding in unanticipated directions and in a unique harmony. A pattern emerged. The music acted as a slight breeze, with bursts of air, and grew into a fierce, roaring wind that first fought, then succumbed to small crosswinds. Next the music performed as a playful wind, like when the air twirls and kicks up dust on the sides of a dry field, as high tones layered upon other high tones that disappeared upward into the twinkling stars; the mellow, deep tones resonated forever while other sounds came in and out of existence. The music evolved into a melody that echoed from one side of the camp to the other as if the flutes talked back and forth.

Eliinka closed her eyes and thought about her harp music. She still had not told Zerin about her gift, that she had the ability to influence others' emotions and actions. She wanted to, but what would he think and would he tell Jereni?

Yes, he would tell. He might reject her. Jereni might use her. If he suspected she had used her gift to add sparks to their love, he might not hold her as close or press his lips on hers again.

The following morning they passed even deeper into the Syrjassa Mountains and reached the river crossing. The wind gusted strongly, branches clattered against each other, and a flute played, oddly. Not like a man blew. It sounded like wind blowing through a flute. As Eliinka searched for the sound, she found a miniature flute hanging from a tree, a short distance downstream. She rode off the trail, reached high up to the branch from the back of her horse, and removed the flute and a pouch that hung next to it.

A blue diamond symbol was carved on the small flute, which was shorter than the length of Eliinka's hand and about the same diameter as her middle finger. She rejoined Zerin and showed him the flute and pouch.

Touching the flute to her lips, she blew, playing three slow notes. She took a breath, reaching into her memory, and played the haunting, five-note melody she had heard the night before—high, sweet sounds, smooth and liquid like a melting icicle on a warm day.

The small pouch held four translucent, colorless, smooth stones. Eliinka removed one stone, thin and round, which fit the center of her palm. It vibrated, yet appeared still. "There is fire and power inside. I can sense it."

"What is it for?" Zerin asked.

Eliinka shrugged. She held it up to the light and tried to look through it. The stones were as peculiar and mystical as the music last night. Maybe Jereni would know why they gave the stones.

"These forests are a mysterious place," Zerin said. "The natives give their allegiance to you as well as Queen Jereni. They've given you presents that must have great value to them, though they are only a simple flute and plain rocks."

They weren't ordinary rocks. Eliinka could tell, but she wouldn't argue with him, not about this. He wouldn't understand. After tucking the pouch into an interior dress pocket, Eliinka placed the flute into her small travel bag that she wore at her waist. She pulled off her boots.

This wasn't how she had dreamed of returning to Pelto, without her token harp. It would only be a short visit, but it was a chance to return briefly. If they signed a treaty, perhaps it would be possible to live in Pelto for part of each year with Zerin.

"This is where we cross the Urho River?" Zerin asked. Cold, gray water rushed by, pounding the rocky edge near their horses' hooves. A few remaining snowdrifts slowly melted under the trees, though the area near the river had been swept clear by the wind. The fast-moving water roared with summer snowmelt.

"We'll warm with at a fire on the other side. Time to cross." Eliinka urged her horse and he lunged without hesitation into the river. Within moments, water soaked her calves, and she shivered, frozen to her bones. Eliinka looked to the opposite bank as her horse swam to Pelto. She hoped the governor would not give her such a frigid reception.

Chapter Twenty-Eight

~ VOW OF IANKAIKKI ~

The pale-faced messenger spoke to them for the first time during their journey as they entered RitVa, "We'll go to the house of Loukku, a member of the council. It's in this quarter of the city."

"Our meeting is with the governor," countered Eliinka.

"Governor Tuli will meet with you tomorrow. This will be a brief meeting."

"Can it wait?" Eliinka asked.

"Loukku wanted to see you as soon as you arrived."

"Take us to him then," Eliinka said, thinking it might be good to meet with a council member. Perhaps he would be willing to help them.

The city had not changed from its subdued nature. It was the same as Eliinka remembered. Yet the inviting smells of early evening meals wafted through the air, and her mouth watered. She looked forward to eating her favorite foods, ones she could not afford when she lived on her own; food such as rich meats, gravies, and savory breads.

The clipping of the horses' hooves clinked too loud on the stones of the almost empty streets, the normal lull between the workday and evening activities. Within minutes they reached a massive estate. Ostentatious for Pelto, the large house and spacious property filled a large portion of a city block, overshadowing the neighboring homes and their adjoining walls. Eliinka grabbed her travel bag as she dismounted from her horse in the courtyard.

"I'll carry your bag for you." Zerin lifted it from her hands.

"Huoli, accompany us." Eliinka turned to the other guards. "Wait with the horses."

No one greeted them at the door, and oddly, there was no sign or smell of food, even though it was the traditional time for a meal. Huoli followed in Eliinka's footsteps. She glanced back once, and his deep, mud brown eyes were alert. The messenger led them through several passageways into a large, windowless hall where a man, dark shadows accenting his scowl, sat near a darkened fire. He rose, facing her, and folded his arms. Two guards stood behind his chair, one on each side. *This must be Loukku*, Eliinka thought.

"I've been waiting for you." Loukku's voice sounded like wind blowing through dry reeds, and his blond-white eyebrows fused above his sullen features. His unusually thin beard hung long from the middle of his chin. Too few candles flickered on a low table. A large candle placed on a side-wall offered only shadowy light.

Eliinka advanced with Zerin and Huoli to the front of the room, their footsteps the only sound. "I'm Lady Eliinka, advisor to Queen Jereni. We look forward to meeting with Governor Tuli tomorrow."

Rakel emerged from a tall-backed chair that faced the fire. Eliinka stepped backward into Zerin and tripped. He caught her. Rakel! What was she doing here?

"I'll explain my views." Loukku scanned Eliinka with his shallow, pale eyes.

We should not have come, Eliinka thought. She signaled Huoli to be alert.

One of the Pelten guards, standing behind Loukku, signaled the sign "danger." A Pelten guard could not know the Virun signs! Her eyes were tricking her. Eliinka placed her hand on her hip, ready to pull her knife if needed.

"We shouldn't have any contact with Viru," Loukku said. "This is a trick, a way to undermine our society. Are you are here to spy on us, to plan an invasion? You threaten our way of life. Our people should not learn of your ways, or of your dress and decorations. They should not be exposed to you." Loukku pointed to Eliinka's arms.

"Do all in Pelto share your view?" Eliinka created an unruffled smile, exuding a calm she did not feel.

The guard behind Loukku signaled the door behind him as the escape route.

Was their situation that bad? Jereni had been wise to teach her the signs. But how did Jereni have her own man in this house?

Two other guards moved around the edges of the room, blocking the entrance at their backs.

"No." Loukku's mouth evolved into an angular smile, the right side higher than the left. "But they'll listen to me after they hear the story of your bold attack."

Zerin put a hand on Eliinka's back.

"You can't be serious," Eliinka said. "We came peacefully."

A fight would destroy any possibility for talks with Pelto. Zerin only carried a knife, and Huoli a short sword. Plus her own small knife. They didn't have a chance! Eliinka turned to Rakel.

"Rakel, will you offer your voice, your protection? I helped you in Viru. I never forsook and will not forsake our friendship."

"You've also become a barbarian." Rakel approached as an unleashed whirlwind, and she shoved Eliinka. Her voice grew louder and louder with each word. "Look at you—your arms, your dress, your hair and face. You're a traitor to Pelto. You're the cause of all the changes in my life."

Rakel slapped Eliinka's cheek. She struck again, with her fingernails.

Eliinka did not block the blows and motioned Zerin to move back. She stood there and faced Rakel, not wanting to do anything to increase her rage, wincing with each strike. Fighting Rakel would make everything even worse. She stood firm as Rakel hit her face again and again in a brief, but silent explosion of rage which dissipated when Rakel stopped on her own accord and looked down at her reddened palm. A broken blood vessel bulged purple on the finger of her right hand.

"I want my brother back." Tears dripped down Rakel's face.

Eliinka swallowed her first retort and stepped back, touching her cheek. It was damp. She dropped her hand to see lines of blood.

"Please, Rakel, we came for peace. Please. Remember our friendship. I'm so sorry. My intent was never to bring pain to you. I came to Pelto for Prince Mikali and Queen Jereni. The red fabric in my saddlebag is a present for you, from them. They wish to visit you. But tonight may unravel their dream."

A flash of uncertainty, mixed with fear, appeared in Rakel's face. Her shoulders sagged. She murmured, "There's no way for you to escape the trap," and she turned away.

"They'll pay a ransom for our safe return."

Loukku laughed.

"Rakel, it appears I'll not be allowed to give you the fabric. It is yours."

"Kill them." Loukku said. His guards drew their swords.

Eliinka pulled her hidden knife from her dress as she leaped two steps to Loukku, dropped him to the floor, and held the blade across his throat. "Rakel knows my skills with the knife. Your men will drop their swords."

Loukku spat at her and Eliinka pressed, angling the blade so the flat edge bit into his neck. "Drop them," Loukku said. Swords clattered to the ground.

"There's no escape!" shrieked Rakel. "Eliinka, spare his life. Please. There are more men outside. Put down the knife, and I'll plead for your life."

Eliinka signaled, and in Virjalo said, "The near door." Huoli extinguished the nearest candle, darkening the room. She hit Loukku hard, on his temple, with the butt of her knife, knocking him out. She caught Zerin's hand, and they moved through sounds of confusion as Huoli fought off the guards behind them.

The covert guard from Pelto waited on the other side of the door. Eliinka hoped she could trust him as they followed him through a maze of rooms. She breathed out in relief when they reached a back window and took the short drop to the ground and the street. "May you find safety, m'lady." He bowed and ran back the way they had come, swinging his sword.

"Our guards?" whispered Zerin as he helped Eliinka through the window. He handed her the bag and dropped down at her side.

"We can pray they will make their escape. Quick! We must move away from here." She turned toward the central city.

"Shouldn't we be leaving the city?"

"They'll search that direction first."

"But we'll be noticed. Our clothing—"

"We'll stay in the shadows." Eliinka pulled her cloak from her bag.

"We have a choice." She worked through her thoughts out loud. "We could make our way back to Viru. Sneak through back ways I do not know, leaving tomorrow. Or stay here." Zerin followed Eliinka into a side street.

Eliinka asked, "What would Jereni choose to do? Do you think we can still fulfill our assignment? Or should we return directly to Viru?"

"She wants peace with Pelto, but is it possible?" Zerin grabbed Eliinka's hand.

The rays of the falling sun still lit the street, and she ducked into the shadows between a tree and a stone wall. She thought through the choices and risks. Could she return and face Jereni without doing all she could? She didn't even know the way. Loukku's men would be searching for her. Plus, her guards and horses? She would not abandon them.

"There's one house where I can request safety, where I can invoke my right to protection." Eliinka navigated through the back streets, through the shadows, hurrying to reach refuge. When she arrived, she rushed to the front door. The house, set back from the street, blended in with the other upper-class homes of the neighborhood.

"Where are we?"

"Trust me." Eliinka pulled her cloak farther over her head and around her dress. Hoping the address that Jereni had given her was correct, she knocked and dropped back into the shadows of a tree.

The door opened a crack. Light streamed onto the ground, clipping her feet. A girl's silhouette blackened the opening.

"May we speak with the man of the house?"

The girl left the door open. In a moment, Timo appeared.

What a relief. This was the correct house.

Eliinka did not extend her hand in the customary Pelten greeting, but removing her cloak, dropped with it as she fell onto her knees and lowered her chin. "I humbly implore you and invoke my vow of Iankaikki and ask you to extend your protection and shelter us within your walls." She held out her hands, palms meeting, fingers pointing upward, and waited. This was a rare request between believers, an appeal at times of greatest need, and was not to be refused. Eliinka lifted her head. "Timo, please. You hold our lives in your hands."

Timo blinked and stepped forward. "Eliinka? You are here? Of course, please enter." After he shut the door behind them, he turned around and held out his hand. Eliinka touched her fingertips to his.

"Eliinka, have you remained true and faithful?" Timo asked.

"Although in defense I've taken the life of men, I have remained faithful. I've kept my everlasting vows."

Zerin stared at Eliinka.

"Your voice is heard. My home is your protection; my walls will shelter you. 'The light of eternity spans all life.'" Timo relaxed his stance.

"This is the first time I've heard the claim invoked. Follow me. You can explain . . . " he glanced again at Zerin, "in the kitchen, over something to drink."

Eliinka took Zerin's limp hand, and they followed Timo into the kitchen where a portrait of a beautiful woman, who looked familiar, hung on the wall. The girl's blue eyes peered at them from around a corner, then disappeared. They sat, their legs touching. Zerin examined Eliinka's wincing face while she clutched his other arm.

"You have no marriage ring on your finger, Eliinka. Yet you are attached. I remember Lord Zerin. Is he the man that Queen Jereni chose?"

"Yes. We were married by a priest of Viru." Eliinka grabbed Zerin's hand and held it tight.

"I'm pleased to see you again, but did not expect your arrival in this fashion or for you to invoke the sacred word of supplication and perform the rites of ingress."

"Explain yourself to me. It is my right to know." Zerin said as he pulled his hand from Eliinka's.

"Timo and I belong to the same faith." Eliinka dropped her hands into her lap and interlocked her fingers, squeezing them so tight that they hurt. "We are of Eleman Puusta. You have seen me in my meditations and prayers. I didn't hide that from you."

Zerin's disappointed eyes creased.

He had a right, at least in Pelto, to a divorce. Eliinka's voice plummeted into a whisper. "I'm sorry. I should've told you before our marriage."

Zerin took her hands in his, and while holding them, rubbed the backs, the diamonds, with his thumbs. His touch was gentle and firm.

"I understand your silence, but I would not have refused you. I didn't consider your faith a possibility. Our records about Pelto say all followers of Eleman Puusta were exterminated years ago." He pulled her hands to his chest. "Does Queen Jereni know?"

"We've not spoken of it."

"Promise me you'll tell her the next time you see her."

"I promise to tell Jereni." Eliinka tensed, grateful she didn't need to worry about facing Jereni until she returned. That would give her time to find the words.

Timo poured three cups of tea. "This is a surprise. I wasn't expecting either of you to visit Pelto."

"An invitation came from the governor," Eliinka said, "and Jereni sent us."

"I did not think that anyone would come," Timo said. "It was a courtesy letter."

"Timo, when you visited, you mentioned that some Peltens want no contact with Viru. The messenger who delivered the invitation brought us to the house of Loukku. He must be one of them. Rakel was there." Eliinka swallowed. "Loukku threatened to kill us. When he ordered us to lay down our arms and his guards pulled their swords, I held him at knife point, struck him unconscious, and we escaped."

"Who hit you?"

"Rakel struck Eliinka several times, and she would not stop her. Eliinka, why?" Zerin scowled. "You could have stopped any of her blows."

"Rakel is the sister of Prince Mikali. It wouldn't have helped us in any way for me to strike her back." Eliinka's face throbbed. "I won't harm her.

She knows I could've stopped her. Perhaps she listened to me. She now carries a bruise on her hand to remind her of me."

Eliinka stood and peeked between the curtains of the nearest window. There was no movement on the streets outside.

"Timo, Loukku trapped us. He would have killed us if we had not escaped and claimed we attacked him. As he desired, he destroyed our ability to meet the governor. He will hunt us down. If we don't return, Queen Jereni will send her armies to Pelto and search for us."

"She seemed peaceful when I met her. Different than what the legends say."

"Timo," Eliinka shook her head. She also remembered the stories that told of a bloodthirsty, barbaric princess. The stories were exaggerated, but Jereni would not be patient, not if her ambassadors were murdered. "Trust me! She will send her armies unless we return safely to Viru. But how can we safely travel? Also, I need to know if my guards escaped."

"You stay here, inside. I'll see if they are still there. Who else was in the room besides Loukku and Rakel?"

"My guard, Huoli. My other three guards stayed with our horses. Also Loukku's guards. There were four of them in the room. The messenger left after he took us into the house." She would not tell him that one of the guards worked for Jereni.

"Toivo," Timo called.

The teenage girl entered the room and stared at Eliinka.

"This is Eliinka and Zerin. Eliinka, this is my daughter, Toivo."

Toivo dropped her head and shifted her feet. Her hair was pulled back away from her face, showing off her high cheekbones and intense eyes.

"Toivo, first bring Eliinka a clean, wet cloth for her face. Second, serve them a hot evening meal. After they finish, show them to the room upstairs and make them comfortable. I need to go out."

"A shared room?" Toivo shot a quick glance at Eliinka and Zerin.

"They are from Viru. They don't share our custom of rings to denote marriage. It's important for you to know that Eliinka is of Eleman Puusta."

Toivo gazed at Eliinka for several seconds before hurrying from the room.

Chapter Twenty-Nine

~ TODAY WILL COMPLICATE OUR VISIT ~

Toivo exhibited the mixed confidence and uncertainties of a girl leaving childhood and trying to enter womanhood as she acted in the role of hostess, trying to make them comfortable. She lit two candles in the small, upstairs guest room. "Thank you for dinner, Toivo," Eliinka said.

Eliinka and Zerin stood, shoulders touching, on a small carpet in front of the fireplace. There was barely enough room for the bed and a narrow cabinet.

"The room is cold. I'll kindle a fire for you."

"You don't need to serve us," Eliinka said. "We can build our own fire."

"Who are you? You speak as a woman from Pelto, yet your clothing is . . . different."

"I'm Lady Eliinka, daughter of Kallela, envoy and confidante of Queen Jereni of Viru, and the wife of Zerin. I'm Virun, although I was born in RitVa." *Is this who I am?* she thought as she said the words. Also, she claimed to be Virun, though she was not sure it was true.

"Your dress is very beautiful." Toivo blurted. "I think you're beautiful too."

Eliinka didn't feel beautiful tonight, certainly not with a bruised and bloodied face. She placed her bag on the bed and rummaged through it until she found her nightdress, which she tossed onto a pillow. She set the harp on the bed. While she took inventory of what she still had with her, Zerin prepared the fire. A wisp of sour evergreen smoke entered the room until the updraft carried it up the chimney.

Toivo stood in the doorway as if she wanted to ask another question. Eliinka continued to search in her bag. When she looked up to see what

Toivo wanted, Toivo said, "Excuse me. I'll be in the kitchen if you need anything."

Deep night had fallen, and rain chattered on the roof. Eliinka walked back and forth across the room, only four steps, glad they could not be seen through the small, high window. She was trapped, with no good choice. The room was small, tight, and she could hardly breathe. The rain increased, banging hard on the roof like horses' hooves.

"I'll go see if Toivo needs any help." Eliinka gave Zerin a brief kiss, one that promised more kisses later.

She found Toivo in the kitchen, balancing several plates from dinner on one arm and two cups in her other hand.

"Let me help." Eliinka took the plates from Toivo and set them in a washing basin. She poured hot water over them and began washing, ignoring Toivo's protests. Eliinka's shoulders relaxed as her hands worked methodically in the warm water. She had not cleaned a dish since arriving in Viru and had forgotten how a simple, daily task gave her time to think. While she worked, she hummed a Pelten tune.

"Do you play the harp?" Toivo carried in the final dish and placed it in the suds.

"Yes. I played for your father in Viru."

"Will you play for me?"

"I dare not, not tonight. Men are searching for me. My songs would be heard, and they might realize I'm in your home."

"I've taken harp lessons."

"Maybe you could play a tune for me instead."

"I'll fetch my harp as soon as I finish." After drying and putting away the dishes, Toivo retrieved a small harp, and as they sat in the warmth of the kitchen, she played a simple folk tune.

Even the music did not ease the throbbing of Eliinka's face.

Toivo struggled through the song, a familiar piece for beginners. "That's my favorite," she said when she finished. "But I need to practice it more." A shy smile appeared, and Toivo replaced a loose strand that had fallen from her pulled-up, dark brown hair.

"I've not heard that tune in a long time. I used to teach harp here in RitVa."

"Here? Why did you leave? And to Viru!" Toivo's eyes were big. "You are very brave!"

"I made a choice, and it led me there."

"What are the people like in Viru?"

"They are like the people who live here in many ways. They spend their lives with their families. They care for each other and spend their time eating, cleaning, working, cooking, and learning. But some things are different. Their fabrics are brightly colored, and their buildings are painted with designs and pictures."

Toivo got a faraway look on her face, like she was imagining a place she had only heard of.

"There are other differences. Marriages are arranged by the woman's family or friends. Marriage is a bond that is not allowed to be broken. Yet women have more rights and opportunities. They can own land and speak for themselves. Of course, the language and clothing are different, and the food is spicy and hot, with more intense flavors. Queen Jereni is a wise, strong ruler who loves her people." Eliinka paused. It was good she had come and not Jereni. Jereni would have killed all in the room and probably died. "She enjoys the hairpiece you embroidered. It's beautiful in her hair." Eliinka tipped an empty pot so she could see her face in the polished metal. Red and purple marred her reflection. No wonder her cheek throbbed.

"My father had not told me who the gift was for or much about his journey. The queen wears it?" Toivo half jumped up and down while she spoke.

"Yes, she does. Your skills at embroidery are extraordinary. It's hard for me to tell the front from the back of your work. Did you create the pattern, the design of the circle inside the square?" Eliinka set down the pot.

"No, it's a family pattern. My great-grandmother designed it. She taught her daughters to embroider and passed down the pattern. It's used by all our family and is in everything we make. I usually use it in borders, but sometimes, like with the hairpiece, I use the design as the main image and embellish it."

"The pattern is also on the bedding in the guest room."

"My mother embroidered that bedding." Toivo paused. She stirred the ashes in the hearth and banked the coals so they would be ready for morning. She brushed a tear from her cheek. "My mother passed through to the other side over a year ago, from the illness. I miss her."

"That year the illness took many, including my parents." Eliinka wanted to wrap her arms around Toivo and comfort her, but she didn't. After what had happened today, she wondered if she would be able to visit her parents' graves like she had planned. "The other side is never far away. I wondered if I'd enter it earlier today." Eliinka touched her swollen cheek. "I've had a bad day. I must rest while I can. Thanks for the music." She pointed to a bucket that sat near the fire. "Can I carry water upstairs for bathing?"

Toivo filled the bucket from the large pot of water hanging in the fireplace, still warm, and handed it to Eliinka. "Who arranged your marriage? Do you live in a palace?"

"Queen Jereni arranged my marriage, and yes, I live in a palace." Eliinka's whole head ached, and it was hard to think clearly. She started up the stairs. "Please, other questions need to wait until tomorrow."

"Sleep well," Toivo called.

Eliinka entered the guest room, set down the bucket, and embraced Zerin. "I'm glad you're here with me."

"I'm sorry." He lightly touched her bruised face. "Today complicates our visit."

"It does. Did I make the wrong choice today?"

"We are still alive."

"Thankfully," Eliinka said. "Jereni would have killed Loukku." She was amazed that they had made it out of the house. The only reason was because Jereni's man had warned them and shown them the way. "Who was the man who helped us, and how does he know the hand signals?"

"He is Pelten, yet he speaks our language," Zerin said. "Queen Jereni has several agents who live in different cities in Pelto, and it's their job to send her information. It's fortunate he was in that house."

"She might be angry with me," Eliinka said, "but I knew that there would be no chance for peace if we fought or killed Loukku."

"She'll be very angry, but you made a wise choice. Perhaps we can still fulfill our assignment."

"Zerin, you don't understand Pelto. We have two very poor possibilities at this moment. We can disguise ourselves and flee, hoping to find our way to Viru. There is a chance we would arrive safely. Loukku and his men will be searching for us along all possible routes.

"The other option is to stay here and try to meet the governor, even though he might refuse to listen to us. Today will also create severe repercussions for me. My actions at Loukku's house violated the law." Eliinka squeezed her hands tight around her upper arms. Now that she had time to think, in the quiet bedroom with Zerin, she realized their situation was much worse than she had realized.

"I don't understand."

"I . . . I struck a man." Her voice choked up. "Perhaps the penalty can be waived."

"What can I do? Though I speak Pelten I don't know this city. I don't know this culture."

"I don't know what to do. Tonight we must rest and wait for Timo." Eliinka clutched his hands and leaned her body into Zerin. "Tonight, hold me."

In the middle of the night a quiet tap sounded on the door, waking them. Eliinka sat up and dropped her feet to the chilly wooden floor. She felt for her cloak in the dark, found it, wrapped it around herself, and opened the door. Light from a candle glanced off the walls.

"We must speak now," Timo whispered as he entered the room. "I went to Loukku's house and arrived at the same time as the watchman. Three of your guards are dead."

"They probably had no chance." Eliinka grabbed Zerin's hand. Her skin felt like it was tightening over all her body. Their deaths were not a surprise, but she had hoped they had escaped. "My other guard? Huoli?"

"Loukku's men said there were only three. None by that name, and that they came into Loukku's house and attacked him."

"What did Loukku say?"

"He said you tried to kill him."

"I did not, though maybe I should have." But she knew she could not have drawn the knife across his neck.

"I'm sure the group he must belong to, Kapina, is searching for you."

"Kapina?" Eliinka asked.

"A group who is working to gain control of the government. At times they are violent."

Eliinka sat on the bottom edge of the bed, curled her feet under her to warm them, and dropped her head into her hands. She drew in her breath. "Is there more?"

"I accompanied the chief watchman when he interviewed each guard."

"And . . ."

"Two of the guards were confused and would only say that they had fought off foreigners at Loukku's orders. The other two guards told of a group, with a woman, which entered the house by invitation. One of these guards said that visitors were unfriendly and escaped. The second guard's story matches yours, Eliinka, with surprising accuracy."

"Timo, that guard is the one who helped us escape." Eliinka lifted her head. "He's why we are alive tonight. What of Rakel?"

"Rakel invoked her right as a woman to not speak without a relative's presence."

Eliinka swung her feet off the bed. That did no good. Mikali was Rakel's only male relative, so Rakel would never give her testimony. She knelt, added wood, and blew on the coals to rekindle the fire. She held her hands over the flames, and shivered. The bitter wood smell filled the air.

"Eliinka, they want to kill you and all Viruns," Timo said. "Hide here for a week or two. When it becomes safe, return to Viru in disguise."

"Father." Toivo stepped onto the threshold, wearing her nightdress, shivering in the cool air.

"Toivo, go back to sleep. We need privacy."

"I had a dream. A dream about Eliinka." Toivo grabbed her father's arm.

Timo pulled her close to him.

"I was in it?" Eliinka asked.

"It's the saddest dream I've ever viewed. Both of you left Pelto together. You were chased and, and . . . I can't say what I saw." Toivo's eyes widened and her body shook. Timo tightened his arm around her and pulled her to his chest in a fatherly embrace.

"We died?"

Toivo twisted her head toward Eliinka and nodded just once. "My dream was horrible. I saw numberless soldiers and armies and death. The rivers turned red, the sky black. Houses and farms and fields burning. RitVa in ruins. Pelto destroyed . . . Tears streamed down Toivo's face.

"It is just a nightmare, nothing more," Zerin said.

"Are Toivo's dreams a foreshadowing, a certainty of the future, or are they a dream of warning that can be altered by our actions?" Eliinka asked. The fire crackled, and large flames shot up the chimney now. Sweat dripped down her neck.

"Toivo has dreamed both types in the past, but nothing of this magnitude," Timo said. "I want to believe this is a dream of warning. She dreams precisely."

Eliinka would have predicted the same situation, even if Toivo had not had a dream. "If Huoli returns to Queen Jereni and is the sole voice she hears, or if no one returns, what Toivo sees is an outcome of her wrath. She won't hold back. If we are killed or delay our return while waiting for safety, peace will not be a possibility. My heart stops cold with the thought."

"But it would be certain suicide for you to attempt to return now." Timo frowned. "Kapina will be searching for you. All roads and the crossing will be watched. It won't be safe for a month."

"There is one other path." Eliinka grimaced. "We'll try to meet with the governor, explain what happened, and request protection for our travels. If we meet with him, we can explain Queen Jereni's desire for a treaty."

"Eliinka, do you understand your peril, what your punishment will be, if you walk into the Hirdahouse after your actions yesterday?" Timo hugged Toivo tighter as she smeared the tears on her cheeks.

"Queen Jereni wants peace, she needs peace. She wishes to visit Pelto, meet Mikali's family, see his home." Eliinka set her jaw. "I'll demonstrate that we of Viru desire peace, that we can create harmony. I'll tread this path, and . . . and if necessary Zerin can return without me." Eliinka touched her still swollen cheek. "I'll suffer the penalty and humiliation. You will vouch for me, and there is a witness, and maybe . . ."

"I'm confused." Zerin said. "What is the danger of going before the governor? We did nothing wrong."

"The law is different here," Eliinka said. "It states that a woman cannot strike a man."

"Our option was death."

"She understands the law well," said Timo. "The penalty is a severe beating and sometimes imprisonment. Not all women survive."

Toivo broke out in sobs.

"No! We can't let you do this. We must return home tomorrow." Zerin wrapped his arm around Eliinka. "Or you stay here, at Timo's, and I'll meet the governor alone."

"They'll know I'm here, track me down, and find me if you go without me. I'd still be punished. Or Kapina would find me first. All other paths lead to either our deaths or a violent war. It is better not to hide." Barely able to give voice to her whisper, Eliinka said, "It is better if I walk in on my own."

She looked down to the thin, white line she shared with Jereni on her inner arm. Their matching scars cemented their friendship. She turned her arm over to trace a blue line and diamond. "I must do this." She gulped and air scratched her throat. "I'll find the courage. Timo, we'll go to the governor tomorrow morning. If he wants peace, he may give me clemency."

"If not?" Zerin asked.

The hot room suddenly felt bitter cold.

"Then there's probably no way to stop the next war between Pelto and Viru."

Chapter Thirty

~ BEYOND A GIFT OF FRIENDSHIP ~

Eliinka noticed every detail as she climbed out of bed: the scratch of Zerin's whiskers on her cheek as she brushed her lips against his face, the shadows on the wall and floor and her skin as she bathed by candle-light, the quiet whisper of the wind in the chimney, the sweet oil polish of the smooth wood floor, Zerin's steady breathing. The small things, the little joys in life. She sat longer in her morning meditations, not wanting to leave the place of peace, but she finally stood, prepared to face the day.

There was one task that Eliinka could do, a task from Jereni that was of critical importance. It had been planned for later during her visit, but today might be her only chance. She found the small box in her traveling bag and put it in her purse. She would do it as soon as she could.

The birds still slept, not yet sounding their morning warble, and she breathed in deeply. The morning air smelled fresh, the after-rain smell, not yet disturbed by the early morning cooking fires. After she combed her hair, she woke Zerin with a kiss.

"You are beautiful." He ran his fingers across her lips. "Only one kiss this morning?"

She kissed him again, on his cheeks, his forehead, the bridge of his nose. He laughed, and they kissed, his lips traveling all over hers, a kiss she would never forget. She held him so close that she could not tell where her skin stopped and his began.

A distant birdsong reminded Eliinka that day truly had arrived. She buried her head into Zerin's chest, trying to shut out the morning. She would rather hide in the room and stay in Zerin's arms all day.

Finally, she knew she couldn't put off the future and slid out of bed. "I'm going downstairs to see if Toivo needs any help."

"I'll hurry. I promise." Zerin gave her another kiss. When he pulled away, he kept his forehead against hers. "I will protect you. Always."

"I love you, Zerin." Eliinka gave his hands a quick squeeze before she left the room.

The stairs creaked more than Eliinka remembered from the previous night. She entered the kitchen where she built up the fire, put on a pot of water, and was warming her hands when Toivo entered the room. Toivo stopped mid-step.

"You are our guest. Let me serve you."

"Please, Toivo, I need to do something to help," Eliinka said. If she thought too much about what she faced today, she would not be able to do what was necessary. Hiding would only make everything worse.

"Could you make the morning breadcake? I'll prepare everything else."

Five minutes later Zerin entered the room, and Eliinka stopped mixing the dough.

"Eliinka, what are you doing? What's in the bowl?" Zerin asked.

"Breadcake."

"Do you know how to cook?"

"You can tell me if I can when you eat this morning." Eliinka chuckled. This was the first time she had made food for Zerin. She hoped he liked it.

"I guess you had to cook for yourself before you came to Viru." Zerin sat at the table.

After Eliinka carefully formed the dough, she shifted several coals to the side. As she placed the breadcakes on the hearth, her thoughts shifted to what they needed so they could return to Viru. They needed horses, supplies, and a map—or someone who knew the way to guide them. She also wondered about Huoli. Where he was hiding. How he would travel.

"Who makes your food?" Toivo asked as she set the table.

"Several cooks work in the palace kitchen." Eliinka sat next to Zerin, who draped his arm around her shoulder and pulled her close. His touch should have comforted her, but instead, she worried about seeing the governor and considered if they should change their plans and not meet with him. Instead, they could sneak back to Viru—but that would be impossible. They needed the governor's protection.

A slight smoky smell overcame the scent of baking bread. Toivo yanked the breadcakes out from the fire.

"The breadcakes almost burned." She raised an eyebrow and shook her head at Eliinka.

"Thanks for noticing. I tend to burn my cooking. I always get distracted. Zerin, it's good you don't have to eat my cooking every day." Eliinka laughed and clutched his hand.

Timo entered the room, but stopped short, wrinkling his brow at Eliinka, who continued to laugh. It was odd to laugh like it was a normal day, she realized.

"Timo of Pelto, I have one mission I can complete." Eliinka stood and gave him a slight bow. "Queen Jereni sends a gift for your daughter, Toivo, to express her appreciation."

Eliinka pulled the small box, wrapped in beautiful fabric, from the purse that hung at her side. She handed it to Toivo.

Toivo peeled back the fabric, opened the box, and held it out for all to see what lay inside. She looked up first to Eliinka, then to her father. "These earrings are beautiful."

The highest quality Virun gems and fine gold sparkled in the rays of the morning light that entered the eastern window. Three squares set on top of each other created each rectangular earring. Emeralds were centered in each square. Sapphires sat at each corner and small diamonds surrounded each grouping, which created an effect of a circle inside a square.

"These are priceless," Timo said. "We cannot accept a gift of such great value."

Toivo set the box on the table and put her hands in her lap.

"Try them on." Eliinka hoped that would change Timo's mind.

After a glance at Eliinka's anxious face, Toivo picked up an earring. "They use my family pattern. Why?" She hung it from one ear and picked up the second one.

"I didn't see the gift until you opened the box. Queen Jereni wants to express her appreciation for your family's friendship." The earrings were more stunning than Eliinka had imagined.

"How do they look?"

"Perfect. You are stunning."

"We can't refuse the queen's gift." Toivo turned her pleading face to her father. The earrings reflected the light and sparkled.

Timo paced the room, occasionally glancing at Eliinka. She sat silent, fingering her necklace, remembering Jereni had said to not pressure Timo.

Finally Timo said, "Toivo will be allowed to keep the earrings, but she won't be allowed to wear them on our streets. Yet Eliinka, we have nothing to offer Queen Jereni in return."

"You've already given much," Eliinka said. "She appreciates your trust and honesty. You've extended your hand of friendship. You are giving us refuge." Jereni had instructed Eliinka on what to say, depending on Timo's response. If he responded positively, she would say more. The goal was a formal friendship with Timo because of his influence in the government and because he was friendly toward Viru.

"Eliinka, we both know a gift of this magnitude signifies something more." Timo shook his head. "These earrings are so valuable that only a princess could wear them. They are beyond a gift of friendship."

"You have great insight, so I'll be bold in my words. Queen Jereni desires an alliance of friendship with your family."

Timo sat at the kitchen table and rested his chin in his hand. Eliinka wondered if he would refuse. Toivo brought over the food she had prepared and placed it in front of them. She sat down, leaning her head against her father's shoulder.

Zerin tasted the breadcake, and Eliinka slowed her growing smile. "Zerin, what do you think of my breadcake?"

He laughed, but his eyes that focused on Eliinka also looked beyond her, perhaps into the distance of their approaching day, she thought.

"It is delightful," he said.

Eliinka took a bite. "A bit overdone." She put down the bread. "Timo, you do not need to answer today."

"This is a very serious offer," he said. "Though I can choose to be a friend and we could perhaps have a family alliance of sorts, I can't work for her or do anything that is not to the benefit of Pelto. What would she expect of me?"

"You can give us influence in Pelto, express our views, push for our positions in your council and laws, and also give us your help, which you are already doing. Queen Jereni wants policies that are good for both her kingdom and your country, such as trade and free travel. She does not request your allegiance and will not ask you to compromise your integrity."

"Eliinka, I must have time to consider the implications of this offer."

"I understand. No matter your answer, she wants to maintain your friendship. Perhaps you can give me your answer before I return to Viru."

"Perhaps," Timo said.

Chapter Thirty-One
~ PENALTY IS REQUIRED ~

In the early morning they walked up the worn, shallow steps that extended the entire width of the Hirdahouse, and Eliinka looked up at it as if seeing the building for the first time. The broad, square wooden building was about two and a half stories high and had a low peaked roof with small square windows running across the front. They passed guards who nodded at Timo. When they walked through two imposing oak doors, the large hinges cried out in tired distress.

Timo left them in a reception room, and in a few minutes he returned with an older man of noble bearing.

"Lady Eliinka," Timo said, "may I present you to Governor Tuli. Governor Tuli, may I present Zerin of Viru, advisor to Queen Jereni."

Zerin gave a small bow, but Eliinka stepped forward and greeted the governor with a firm handshake, in the manner of Pelto. "I look forward to our discussions, Governor Tuli."

He pulled his hand away. "Did Queen Jereni send a woman to meet with me?"

Eliinka tossed a tight smile. "I'm the voice designated by Queen Jereni. I've come at her command and in response to your kind invitation."

"You speak for Queen Jereni?"

"I have authority to conduct negotiations. Queen Jereni wishes to sign any documents." Eliinka took a deep breath and looked directly into Governor Tuli's face.

He averted his eyes.

"I regret to say that an unfortunate incident occurred yesterday, removing from my hands a valuable gift for you from Queen Jereni." She ignored the gasps of Timo and Zerin. "I wish to explain, before rumors of my actions reach your ears."

Two well-dressed men burst through the doors.

"Why do you interrupt?" Governor Tuli demanded.

One said, "We have just cause against these foreigners," at the same time that Timo said, "I request private council with you, Governor Tuli."

"It's good we came early," Eliinka whispered. How did they know to find her here? Her shoulders sagged.

"Order! Be quiet!" Governor Tuli commanded. "Wait in the Central Hall. I'll hear your accusations later." The two men hurried from the room.

As Timo walked out, following the governor, he paused and said to Eliinka, "I'll return soon."

"It's better the governor hears our story from Timo," Eliinka said. "It is more likely he will listen to him." She sat at the front edge of a chair at the side of the room and leaned her head on her hands.

"Will the governor hear us?" Zerin asked. He gently touched Eliinka's shoulders until she sat up. While remaining standing, he leaned down and gave her a hug. It made her wish they were in Viru and that the previous day had not happened.

"I don't know," Eliinka said. "The government is very different in Pelto. They are elected in their communities, yet almost all fill the post of their fathers. Timo and another man were chosen from parliament to form the governor's council. They have the daily governing responsibilities. Timo has been on the council for much of his life, as was his father."

"Timo must have great influence."

"He does, but Governor Tuli prefers to rule by consensus, so few decisions are made unless parliament is in assembly, and any change, any real decision is unheard of. Parliament only assembles four times a year."

While they waited, Zerin wandered and examined faded portraits of men that covered the walls of the reception room, occasionally glancing over his shoulder at Eliinka. She tapped her right thumb against each fingertip in turn, again and again. If she knew how long they would be waiting, she would get out the harp and play, but they might return at any time.

When Timo and the governor returned, Timo stopped just inside the door and gave Eliinka a low, solemn bow.

The governor continued forward. "Are the words of Timo true?" he asked Eliinka.

"I did not hear his words," Eliinka answered.

The governor acted as if she had said nothing. Timo nodded for her to speak.

"We were led into a trap because the men wanted to destroy our opportunity to meet. Yet I trust Timo's words are true."

"Do you understand what you have confessed?"

"I was born and raised in Pelto. I understand your laws."

A corner of the governor's mouth twitched. With obvious distaste, he shook his head while gesturing at her Virun dress, arms, and loose hair, which was not put up on her head like Pelten women. "Who are you?"

"I'm Lady Eliinka, daughter of Kallela, envoy from Viru, and personal advisor to Queen Jereni." Eliinka held her head high.

"Let's hear your accusers."

As she passed out through the door, Timo whispered, "You'll only have one chance to speak for yourself. I'll let you know when."

The audience stilled when Eliinka entered the Central Hall. It was her first time inside. The hall stretched almost the length of the building and reached to the roof. The two men glared at her. Timo guided Eliinka and Zerin to the front, left of the hall. The governor sat in a plain wooden chair at the front and called the men forward.

"This foreigner came into the house of Loukku and struck him to the ground." The larger man pointed at Eliinka.

"My report says three men entered the house of Loukku and that his men killed them in his defense." Governor Tuli pulled a parchment from a table and held it up.

"That was the official written report," the man said. "But this woman was there and injured Loukku. Ask her. Will she deny it?"

Timo gave Eliinka a slight nod of his head. This would be her only chance to speak. She stepped forward.

"The messenger brought us into the house of Loukku where he threatened us with death. I was struck many times." She motioned to the bruises on her face. "I struck Loukku so we could escape with our lives, yet I spared him because we desire peace. My guards who waited with my horses were murdered, and my horses and goods stolen."

"She twists the truth, Governor. Yet she admits breaking the law."

"You have been wronged, yet the law is clear. The penalty is required." The governor's announcement echoed loud and clear.

Eliinka walked across the front of the room and stopped an arm's length away from the governor. She said the words she had rehearsed in her mind as they walked to the Hirdahouse.

"Governor Tuli, consider my words. I've come here because of this document." She handed him the parchment of invitation with his signature. "As envoy to Viru I expected safe passage, like we gave your people

179

during their visit to Viru for the royal wedding. We gave them the very best hospitality. Queen Jereni will be furious when she hears we were waylaid and assaulted by a government official; she will be angry her men were killed. Yet when she hears I've been punished for protecting my life, I may not be able to check her unrestrained anger. The chance for trade relations she hopes for will be gone. The unofficial peace our lands have enjoyed for many years will disappear."

The governor did not respond to her words. Eliinka spoke in a soft, clear voice. "I do understand I don't have sufficient support to clear my name."

"I'll meet with my councilors, Timo and Gervald, to determine your penalty. Who struck your face?"

"A woman who was my childhood friend," Eliinka answered. "I desire no punishment for her. Her name is Rakel, the daughter of Aalto, sister to Prince Mikali."

"Send for Rakel," the governor ordered a guard. "And take this woman to the holding chamber."

The guard reached for Eliinka's arm, but she knocked his hand away, and Timo snapped out, "Don't touch Lady Eliinka."

She stalked after the guard through a side door into a tiny, plain room. Zerin followed her. Another guard entered behind them, shut the door, and crossed his arms.

"Our meeting with the governor is going poorly," Zerin said in Virjalo.

"The governor wants to please both the people and me, and uphold the law, yet he can't. Pelto can't adapt to unusual circumstances, and in this case, make logical exceptions to the law." If there had been a way to leave, escape at this moment, Eliinka would have taken it. Yet it would be impossible to leave the Hirdahouse unnoticed.

"I don't understand the laws here."

"And I can't explain them to you, not easily."

Zerin closed the gap between them until their feet touched and whispered, "Eliinka, I want to protect you, but we are in a place where I can't. What can I do?"

"Remember your first duty. Our first duty is to Queen Jereni." Eliinka said this as much to remind herself of her duty, of what she must do, and of why she was making the sacrifice that would be required. If only it was not a waste of a sacrifice. That was the best she could hope for.

Zerin swung his arms forward and his hands clung to Eliinka's.

"Eliinka, I love you." His lips touched hers, a gentle whisper that reminded her of their first kiss.

The guard coughed.

Zerin pulled away, his face red, yet he didn't let go of her hands.

"I'll be fine." She tucked her head under his chin, hoping what she had said was true. After a minute, she said, "Pelto's leaders are not known for making fast decisions. Music will make us feel better, help pass the time." She pulled the travel harp from her bag.

Eliinka played the simple folk tune that Toivo had played the previous night. Extra notes and chords mingled and soared into variation after variation. The music diffused throughout the building, caressing not only Zerin, but also all who were within its walls. It flowed through the windows and spilled into the streets. She weighed the risk of using her gift to protect her; it would be a certain death sentence, so she played from her heart. She thought of Zerin and their future together: that thought gave her courage for what would soon come. After twenty minutes, Eliinka rolled the final chord. The overtones faded, softer than a whisper.

Zerin moved the harp aside and drew Eliinka to his chest and held her tight. His arms created a safe haven she wished were permanent. They broke apart as a guard approached, and after she put the harp back into her bag, they followed the guard back into the Central Hall.

"Rakel." The governor leaned forward in his chair. "You are allowed to speak."

"Eliinka has sworn herself to the Queen of Viru. Don't trust her. Viru trained her to fight. Look. She bears scars of violence on her left shoulder."

Eliinka swirled toward Rakel.

Rakel took a step back, tripping on her feet, but she kept her balance and glared at Eliinka.

"You broke your promise to Queen Jereni! Never again set foot in Viru for now my voice asking for your protection will not be heard." A tremor rushed through Eliinka's veins. This knowledge of her injury couldn't really make a difference.

But she wasn't sure.

"Bare her shoulders and back," Governor Tuli said.

"This is not right." Eliinka raised her chin in defiance. She would not, could not. But this was not a surprise: all punishments were given in public.

Quiet murmurs arose from the onlookers.

"Did you come here planning to undermine my government? Were you trained to assassinate me?"

"No! I came at your invitation as a representative of Queen Jereni—"

"Your first action upon arriving was to break our law." Governor Tuli motioned a guard to Eliinka's side.

If Eliinka didn't expose her back, he would, so she removed her arms from the sleeves of her dress so both shoulders and her back showed and held the front of her dress with her arms to cover her chest. The upper segment of her scar showed vividly, skin fused to skin across a horrid, jagged line. Gasps came from all across the room.

"You must have seen scars of battle before." Eliinka frowned at the Governor Tuli's stare.

"Never on a woman. How?"

"Protecting my queen. I was trained to protect myself after I almost died." Eliinka stood straight, scar in open view as if daring him to continue in his gaze.

"The law offers no exceptions."

Timo hurled a black look at the governor. Zerin protested in Virjalo, and Eliinka stepped to his side. "Speak in Pelten. Don't interfere. It will hurt our cause."

Zerin reached up and stroked Eliinka's injured cheek. His face and body sagged.

"I spoke strongly for your case, but the governor won't listen," Timo spoke under his breath. "He doesn't comprehend who you are."

"Zerin, you must understand what I tell Timo. I don't want to be parted from you. Ever." Eliinka squeezed Zerin's hand. "Timo, I give you permission to restrain Zerin if needed. I don't want to learn the consequences of interference."

Eliinka turned around. "You may continue, Governor Tuli."

"I took in consideration your bravery of walking into these halls today and your willingness to be the first to inform me of your actions. We give you the lightest punishment. You can tell your queen I showed mercy. It will be done with a light hand and the smaller whip. In recognition of the demands of my councilors, you will not be touched by our actual hands, bound for the whipping, or imprisoned."

It did not sound like mercy to Eliinka.

"Governor Tuli, I'll explain your judgment to Queen Jereni. I doubt she'll accept your definition of lenience. You do not understand my position! Does the law apply to Loukku for the murder of my men and stolen goods?"

"Loukku has immunity as a government leader."

Eliinka nodded her head. *Why did immunity not apply to me*, she wondered. But they would not count her as a government leader. They only viewed her as a woman who had no rights.

The governor motioned, and a lean, muscular guard stepped forward. The simple whip was larger and longer than Eliinka had expected. The whipping would be more than symbolic, which had been a faint hope. This punishment would draw lines of pain she would carry for the rest of her life.

Eliinka tried to distract herself by thinking about her harp.

The fibers in her arms quivered. Her mind seemed to separate from her body. She bit her lips and tightened her fists, but as she tried to control her muscles, the invisible vibrations turned into spasms. Eliinka did not know where the convulsion came from, because she felt no fear. Her body would not obey her commands; her nerves had a mind of their own. The spasms spread throughout her body until she shook uncontrollably. Frustration worsened the spasms, which grew until she was uncontrollably shaking. She was scared by her failure to control her body and her muscles, by her failure to command her body with her mind.

Voices commented on her trembling.

The whip whistled through the air.

It spliced across her upper back. Her skin tore open.

Eliinka gritted her teeth and managed to stay on her feet, forced herself to stand upright, although her body shook like a sapling in a storm.

The whip sounded again. Her lower shoulder blades fought against the rough whip as an unexpected screech escaped her mouth.

Shooting pain seared her brain. She suppressed her vocal chords and looked down, focusing on the blue diamond on the back of her right hand. She breathed through her nose. The whip screamed. Her blood splattered across the floor, and she closed her eyes as if that could diminish the fire in her flesh. She did not count the fifteen stripes she received, but focused on standing upright, refusing to collapse in a heap, refusing to vocalize her agony.

"It is finished," announced Governor Tuli.

Zerin rushed to Eliinka, and he tenderly draped a clean cloth over her hanging strips of skin and flesh. He pulled her dress up over her back and shoulders, and helped her arms into the sleeves, all the time glaring at the governor.

Rakel, her face white, held onto a wall for support. She turned her head away from Eliinka's gaze.

"Now we will speak about your visit," said Governor Tuli.

Eliinka swelled in disbelief. She fought to stay conscious.

"I will listen to your requests in the Parliament Room." He droned with a slow voice.

"I am not in a condition or temperament for a discussion." A violent riptide dragged Eliinka into a current of an unfamiliar emotion—anger. "I didn't bring requests, but came to promote dialogue between our lands. It is now prudent for you to request peace with Viru. It would be wise."

Governor Tuli sat speechless.

"Lady Eliinka is very powerful," Timo said. "We must give her an agreement or face dire consequences."

Gervald, the other councilor, stepped to the governor's side and whispered, "We, the councilors, want to work toward a treaty."

Eliinka narrowed her eyes, and the governor again diverted his gaze.

He nodded his head as he made a rare, pressured decision of consequence and said, "We are willing to enter into an agreement. But we must first speak with parliament."

When Eliinka spoke, she relaxed her glare, but not her voice. "I don't have the time or patience to wait for you to convene."

The crowd shifted. The guards leaned forward. The counselors and governor looked at each other.

"I'll state our resolute desire for trade and free travel between our lands. I'll inform Queen Jereni of your intentions and explain that she should expect a draft of a formal treaty in the near future. I must leave immediately to avert her anger.

"I demand an escort and protection to the borders of your land. I demand the replacement of my horses."

The governor's voice strained as he tried to regain his power. "You will need no protection here in Pelto. And Timo will direct you to where you may buy horses."

Eliinka gave no act or words of parting. She turned her back on the governor. Every silent eye watched her every step as she walked the length of the room toward the archway that led to the exit of the Hirdahouse.

Chapter Thirty-Two

~ MY PRICE FOR PEACE IS TOO HIGH ~

That may have been the best performance of my life."

Eliinka took a deep, painful breath. Tears she was holding back glazed her eyes, giving a hazy film to the room and everyone's faces. Every step she took fused with pain, pain she must hide. She grabbed Zerin's hand.

He helped Eliinka down the broad stairs of the Hirdahouse. The brisk air took her breath away. When they reached the bottom step, Timo caught up, breathing hard.

"Lady Eliinka, may I accompany you?" Timo bowed to Eliinka. "Please continue to grace my house with your presence."

"Thank you, Timo. A verbal agreement to work toward a treaty is more than I'd anticipated." Blood dripped onto the cobblestones. Though she had hoped for better, the events were not the worst possible. She was alive, and she could walk.

"It is not right," Zerin said. "That was not justice. Loukku should be punished. If he lived in Viru, he would face death."

"Justice is different in Pelto. Zerin, let's leave for Viru today. We'll buy horses, and maybe we can hire guards to protect us."

"Can you travel?" Timo asked.

Eliinka nodded her head as she continued forward, careful to avoid stepping on the most uneven stones.

"It might be wise, Eliinka," Zerin said, "to stay for a week so you can regain your strength."

"Nothing remains for me to do here. Except to visit my parents' graves as we leave." Eliinka slowed her walk. Each step was like ice burning across her back. If she could play her harp, it would hurt less, yet it would take days for them to return to the palace.

"A healer should care for you first," Timo said. "We could visit your parents' graves in two days and you could leave a week after that."

"That would give us time to buy good horses, maybe even get our horses back," Zerin said. "It will also take time to hire guards."

"I don't want to stay in RitVa." Eliinka stubbed her toe. Her back muscles tightened and she grimaced.

"Please, Eliinka." Zerin kept hold of her elbow, helping her walk. "Only for a few days. So we can prepare."

Perhaps Zerin was right. Every breath seethed with fire, and blood dripped down her skin. Eliinka paused, steadying herself. If Zerin weren't helping her walk, she would have already fallen, and now she felt faint. "Zerin, I don't feel well. I might . . ."

"Eliinka," Zerin yelled as he shoved her hard.

She screamed as she landed on the ground. Zerin fell at her side. A short, red-shafted arrow with yellow fletching impaled his ribs. He groaned. Blood flowed through his shirt around the arrow shaft.

"Pelto doesn't want peace," Eliinka wailed. She grabbed his hand. "Zerin. Zerin! Please, stay with me!"

"Can you stand?" Timo lifted Zerin to a sitting position.

His eyes were saturated with deeper hues of gray and his pupils had shrunk tiny. His mouth opened, but he didn't speak.

Timo waved to two sturdy men who had joined the growing crowd. They hesitated, yet when Eliinka flashed a gold coin, they helped Zerin to his feet.

Unbalanced, Eliinka stood up. "Timo, please," her voice broke, "Help me walk." Timo helped her, and the men followed, carrying Zerin.

They entered Timo's home, and the men laid Zerin on a quilted pad that Timo rolled onto the floor. The men hurried away after Eliinka handed them the gold coin.

Toivo froze in the doorway to the kitchen. She clutched her stomach.

"Toivo, run! Hurry! Bring a healer!" Timo said.

Toivo dashed across the room and flung the front door wildly open. She did not glance back.

"What can we do?" Eliinka collapsed at Zerin's side, touching where blood soaked his shirt. "The arrow, how can it be removed? Will he live?" She grasped Zerin's hand with her left hand and stroked his brow with her right.

"Zerin, a healer is coming," Eliinka whimpered in low tones. "Say something. Squeeze my hand. I'm here. I need you. Please."

Timo left the room and returned with clean cloths. "This will slow the bleeding." He took the top cloth and wrapped it around the arrow shaft. He held it firmly in place.

Eliinka tightened her grip on Zerin's hand and brought it to her chest. "Zerin, speak to me, please," she wailed in Pelten. She repeated the words in Virjalo. "Speak to me. Don't leave me!"

Zerin opened then shut his mouth. He turned his face toward Eliinka, and his eyes locked with hers. "Eliinka, the pain is leaving."

"No, no . . ."

"I see clearly now." Faint words crossed his struggling lips. "Tell Jereni my voice is for peace."

Zerin closed his eyes.

She leaned down, brushing his lips with hers.

"Please meet me when it is my turn to pass through to death," Eliinka whispered into his ear. "Please! I'll miss you so much." She sat at his side, holding his hand tight as he took his last breath. "My price for peace is too high."

Chapter Thirty-Three

~ ZERIN'S HAND ~

The healer arrived.

"No," Eliinka insisted. "He should go."

Timo sent him away.

Eliinka still held Zerin's hand.

Toivo slid through the room to the back of the house.

Eliinka still held Zerin's limp hand.

Shadows darkened.

The room grew dim.

Eliinka held his cold hand to her lips.

Chapter Thirty-Four

~ TAKE BACK YOUR VOW! ~

Eliinka still held tight to Zerin's hand. Her life was ending. It would have been better for her if it had ended at Loukku's.

Timo lit two candles. Shadows intensified around the edges of the room.

"Lady Eliinka, I'm sorry," Timo said. He lit another candle. "Zerin saved your life today. He was a good man."

They had been married for so short of a time, and their love had become real. Using the gift had only increased their love, made it deeper and now—

"Do you want to stay at my house?"

"No. I must return to Queen Jereni." Eliinka didn't want to stay in Pelto a moment longer than needed. She could not stay. She did not belong, and they would kill her too. Yet there was risk in leaving, in traveling. She hurt so much. Now, it didn't matter if she did not make it back to Viru. Nothing mattered.

"When are you planning to leave?"

"Soon. Today if possible, but Zerin . . ."

"I'll bury him in my family's plot." Timo lit another candle, mounted on a wall. The flickering light deepened the lines that creased his forehead.

"Thank you. Thank you very much." Eliinka did not move.

Her husband. Zerin. He would be buried in a foreign land.

She would never be able to return to visit his grave, never be able to finish the rites of her faith for him or her parents. Her whole body ached, every muscle, every vein, every single cell.

"Lady Eliinka, will you still give Queen Jereni your voice for peace?"

"I don't know if I'm able," Eliinka said in a choked voice. How dare anyone think about peace at this moment? Zerin! They needed more time, years together. It couldn't end, not like this.

"Who did it?" Eliinka asked. "Loukku?"

"He would not be that brazen, I don't believe. But Kapina is likely involved."

"Pelto needs to find them all, punish them all! If not, Queen Jereni will destroy Pelto. Her anger will not be turned."

Timo touched Eliinka's shoulder, gently. "Please consider two things. War is always the most unfair for the innocent, the women and children. Look what anger and fear have done today. Also, consider Queen Jereni and Mikali's union. Can their marriage withstand the stress of war between their native lands?"

"Zerin . . . " This moment could not be real, but he did not move. His skin was cold. Eliinka looked blankly toward Timo, not focusing, not seeing anything.

"You need to let go."

Eliinka removed Zerin's signet ring and placed it on her finger in the manner of a Pelten wife. She leaned over and was kissing him on his brow as Toivo peeked in through the door.

Timo waved her in and said, "Lady Eliinka, by my vow of Iankaikki, I ask you to take my daughter Toivo, as your sister, with you to Viru for twelve months and teach her the harp, your language, and the ways of your people."

Toivo stumbled backward into the wall. She opened her mouth, but released no sound.

"Please, Timo, take back your vow!" Eliinka tightened her shoulders. She winced as her broken skin screamed. Why would he vow this? "She'll be in danger with me."

"If she is with you, you'll arrive safely. Queen Jereni needs you alive. Dare you refuse the vow?"

"No." How could Timo ask this of her? "Will Toivo be willing?" Eliinka rose, not looking away from Zerin. She should not take Toivo, but even though it was dangerous, there was no reason to refuse this request.

"Peace begins with understanding. She'll be as your sister." A tear dripped onto Timo's cheek.

"Toivo, are you willing to come with me?" Eliinka asked.

"My father invoked his vow," stuttered Toivo, in a halting whisper of disbelief.

"I want you to choose," Eliinka said. She would not force Toivo to come with her.

Toivo swept her eyes over Zerin and back to Eliinka.

"I'll obey my father. I'll go with you."

"I was willing to risk traveling alone, but now I need protection." Eliinka took a deep breath. "We need an escort and a guide. I don't know the way." Eliinka jerked toward the wall to try to hide her pain and the brimming tears that she held back.

"Lady Eliinka, your back must be bandaged," Timo said, in a calming, fatherly voice. "Allow Toivo to care for you. I must go out now."

"No," Eliinka whispered.

Timo covered Zerin with a large cloth, draping it reverently over his entire body. Eliinka froze as she gazed at the rumpled cloth, the contours of Zerin's body. Timo nudged Toivo, nodding his head at Eliinka as he handed her Eliinka's bag and Zerin's money pouch.

"Come with me to the kitchen," Toivo said.

Eliinka shook her head. How could she leave him?

"Come," Toivo repeated. She grabbed Eliinka's wrist and drew her out of the room into the kitchen. "You must sit down." She sat Eliinka sideways on a bench, near the hearth. Eliinka hunched over, elbows on her thighs.

"I'm in so much pain," Eliinka rasped. The flames, too hot on her face, burned a burning heat. The moment replayed in her mind: Zerin falling, the red and yellow arrow in his side.

"My father says I must care for you." Toivo touched Eliinka's back and shuddered.

Eliinka tried to block out the pain to her piercing nerves as Toivo removed Eliinka's arms from the sleeves and pulled the bodice down to her waist. The cloth that Zerin had placed on her back stuck to her flesh. When Toivo peeled it away, it felt like she was ripping skin and reopening the wounds. Moisture dribbled down Eliinka's back. She reached around and touched it with her hand: fresh blood dripped from her fingers. She tried to focus her vision on the fire, yet the flames blurred.

Toivo poured hot water into a bowl and placed clean cloths next to it. "I wish the healer were here to take care of you. I don't like blood." She dipped one cloth into the water and lightly sponged the flayed skin. Eliinka quivered as Toivo touched the raw flesh again and again; her ribs tightened; her stomach tensed. She clenched her teeth. *I might vomit*, she thought. Toivo repeated the process again and again until she washed the dried blood away. After she dumped the red water outside, she refilled the bowl.

"Should I? . . . Some of your skin is still attached. I'll lift the large strips back into place. Is that what I should do?"

Eliinka stared at the fire, fighting a spasm of pain.

"It's still bleeding," Toivo said. "But it's slowed. Wait here. I'll get some healing balm." In moments, she returned, holding an oblong, stone box.

The flames died down as the wood burned away into nothingness.

"This will help you heal. It also reduces scarring." Toivo showed Eliinka the light brown balm, and dabbed it on her wounds. Gently, like she was afraid to touch the raw flesh.

The first smear of the balm was cold, and Eliinka jerked forward, inhaling her scream. Wouldn't this ever end? Toivo was trying to be gentle, she knew, so she held still until after Toivo had bound cloths into place. "I should have used this last night," she said as she gently smoothed it over the injured cheek.

"May I apply the balm to this other scar?" Toivo pointed to Eliinka's left upper chest. "It may help it fade."

Consciously directing her head to move, Eliinka twisted and looked at her scar. She nodded.

Toivo spread a thin line of balm on the skin and massaged it into the scar. Then she draped a length of cloth around Eliinka's shoulders and noticeably relaxed.

As the light fabric fell heavily over Eliinka's bare skin, she shivered.

"Come upstairs and change your dress." Toivo picked up Eliinka's bag.

Eliinka could not move. It was too hard. It hurt too much. The red spots on the coals blinked out, and the coals collapsed into dust.

"You can't stay in that dress. You must change." Toivo grabbed Eliinka's wrist and pulled her upright. Eliinka let Toivo pull her across the room and up the stairs. Each step pulled at her skin. Her feet automatically moved one after each other and somehow remembered how to walk. The guest room door opened, and the last day all returned in a flash: the trap at Loukku's, Rakel, the harp, this bed, the snapping whip, the arrow, Zerin.

Zerin.

No, no, no, he couldn't really be gone. But the pain of each breath—it was real, all too real.

"Which dress do you want to wear?" Toivo held up the two dresses that Eliinka had hung up the night before.

Eliinka pointed to a Pelten-styled traveling dress, the one she had worn to Kaikula. She had packed it last minute, but hadn't thought that she would wear it. She ran her finger under an eye. It was dry. She had expected tears, perhaps tears she could not feel.

"Eliinka, I need you to talk to me," Toivo said. "If we're going to leave today you need to move, you need to do something. Please. I can't guess what you want."

"Where can I find the strength to continue?" Eliinka spoke so low, she hardly heard her own words. It took so much energy to think. To speak. To move.

"I'll help. What do you need?"

"I normally dress myself, but I . . . I don't think I can today."

Toivo helped Eliinka slip off the stained dress, which they dropped to the floor. "You are pale. Lay down and rest."

"No. I can't rest. We must prepare to leave." Part of Eliinka wanted to collapse on the bed, stay here in this room where she and Zerin had last slept. But Eliinka knew if she did, she would bury her head in the pillow and smell his lingering scent and never get up again. She couldn't stay the night in this room.

Even though Eliinka moved her arms, shoulders, and back as little as possible while she put on her traveling dress, and Toivo helped, each minor movement released another avalanche of pain.

Eliinka didn't move to help as Toivo repacked her bag, putting the travel harp in last. Only the bloodstained dress remained, crumpled on the floor. When Toivo picked it up, she crinkled her eyes. She ran her hands down the fabric, stopping at the hidden pocket. She gasped and asked, "A knife?"

"A gift." The knife was for Eliinka's protection, and she had not used it. How different would life be if she had? Her hands wouldn't move to reach for it.

Toivo handed Eliinka the knife, picked up the dress, and grabbed Eliinka's wrist. She pulled Eliinka down the stairs and placed Eliinka's open bag on a chair.

"We can't stop living," Toivo said as she dropped the dress into a tub of water. She washed her hands, and as she dried them on a towel, she added, "That's what my mother would say when everything went wrong. It was one of the last things she told me. Now, come! Wash your hands too. Get the blood off them." She brought the bucket from in front of the fire and set it in front of Eliinka.

Hands, fingers, fingernails, cuticles, the lines in her skin: all blood-stained, caked with cracked, drying blood. Eliinka washed blindly in the steaming water, not looking down. When the water had cooled, she sat at the table and dropped her head onto her arms.

Toivo scurried around the kitchen and set bread, cheese, and soup in front of Eliinka.

But Eliinka did not eat. She stared blindly at her food and bowl. She was not sure she would ever focus her thoughts again.

"You must eat." Toivo shifted the food closer. "Please eat."

"I can't."

Toivo sat across from Eliinka and ate her own meal, quickly, gulping down the food. When she finished, she drummed her fingers on the edge of her plate. After a minute, she jumped up. "I'll gather our food. How many days is our journey?"

"Six, maybe seven."

"That far? I've never traveled. I've never had to pack before. What should we take?" Toivo opened a cupboard and gazed at Eliinka, waiting.

The back door swung open. Toivo dashed to the doorway and while hugging her father, said, "Eliinka won't eat."

"She'll eat when she's hungry."

Timo stepped inside and bowed until his head reached the height of his knees. When he rose up, he said, "Lady Eliinka, I've brought you an escort."

The guard who had helped them escape Loukku's house knelt on one knee. "At your service, m'lady. My name is Ritari. I'm told you need help to return you to our queen."

Eliinka sat up straight, slowly, and traced the blue diamond on her left hand. She must find the strength to do what was necessary, no matter how painful it was. "Thank you, Ritari, for saving our lives yesterday. Yes, I need to return to Viru. Can you act as my guide?"

"I'll make arrangements for a brief absence. It'd be better if I meet you outside the city. We'll travel to the southeast, on roads where they're not searching for you. This'll lead us to an uncharted route to Viru of which I've heard mention."

"I'm leaving this afternoon. Can you meet us in the countryside tomorrow morning?"

"I have a friend who owns the ValkoPuu Inn, on the Katu road," Timo said. "It's a three-hour ride southeast of the city. You should stay there tonight where you can enjoy a comfortable room, good food, and safety." He placed his arm around Toivo, who clung to his side. "Ritari can meet you tomorrow morning after you leave the inn, while you continue south on the Katu road."

Eliinka nodded her approval. Her voice stuck in her throat.

"My pleasure to serve you, m'lady. I'll find you on Katu road before the midday meal." Ritari bowed again and slipped out the back door.

Eliinka picked up a piece of cheese that Toivo had placed in front of her. She took a bite, and strode to the open cupboard and pulled out food that was easily transported. If she kept busy and focused, she would be able to keep moving. But if she began to cry, she would never, never, never stop.

"You need to pack." Timo hugged Toivo. "Don't take much. You should travel light."

"We'll use the back paths to the edge of the city where you can buy horses." Timo glanced at Eliinka's open bag. He moved the harp aside and looked inside. "Though they will not expect you to leave so soon, we still need to be careful."

"When did Pelto become such a dangerous place?" Eliinka asked.

"The people do not trust those who are different."

Eliinka shut the cupboard door. The wood clacked hard and the cupboard bounced back open, and she shut it firmly, almost slamming it. "Are you certain we can arrive in safety?"

"Yes. Trust my words."

Eliinka twisted Zerin's ring. She hoped Timo was right, that the men who wished to kill her would spare Toivo if they found them. It would only do harm to express her fears, so she would say what was appropriate. "Timo, I'll do my best to teach Toivo. She'll be as my sister. You are welcome to visit us in Jalolinna whenever you wish. Queen Jereni will wish to honor you for helping me." Eliinka scanned the mound of food. "This will be enough."

Toivo's feet clipped down the stairs and she burst into the room, her bag slung over her shoulder, her cloak over her arm.

"Is there a way to write to Toivo?" Timo asked.

"Queen Jereni will send messengers. They can carry any letters you wish to send."

"I'll also write to Queen Jereni," Timo said.

Toivo leaned against her father's shoulder.

"Do you need to. . . ?" Timo's voice trailed off, and his eyes moved from Eliinka to the other room.

Before he could say more, Eliinka rushed through the door. She collapsed at Zerin's side and stroked his cold cheek and wished with all her heart that he were alive. How could love hurt so much? Why did he leave when they had so much life in front of them?

Taking his hand for one last time, she intertwined her fingers with his. She didn't want to forget how his fingers fit between hers, how their hands were made for each other. She didn't want to ever forget his gray-green eyes, his hesitation to smile, and how she felt when he wrapped his arms around her and pulled her close. Could she memorize every detail of his face, and somehow, never forget every moment they had together?

Was it possible to leave, knowing she would never have a chance to visit his grave?

If only she could stay with him. She laid her head on his still chest and whispered, "I'll always love you, Zerin."

Chapter Thirty-Five

~ NOT THE COMMON WAY ~

Is there a way through?" Eliinka asked. She twisted Zerin's ring as she sat on the back of her horse and stared at the dense undergrowth, jumbled with interlocking branches and weaving vines, engulfed by towering evergreens. She pushed aside the nearest branches, releasing a deep mossy smell. At least most of the snow had melted. But they could not pass through this forest, not without a trail.

"M'lady, this is the only way for you to cross into Viru." Ritari wiped the sweat from his forehead. "Loukku has twenty men searching for you. They don't know you've left RitVa, at least they didn't yesterday evening. They're waiting at all western intersections and at the river crossing. This route to the south hasn't been used for more than a century." He rode a short distance to the right, came back, and rode to the left, looking into the trees for a sign of a long-lost trail.

Eliinka dismounted and handed Toivo a slice of fresh bread, given to her by the innkeeper before dawn when he had met them in the stable, their horses saddled and ready. She took a bite and drank from her water flask. They had already ridden for over six hours today, Ritari catching up to them only an hour earlier. They should be safe after they entered the forest.

He rode up the path, away from them, in the direction they had come. After a couple hundred paces, he turned and studied the forest. He returned. "Do you see the largest trees, m'lady? They were planted next to the path."

"But how?" Toivo asked as she gingerly stretched her legs. "It's impassable." She grasped the reins with clenched fists and nodded she was ready to go, although she shifted forward and back, adjusting her seat.

"Perhaps after we pass through the outer edge, the undergrowth will be less." Eliinka remounted her horse. A surge of pain spliced through her entire upper body. She was sure her back was bleeding.

They pushed in, following an imperceptible deer trail, picking a path, finding a way through the vegetation, under, over, and around shrubs as branches tugged at their bodies, thorns caught on their clothing, and leaves tangled their hair. The trees were massive, wider than three horses, and towered upward, demanding their place in the heavens. They pushed through the underbrush, which lessened in the dense shade, and found what seemed to be a path, a path blocked by immense fallen logs, too tall to climb over, and fast-moving streams to ford.

The constant pain in Eliinka's back increased with each sharp, jarring hoofbeat. She held tight to the reins. She concentrated: *I will not faint. Will. Not. Fall. I should block the pain out, somehow*—and she did, by sheer willpower.

After a long afternoon, they emerged at the top of a high canyon. Ritari helped Eliinka down from her horse, and now that she stood still, the pain burst to the forefront of her mind. She let down her hair, which she had tied up a few minutes after entering the forest, and ran her hands through it, glad to wear it loose again, instead of having it tightly restrained. She folded her arms, set her jaw, and whispered to herself, "Ignore my wounds. Pain is temporary. It will be gone someday." But she did not believe her own words.

"M'lady, I apologize. I brought no tent."

"We'll be fine, Ritari. This canyon?" Eliinka asked. "Is it supposed to be here?" It was a breathtaking view, the most amazing sight she had ever seen. Standing here was like perching in the tallest tree. This massive canyon appeared even more impassable than the forest. Viru was like an unreachable note, a string that was a note pitched higher than the highest string on a harp.

"Its size is why this route was abandoned. I didn't realize how large the Kahlaamo Canyon would be, m'lady. There's still time before the sun sets. I'll search for the ancient trail after I care for the horses."

Toivo dismounted and tumbled to the ground. She pulled herself to her feet and swayed.

Eliinka supported her as they walked around a snowdrift toward a patch of flatter, clear ground, sheltered by a large pine tree. "This is a hard journey, Toivo, especially at the pace we took today. You rode well. Look across the canyon. That is Viru. Travel will be easier on the other side." She wished they could enter Viru now and not have to spend the night in Pelto. They must have left tracks in the forest. Could they be followed?

Toivo collapsed under the drooping branches, dropping her head into her hands. A thin sliver of words ascended through the air like a tremulous high note. "My father, why did he give his vow?" Toivo talked faster and faster. "Something changed my father. Something that has to do with you, or something you said or did. He's sending me to Viru for an entire year." She pulled her arms close to her chest and blurted, "I'm so sorry. Don't be angry with me. But I just met you this week, and you're a stranger, and Viru is so far away and . . ." Toivo's voice trailed off. She twirled a strand of hair.

"I don't understand why your father sent you with me either." Eliinka considered several possibilities. It was too strong of a way to show he accepted the alliance with Jereni.

"Where will we sleep?"

"We'll sleep under this tree tonight," Eliinka said.

"But, your back?" Toivo questioned. "How will you sleep?"

"In Viru we don't let others see or even know of our wounds." Eliinka nodded toward Ritari, who was tying the horses to a low tree branch next to a bunch of tall grass. "People in Viru believe this knowledge gives others an advantage in battle and disagreements. Even though it will be known throughout Pelto, will you promise to not tell others of my wounds?"

"I'll not speak of it. I promise. Let me apply balm to your wounds while Ritari searches for the path."

Eliinka nodded.

"I'm sorry about Zerin." Toivo opened the box and began to gently dab Eliinka's flesh.

"I miss him." Eliinka murmured. She shuddered at the cool cream and Toivo's light touch. "We are just parted, and yet I long for him. I miss the sound of his voice, the rumble of his laughter. I miss the glance of his eyes, the touch of his hand against mine. I miss his kiss." Eliinka closed her eyes, seeing him in her mind the way he had appeared all the times he sat in the White Room across the table from her.

"You'll see Zerin again."

"Yes, I believe what our faith teaches, yet he's gone. Gone." Eliinka pulled her dress up and over her back and shoulders. "You'll miss your father. A year is not short."

They ate a light evening meal of bread, boiled eggs, and dried meat while they looked over the canyon. When they finished, Eliinka took a cheese bundle from her bag and pulled out her knife. She unfolded the cloth and held the nightmilk cheese in her hand. She measured it with her fingers to make sure she would have enough for each day of their travels, then cut two thick slices.

"Here, have a slice." Eliinka's hand trembled with fatigue as she held out one piece. Eliinka nibbled her cheese.

"It wasn't long ago when I first entered Viru. When I first arrived it was overwhelming, a blur. Everything was so different." She paused and lifted her water flask. "Now Viru is in my blood. The land, city, and people are so beautiful, so colorful, so happy and content. I hope you enjoy your time with us."

Ritari returned as the brilliant hues of sunset scuffed the canyon walls. "I didn't find the trail. I'll continue my search in the morning, M'lady." He sat nearby, on a small incline where he kept watch.

Eliinka hoped her exhaustion would make it possible to sleep on the uncomfortable piece of ground. But she did not fall asleep. It was painful to move; it was painful to lie still. The events of yesterday repeated again and again whenever she closed her eyes.

She could not escape what she wished was a bad dream.

Her voice could tip the scales if she made it back alive. But could she honestly give Jereni her voice for peace? After all was silent and she believed Toivo to be asleep, Eliinka quietly hummed the lullaby over and over and over until she fell into an intermittent, restless slumber.

Eliinka woke before daybreak. Her back screamed as she walked to the canyon edge. The angle of the pre-morning light accented the vertical clefts and ridges. How would they cross? It was deeper than the height of a hundred men and so wide she doubted anybody could throw a stone to the other side.

Ritari appeared and bowed. "M'lady, I searched to the east yesterday. I'll search to the west now. The trail must be nearby."

He walked away, pushing through the dense brush.

The canyon wound as far as Eliinka could see in both directions. The forest closed in on top of the vertical walls. After finding an open spot overlooking the canyon, she settled on the ground. "Elavaksi," she murmured.

"Give me peace and understanding." She breathed slowly, deeply, and relaxed into her morning meditations. When the sun reached halfway up the bright blue sky, Eliinka shook Toivo awake.

Toivo groaned as she sat, but she gasped when she saw the sun. "How did I sleep so long?" She stretched and rubbed her hands up and down her thighs. "The canyon! What a steep drop! Eliinka, how will we cross?"

"I don't know."

"Will we need to turn back? Toivo asked. A breeze blew, and she pulled her cloak tight around herself. "This is the most beautiful view I've ever seen."

Ritari came running toward them. "I found the trail, but we'll need to be careful and lead the horses. It's steep."

After he saddled their horses, he led the way, disappearing into a thicket of brush. Toivo followed, and Eliinka came last. She wondered how Ritari had found the trail. It was hidden very well by decades of disuse. They led their horses back and forth, down switchbacks carved in the rock wall, making their way slowly. Occasionally, loose rocks clattered over the edge, dropping from view. Eliinka only relaxed her grip on the reins when she reached the bottom, where her horse joined the others who drank from the river.

Eliinka scanned the terrain, looking back up the cliff they had just descended, amazed that there was a trail on that cliff wall and that they had made it down safely. The way up the other side of the canyon, luckily, appeared less steep. The river here was wider and not as deep as the other crossing. Under the clear water was solid riverbed rock.

When her horse lifted his head, she flicked the reins and he walked into the river. Even halfway across, the water remained shallow. She urged him forward, into the deeper water on the Virun side.

"How do I cross?" Toivo called out. She had stopped her horse at the edge.

"Trust your horse and guide him to follow mine."

Water only splashed at her boots as Eliinka's horse trotted the rest of the way across the river. Within a moment Eliinka and her horse were on the rocky beach. She was in Viru! But the tension didn't lift. It was still a long journey to Jalolinna, and they didn't know the way through the rugged Syrjassa Mountains.

Toivo had wrapped her arms around her horse's neck and closed her eyes. Her horse started to trot downstream, and the higher water slapped at her feet.

"Toivo," Ritari called. He turned his horse and followed her.

Eliinka's horse galloped down the bank and back into the river on the downstream side of Toivo. Eliinka lunged, grabbing Toivo's reins, and guided both horses back to land.

"I'm sorry." Toivo slumped against her horse's mane.

"There is hardly a current here. You didn't tell your horse which way to go!" Eliinka wheeled around and started up the trail, moving away before she yelled at Toivo, who hadn't even tried to make it to shore. She hadn't even kept her eyes open. Eliinka's back felt like it had ripped in two, and she wished for a place to rest, but that would have to wait.

At least the riding was easier now: the cliff on this side of the river was half the height of the one they had descended and not as steep, with a wide enough natural trail where they could ride their horses.

"Ritari, where are we?" asked Eliinka when they reached the top.

"This is the Urho River, the same river you've crossed before, but we are farther south. The old books say it's a two-day ride to Turvallisuus, the nearest town in Viru."

"Does that return you to Pelto in time? Will they miss you?"

Ritari patted his horse's neck and looked away.

"You must return soon."

"I can't leave you alone in the wilderness."

Eliinka circled her horse as she took in their surroundings, and she rode up a small knoll to a large fallen tree. She halted and bit her lips. "I'll allow you to take us a little farther today. But I need to do something first."

She dismounted and handed Ritari her reins. She dug through her saddlebag and, after pulling out her small flute, considered the possibilities. If she played, called the Flute People, would they come and help her? Could she use her gift while playing the flute?

She must be certain of a safe return to Jereni.

After climbing up the log, she brought the flute to her lips and warmed it up with her breath, making no noise, gathering her thoughts. She played one note, then a simple tune: a sorrowful, mournful melody of just seven notes. How could she play the airy, high notes, the ones that resonated above the normal tones? Eliinka blew slightly faster, adding more pressure, slightly spinning the flute toward and away from her until she got the overtone to sound smooth and clear. She repeated the melody, using the overtones, making a haunting, piercing melody.

Eliinka clambered off the log she was standing on. "Let's ride to where we'll camp tonight."

"Why did you play the flute?" Toivo asked. Her teeth chattered.

"The music will bring us help," Eliinka said. "Keep riding. That will warm you up."

They rode south for several hours, Ritari determining their direction from the sun because there were no remnants of a trail. The clomping trot · of Eliinka's horse reopened more wounds on her back, but she said nothing. She knew if she did, they would stop, which would slow their journey.

Late in the afternoon they came upon a large rock that protruded from the ground, thrust upward like a giant fist. It was the height of ten men, flanked by several trees. The back was uneven: vegetation grew along a series of natural giant steps. Below squatted several large boulders that had chinked off.

"This is where we'll camp, here, in front of this rock," Eliinka said as she examined the front, the cliff-like rock face.

Eliinka climbed the rock from the rear side, finding a path to the top, a flat surface. She sat at the same height as the tallest trees and played the flute in the same manner as before, the tones calling above the trees, ascending to the sky where they were carried away by the wind. When finished, she climbed down the rock steps.

"Ritari, where are we?" Eliinka asked.

He drew a crude map on the ground. It showed the Urho River, the forested region they would travel through, the town of Turvallisuus, and the capital, Jalolinna. He marked where he thought they were and pointed the direction they would need to take the following day.

Eliinka looked toward the setting sun and with a long stick drew an arrow on the map and outward in the dirt in the direction they would travel. She walked past the dirt line into the forest.

"Use caution, m'lady." Ritari followed her into the woods, his eyes alert. Toivo caught up with them, and she jumped at a crash of a falling branch.

"Ritari, you will return tomorrow." Eliinka spun to face him. "You can't miss your duties in Pelto."

"I won't leave you alone in this forest, m'lady. I must stay with you until we find Turvallisuus."

"But we are not alone."

Eliinka retraced her steps to the mossy ground in front of the rock. She sat and lifted the flute and played the same haunting tones, hoping. After she finished the melody, she tipped her head to the side. In the distance, quiet sounds passed through the air, indistinct from the wind to untrained ears. She jumped up. "Listen. Do you hear? We're safe now. We can have a fire tonight."

Ritari clapped his hands together. It looked like he might argue with her, but he didn't. He kindled a small fire in the shelter of the rock.

They sat near the edge of the flames, enjoying the warmth, the flickering light and the quiet crackling sounds of fire eating away at wood. A light column of smoke rose and the scent of campfire filled the clearing. In a short time, the sun dropped below the tops of the trees.

After their evening meal, Eliinka took out the nightmilk cheese and again shared it with Toivo. She chose a comfortable spot to sleep and settled down near the fire on a natural bed of thick, moss-filled grass. Toivo fell asleep within moments. The rising full moon brightened the clearing. Wishing she could so easily slide into a peaceful slumber, Eliinka peered into the woods, hoping the sounds of her flute had carried her message and that she wasn't just hearing imagined melodies on the wind.

Hollow, haunting sounds vibrated the moment between night and day.

Toivo sat up with a start, but Ritari did not budge from his deep slumber.

Eliinka's flute echoed. She sat in the same spot she had the previous evening, overshadowed by the large rock face, next to where she had slept. After finishing the melody, she set the flute down.

Toivo shook her head and lay back down.

The air was chill and still, and Eliinka's breath blew out like wisps of smoke. She played the melody again, waited, and played it one more time. Then standing, she looked out into the forest and motioned with her hands.

A wiry, barefoot man in threadbare clothes slipped into the clearing and knelt before Eliinka.

Toivo sat up.

Ritari jumped to his feet.

Eliinka signaled for him to sit, then spoke to the man.

"I am Eliinka. Thank you for the flute. I need a guide to Turvallisuus, or the nearest town in Viru, so I can return to Queen Jereni."

The man pulled out a flute, a larger flute than hers, from his clothing. He played one long note that wavered up and down. A response rose from the surrounding forest, encircling them with a chorus of singular drawn out notes.

Ritari rushed to Eliinka's side, his hand on his sword's handle.

"No. They will help us," Eliinka said.

The man played another melody, short and rhythmic, and the melody turned into a call and response that echoed back and forth from his flute with the forest.

When he finished playing, he spoke. "You take not the common way." He had an odd, slurred accent to his Virjalo. "We have not horses, so follow our flutes. You will see not us."

"Thank you. What name can I give to Queen Jereni?"

"She knows me as the man of the blue tree." He bowed again, then ran into the forest.

Eliinka smiled and turned to the others. "See, we have our guide! Ritari, saddle our horses."

"But that man is on foot." Ritari shook his head. He rubbed his short beard.

"Saddle our horses. You can return to RitVa. We'll leave as soon as possible."

While Eliinka and Toivo ate a hurried morning meal, Ritari prepared the horses.

Eliinka grabbed the reins and said, "Ritari, thank you for guiding us this far. You must return to RitVa now, before they miss you. Your duty is to Queen Jereni."

"I can't leave two women alone and unguided."

Eliinka mounted. From the top of her horse, she motioned for Toivo to mount.

Toivo looked from Ritari to Eliinka and hesitated.

A flute sounded from the south. "Listen. The flutes lead us. You don't know the route, but the people of these woods do. They are now sworn to Queen Jereni and will lead us safely through the forest. You'll soon receive word of our safe arrival."

"I should accompany you."

Shifting in her saddle so she leaned over Ritari, Eliinka spoke in a commanding voice. "Ritari, this is a direct order. Return at once to your duties in RitVa. Queen Jereni needs the information you gather. Find out more about Kapina." She gave him a hand signal, telling him to listen and obey.

"I'll follow your orders, m'lady." He bowed low.

Eliinka wheeled her horse in the direction of the rising flute sound. Toivo followed close behind.

As they left the clearing, Eliinka glanced back, glad to see he did not follow them, but that he returned on their tracks from the previous day.

The flutes called them forward, and they continued south all day, never seeing the flute players, yet always following and moving in the direction of the sounds. The terrain was easy, so Eliinka's back didn't hurt as bad as from the riding the previous day. At dusk they found a blazing fire in a clearing, fresh bread of an unusual grain, and cut, fern-like branches spread for a soft bed.

First, Eliinka helped Toivo care for her horse and tied both horses near two wooden buckets of fresh grain. Then they ate near the fire, and after Toivo applied balm to Eliinka's back, they continued their nightly ritual of silence and mixed conversation, with Toivo doing most of the talking.

Toivo fell asleep, but Eliinka watched the dwindling fire. She wondered if she could extinguish the flickering flames and quench her pain if she released her emotions and let herself cry. She sat for a long time in the darkness, reluctantly awake, unable to sleep. She wished for the desired sleep to come, for the distant slumber that would temporarily deaden her grief.

The following morning a flute woke them.

Eliinka was surprised she had slept past sunrise.

Their travels followed the same pattern as the previous day, riding in the direction of the flute's call, listening for the next tone, and continuing on. The trees thinned, and eventually the angled afternoon sun glowed on open, cultivated fields.

Which way? Eliinka wondered, but a flute called to her right and they turned their horses toward what must be Turvallisuus. She played a short melody on her flute and waved to their unseen guides.

Within minutes they were on a narrow road, not much more than a path, and Eliinka said, "Toivo, I want to be in my own room, in my own bed tonight, but Jalolinna, the capital, is still a day's ride away. We'll have to spend the night in Turvallisuus."

She traced the diamonds on her shaking hands. She had no treaty, little hope of peace, and most, if not all, of her guards were dead. Her quiet hope of a peace that would make it possible for her to spend time, perhaps live in both lands, had crumbled. She would never return to Pelto again. As she breathed in deeply, the muscles on her back and the skin pulled, and it felt like tiny knives sliced her flesh.

And Zerin . . . She kicked her heels into her horse, urging him forward to a place she both wanted, but feared. She spoke out loud to herself, "How can I tell Jereni of my failure? What will I say?"

Chapter Thirty-Six

~ WHERE IS HE? ~

"Eliinka!" Jereni exclaimed. Though almost a whisper, she sounded surprised. "Welcome home."

Eliinka forgot all she had planned to say, so she advanced without a word through the Great Hall, followed by Toivo who walked in her faint shadow. Those who waited to speak with their queen backed away. Though they had ridden at a quick pace, it had taken until late afternoon to get to Jalolinna. The hard riding had broken open any healing that had begun. She tightened her shoulders, tensing from every jolt of each step, and kept her chin up high.

"How did you return so soon?" Jereni jumped from her throne.

Eliinka stopped short, sure all the blood drained from her face. She interlocked her hands and bowed her head. The room was too quiet; there was not even a whisper or a scuffle of feet.

"Lady Eliinka, you have brought—" Jereni paused and waited.

"Queen Jereni, this is Toivo, daughter of Councilor Timo," Eliinka's faint voice filled the expanding silence. Toivo gave an awkward bow.

"You returned alone, just the two of you? Where is Zerin? Toivo crossed into Viru with you?"

"We came here as quickly as possible, only Toivo and me," Eliinka said. Only. Pained words shot out like misspent arrows.

"But how?"

"We took the unknown way through Kahlaamo Canyon. After we entered Viru, we found the way to Turvallisuus, where we stayed last night." Eliinka struggled to breathe. Her hands went to her chest, her legs gave out, and she collapsed to the floor. The crowd gasped.

Both Toivo and Jereni rushed to Eliinka's side.

Toivo reached Eliinka first. She dropped to her knees and grasped Eliinka's hand. "Eliinka. Eliinka, you're safe. You're home. Everything will be all right now."

"What happened? Are you feeling ill?" Jereni lifted Eliinka up and greeted her with a hug and a kiss.

Eliinka flinched at the touch of hands on her back.

"Toivo, welcome to Jalolinna." Jereni now spoke in her perfect Pelten, in a softened voice.

Toivo gave a small bow of her head.

A curious smile grew and lit up Jereni's face. "The songs of birds will be more melodic and the perfume of the flowers more heavenly in the gentle breeze of your voice." She motioned with her hand for a servant to take care of Toivo.

"Come with me." Jereni supported Eliinka, keeping her on her feet, and started to walk her from the hall.

"Wait!" Eliinka said. "Toivo stays with me. She's scared. She doesn't understand Virjalo, and you may need to question her."

Jereni raised an eyebrow. She took Eliinka again by her arm and nodded for Toivo to follow.

As they exited, Shimlon spoke to the people. "Queen Jereni will be happy to speak with you later . . ."

The palace seemed as a steamed mirror, and Eliinka blinked, trying to bring everything into focus.

They paused at the study; Jereni glanced at Toivo and continued to Eliinka's room.

"I brought messages," Eliinka said, after they entered. She did not sit, but gripped the back of her favorite chair for support. "Also, Timo asked me to teach Toivo the harp and our language. She'll live here for twelve months. He wants me to treat her as my sister."

Jereni put her arm around Eliinka's shoulders. She jerked at the touch.

"You can explain after you deliver my messages," Jereni said in Virjalo. She ignored Toivo. "Sit down so you can rest."

They sat in front of a dead fire, Eliinka sitting at the front edge of her chair to keep her back from touching anything. Toivo remained standing in the center of the room.

Eliinka's hands tightened into clenched fists, her fingernails biting her palms. She knew what she needed to say first, but how . . . how could she say his name? *Courage, find the courage*, she thought.

"Zerin said, 'Tell Queen Jereni that I see clearly now. My voice is for peace.'"

"Where is he?"

"He asked me to first inform you of another item, something about my personal life." Eliinka flexed her hands, spreading her fingers first wide open, then shut. "I am of the ancient faith of Eleman Puusta. I believe you already had discerned this."

Jereni nodded.

"The other message is from Governor Tuli. They are willing to enter into an agreement, but parliament must meet first."

"You did not stay to represent Viru. Why?"

"Parliament does not meet for several weeks. Timo will press for our point of view, I hope."

"Did he send me a message?"

"I left rather suddenly." Eliinka blinked hard and stared at the dead, gray ashes.

"Now tell me of your journey. Where is Zerin? Why didn't he return with you?" When Eliinka didn't respond, Jereni patted Eliinka's hand. "Eliinka?"

Eliinka gazed into the fireless hearth and frowned as she considered where to begin. She slumped in her chair, grimacing as it bumped against her torn back, which felt like it had begun to bleed again. "The messenger led us into a trap at the house of Loukku. When Loukku was about to kill us, one of your men, Ritari, signaled the way for our escape. I struck and injured Loukku. Zerin . . . " her voice caught in her throat. "He and I requested refuge at Timo's house, but our guards, the three who stayed with the horses, were murdered. I believe Huoli escaped and is trying to return to report, which is why I hurried back."

Anger grew in Jereni's eyes, but her voice remained calm. "You said you spoke with the governor."

"It wasn't safe to stay, and it wasn't safe to leave because men opposed to peace with Viru were searching for us. I chose to try to speak with him instead of immediately fleeing back here. That was a mistake." Eliinka swallowed, tightening her throat. "Jereni, it's a crime for a woman to strike a man as I did."

"They should fear me more," Jereni said. "Did they harm you? Did Loukku receive punishment?"

"He's a member of parliament. He's immune from the law." Eliinka's voice rose then fell to a whisper. "Timo's demands kept me from being bound for the whipping, or imprisoned. The governor gave me the lightest sentence, but still, I was whipped in the Hirdahouse, in public view."

"Let me see."

Eliinka sat on the floor in front of Jereni's chair, her back toward her. Toivo moved closer. Jereni pulled the fabric down off her shoulders, and when she lifted away the bandages, Eliinka's muscles contracted. It was as if her nerves ripped apart and scattered in pieces throughout her flesh.

"Fools! They had no right to touch you." The crescendo in Jereni's voice matched Eliinka's anguish. "How dare they treat you in this manner? I swear upon my very kingdom that the man responsible will suffer and pay with his life!" Jereni smashed her fist so hard on a side table that the wood cracked.

"Did no one come to your defense?"

"I didn't allow Zerin to interfere so he could remain free."

"Where is Zerin?"

"He . . . we . . . Jereni, I understood the probable consequence of approaching the governor after my encounter with Loukku. I hoped he would withhold punishment. After the punishment, he agreed to consider an agreement. I requested protection for our return to the border and compensation for our stolen horses." Eliinka's voice dropped to a grave whisper. "The governor believed there was no need."

Eliinka groaned as she pulled her dress up over her shoulders.

"You must rest. It appears Toivo's been caring for your wounds."

"She spreads a healing balm on my back, and also on my scar. Toivo made it possible for me to return alive."

"Alive and badly injured! There will be an emergency meeting today and plans must be made." Jereni paced back and forth in front of the fireplace. "Tonight Mikali will learn of the ignorant, barbaric actions of his people. They should not have touched you. Ilari will gather men. Pelto must be punished."

Eliinka's mind spun. Gather men already?

Jereni was already thinking of war.

And she did not yet know about Zerin. Eliinka had not rushed back to instigate war.

The more she thought, the more sick she felt. What she needed was a night in her own bed and some rest. Time and a chance to play the harp would help Eliinka sift through her feelings and figure out what to say to Jereni. Decide if she could ask for peace, the peace Zerin wanted.

"I'm afraid." Eliinka didn't realize at first that she said the words aloud. What if she asked for revenge, asked for war? She struggled to steady her emotions.

"You're safe now. They'll never touch you again, and all of Pelto will pay for their governor's arrogance."

All of Pelto. A war!

Zerin.

All of sudden, Eliinka's emotions crested, spilled out and broke through the dam she had built. Moisture trickled out of the corners of her eyes. She dropped her face into her hands and sank to the floor.

"Eliinka." Toivo rushed across the room. "What's wrong?" She knelt at Eliinka's side. "She's in much pain, Queen Jereni. I'm very sorry. Her loyalty and devotion to you is what gave her strength to travel. My father asked her to bring me to Viru." Tears glistened on Toivo's cheeks.

"You will be rewarded for your efforts," Jereni said, in a cold voice, in Pelten.

Eliinka lifted her head, switching the conversation back to Virjalo so Toivo wouldn't understand. "My sacrifice is given. I'd thought to only be wounded physically, but I gave much more than I thought possible. My heart has been ripped apart. My sacrifice can't be . . . it can't be ignored." She twisted Zerin's ring. "I make my choice. I don't wish my pain to be shared by all. I'll respect your decision, but I add my voice to my husband's for peace."

"Where is Zerin?" Jereni's surmising whisper did not disguise her growing impatience of repeating the question.

Eliinka shook her head. She could not say Zerin's name again or explain what had happened. It hurt too much.

Jereni sprang toward Toivo. "Where is he?" she yelled.

Toivo stepped two steps backward.

"Where is he?" Jereni grasped Toivo by both wrists.

She tried to pull away.

Jereni gasped and switched to Pelten. "Where is Zerin?"

Toivo paled and hurriedly spit out the words. "Zerin noticed an assassin in the streets when they left the Hirdahouse. He saved Eliinka's life, but the arrow hit him. My father buried him."

Jereni released Toivo's wrists. She shouted words in Virjalo, words Eliinka did not know, threw open the door, and stomped away.

Eliinka jumped to her feet, gasping in pain as she rushed to the still-open door.

"Jereni. Please, listen to me." Eliinka held the door open, trying to catch her breath.

Jereni angrily rushed down the hall.

"We will not wait. My armies will attack Pelto!" Anger filled Jereni's discordant, off-pitch voice that echoed throughout the corridor.

Eliinka sagged against the doorframe. Her wounds would split her body into two.

Chapter Thirty-Seven

~ THERE IS ALWAYS A CHOICE ~

Eliinka slipped into the study, thinking to find it empty in the mid-morning, but Jereni was already there, sitting in her chair, watching the door. Behind her, the fire flamed in the hearth. Eliinka gave a small nod of her head and walked over to her token harp, the harp she had not played since before she had left for Pelto.

Jereni shoved a book aside. It fell on the floor. She left it on the carpet and stared at her parents' portraits.

Eliinka pretended not to notice. She brushed her fingers across the strings. The music fell flat. No energy, no life. The strings would not respond to numbness. She struck the strings hard, started another song, trying to find her music.

Her fingers failed before she finished the first phrase. She leaned her forehead against the top of her harp and plucked random strings, listening, hoping that somehow, some way, a melody would emerge—that music would deaden her pain.

She tried playing another tune. Every combination of strings created a harsh dissonance.

She would never be able to play a real song again.

Jereni's hand fell on her shoulder. Eliinka gave a start.

"Your thoughts, your emotions are scattered. Come sit with me." Jereni didn't sit, but picked up her nightmilk, circled the table, and almost dropped the mug when she slammed it back on the table, spilling several drops.

"I'm sorry my music is lacking." Eliinka had never been unable to play before. If she had more time and peace and quiet, she could find the notes. If only she could find the heart and energy to play.

But how could she play her hollowness? Her fears?

Eliinka twisted Zerin's ring back and forth on her finger. Could she convince Jereni that beginning a war was not for the good of Viru? She sat, avoiding the chair she had shared with Zerin, and she picked up the fallen book and held it on her lap.

"Why did you accept Toivo as your companion, as your sister? Why did you bring her to Viru?"

"I had no choice," Eliinka said. Toivo should not have come, even if it would have meant Eliinka traveling alone, running into Kapina, perhaps dying. That would have been better than this pain. Now with Toivo here . . . how was she supposed to care for her? Even last night Eliinka had not known what to do with her and had fallen asleep before asking Milla to put her in a guest room. Toivo had slept on a cushioned sofa.

"There is always a choice," Jereni said. "It was a poor decision to bring her here."

"But I can't choose the consequences of my choices."

Jereni lifted an eyebrow. She took off her wedding ring and examined it.

"Timo insisted by a vow and convinced me to take her, and there was no reason for me to refuse." Eliinka sighed and Jereni nodded for her to continue. "I gave Toivo the choice. She didn't dare refuse her father. She expressed her qualms about coming with me during our journey, but seems determined to make the best of her situation."

"Did he send her here to protect her, believing my armies would raze Pelto? He knew men were searching for you, which placed Toivo in danger." Jereni tapped a finger on the table, and Eliinka braced herself for hearing more about war and Jereni's plans. "He knows the journey through the wilderness is challenging in the best circumstances. The route you took, a route not traveled in over a hundred years—without a guide—was not a wise choice."

"Timo thought we had a guide," Eliinka said. She must find a way to bring up reasons to not attack Pelto. Something else was bothering Jereni, but what was it? "He brought Ritari to lead us. But I ordered Ritari back after the crossing. I wouldn't let him risk his mission."

"Thankfully you returned safely, and Councilor Timo accepted my offer."

"He did not fully accept. He asked for time to consider the implications of an alliance. I believe we can assume he accepted, because he sent Toivo." Eliinka shifted forward in her chair. "Jereni, the real danger is a group inside Pelto. Loukku, the man whose house we escaped, is of Kapina, a group trying to create discord in their government. I'm sure they murdered Zerin. They are the problem. Please, understand Pelto. My treatment, though wrong, is understandable when one understands the culture. Their treatment of women is different." Her voice dropped to a whisper. "Please, don't send your armies. You know what Zerin wanted. You know what I desire."

"Your nightmilk is cooling. Drink!" Jereni handed Eliinka the other steaming mug of milk and took a gulp of her own. Eliinka sipped the hot milk, but it did not comfort her.

"In two days there will be a memorial service for Zerin and the fallen guards. You will play one song in Zerin's memory."

No! Eliinka wanted to say. She couldn't play, couldn't face the memories, the pain.

Not that the pain ever left. Every night she relived the moment in the street; every time she shut her eyes, she saw Zerin dying. Eliinka forced herself to slowly sip the nightmilk, exhibiting a calm her vibrating muscles, cold skin, and racing heart didn't have. She measured slow, shallow breathes, forcing herself to relax.

Jereni picked up a split log and threw it at the fire. Sparks leaped in all directions. The half-burnt wood of the already burning log collapsed on itself. "Eliinka, you are upset with me."

Eliinka set down her half-full mug, while Jereni glared at the fire.

"Mikali is angry." Jereni threw another log. More sparks leaped, and the bark caught fire. "War appeals to me now. It never did before. Zerin's final words, your plea, and Mikali, his demands . . . Eliinka, you speak so strongly for peace. My heart is as torn and shredded as your back. My armies should march tomorrow, yet peace, formal peace with Pelto has been my deepest desire since I was a little child."

Jereni sunk into her chair, another log in her hands. Tears trickled down her cheeks.

It was the first time Eliinka had ever seen Jereni cry. She wasn't sure what to say. But there was a glimmer of hope that Jereni would not attack Pelto.

"Strong words, loud words, words of anger, words of frustration were spoken last night between Mikali and me. He doesn't want war. Our words tear at our friendship; our angry voices pull apart our love. This morning we both apologized for our fiery words, but the ache remains." Jereni stared at the fire.

Eliinka knew Jereni's apology was probably the hardest thing she had ever done.

"We reached an agreement. The agreement we made will be most diffi-cult for me to keep. My heart wishes to keep it, yet if there was any possible way, my agreement with Mikali would be shattered today." Jereni tossed the log over the table and into the fire. Few sparks came from the now flat-tened, dying blaze. The logs she had thrown lay cold, flameless.

"What is your agreement?"

"We agreed that my best efforts will be used to reach an understand-ing with Pelto. After six months have elapsed, if my best efforts have been exerted for an agreement (you, Eliinka, are to be the arbitrator), then Mikali will support me in a war. He believes time will soften my anger. For now we will send a formal complaint denouncing your treatment, request the return of my horses and supplies, and demand that justice be brought to those who murdered Zerin."

Six months! Eliinka hoped that would be enough time to dissuade her from war.

Jereni took the book from Eliinka and placed it back on the table. "War and peace tear at my soul in the same way spring and winter battle for the days that fall between them. Eliinka, help me find the will to pursue peace and keep my word. Mikali . . ." Jereni frowned.

"How can we reclaim our love? My kingdom needs me to bear heirs to the throne. There is now such distance between us. We poured water on the fire of our love, but it must not be extinguished. Not with so few thoughtless words." Jereni shoved her mug of nightmilk away.

"I'm the cause. I'm sorry," Eliinka said. "I wish I could take away your pain. Friends sometimes disagree and hurt each other. Perhaps it helps us remember how important love is." Eliinka hoped she was saying the right words.

"Jereni, you worked out your differences and found a solution accept-able to both of you, or at least a solution you agreed would be acceptable. Tell Mikali of your hope for peace. Show Mikali increased love and atten-tion. Make plans for what you will do, where you will visit when a formal peace is accomplished."

"You still believe a formal peace is possible," Jereni murmured. She tucked a strand of hair behind an ear. "We want to spend time at Mikali's lodge in Metsakauni. We can make plans for that trip, and perhaps he can send letters to friends of influence as we pursue peace. He can help." A coy smile grew on Jereni's face. She jumped up, gave Eliinka a quick hug, and dashed from the study.

Eliinka returned to the token harp, and longed for Zerin as she played. The empty notes grew into angry notes that played themselves out and transitioned into a song of mourning, a song of remembering. What song could she play for his memorial? Her tears flowed over her hands and down the trembling strings.

When Eliinka entered the White Room, it seemed as if her heart collapsed. She swallowed hard. She would find a way to make it through the day.

Jereni leaned against Mikali's chest, and he wrapped his arms around her. He lifted an arm and motioned a brief wave of thanks to Eliinka, then he replaced his hand at the small of Jereni's back and pulled her close. Jereni leaned up and whispered into Mikali's ear. He kissed her cheek.

Eliinka clamped her eyes shut for a moment. How could she play today in front of an audience? Would she even be able to see her fingers?

Jereni and Mikali's hands did not separate as the families of the slain guards entered the White Room where they were gathering before the memorial service began. Mikali said only a word or two as he stood at Jereni's side, but he listened. He had learned sufficient Virjalo to understand, but was still uncomfortable speaking the language.

Though Eliinka hesitated at first, she joined Jereni to greet the other widows. She knelt down and gave hugs to their young children and thanked the women for their husbands' loyalty and spoke with them about their futures.

It was too much. Their pain. Her pain. So much sadness.

Eliinka needed space, to be alone, but if she left the room, she would upset Jereni. These women had also lost their husbands. They also would never be able to visit their graves. They would not be buried near their beloveds. She turned to a wall and focused on a spot of nothingness. In a moment, Jereni's firm hands grabbed Eliinka's shoulders and turned her around.

"My choices brought sorrow to so many people." Eliinka's chest heaved. Her shoulders shook. "I should have gone directly to our lodgings and not followed the messenger."

"Don't blame yourself. You didn't realize it was a trap; none of us did. Your playing today is not only for those who come."

"I can't play today."

"You need to play. It's as if the clouds obscure the stars on a rainy night. For a moment we can only feel the pains of life. Your music will help you mourn. In time, life will reenter your music and your heart."

"You believe in me more than I believe in myself." Eliinka collapsed into Jereni's arms. She held back her tears, but lost control of her shaky voice, which shattered on each syllable. "Jereni, Zerin loved me and now he is gone. The problem is—well, my music is broken."

"Do not worry. While you play, remember Zerin's last smile, his last embrace, and his last kiss. Remember your beliefs, for they will give you strength."

Eliinka glided toward the door, sliding past the other sorrowful faces, the people also holding back their tears.

Life would move on. She would be swept forward by time and the greatest pain would be left behind like a giant log thrown on a beach, unmovable, half-embedded in the sand after a violent storm, something to walk around on sunny days with bare feet scuffing the sand and a light wind bringing back only the desired memories.

Half numb, Eliinka found herself in the Great Hall, half-listening to the eulogies.

When it was her turn, she sat at the harp and stared at the blue diamonds on her hands, hands she clenched tight, her nails biting her palms. She couldn't play. How could she even touch the harp?

After a long pause, Jereni came to her side, and whispered in her ear. "You must play away a portion of your grief and sorrow so you can begin to live again. You are needed here." Jereni picked up each of Eliinka's hands in turn and placed her fingers on the harp strings. "Play for Zerin." Jereni backed away.

The first chord was the hardest to release. Eliinka played the next chords, which sounded dry and flat, and added a melody, even though it had no life. As she let her hands do the work, the music took over without her directing it. The piece began with a grief-stricken air, expressed her anguish, and developed into a brief memory of Zerin and the beauty of Viru. As she thought of him, everyone in the room disappeared from her consciousness. It seemed as if he sat at her side. The strings vibrated under her fingers, a warm calmness flowed through her body, and she felt alive again. Large vases of sweet lehti flowers filled the room with a rich, floral scent. She played with such emotion that, as she finished, she wondered at how well she had played and sensed an unexpected, unseen kiss from Zerin on her cheek.

Eliinka returned to her seat, touching her cheek. Toivo reached over and patted her hand. Jereni whispered, "Your heart is already returning to your music."

Chapter Thirty-Eight

~ QUIET DISSONANCE WITHIN THE MUSIC ~

ere is a note from Timo for Toivo. Find out what it says." Jereni
handed Eliinka a letter.

They sat in the study where Eliinka planned to stay and play the harp
until it was time for sleep. A cool evening breeze brushed the curtains in
the windows. "Does Toivo still put that balm on your back every day?"

"Yes, she says it reduces the scarring. I still don't have courage to look
at my back with a mirror. I don't want to see my scars. I want to forget
Pelto."

Jereni edged to the front of her chair. "Let me see them then."

As Eliinka moved to the floor in front of Jereni, she expressed what
had been on her mind all day. "I thought Toivo was adjusting to living
here—it's been two months since she arrived. But today she broke down.
When she stopped crying, she told me she doesn't think she can learn
Virjalo or ever make friends."

"Maybe the letter will help. It isn't easy for Toivo. She misses her father.
You'll find ways to make her comfortable." Jereni pressed on Eliinka's scar
tissue. "New skin is growing. How does it feel?"

"I have no pain when I move." Eliinka wasn't sure how she could help
Toivo become comfortable in Viru. She herself had never felt fully at home
here, and now with Zerin gone, could she?

"The scar on your upper chest has faded. At least all your scars are
covered by your clothing. We must get some of that healing balm. Find
out what is in it; see if Toivo knows." Jereni picked up her mug of steaming
nightmilk.

"Your flesh is healing, but how is your heart?"

Eliinka tried to smile. "It is like part of me is missing. It's hard to fall
asleep at night." She swallowed. Nights were bad, especially the quiet time

when she fought sleep and her mind flashed replay after replay of the arrow flying. "I view it as a long separation from Zerin."

"Your beliefs dampen your pain. Many would like to know their loved ones still exist and live on after they have passed through to the other side."

"I do believe I'll be with Zerin again. But how do you know what I believe?"

Jereni sipped from her mug and then continued to hold it between her palms as she spoke. "Not only was I taught the language of Pelto, but I learned what I could about Pelto's culture."

"But my faith, although ancient, is rare and has few believers," Eliinka said. "Who taught you of Eleman Puusta?"

"We study all aspects of Pelto and its history. Timo also sent me a note. You may read it." Jereni handed Eliinka another letter.

In the note, Timo thanked Jereni for her hospitality and kindness toward Toivo. He apologized for the treatment of Eliinka. He mentioned his efforts with parliament, commented about an upcoming election, and as an afterthought, noted the disappearance of Loukku.

After reading the note twice, Eliinka turned the paper over, looking to see if she had missed anything. "He didn't mention an alliance."

"No. That would not be safe to write in a letter that might be read by others."

"Timo will make a powerful ally." Eliinka handed the letter back to Jereni.

"Another message came this afternoon that will be discussed in my meeting tomorrow. You should know of its contents." Jereni's eyes darkened like an approaching storm. She threw a parchment on the table.

"Who is it from?" Eliinka set down her nightmilk.

"The message is from Governor Tuli. He sent it with my horses and tents, but no other supplies were returned. He claims they have no information about who murdered Zerin and no way to discover the culprit."

"That's what I suspected." Eliinka shrugged.

"Eliinka, there is no apology for your treatment!" Jereni slapped the parchment onto the table.

"They don't view it as wrong."

"Then they are stupid. They underestimate me." A sly look appeared on Jereni's face. "They also insulted you and me by requesting that if . . . if an ambassador is sent again, that it would be someone higher in my government, someone with more authority. My patience is fast disappearing."

"What will you do? What else can we do, send more letters?"

"Eliinka, at times when you play your harp the listener is lulled into complacency with beguiling melodies and rich harmonies. You can slip in other melodies, or add a minor dissonance, without their realization, or they can be shocked with sudden jarring changes and an obvious switch to a different tune. At this time, the first approach, quiet dissonance within the music, is my choice." Jereni leaned back in her chair. "Actually, this method has the potential to more effectively achieve my goals and will be more interesting. The Peltens will give me what I want."

Eliinka would not ask what Jereni planned. She did not want to know.

Chapter Thirty-Nine
~ AN UNPLANNED COMPLICATION ~

"A re you preparing for war?" Eliinka scowled. Over twenty large tents were scattered under pine trees, and there were more men than Eliinka could count in the mountain camp: men with beards like men of Pelto, instead of being clean-shaven. It had only been three months since Eliinka had returned from Pelto. Jereni couldn't be preparing to attack already.

Jereni wheeled her horse around. She steeled her eyes at Eliinka, daring her to comment more. But then she shook her head. "Actually, we're not fighting a war; think of it as a series of operations. The guilty are being brought to justice."

"I'm not trained in tactics of war or whatever you say you are directing." Eliinka's voice tightened. "I doubt I'll ever understand much of it."

"You are disturbed," Jereni said. The men bowed to her as she rode into the camp. Guards took the reins and they dismounted. "Today you will see all that has been accomplished so far, which is little. You understand much more than you will ever admit. You are here to verify the name of a man."

The soldiers or guards—Eliinka wasn't sure what they were—dispersed, one of them leading their horses away, while the leader of the camp, a tall, sturdy man, remained.

"Show him to us," Jereni ordered.

He led them to a tent and lifted the flap.

Eliinka had not even stepped inside before she spun around, stumbling away from the doorway.

"No!" she whispered in Virjalo, pulling Jereni away from the entrance.

As Jereni opened her mouth, Eliinka said, "Sh! Don't go in!" She motioned Jereni to follow and ran from the tent, her feet thumping on the needled forest floor, only stopping when Jereni caught up with her on the far side of the camp.

"Eliinka—"

"Rakel! I'm sure Rakel is in that tent. Tied up! She might have seen me. Why did you capture her?"

"That isn't possible!"

"I'm not going in there. If it is Rakel . . . what do we do?"

"It can't be her," Jereni said. They walked back to the center of camp, toward the largest tent.

Moments later, when the guard leader joined them, Jereni asked, "Was a woman captured?"

"Yes," he answered. "She was in the same room, so my men also took her."

"Find out her name and bring the male prisoner to me."

Jereni turned to Eliinka. "We came here for you to identify a man. If Rakel is here . . ." She shook her head, "it would be an unplanned complication." She sat on a chair in front of the largest tent and pulled a stack of parchments onto her lap. To her left was a table laid with breads, cheeses, fruits, and drinks.

A few minutes later, two guards dragged a bound man across the camp. The guard leader said, "The woman's name is Rakel."

"He ran. He didn't even try to protect her," said the guard who removed the covering from the man's head.

Eliinka stepped backward, almost falling. Loukku gave her a poisonous sneer and tried to speak through his gag.

"So you recognize him, and he recognizes you," Jereni said.

"Yes, he is Loukku." When Eliinka said his name, he struggled at his bonds.

"Is Rakel, Mikali's sister with you?" Jereni spoke in slow, even Pelten. Loukku turned away.

"Nod your head if she is here." Jereni said.

He didn't move.

"Answer me, fool." Jereni grabbed a staff from a nearby guard and struck Loukku on the back of his knees. He crumpled backward. Pressing the staff on the front of his neck, she demanded, "Answer me. Is it her?"

Loukku mumbled through his gag and nodded his head.

"Take him away, but take him to the far side of camp. Don't let him near Rakel again." Jereni poured wine into a mug, sloshing some over the side. But she didn't drink it; she pushed it away.

"Rakel did nothing worthy of punishment," Eliinka said. "Although I dislike her, she doesn't deserve this."

"She struck you," Jereni said. "But you are right. She is not guilty. Unlike Loukku, who will be punished."

"Does she know she's in Viru?" Eliinka asked.

"She shouldn't. The guards dressed like Peltens and grew beards. They were careful, as we did not want anyone they came in contact with to know Viru is involved. Today is the first day that Loukku realized he is no longer in Pelto."

"Can Rakel be released? Do we keep her here indefinitely?" Eliinka rubbed her temples. A headache was coming on.

"It's too risky to release her right now. My men are still quietly working in Pelto, trying to find all who attacked you. She may go back to those who are Loukku's friends. Though the chance is small, we can't risk accidentally taking her again."

The smoke of the campfire sifted through the late summer breeze, and the smell of cooking meat slashed at Eliinka's queasy stomach. She tipped her head up, but couldn't see the top of the towering trees. "What will we do with Rakel?"

A troubled look flickered over Jereni's face. She narrowed her mouth. "We cannot hold her for long."

Eliinka drummed her fingers on her thigh. She leaned forward, her left hand cupping her chin, her elbow pressing into her leg. Insects buzzed her head. She fingered a just-fallen pine needle. "Have your men perform a fake rescue and bring her to the palace where she'll be safe."

"Mikali wrote to Rakel," Jereni said. "She never answered, but from all we heard, she thinks she can only be satisfied in Pelto."

"Could she be moved and held in a more isolated area as we wait for a better time?" Eliinka asked. "And then your men who can speak Pelten could rescue her. They can see if she has any suspicions about who captured her. They can either return to Pelto or if she knows anything . . ." Eliinka's words trailed off. "Never mind. There are too many chances of failure."

"Moving her to a more isolated area is a good choice," Jereni said. "It is the best solution. Even though the guards will dress as Peltens, they can never talk to her, nor have their voices heard. Those who speak Pelten have accents she will notice. Luckily, her eyes have been covered at all times except when she has been inside the tent. She may wish to live in Viru someday and can't know who is responsible!"

Jereni ordered a map and within a moment it was brought to her. She unrolled it, spread it out wide, and skimmed her fingers across the parchment. "Here," she pointed. "The appearance of the land is similar to parts of Pelto. Rakel will be taken to this valley, near Piilo, one day north of us on horseback. She'll be able to walk outside, get fresh air, and assume she is still in Pelto." Jereni rolled up the map.

"Your men are skilled to capture Loukku from RitVa," Eliinka said, while shuffling her feet back and forth in the dirt. "Though they shouldn't have taken Rakel, even by accident. Are you sure no one in Pelto suspects us?"

Jereni took a long drink of her wine. She poured juice into a second mug and handed it to Eliinka. "The one man who may possibly harbor any suspicions will say nothing as his daughter is our visitor. My men left no traces. The Peltens are confused."

"Actually, I think Timo would agree that punishment is justified," Eliinka said, glad that Jereni cared that her men had captured the right man.

"Sit and eat. Afterwards we will talk about Loukku's punishment."

Punishment? What did Viruns do to their prisoners? Eliinka had been hungry, but now, the bread, the cheeses, and meat, none of it had any flavor. Bitter pine smoke blew their direction. She only nibbled, while Jereni ate her fill. Eliinka was taking a sip of juice when Jereni said, "Loukku will first be punished for the results of his actions against you. Eliinka, you have the right to give the first strike."

Eliinka choked on her juice. "Must I claim this right?"

"Does he deserve consequences for his actions?"

"Undoubtedly." Eliinka's stomach curdled.

"According to the law in Viru, he will be punished for his attack on you, plus he will be punished for what the government inflicted on you. The first strike is a responsibility you must take."

Eliinka covered her mouth with her hand and spoke through her fingers. "I don't think I can. What will this do to my music?" Would she still be able to play? She traced each diamond on her hands in turn.

"Is it correct that the punishment for murder is death in Pelto?" Jereni asked.

"Yes," Eliinka said, through her almost-closed teeth.

"The punishment is the same in both lands then. Loukku ordered the murder of my guards. He also sent the man who shot the arrow. He is responsible for Zerin's death." Jereni thinned her lips. "He admitted his guilt and will be punished."

Anger upswelled and Eliinka fought it. How could she want to take revenge? Would she really be happy to see Loukku in pain, even if he deserved it?

"How is the first strike to take place?"

"You will use a whip."

Eliinka flinched. Her back echoed pain. "I've never held a whip in my life."

"You will be instructed in its use. You need strike only once as it is ceremonial in nature."

After Jereni pulled a whip from a bag, she stepped into a clearing, away from the tents. She unrolled the whip, moved her arm above her shoulder and head, and with a quick movement, brought her hand down and sent the whip flying forward.

The whistle-snap sent cold chills slicing across Eliinka's scars. The skin across her shoulder blades burned. The snap echoed in her mind, even though the whip had stopped moving. Jereni snapped the whip two more times. She handed it to Eliinka.

Eliinka hesitated before taking the handle. She sent the snakelike cord in a general direction, but it would not snap. Limp as a broken harp string, it would not fly through the air. The whip was as fluid as water and unlike any weapon she had ever before used. It didn't hit anything. It was impossible to control. She wound up the whip and tugged on the circle she made. Discouraged, she handed it to Jereni.

"Snap your wrist at the last moment. Like this." With a quick movement, Jereni stripped leaves off a branch.

Eliinka tried to imitate Jereni's arm motions, but couldn't make the whip strike where she wanted.

"You're making it harder than it is. You need to move your whole arm." Jereni stood behind Eliinka, put her left hand on Eliinka's shoulder and placed her right over Eliinka's hand, on the handle. The movement was quick and powerful. Together, they repeated the motion several times. "Now try it by yourself. Do it by feel and focus on the tip of the whip. You'll learn with practice." Jereni moved a safe distance away and leaned against a large tree.

Eliinka swung the whip, using the same motion she had just felt. She coaxed a light popping sound out of the tip. Although she practiced until she didn't want to lift her arm again, she only got a little pop—no slicing speed or cracking sound. She wound up the whip and dropped it on the ground.

"Good enough," Jereni said. "He will be punished tomorrow, after Rakel is gone."

Tomorrow! Eliinka kicked the whip that lay at her feet. Its coils scattered. "Do you think I'm capable with the whip?"

"Though you can barely swing it, you should be able to hit his back. If you miss, just take another swing."

Eliinka cringed. "What I mean is, do you think I'll be able to swing a whip toward a man when I'm not defending you? I don't want to harm anyone. My faith . . ."

Jereni grabbed Eliinka's wrist. She scrutinized her face. "You have always managed to do what is necessary. You even crossed the wilderness without guards. You're not as innocent or as inexperienced as when we first met—don't pretend to be. His punishment is required." She released her wrist. "The guards have heard of your bravery. They will watch your ability to administer justice."

"Justice?" Eliinka shook her sore arm, loosening the muscles and picked up the whip from the ground. Zerin would not be brought back, no matter what they did to Loukku. Where was the justice for herself? There was none, so she went to the middle of a clearing to practice making the whip fly properly through the air.

Chapter Forty

~ BURDEN OF DECISION ~

Dawn still arrived even though Eliinka lay in bed, trying to delay the morning. When Rakel's screams passed through the tent walls, she rose and peeked through a slit in the tent and was slapped by nippy air.

A guard forced Rakel onto a horse. Her head was covered and her wrists were bound together with twisted fabric. A female guard mounted behind her.

Although Eliinka was relieved she would not have to see Rakel again, she felt neither malice nor happiness as she watched Rakel being carried away. She wondered if her ability to feel emotions had been deadened? Perhaps she would be able to swing the whip after all.

Eliinka walked through a knee-high fog with Jereni to the central area of the camp. Wisps of mist seeped around the trees.

Loukku's mouth was gagged, his back was bare, and his hands were bound to a tree. He turned his head and glared; his hatred arced through the air toward Eliinka.

Jereni handed her the whip.

Guards stood at attention.

The expectation hung heavy, like a repeating bass note pounding, pounding, pounding a beat that would not stop.

Eliinka stood as if in a dream, looking on the scene, seeing herself. Her mind disconnected from her body and she swung the whip like she had practiced. Everything moved in slow motion: the pulling back of the arm, reaching above and behind, swinging forward, snapping the wrist. Speed burst forth from the whip; the end sliced across Loukku's back, leaving a red, shallow slash. Eliinka's own back tensed.

"He'll receive fifteen lashes in total, the same number you received. You have a right to deliver them all, if you are willing." Jereni reached to take the whip from Eliinka.

A large, muscular guard flexed his muscles. He held a larger whip.

Fifteen lashes. Eliinka did not release the whip when Jereni took the handle.

"Really?" Jereni asked.

"Please allow me a moment to prepare." Eliinka walked to a towering tree and sat with crossed legs, hands in front with fingertips touching.

The mist still swirled. The moisture pressed in on her skin, dampening her hands and wrists and face. In a minute she rose. She took one swing toward nothing.

Jereni waited, hands on her hips, her eyebrows raised.

Eliinka gave Jereni a slight nod.

Concentrating on Loukku's back, an exact spot where his right shoulder blade protruded the most, she swung her arm swiftly, whipping her wrist as the whip lowered in the air. A loud echo boomed across the clearing as the tip precisely, but barely, touched Loukku's back, leaving a bright red mark. She drew no blood.

Each strike left a similar red welt. Eliinka counted each time she let the whip fly. After the fifteenth strike she dropped the whip to the earth of the silent grove.

"Enough people have suffered in this world. Justice is served. Although he threatened me, he never touched me. The remainder of his punishment is just." Eliinka turned away. "His death for Zerin's."

But she did not want to see death, so she walked away from the chatter, from the fear, and into the dappled shadows of the trees.

Just a few minutes later, Jereni's hand fell lightly upon Eliinka's shoulder. "You said correctly that you harbored no ill will."

Eliinka continued walking, but Jereni did not loosen her grip.

"Would you have chosen differently?" Eliinka asked as she glanced to Jereni.

"Suffering is not pleasant to receive or inflict," Jereni said. They stopped near a giant of a tree where Jereni pointed to a small, white, three-petaled flower growing between its large gnarled roots. "You are like the trillium, able to grow in challenging terrain, able to keep your roots in the ground despite heavy rains, able to bloom despite lack of sunlight, able to remain white and pure although the ground around you is littered with fallen giant trees that decay."

As Eliinka knelt in the soft, spongy humus and stroked the flower petals, her skin tightened on her aching back. Her necklace thudded with her pulse. "Jereni, I never want to touch a whip again. Never again."

The crisp mountain air was no longer fresh, but smelled of mud and old leaves. Flowers lost their brilliance and faded as if they grew in the shadows. Hooves beat the dry, dusty road. Jereni rode slightly ahead. Eliinka sat with unsettled ease on the back of her cantering horse. What she had thought was going to be a relaxing outing in the mountains, an escape from the nightmares that haunted her, had not been. How could she accept her choices?

"Jereni," Eliinka called. "So many of your choices require hard decisions, often decisions with no right or wrong answer, or decisions with no possible positive outcome. How do you bear the responsibility of your people on your shoulders?"

Jereni slowed her horse to a trot. "Your music lightens my burden and diverts my mind for a moment. My love for my people and Viru is all encompassing, yet the load is too heavy for one to bear." She halted her horse near a large, ripening field of grain and gazed toward the distant mountains.

Eliinka turned her horse around and returned to Jereni's side.

"This is the time," Jereni said. "You now carry weight, enough weight, enough burden of decision that you need to know what everyone, what every man, woman, and child in Viru knows. You will hear my words, my explanation."

"There can't be something that everyone knows that I don't."

Jereni's face grew more serious than Eliinka had ever seen. "As requested by me, Zerin never explained all aspects of the royal house and the ceremony of Vala to you. As it stands at this time, if anything happens to me, you would take the throne."

Eliinka gripped her saddle in shock, keeping herself from falling off her horse.

"If I should die after I have children, you would be the ruler and their teacher, until they come of age. You would be required to perform the tasks which you have so innocently achieved."

"This can't be true."

"Notice how all the people treat you. They see what you have not. You became my sister by a ceremony of blood. My impulsiveness, my rashness, in this case was a wise decision. But could you be trusted with this knowledge at that time? No.

"You brought back Toivo. This fulfilled a requirement that you were unaware of, a requirement that one of royal blood must bring a Pelten to Viru to proves one's bravery without the help of others in the royal family. This task is required for one to wear the crown. To return with a Pelten at your side without the help of any guard is unprecedented in our history. It is a feat that is becoming legend."

Eliinka laid her head against her horse's neck. His hair tickled her nose. She was not even sure if she had become Virun, and now the kingdom . . .

"You have shown devotion, loyalty, and the ability to act in my stead. You choose to enact my will, even when you would prefer to do otherwise. Your ability to administer fair punishment will be spread by the guards. Your esteem will rise even higher among all the people, for they know you are fair and also merciful."

"I never want a crown or the burdens it brings. You must outlive me and bear many children." Eliinka sat tall and jerked her head back toward Jereni.

"You searched me out! You brought me to Viru so you could take the throne, so you could wear your crown. It was required by tradition. I understand now."

"Yes. It was necessary," Jereni said.

She'd hoped it was a lie, but it was true. Eliinka gulped. "You planned to forcibly bring me here, perhaps forcibly keep me here. Is that true?"

"As my father did my mother. As did all the rulers before me. My men listened to my instructions and searched for the fine gem hiding in the cliffs, the one perfect pearl on the beach, the stray flower in a weedy pasture. They searched for a woman with musical talent, with intelligence, a woman who would not have close family to miss her. They returned with many possibilities, but you were the perfect match.

"When you somehow heard my steps and turned in your room and looked at me with your pure eyes, my tactics changed to persuasion. The thought entered with power into my mind that you would become a greater musician and a greater asset if you played because you loved music, not because you were forced to play. Persuasion had never been used before, but traditions can be altered. Your coming willingly has changed the course of my life, the history of Viru, and has given me a marriage of love." Jereni's face reddened. "But there is much more for you to learn. It is now necessary for you to attend all my meetings as an advisor, even though you would rather not be involved in daily governing."

"Does Mikali understand what you have told me?"

"Mikali knows you are close to me, but not your true position. We will inform him when we return. This evening, you will also be given a ring with my royal seal. Perhaps you should have begun wearing it earlier, but now it is the proper time."

Chapter Forty-One
~ WHATEVER IS NECESSARY ~

The gentle morning rain glimmered as the rising sun peered through a crack in the clouds. Eliinka couldn't fall back asleep, so she rolled over and hung her feet over the edge of her bed. Life had settled into a regular, predictable schedule. Still, it was hard to get out of bed each morning— usually Eliinka would lay on her back for a long time, thinking.

It had been more than three months since she had been in Pelto, but Eliinka still avoided conversations when possible and never entered the White Room, where she had spent so much time with Zerin. Instead, she often took other routes around the palace so she wouldn't have to pass through that hall. She often chose to be silent, knowing that if she spoke, sobs might leak out. She played the harp every day, but her music only temporarily deadened the pain.

The rain pattered against the window, and Eliinka sat up, watching the water droplets chase each other down the glass.

Her bedroom door swung open and Toivo dashed in, spouting off the gossip she had learned the previous day, breaking into Eliinka's thoughts. Toivo was now so busy with friends that the only time Eliinka spent with her was their morning meal that they ate in Eliinka's room and a short harp lesson afterwards.

Milla placed their bread and fruit and juice on the table, and after bowing, she left the room. A moment later, Jereni's bedroom door opened, and she entered, greeting Eliinka with a kiss to each cheek. It was unusual for Jereni to enter her room, but Eliinka contained her surprise. This visit brightened her morning.

"Good morning, Jereni," Toivo said. "Are you eating with us this morning?"

"Eliinka!" Jereni's face glowed. She patted her flat stomach. "Mikali is so happy! We so hoped we would not have to wait long."

"A baby! Congratulations." Eliinka grinned. She had hoped for this. She poured a glass of juice for Jereni and a glass for herself.

"Oh, and a letter from Timo arrived last evening."

Jereni handed Toivo the letter. She took a bite from the wedge of sweetbread that she scooped into her hand and sat near the window that faced the cloud-cloaked mountains.

Toivo broke the seal.

"We'll need to prepare a nursery," Jereni said. "Clothes need to be made. There's so much to plan."

Eliinka sipped at her juice. It was the peak season for the marja fruit and the juice tasted sweeter this morning, almost too sweet.

Toivo read and reread the letter. She ran her tongue over her upper lip.

"What did your father write?" Eliinka asked.

"He's very worried that some men in government positions have disappeared." As was her custom, Toivo handed them the letter, and they leaned close together. Eliinka glanced at Jereni as they finished. Her face was unreadable.

"I'm scared that he might also be taken, or killed." Toivo pushed a finger against her front teeth.

"Don't worry. He's well respected by everyone," Eliinka said.

But Eliinka still felt unsettled. She set down her glass in the windowsill and nodded at Jereni, hoping she could comfort Toivo.

Toivo tore her bread into small pieces. She pushed them around her plate.

"Toivo, your father is safe," Jereni said. "Timo is under my protection, under the watchful gaze of my best men at all times. He doesn't know he is being guarded. Do not tell him."

But Toivo did not listen. "It's happened before. My grandmother's younger sister, my mother's favorite aunt, disappeared when riding to a neighboring town. My mother said they searched for her and never found a trace. My grandmother would tell me stories of her when I visited. She was beautiful and talented with cloth. I know it was over twenty years ago, but I don't want my father to also disappear."

Eliinka patted Toivo's hand. "Jereni's men will keep him safe."

"Jereni, you are so nice and good," Toivo said. "Thank you."

Jereni picked up her glass of juice and took a long, slow drink as Toivo continued. "I grew up hearing the stories, you must have heard of them. They tell of Viru, but they are untrue. Anyway, my father wouldn't have sent me here if the stories were true. You are not the princess the legends speak of. The princess who kidnaps people and fights fearlessly in battles, slicing through enemies swifter than a falling star."

Eliinka touched Jereni's elbow.

"You are not the queen with a temper that topples both friend and foe. You are patient and caring and peaceful. You treat me as a friend."

Jereni's eyes glazed like a frosted mirror. She set down her glass, but did not let it go. Instead, she gripped it tight as she stared at Toivo. She spoke in her calmest, most lyrical voice. "That is very kind of you to say. My love is for my people and my kingdom. Whatever is necessary, whatever is required for the welfare of my kingdom will be done." Jereni released the glass. "Toivo, your mother must have taught you well, for you look for and find the good in people."

"I was very close to both my mother and grandmother. My mother always wanted another child. Now it is like both of you are my sisters as well as my best friends." Toivo gave Jereni a quick hug. "Jereni, you've never mentioned your mother to me, only your father. What was she like?"

Jereni's face lost all color. Silence hung like a wilted flower.

"Toivo, it's time for your harp lesson," Eliinka said.

But Jereni spoke in a faint whisper. "Toivo, my mother also looked for the good in people. She was extremely beautiful—as beautiful as the long-awaited spring blossom—and loving. The encircling of her warm arms comforted me, and she was a friend who heard what was not expressed. But my mother was also very sad. She would wish to see her grandchild." Jereni patted Toivo's cheek, then gave a long embrace to Eliinka. She dabbed her eyes as she returned to her room.

Toivo pressed her fingers against her upper cheek. "Jereni is so emotional today. I didn't mean to upset her."

"It must be because she is missing her mother," Eliinka said.

Chapter Forty-Two

~ COMING HOME ~

The large doors of the Dining Hall slammed open. The nobles seated at the long table shifted in their seats and strained their necks. A woman—Rakel?—pushed her way in, wearing a deep-red dress that was Pelten in design but made from Virun fabric.

It was Rakel! Eliinka's laughter tapered into choking coughs, and Jereni frowned.

Two palace guards escorted Rakel up the hall, staying close to her sides, and a broad, tall, bearded man trailed behind her. Eliinka had not expected to see her again, not after the glimpse of her at the camp two months ago.

Jereni nudged Mikali, whispering in his ear, and he jumped to his feet.

Rakel lifted her skirt and ran the rest of the length of the hall. She wrapped her arms around his chest. "Mikali, protect me," she stuttered.

Eliinka shoved her plate away and stood. She stepped away, planning to leave, but Jereni pulled her back.

"No! Stay."

Eliinka sunk low into her chair and stared at her food.

"Let me live here with you." Rakel spoke in a higher-pitched voice than normal.

"You never answered my letters." Mikali pulled away from her arms. "You never even said good-bye."

Jereni shifted her chair, angling it toward Rakel.

Eliinka stabbed her bread with her knife.

"Please, please take me in and protect me." Rakel knelt at Jereni's feet. She motioned to the tall man. "I was kidnapped. They held me captive for months, and this man rescued me. I'm scared to go back to Pelto. I'll not be safe there." Her voice faltered.

Jereni waved a hand to the nobles, who had stopped eating. They returned to their meals and conversations.

"Queen Jereni, I apologize for my past behavior and my rudeness when you extended your hospitality to me. I broke my promise to you. I'm sorry." Rakel shifted her weight and bowed lower so her forehead almost touched the floor. "Pitka, the man who rescued me, doesn't speak Virjalo. I insisted that he bring me here. Please show him kindness and allow him to return to Pelto."

"He will be questioned—by me if necessary. Take him away," Jereni snapped.

Her guards escorted the tall man from the hall.

Eliinka skewered her tiny pieces of bread, breaking them into crumbs.

"Rakel, why are you here?" Jereni narrowed her lips.

"Please let me live in Viru." Desperation tinged Rakel's voice. "I'll live with the weavers and work for Taina, or go anywhere. Just inside your kingdom. Please forgive me."

"Your greater wrongs are against Lady Eliinka. She will decide."

Eliinka dropped her knife. It clattered on her plate.

For the first time since entering the room, Rakel glanced at Eliinka. She visibly shuddered. But she approached Eliinka, her gaze to the ground.

Frustrated, Eliinka stared at Jereni, trying to get her attention. Jereni ignored her. Eliinka knew her decision would be final.

Rakel straightened into a standing position. She twisted her face, chewed on her lips, and her shoulders sagged.

Eliinka curled her fingernails into her palms. She would control her anger. She would not make a scene, she would not strike Rakel, and she would maintain control over her temper like she had in the forest. She had wanted to forget all about Rakel. "Come with me. I guess I'll have to use the White Room." It was closest. She stomped out of the Dining Hall. In her peripheral vision, she saw Mikali lean and whisper into Jereni's ear.

"Enter." Eliinka motioned to the closed door. She had avoided the White Room since Zerin's death. Rakel held it open for her, and Eliinka entered and glared at the walls. Tomorrow she would insist they be painted a different color.

She spun and confronted Rakel. "Why did you return?"

"I'm sorry," Rakel sputtered. "I abused our friendship. Show me mercy. Please give me the privilege of living in Viru for the rest of my life. Please."

"Last time you were here, you rudely left and publicly disowned your brother. You broke your promise to Jereni and told of my injury. You abused me when I was helpless and would have allowed me to be murdered. You attacked me! You humiliated me in the Hirdahouse! You saw my blood spray to the earth and viewed my ripped flesh! My skin is scarred for my entire life! My beloved husband is dead! How will I know you won't turn against us again?"

With every sentence Rakel cringed as if she had been given one more lash with a whip.

Eliinka yanked a chair that was next to the table, let it crash to the floor. Then she righted it, sat down, and clenched her fists. She choked on her rising grief. Rakel's return had dredged up the pain she wished to keep buried.

Rakel's knees plummeted to the marble floor. She wiped her eyes, but tears continued as she begged through her sobs. "I'm sorry. I did you wrong. I've changed. Ask whatever you want from me, and I'll do it so I can stay. Have me guarded. Put me in prison. I'll suffer any punishment. Have me whipped."

"The sister of Mikali will not be so abused," Eliinka muttered. Jereni would not allow it. Plus, it was not just.

"Then I'll be your servant."

"Would you keep your word if you were allowed to stay in Viru?" Eliinka leaned closer.

"I swear on my life to obey you! Please! Hear my plea! Let me stay! Please! Where is the girl who could not even harm an animal, my friend who said she would never forsake our friendship? Can she remember me, who I was?"

Rakel collapsed the rest of the way to the ground. Her head hit the marble. She tugged on her hair. Her body shook as she rose up from the ground and supported herself on her hands.

"I beg you," she whimpered. "I plead with you. Have compassion on me." Her voice lowered to a faint whisper, "Or if not on me, have compassion on my unborn child. I wish him to be born in Viru, to be Virun." Rakel pulled herself up so she sat on her heels, hands clenching her knees, her mouth quivering, her head down. Teardrops splotched on her red dress, like drops of blood.

Eliinka gave a start. Rakel's abdomen was slightly rounded. "Were you abused by your captors?"

"No. Loukku, the man I was with when I was captured, he's the father." Rakel stifled a sob. "He insisted I prove my devotion to him and his cause. I hoped we would marry. I worked with him to try to force changes on Pelto. I wanted the power to take Mikali back."

"It is dangerous for me to be in Pelto. And now I'm back in Viru and near Mikali, at least for a day." Rakel finally looked up.

Eliinka softened her voice from steel into roughened velvet. Rakel never made anything simple. "Do you have any other information that I should consider?"

"I had such a great desire to return." Rakel sounded confused and her sobs faded. "When I entered Jalolinna, it felt like I was coming home."

Rakel shifted forward on her knees and lowered her head. "Lady Eliinka, no matter your decision, I promise to never be involved in politics again, or harm or speak ill in any way about Viru. I'll keep my word. I'm sorry. I know I can never make full amends or change the past. I can never take away your pain."

"Is it only for your safety that you come here now?"

"I am afraid to return to Pelto, yes. But also, I came to realize that Viru is a good place. I refused to accept that when I was here last time. I also want to live near Mikali and Jereni."

"Can I trust you? You broke your word before."

"Please, I promise I'll obey Jereni. I'll obey you. I won't fail like I did in the past."

Eliinka waited for a moment. She needed time to think. "I'll inform you of my decision later today."

"Thank you."

Eliinka opened the door and instructed a guard, "Take Rakel to a room. I want one female guard with her at all times."

Rakel did not move from her knees.

"You may stand. Follow the guard."

Rakel rose. She bowed again as she left the room.

Eliinka laid her head on the desk, wishing for a harp. She only felt whole when she played. It was the only way to forget the pain.

Rakel was always a problem. Always! Why should she show her any mercy? If she allowed her to stay, she'd have to see her face every day. It would be one more reminder of losing Zerin in Pelto. But if not . . . She tapped her fingers on the desk, wishing this day did not exist, that she didn't have to make such hard decisions.

Eliinka jumped to her feet when Jereni entered.

"Jereni, do you know what would have happened if she had returned to Pelto?" Deep-seated bitterness edged Eliinka's voice. "What I received is as a broken fingernail to what they would do to her. The man is not even reprimanded, but the woman is given a slow, tortuous death."

"Explain your words."

"She's going to have a baby, but isn't married. The father is Loukku."

Jereni gasped.

"Is it also a crime here?"

"No. They are given an option to marry, which they usually do to avoid shaming their families' names. If not, the infant is given to a married couple who is unable to have children, to raise as their own."

"Will you take Rakel's child away?"

"No, she can keep her baby."

"Should we send her back after the birth?"

"This is your decision." Jereni headed for the door.

Eliinka sucked in her lips, then breathed out. "She doesn't deserve to live in Viru. What is your advice?"

Jereni paused in the open doorway. "Be compassionate. A guard will bring Rakel to you in one hour. She waits in her own room. It is better for me to be here when you tell her your decision."

"Thank you. I want no misunderstandings."

Jereni passed Eliinka an uncertain smile.

As the door clicked shut, Eliinka retrieved two types of parchments and a quill from the small cabinet. An agreement, that Rakel signed, would help ensure she kept her word. She set them on the table, but then paced the room instead of sitting, listening to the fighting voices in her head.

Could she handle seeing Rakel every day?

Eliinka slapped the table as she lowered herself back into the chair. Her back bumped the wood. Her scars on her back! The raised streaks of flesh that she touched every time she bathed.

She tapped the quill on the table. She scribbled notes on the lower-quality parchment, considering the possibilities. Finally, she dipped the quill into the ink once more. She wrote word after word, slowly and clearly, and after she finished, she took a deep breath and walked around the room. A book rested on a side table. Reading might distract her, especially since she had recently learned to read Virjalo.

When the time arrived, Rakel returned. She bowed deeply.

Ignoring her, Eliinka attempted to focus on the page. The difficult symbols swam in the parchment. She blinked hard and glanced up from the book, pleased to see Rakel's choice of clothing, surprised to see her hair released from its ties. Rakel stood awkwardly, shifting her hands from her front to her back, to clasped at her waist. She had bathed and her still-damp hair, draped over her shoulders, tumbled onto one of the Virun dresses she had refused to wear during her previous stay. Her eyes flicked around the room, then settled on Eliinka.

Eliinka turned back to the book and worked harder on her reading, postponing the inevitable. She finished the page before she spoke. "Jereni will come to hear my decision."

Rakel paled and bowed her head again. Eliinka turned the page and continued in her struggle to read.

After several minutes, Jereni entered the room.

Rakel dropped to the floor, prostrate in her kneeling, her entire body stretched out on the marble.

Jereni raised an eyebrow.

"Rakel, you may come read your agreement." Eliinka traced the diamond on her left hand.

"An agreement!" Rakel rushed to the ink-covered parchment. "I have a chance to stay. Thank you, thank you so much!"

"Read it aloud. You must understand what you are signing." Eliinka would have rather banished Rakel, but that would have been too harsh a punishment.

Rakel nodded.

Rakel renounces all loyalties and attachment to Pelto.

Rakel becomes a subject of the Kingdom of Viru and Queen Jereni. She is given all the associative rights and obligations including being productive and industrious.

Rakel will learn and speak Virjalo and will follow the customs of Viru.

Rakel swears allegiance to Queen Jereni and her heirs to the throne and agrees to follow instructions given by the queen or her representatives.

Rakel will give her child to serve the kingdom as the queen sees fit.

Rakel retains her rights and privileges as the sister of Prince Mikali.

Eliinka gives Rakel protection, shelter, clothing, and food.

Amnesty will be given to Rakel for past actions, and no mention will be made of these wrongdoings.

"Thank you." Rakel said.

Eliinka stretched her mouth into a narrow line. "Do you understand your agreement?"

"Yes," Rakel said. "Please, I wish to sign now."

Eliinka handed Rakel the quill.

After signing the parchment, Rakel bowed again. "Thank you for your mercy."

Eliinka swallowed hard. It was not a contract, not yet. She hesitated, dipping the pen in and out of the ink several times before blotting it. She held the pen above the parchment, hesitating. A drop of ink fell and splattered. There was no use delaying. She signed the document and Jereni gave her an approving nod. At least Jereni was pleased.

Jereni removed her ring and affixed her seal to the contract.

After bowing, Rakel said, "Queen Jereni, thank you for your generosity and fairness. I do believe that my brother chose the most beautiful and intelligent woman to be his wife." Rakel turned to Eliinka. "How do you wish me to address you?"

"You will address Eliinka as Lady Eliinka until, or if ever, she indicates otherwise," Jereni said. "When her wounds are healed, she may allow you to reclaim your friendship. You must understand her position. Eliinka is not only my most trusted advisor, but she is a member of the royal family. Rakel, you may dine with us in the Dining Hall when we have formal dinners. You will have your room from before. The weaving supplies are still there.

"Mikali wants to see you. We'll come to your room this evening." After a quick glance to Eliinka, Jereni said, "Rakel, welcome home."

Stepping closer, Jereni gave her the Virun embrace and kisses on her cheeks. "I take you as my sister. Call me Jereni." She did not let go, but whispered in Rakel's ear. "Eliinka still has much pain. Give her time."

Hearing Jereni's words, Eliinka considered leaving the room, but instead asked, "When will your baby be born?"

"In four months or so, I think."

"Go and ask for food from the kitchen if you are hungry. Remember, we expect you to speak in Virjalo. I realize it won't be easy at first."

Rakel nodded. "Lady Eliinka, would you be so kind to remind me how to say the words bread and juice?"

"Bread is pylla and juice is mehu."

Rakel bowed again to Eliinka, whispered "Thank you" to Jereni, and exited the room.

Jereni placed her hand on Eliinka's shoulder. "You were generous. Why do you think you received this task? Mikali will be very pleased."

Eliinka had not wanted to offer a contract at all. But it was right, and it was fair, even if it would hurt. She would avoid Rakel as much as possible.

Laugh lines stretched from Jereni's smile. "Maybe we can find a husband for Rakel. Meet me tonight in my study. The stress of today will melt away if we drink nightmilk and play our harps."

Chapter Forty-Three

~ THOUGHT I COULD NOT SEE ~

Eliinka spun her signet ring, and ran her fingertip over the royal seal perfectly carved into a blue-gray gemstone, the reminder that this morning she had publicly promised to give her life to serve the people of Viru. She sighed. Life used to be simple. Her childhood, even her time in her room by herself in Pelto, had been easier. Could she ever return to Pelto? But, even if she did now, it would never be home.

Eliinka examined her narrow golden crown, its engravings of Virun symbols, and the too-bright jewels. She fingered the necklace she never removed from her neck, the original necklace given to her as a token. She had wanted to refuse the crown and the title of princess, but Jereni depended on her. She insisted it was necessary.

Since Zerin's death she had immersed herself in her music, trying to escape. But the pain remained . . . even though she played the token harp every evening. Jereni had drawn her out, insisting she attend meetings, insisting she take on some of the responsibility, and insisting she mingle at social functions. Now that the Festival of Light was over, the palace would be quieter.

Maybe if she visited Zerin's grave, she would feel more at peace, even if it meant not playing her token harp for two weeks or even longer. It might be worth the risk. Occasionally messengers traveled back and forth with notes to Timo. Perhaps she could go with one of them, keep herself hidden and safe. Perhaps she could take a quick trip, visit her parents' graves and see where Zerin was buried. Eliinka decided she would talk about the possibility with Jereni this evening when they met in the study.

"Timo sent another letter," Jereni said as the door shut behind her. Her pregnancy was now obvious.

"Another man in parliament, Kettu, spoke with Timo. He also wants relations, trade relations with Viru. Timo also wrote that he believes the government will now accept a representative, but doubts we can come to any agreement."

"Do you think it's possible?" Eliinka was happy that Jereni was no longer considering war.

Jereni walked along the row of portraits, pausing for a moment to look at her mother. "A treaty? No. Still, Mikali wants to visit Pelto. He wants to show me his favorite places." She leaned out the window, the one that looked north toward Pelto. "He also wants me to meet his mother. He doesn't think she could survive the rigors of travel, so we won't bring her here. But we refuse to travel in disguise. A treaty is required before we travel to Pelto."

If there were peace with Pelto, Eliinka could also travel back and forth. When she died, she could be buried at Zerin's side, like she should be.

"Jereni, I think you would love seeing Pelto," Eliinka said. "You could visit Mikali's lodge. Go to RitVa. Eat the food." It was a minor thing. Though Eliinka now preferred the food in Viru, there were some foods she really missed. Right now she craved hedelma juice.

"It's impossible. It can't happen in my lifetime," Jereni said.

Jereni's maid entered the room and set three mugs of nightmilk on the table near the fireplace.

"I could go," Eliinka said.

"It isn't worth the risk."

"If there were a treaty, if Viru and Pelto developed a friendship, then you could meet Mikali's wonderful mother." A swell of homesickness for Pelto grew in Eliinka.

"Peace is impossible."

"If I went, I could meet with Timo. I could visit Mikali's mother. I haven't seen her in a very long time. And maybe I could speak with the government and see if there is any way to agree to trade relations. That would be a start."

"But there's no reason to go." Jereni shook her head, frowning. "Remember last time? There can be no peace." She settled in her chair and put her feet on the table.

"Peace may be possible. Also," Eliinka lowered herself into the large chair she had shared with Zerin. "I need to visit Zerin's grave." She drank half of her nightmilk in one gulp. What was she saying? How could she even think of this? But as she spoke, she realized that she needed to go back.

"Returning to Pelto is something I must do. It will help me heal."

"Eliinka—"

"I never saw where Zerin rests. As his wife, I'm supposed to anoint his grave with my tears. Plant the huuttaa tree. Do what is needed for him to rest in peace, both here and in the next world. Ensure he will remember me."

"But he isn't of your faith. There's no need."

"It does not matter. Who am I to judge his beliefs?"

"So you wish to travel in our enemy's land, even after they abused you?" Jereni asked, twisting the hairpiece and pulling it from her hair.

Eliinka waited patiently.

"If you go, you must be careful. You would travel with more protection, with a minimum of twenty men, plus there are many others who will reveal their identities, if needed, to protect you."

"Could the men be ready to leave the day after tomorrow? Perhaps I can also speak with Governor Tuli and encourage a treaty of peace." Visiting Pelto! Anticipation of returning rushed through Eliinka's heart. She picked up her nightmilk and savored a long sip.

"Wait!" Jereni fingered her mug, picked it up and set it down without lifting it to her mouth. Her lyrical voice tensed like a pulled harp string. "Your safety is paramount. You will take no risks."

"I'll be careful."

"Only visit Zerin's grave and talk with Timo, if that is all that appears safe to do," Jereni instructed. "If the situation appears hopeful, talk with the governor to see if they are open to a treaty, trade, or more discussions."

"They are slow to make decisions, so it is unlikely. But if it is possible, I'll meet with the governor."

"You will have authority to act in my name, in case they choose to act, but take no risks." Jereni picked up her mug and took a long drink, peering over the rim.

"Eliinka, you can only go under one other condition. You *must* use every available resource. You must protect yourself." Jereni set down her mug with a thud and she stood. "We both know your gift is music. Your abilities have grown."

How could Jereni know? Eliinka gripped her mug tightly between her hands. The fire crackled and popped.

Jereni's eyes intensified. "You can use your gift to bring me peace, to create harmony. You can use your gift through your music so you are able to use your music to affect people, not just entertain them. You can influence their thoughts. You are able to guide others' emotions and control their actions."

"My music is not that powerful."

Jereni took Eliinka's mug from her hands, set it next to her own, then leaned into the space above Eliinka's chair.

Fear flowed into Eliinka's bones. She had not been afraid of Jereni for a long time.

"Eliinka, do you not see your gift?" Jereni spoke in a slow, steady voice. "Have you not been taught? Do you not feel it when you choose to use your gift with your music?"

Eliinka turned her head away, fighting the sinking sensation that filled her.

"You do understand, but thought you could hide it from me. You never told me of your gift because you thought it would be misused. You thought no one would notice when you used it so carefully and so rarely."

Eliinka could pretend she didn't understand what Jereni spoke of, but Jereni would know that she was lying. So she said nothing as she stood and walked around the table to the warm hearth. She held her hands over the flaming fire. Still, a chill swept over her.

Jereni's voice started as a whisper, but increased in volume with each sentence. "It was very foolish, but you tried to use your gift on me your first week here. You also used your power, your gift, that night with Zerin. You encouraged him to do what he wanted to do, but he could not move forward without prodding. You hesitated. You held back your power when you could have created a passionate love. You used your music to kindle the first sparks of desire in his heart in hopes he would come to love you. Do you deny it?"

Eliinka jerked around to face Jereni. "How could you see? How did you know?"

"Remember my mother was Pelten. She was also of Eleman Puusta."

Eliinka sagged back against the edge of the fireplace. "Yes, I used my gift that night. But now the ache of Zerin's passing has been harder to bear. And, and . . . " Eliinka looked up. "I also used my gift to bring Toivo and me safely back to Viru."

Jereni nodded knowingly.

"I was so desperate and so scared. I was in so much pain. I had to use it. I discovered my gift also worked with the flute. I was able to call the Flute People when I needed a guide."

"Your gift was the only way for you to pass through the wilderness unaccompanied." A small grin grew on Jereni's face. "You also used your gift one other time."

Plopping down in her chair, Eliinka rubbed the diamonds on the back of her hands. She didn't speak until Jereni reached over and patted her arm.

"Yes, I did," Eliinka confessed. "But I only use my gift for good and the need was great. I discovered my gift can be used to acquire knowledge, answers. I could find no solution, and the issue was so important, so critical. It took hours of effort, but the name finally came of who should be your husband. The knowledge came as a piercing ray of light." Eliinka picked up her nightmilk, tucked her legs under her, and turned sideways in her chair toward Jereni.

"The use of your gift that night, your energy flowing through my palace, was so strong that it woke me."

"So, your mother was of my faith. How did you sense my gift when you were asleep? How?"

Jereni ran her fingers down Eliinka's forearm, over the azure-blue, intertwining lines. "'The light of eternity spans all life.' Eliinka, my mother taught me well in the doctrines of *our* faith."

Eliinka could not keep the shock she felt from entering her expression.

"Yes, Eliinka. I share your faith."

"Why didn't you tell me earlier?"

"My mother wished me to keep my faith private in Viru. Also, I do not live its precepts as I should."

Eliinka nodded. "I have heard that some of our faith have gifts, but not all. Do you have a gift?"

"My gift is the gift of language, and it is twofold. Mine is to sense people's thoughts and intents."

That explained why Jereni could so easily detect when Eliinka used her gift.

"My gift can also persuade or force others' actions with my words. When young, my gift, well, it was powerful . . . My mother insisted that it be used only to influence others, not force them."

"Have you used your gift on me?"

"Yes."

Eliinka pinched her eyes shut.

"Only to understand your thoughts, Eliinka. Knowing them made it easy to convince you to sign our agreement. My gift was never used on Mikali at any time." Jereni laughed. "It was so easy to see his thoughts, on his face, in his actions, and in his words."

Jereni placed her hands on her stomach and smiled. "He's kicking. Would you like to feel?"

Eliinka placed her palm next to Jereni's. Her stomach bulged under Eliinka's hand as several little kicks pushed outward.

"My children need to be taught in the ways of Eleman Puusta. Please help me so the teachings they receive remain pure."

Jereni placed her hand on top of Eliinka's. "Take no risks during your travels, but Eliinka, use your gift throughout Pelto. Use it to keep you safe. They won't notice if you use it with a subtle touch. Encourage the desire for peace. Plant seeds for the future. Encourage the peace that Peltens want deep down in their hearts. Help them forget their anger over past wars. Use your gift wisely. We don't want them clamoring to be part of Viru. We don't want to create unintended consequences."

Speechless, Eliinka nodded. How could she use her gift in this way?

Jereni relaxed back into her chair and was finishing her nightmilk when Mikali entered.

Taking Jereni into his arms and beginning at her high cheekbones, he worked down to her lips with a series of slow kisses. Jereni murmured, "Mikali, this is my study."

Eliinka gulped down the remnants of her nightmilk and left the room, twisting Zerin's ring back and forth on her finger.

Fourth Crossing

Chapter Forty-Four

"Zerin!"

Eliinka fell to her knees. She cleared the layer of snow from this spot of earth, noting that there was room for two in this plot, like was always given to one who was married. She planted the huuttaa tree and watered the dirt with her tears, a rite she had not fully understood until now. In a way, it allowed part of her to stay with him.

"Zerin," she whispered, "I feel so alone without you. I wish I could see you. It might be so long, so long, for me to wait, for me to be with you again." She said all she had been holding inside herself, all she wished she had said before.

If there were a treaty, she would be placed next to him someday. She piled a layer of fallen leaves and snow around the base of the dormant tree, thinking. This visit to RitVa was her only opportunity. It would be her last time ever in Pelto unless she acted. It would involve more risk than Jereni wished her to take, but this was her only chance to make change so she could return in the future.

After she planted several seeds of the lehti vine that would sprout when the warmth of spring arrived and placed a handful of Virun soil on the grave, she sat for over an hour, remembering their time together. These Virun seeds would grow into a flowering, bushy vine that would thrive in the Pelten climate. Now, when she walked through the Garden Courtyard in Jalolinna, she could sit at the bench near this bush where she had gathered the seeds and remember Zerin. Plus, it gave him a piece of Viru.

She had rushed to visit Zerin's grave when she first arrived in RitVa. Next, she visited her parents' graves, planted their huuttaa tree, and walked by the room she had lived in and the home she had grown up in. They had not changed, though they were much smaller and more drab than she remembered.

"Governor Tuli, I'm seeking an agreement between our two lands," said Eliinka, from where she stood flanked by two of her guards in the doorway to his office in the Hirdahouse. Timo stood just outside the room. It was not what Jereni expected her to do, to visit the governor so soon after she arrived in Pelto, but Eliinka was still angry about the way the governor had treated her the previous time. Perhaps he would listen if he were alone.

His quill fell to the desk. He stared at her crown and glared at her guards. "Why do you need your guards in my office?"

Eliinka ripped off her fur-lined cloak and tossed it to one of her men. She strode across the room and placed her hands on the governor's desk. "They are here to protect me from a repeat of the treatment that occurred at our last meeting."

The governor shifted away from Eliinka's patterned hands. He refused to look up at her.

"Queen Jereni has been more than patient with your excuses. An agreement will be good for both of our lands and all people. Trade will increase prosperity for all who live in Pelto and Viru. I have the authority to negotiate and sign our agreement, and I will stay in Pelto until we reach an accord." The only way to force the peace, Eliinka knew, was if she demonstrated strength. Governor Tuli would give in with enough pressure.

The governor shuffled parchments on his desk. "I see no pressing reason, yet perhaps an agreement would be good. I need to speak with parliament. We can discuss this later."

"You've had a good part of a year to speak with them." Eliinka slapped his desk. She tapped her fingers on the wood with increasing speed. "I'm less patient than I was a year ago."

The governor still did not look up. "My government has had a challenging year. We have many new men in parliament."

"Let me speak with them."

He moved his quill from one side of his desk to the other. "They are not here."

"Your meetings begin in a little over a week." Eliinka straightened and in a sweet, coaxing voice said, "You are intelligent and capable of negotiating for your people. I'll return in two weeks. I'm sure we can reach some sort of agreement. I have great hopes for a productive discussion and look forward to our next meeting."

Governor Tuli grasped his desk.

A woman had never spoken in such a way to him, Eliinka was sure of that. She paraded from the room.

Timo jumped from his horse and helped Eliinka dismount outside the villa he had rented for her and her guards. It was in a quiet neighborhood, between the Hirdahouse and the south side of the city. Eliinka clutched his arm. "Timo, thank you again for gaining me entrance. Please let me know if I take a misstep."

"Your words were well chosen."

"Thank you."

"What will you do for the next two weeks?" Timo asked as they walked to the front door.

"I'll travel and see Pelto. I leave in the morning."

Timo frowned. "Travel? I'd hoped for more time with you."

"We have now. Come inside. Join me for an hour."

Even though her guards had had only an hour to prepare, the large sitting room welcomed them with Virun carpets and a roaring fire. Eliinka rolled her shoulders and stretched her legs. She gave Timo a warm smile. "Please sit and make yourself comfortable."

A guard poured spiced hedelma juice into tall, narrow glasses. A fruity aroma filled the air.

She took a glass, and it warmed her hands.

"Eliinka, our alliance at times puts me in awkward positions," Timo said as he remained standing. "Why does Queen Jereni want an agreement? If she really wanted, she could conquer the land of Pelto. Her father did not press; that is the reason Pelto did not fall to Viru."

Eliinka nodded and sipped the warmed juice. It was as good as she remembered.

"Trade between our lands will help us in Pelto much more than you. Mikali sold his trade business. Why? He would profit if trade begins." Timo paced to the fire and back. He grasped the back of one of the chairs and continued to speak. "In all of its history, maybe a thousand years, Viru has never considered the peace that Queen Jereni wants. Why now? Her words are not logical."

"Mikali is Pelten. They'd like to visit here together. He still owns much land in Pelto." Eliinka would not mention that Jereni did not believe a treaty was possible.

"That's a good reason, but not strong enough to explain this illogical pursuit, this obsession. It's like choosing to step into a stream to catch the fish with your hands, rather than using nets to easily harvest them all. Toivo told me she does not want to return to Pelto. Jereni has captured your heart and Mikali's. I fear she has captured Toivo's. Does she want the hearts of all Peltens?"

"Queen Jereni has a deep love for Pelto."

"Why?"

"Her reasons are perhaps more complicated than I fully understand." Eliinka turned the glass around in her hand, making small bubbles in the reddish liquid. "Why did you send Toivo with me? Can you explain?"

"I wanted you to return safely," Timo said. "I knew if you were responsible for her you would not take risks. That day you did not care if you lived or died. I've experienced similar loss."

"The loneliness, the pain, does it ever disappear?" Eliinka turned to wipe away the uncalled-for tears.

"The pain fades, the loneliness recedes. I still remember Kiikki every day. And yes, eventually the pain is gone, but never the joy of the memories." Timo described his wife at length with such vividness and love that it was hard for Eliinka to believe that Kiikki had died five years earlier.

Eliinka encouraged him. A guard served a meal and they ate and talked.

Pleased to have a willing listener, Timo told stories and memories of their life together and told her of Kiikki's family. Eliinka thought about Zerin and wondered if their love would have grown that deep if he had lived longer, if she would have finally found a place she belonged. Perhaps her mother had been correct in warning her about unintended consequences. The heartbreak when he had died . . . when would the pain diminish? Maybe she should not have used her gift like she had with Zerin, but she was glad she experienced the love they had.

The lengthening shadows grew, and the sun glimmered through tall windows and cast a sunset hue on Eliinka's hands and dress. "I'd like to hear more about Kiikki—next time we meet—but I must prepare so I can leave in the morning. But have no doubt—Queen Jereni loves the land of Pelto. Trust us."

"You have sidestepped my question. You are becoming a politician."

Eliinka tried to hide her smile.

"Thank you for the meal. Is Toivo this spoiled?"

"Yes, and she hasn't cooked or cleaned since she arrived."

Eliinka worked from before the sun rose until late at night as she traveled to all the major cities and as many towns as possible throughout Pelto. Most were places she had never before visited. Jereni would think this was risky, but Eliinka enjoyed her travels, even though it was winter. She found the ingredients for the balm, suklaa, in the far north. She made a very generous trade of several lengths of beautifully woven fabric with the woman and took her name, Sirka, for future trades. They both left the transaction more than satisfied and Eliinka stowed ten vials of suklaa in her bag.

The people flocked to see her and to listen to her evening harp concerts, where she played a small travel harp and used her gift with a light touch. As far as she could tell, no one suspected her, but only believed they were moved by her music.

Most of the time she ate at a local café or restaurant, enjoying the Pelten food that she didn't get to eat in Viru. But every night she pulled out the round of nightmilk cheese, carved off a slice, and savored each bite.

By the time Eliinka returned to RitVa, it was common knowledge that Viru extended a hand of peace and desired a treaty.

Chapter Forty-Five

~ MY HAND ~

I don't believe we've met." Eliinka stretched out her hand to yet another guest who had come to the banquet held at RakennuTalo, the second largest building in RitVa, the building used for concerts, banquets, and large gatherings. She was moving around the room, mingling, meeting people. This building didn't look large to Eliinka anymore, not after living in Viru. The governor had invited her to this evening's banquet as the guest of honor, Timo had explained. Perhaps, she thought, it was his way to apologize.

The man refused to shake her hand, but he stepped closer. "I am Kettu. I'm glad you came. We need to speak about trade."

Eliinka recognized him now. He was the quiet, narrow-faced man from parliament. She had spoken to them as a group briefly this morning, but Kettu had not said a word at that time.

"I hope we can find common ground in our discussions tomorrow." Eliinka ignored his affront at refusing to shake her hand.

Kettu showed a fake smile. He stepped too close to her, just a breath away, and she stepped back. He did it again. "We do need to speak," he said as he moved too close again and again, guiding her to the side of the room, until Eliinka was fully aware of his intention to speak to her in the shadows.

Her heart raced. They were in a corner, behind a pillar. She looked for her guards.

The background noise almost drowned out Kettu's quiet voice. "I believe you have a hidden agenda. You want to control our government. You appeal to the common man. Already you have Timo. How much do you pay him?"

"This is not the time for accusations. Anyway, you're wrong. We do not pay him. It isn't our goal to control Pelto."

"It isn't? All that Viru does shows that it is."

Her back met the wall. "I need to greet others now," she said, trying to make her strained voice sound confident.

"This is the best time for our discussion. A crowded room allows for greater privacy." Kettu stood too close, his body squared on her. "I know your background. You came to power quickly in Viru. If you give me what I want, I'll smooth your path. I'm powerful. With both Timo and me working for you, you'll walk away with your treaty."

"What is it you want? It must not be in everyone's best interest or you wouldn't discuss it with me in this way." Eliinka tried to step sideways, but he moved within inches of her face and blocked her from leaving by putting his hands on both sides of her.

"Viruns have different values and they'll be a bad influence on Pelto. We should not have any relations with our enemy."

"Then why did you say you wanted to trade with us?" She glared.

"You are from Pelto and will work with me. My father was killed, and his lands were destroyed by Viru. If I control the trade in Pelto, I can regain his lost wealth."

Where were her guards? Only four had come with Eliinka tonight, and they were posted at the doors. The crowds obscured her from their view, so she couldn't signal them.

Kettu laughed, slow and low. "You realize your guards can't always protect you. I will regain my family's status, our wealth. I want exclusive trading rights with Viru. You will help me." His hand opened to a jeweled gold bracelet. "Plus, I'll give you a percentage of all trade value. You would have even more power, wealth, and jewels if we join together and control the trade."

"A bribe?"

"It's not a bribe. It is a token for a contract we will make. I'll give you what we have spoken of and more."

"I'm not sure an exclusive contract is for the best."

His eyes collapsed into slits, and he whispered into her ear. "You'll not be safe unless you agree to work with me. Even your footprints will be in danger. There are ways I can destroy you."

"I'm not afraid of death," Eliinka said. But it was like a drop of cold water fell on her back and dripped down her spine.

Kettu muttered through his narrow lips. "We'll see what you're afraid of. Realize this. No one will believe our conversation tonight. My reputation secures that. You have until the meal ends to change your mind."

"I'm here to do what is best for my people and my queen. I won't deal underhandedly."

"Hm—there's something you fear. It's deep in your eyes. I'll arrange for it, unless you agree to work with me." As he turned to face the crowd, he pointed at the diamond on her right hand, and in a sarcastic voice said, "Enjoy your evening, Princess." He walked away, a pleasant smile curling on his face.

Eliinka was sure her face was pale. Her hands felt cold and clammy, and she tried to shake off her unease as she greeted more people; she struggled to smile as they eagerly met her. All evening while she mingled, she watched Kettu; he always stood so he could see and hear her.

Not soon enough the meal arrived. With relief, Eliinka sat in the seat of honor at the lengthy head table, actually several tables placed end to end, which seated the entire parliament. Governor Tuli sat at her right. Timo chatted with Kettu at the far end.

At her left was a man who tried to tidy his light brown tousled hair. "I'm Kivi, son of Kivi," he said. He reached out and shook her hand, his deep brown eyes surveying her. "I'm from KesKi in the north. I enjoyed what you said today during the meeting, so I requested to be seated next to you. I'd like you to clarify Viru's views?"

He was the only Pelten man without a beard, but as Eliinka looked closer, she realized he was probably only twenty, the youngest council member, and probably couldn't grow a good beard yet. He leaned toward her. "I'm the luckiest man tonight. A beautiful woman sits at my side."

Eliinka smiled. He acted like a typical Pelten man.

The first course, a thick stew, was served. After a brief greeting, the governor ignored Eliinka and conversed with others.

So Eliinka spoke with Kivi. He asked many questions and managed to steer their conversation. Even though she was conscious of this, his easygoing manner made her comfortable. As she tasted the last course, a rich pudding, Kivi pointed to her full glass of wine and asked, "Aren't you going to drink?"

"No. I prefer other drinks."

He shifted his chair closer to hers and touched her arm.

She dropped her spoon.

"You are a fascinating woman." Kivi cupped her left hand inside his hands.

No, not now. Eliinka's heart beat as an uneven drum. It had been so long since she had been touched; she enjoyed the warmth of his hand and his attention. Forwardness such as this, though common in Pelto, was unheard of in Viru. Yet in situations such as this, to refuse the touch would be considered rude. Her hand nestled, hidden, inside his. *I'm not ready. Not yet. He surely doesn't mean to express this much interest in me.* She should pull her hand away, especially as she represented Viru. But the part of her that was Pelten wouldn't let her.

"My markings don't deter you," Eliinka said.

"They are unique, but beautiful."

"They're a token I've given Queen Jereni that express my devotion." Eliinka glanced down the table at Kettu who was still watching her. "Kivi, this is awkward for me." She stuttered, "You . . . you have not released my hand. It seems you desire to claim me."

"How can one claim the heart of a princess? Her heart is already taken by her people."

Eliinka's hand tingled. She had not realized how much she missed a simple touch, and told herself, *I must think straight.* I'm not here for attention, not for love. And what about Zerin? With her other hand, she picked up her goblet and took a drink of her juice, trying to get courage to speak again. "Since you will be so familiar, if I'm to allow you such liberties, you may call me by my name, Eliinka.

"Kivi, I know it is just my hand—but to be blunt, in my land, in Viru, only a husband would dare touch his wife in this manner."

"You don't pull away."

"Well, I should."

As Eliinka started to remove her hand, he tightened his grip. "Wait, I must know for myself." Leaving his left hand under hers, he placed his right hand on top of the diamond.

Power flowed through his skin. Eliinka jerked her hand away. "How dare you be so bold?" He had a gift and used it on her. How dare he? He must have assumed she would not notice it. Now she knew what her mother had meant by not using her gift.

"You have pure intentions! Your motives are for the good of both our peoples." Kivi turned to face her. "It isn't possible. It can't be. You're Virun, but you're one of us. I'm also of Eleman Puusta. I'll support you."

She rubbed her hand, the one she had just removed from his as if she could erase his touch. "Thank you." She safely put both hands on her glass of juice so he couldn't hold her hand again.

"Kivi, I was born and lived most of my life here in RitVa. Pelto has not changed, yet it is not the place I remember."

"You became a Virun after growing up here? I thought it was just a tale that you were born here. You wear a crown. How are you the princess? I assumed you were from Viru."

"It is my path. I work for the good of those who live in both lands." As she said this, she sadly realized Pelto could never again be her home. She could never belong here.

The banquet ended, the dishes were removed, and the dance music started. "Eliinka, you grew up here—do you know the Pelten dances?"

"Yes."

"I assume you will dance with many tonight."

Eliinka tried to hide sadness from entering her voice. "Yes, I'll dance. It's part of my duty."

Kettu still watched her, from where he sat with Timo. Should she agree to work with him? All it would take is one hand motion or a nod of her head, a signal that she wanted to speak with him again. It would make it simple to bring Jereni a treaty.

"May I have the first dance?" Kivi jumped up, helped her with her chair, and grasped her hand. The physical contact that commonly occurred between men and women in Pelto shocked her after being away so long, but her heart leaped as he led her to the cleared floor and they began to dance. The evening would perhaps be enjoyable after all.

The music finished, and Kivi grudgingly allowed another man to take her for the next dance. Later in the evening Eliinka danced with Timo.

"I met Kettu," she said. "He has strong opinions."

"That's true. He is also a good negotiator and likes to bring opposing sides to agreements."

"Is he trustworthy?"

"Kettu is one of the best men in parliament," Timo assured her.

"I don't trust him," Eliinka said. The dance finished before she could say more, but it was as Kettu said. No one would believe her word against his.

During the whole evening, Kivi hovered in Eliinka's vicinity, like a moth near night flowers, and secured two more dances.

Kettu caught her eye once halfway through the evening. She could have danced with him, told him the answer he wanted to hear, but she turned away. Trade with Pelto would help create ties between the two lands. It would be easy if she worked with Kettu, but he did not seem honest. As she danced with other men, she continued to think about Kettu's offer.

Finally, she decided she would not give in to his threats. She waved to him and he approached.

"I'm glad you decided to work with me."

"Viru would be glad to trade with you, but under different terms. An agreement needs to be between our two lands, by treaty. It will be made with the knowledge of parliament and trade will be open to others. My answer is no."

"You have made a choice you will regret." Kettu walked away, not looking back at her.

After another hour of dancing and mingling, the governor came to Eliinka, smiling, friendlier, his hesitations gone. He took her hand. He was drunk.

"If you'd be s'kind t'play a song for us."

Eliinka was not sure if she understood Governor Tuli's slurred words. Would he really ask the honored guest to perform?

"I insist. I want t'hear y'play. The harp. Over there."

Before Eliinka responded, she heard her name announced to everyone in the hall.

"I didn't know you were going to play," Kivi said. She gave him a frustrated look.

He reached her side in two steps, wrapped an arm around her shoulders, and walked her to the front side of the room where the large harp sat. He spoke in her ear. "Everyone wants to hear you play. We've heard of your music. Every single person came that was invited, not only to meet you, but in hopes you'd play for us. This will be a delight."

Eliinka checked the tuning and listened to the harp's tone and response. She considered her opportunity to play for this large group of people, which included essentially all the leaders of Pelto. Because of her time traveling and experiences performing throughout the land, she now knew how to control her gift and play so its influences were subtle. But would it be safe to use her gift, even subtly?

Kettu sat near the front, near Timo and the governor. Eliinka would talk with her guards, and they would take extra precautions as they returned to the villa.

"I'll play a song that springs from the desires of my heart," Eliinka announced. "You will recognize one melody, a common Pelten song, but the other tune is from Viru. When interwoven, these two melodies make a greater piece of music, the same way I believe our two lands working together can enrich our lives. Harmony will bring us greater peace."

She started off with a phrase from the simpler melody of Pelto and followed it with the first line of a folk tune of Viru. Next she combined the two tunes, playing the melodies off each other at times, melding them into a greater melody, always supported by complex harmonies of arpeggios and chords. She looked up and out at the audience. They were moving in time with the music, and one woman in the back was dancing.

Even if Eliinka used her gift for a brief moment, using a touch so light it might be confused with the power of music, it would not be safe to add her gift. Not here. Someone would detect it. So Eliinka only played her pure music, music filled with energy and light—

A small flash of movement flew through the air.

A burning, a fire!

An arrow.

Her right hand pierced.

Automatically, Eliinka reached for the hidden knife in her dress, but stopped. Although her left hand was now accurate, the room was crowded. Pain coursed through her veins, and several men seized her assailant, a man she had never before seen. A quiet buzz ran through the crowd.

Her shock increased tenfold when she glanced down. The arrow shaft speared through her hand. The shaft was red.

Timo and Kivi reached her side. Timo grabbed her, held her steady.

"Help me to another room," Eliinka commanded, "without people."

Two of her guards helped Timo carry her to a small room, just off the hall. They laid her on a carpet.

"I'm glad he missed and that your life is spared," Timo said.

"The arrow didn't miss. He hit what he aimed for." Eliinka removed her crown and handed it to one of her guards. "Put it in my bag."

"Why do you say that?"

"Kettu threatened me, tonight."

Timo and Kivi looked at each other and shook their heads.

"He would never do that," Kivi said.

"Kettu was quite bold. He said, said . . . no one would believe." Eliinka's breath came out uneven, halting. "I need to go . . . to our meeting. Tomorrow. Morning." Her hand! Would she be able to play the harp again?

"There's a healer among the guests," said Timo. "I'll bring him to you."

Kivi stood behind Eliinka, rubbing her shoulders, whispering in her ear, telling her she'd be fine.

The healer rushed into the room. After he opened his bag and pulled out his tools, he cut off one end of the shaft and removed the arrow. When the wood moved, it was like Eliinka's hand ripped apart. She held in her scream. Even though the pain surged in great waves, Eliinka's body seemed disconnected from her mind. She did not flinch as he cleaned the wound. She did not move her hand. The fletchings were yellow.

Like Zerin's! Eliinka realized as she felt a cold chill rush through her veins. Her muscles began to loosen; it felt like they were separating from her bones. It seemed as if she were sinking downward. The men's faces began to fade and became blurry.

"I'm weak. I'm not . . . going to make it." Her voice cracked with pain.

"We'll take you to your villa," Timo said as the healer bandaged her hand. "It's close. You will rest better there."

"I must . . . must give you . . . instructions. Follow them. So Queen Jereni . . . will not destroy . . . Pelto. When I die."

"You won't die," Kivi said.

Eliinka continued to stutter. "Timo . . . the arrow. It looks . . . the same as . . . the one that . . . killed Zerin."

How long had Zerin lasted? Eliinka struggled to breathe. The burning!

"Timo . . . please . . . bury me. Next to . . . Zerin." She would be with him soon. If only Jereni would control her anger and not destroy Pelto.

"Kivi, Eliinka needs more than a normal healer," Timo said. "Meet us at the villa."

Chapter Forty-Six

~ FOREVER ENTANGLED ~

Eliinka struggled to speak. It took enormous effort to form each sentence, to think her thoughts, to say each word.

"Treaty. Timo . . . Peace. Jereni," she said. Her strength ebbed away.

"Shh." Timo said, stroking her cheek. "I'll be your advocate in the meeting. It will be as if you were there."

"Lay me . . . next to . . . Zerin . . . when . . . I die," Eliinka gasped.

Kivi burst through the open door, a young woman at his heels.

She gave Kivi an accusing glance as her chest heaved and she gulped for air. He grabbed her hand and drew her toward Eliinka.

"Eliinka, this is my younger sister, Karelia."

Karelia took a backward step. "She is Virun."

"She's one of us." Kivi grabbed Eliinka's good hand.

"How can a Virun be of our faith?" Karelia crossed her arms.

Eliinka whispered through her now dry mouth. "Light . . . eter . . . nity spans . . . life.'" She closed her eyes and her body shook.

"My . . . my pain . . ."

"Karelia has the gift of healing," Kivi said. He grabbed Karelia's hand and placed it between his and Eliinka's.

Eliinka's eyelids fluttered. She cracked them open.

"Please . . . heal me."

"I touched Eliinka, Karelia. She is pure. Help her." Kivi moved his hand to Eliinka's shoulder.

"I'm so . . . so weak . . ."

Eliinka sank farther into her blankets. She could not fight any longer.

"Zerin, . . . I'll come . . . soon."

Karelia sucked in her cheeks. She touched Eliinka's forehead. "I agree to care for you." She felt the pulse in Eliinka's neck.

"The wound is only in her hand." Timo unwrapped the bandage. "Yet her face turns gray. She can barely speak. Zerin was her husband. He was murdered in the streets during her last visit here. They had only been married a month."

"Why did she come back?" Karelia examined Eliinka's hand.

"She said the arrow looked like the one that killed her husband."

"Her hand is damaged, but not enough for her to be this pale and her breathing this labored." Karelia tore open her bag. "The arrow must be poisoned. Bring me a cup of warm water."

Kivi tightened his grip on Eliinka's shoulder.

"She said she was threatened this very evening," Timo said.

Kettu, Eliinka thought. She wanted to scream his name, but she couldn't force the sound out.

"This powder is an antidote for the most common poison," Karelia said. The chink of a spoon hit the cup again and again. "I hope that's what they used."

Timo lifted Eliinka to a sitting position and poured liquid into her mouth. She gagged on the coarse, pulpy substance.

After laying Eliinka back onto her pillow, Karelia lifted her eyelids and looked into her eyes. "That may not act fast enough. I'll make it more concentrated; perhaps direct contact will help." After a moment, Karelia poured liquid ice through the wound, moistening both sides of Eliinka's hand. "How long did her husband last?"

"Less than an hour, but he was shot in his side, near his heart."

"I might be able to save her. But I work better in solitude."

Timo leaned down, kissed Eliinka on her forehead, and murmured encouraging words into her ear. Though her eyes were closed, she continued to listen.

Kivi said, "Karelia, you must save Eliinka. Tonight could alter the future of Pelto."

"How?"

"With my gift I sensed that if Eliinka dies, her queen's restraint will die and there will be a war beyond what we've learned of in our history books. Pelto will be destroyed. I hope you can save her."

Eliinka fought to stay conscious. Kivi was not certain she would live.

"Timo, her guards? Will they stay?" Karelia asked.

"They will stay."

Karelia huffed, then placed another pillow under Eliinka's head. She forced her cold lips to part and trickled more liquid into the shivering gap. Eliinka struggled to swallow. She choked on each tiny sip.

After cleansing the wound, Karelia immersed Eliinka's hand into a bowl of the antidote mixture. The coolness chilled Eliinka's hand . . . she couldn't move her arm. After a minute, Karelia removed it, patted it dry, and held Eliinka's right wrist between her thumb and middle finger. She placed a hand on Eliinka's forehead.

A warmth, an essence of pure energy, flowed into Eliinka's body.

A guard moved about the room. Logs dropped onto the fire. Light from candles filtered through Eliinka's closed eyelids.

Karelia did not move her hand from Eliinka's forehead.

Though Eliinka fought the sleep that threatened her, though she fought unconsciousness, she could not stay awake any longer.

Eliinka half-opened her eyes.

"Thank the heavens." Karelia breathed a sigh of relief.

"You wouldn't let me pass on," Eliinka accused in a faint whisper, like she was finding her voice. "You held me back."

"It is not your time or I couldn't have kept you here. But part of you still tries to leave. You must live so Pelto can live." Karelia touched Eliinka's forehead, her golden eyes worried. "Trust is part of healing. Will you trust me?"

"I want to trust you. I need to trust you." Eliinka said as she choked on her own breath.

"I can help you heal."

Karelia's face whirled and shifted away.

Unconsciousness battered at Eliinka's mind, finally invading it.

She balanced as if standing on a threshold, which appeared as a field of two colors, one foot on either side. It would be so easy to escape the pains of life. She would see Zerin and her parents soon if she chose the side of white flowers. The sweet smell of joy beckoned. She could have freedom from worry and challenges.

Looking at the other half of the field, the side that was as green as the forest, Eliinka could somehow see Jereni within her room in Jalolinna.

How was this possible? *Am I still alive?*

Eliinka had never entered Jereni's room before, even though it was attached to hers. Not only did a collection of Pelten dresses hang in an open cabinet, but paintings, jewelry, and furniture, all items of Pelto, surrounded Jereni as she sat on her floor, on the only Virun item, a carpet obviously designed and woven by her mother.

Jereni sat in the center of a large blue diamond, in deep meditation. Her arms embraced the token harp. Slowly, she picked out the lullaby, so slow that each note almost died away before she plucked the next note of the melody.

Eliinka sensed Jereni's thoughts reaching into her mind: *Eliinka, please stay here. I need you.*

Could Jereni send her thoughts? It was not possible. Eliinka had never heard of any gift that could do this. It must be her mind imagining this, her mind creating desires and words.

Eliinka edged toward the white flowers. Only take one step and she would journey to peace . . . to belonging.

Eliinka, please, please do not go. Not now. Accept the pain.

A single note, deep and clear, rang from the harp.

Tears poured down Jereni's face. *I invoke my vow of Iankaikki and ask you to wait a moment and consider your choice. The woman who sits beside you has the power to heal you. Please trust her.* Jereni dropped her head with her falling tears as if another force touched her.

The vision of Jereni and the harp withdrew from Eliinka's mind, leaving the words: *I can interfere no more. The choice must be yours and is yours alone.*

The sudden sense of loss was so great that Eliinka turned her back on the white half of the field. It felt as if the dream cracked as glass and the field dissipated like smoke.

With great exertion, she surrendered her hesitations and a near voiceless whisper seeped through her lips. "I'll trust you."

Karelia's fingers exerted a light pressure on Eliinka's head. "I lost you. You went somewhere else." She cupped Eliinka's face and peeled up both eyelids. "Look at me. Keep your eyes open for now. How do you feel?"

"Afraid." Eliinka shivered.

Karelia touched Eliinka's temples with her fingertips, her thumbs meeting just above the bridge of Eliinka's nose. She pressed firmly.

"I'm afraid," Eliinka said.

Karelia glanced at the guards.

"I'm afraid for those who have helped me. I've placed you and Kivi in danger. I'll reward you. I'll try to protect you." Eliinka sucked in a shallow breath. "I choose to live, to experience joy and sorrows, but I'm afraid I'll never play the harp again."

It was like her harp and music were thrown into a roaring bonfire and went up into a chasm of flames—all future notes dissipated into thick smoke.

"I thought I'd sacrificed all I had to offer, but I realize there is more . . . "

Flames crackled in her veins. *No! No!* The loss was so great. She tried to go back to the white field where the pain would cease, but she couldn't find it. She couldn't return.

"I can't feel my hand."

Karelia gently touched Eliinka's right palm, on the front and then the back of her hand, and examined her long, narrow fingers. "Your flesh is torn badly, but nothing is severed." Karelia touched the ring with a diamond shaped outline. "Your ring, is that the seal of Viru?"

"Yes. Karelia, I'm cold."

"So you're truly a princess, a princess of Viru."

"I am."

"I believe I can bring feeling back to your hand. Could you ask your guards to leave while you change? You'll rest more comfortably in other clothes."

Eliinka ordered her guards to leave. They hesitated, but then left the room.

Karelia helped Eliinka sit upright.

"I'm so weak."

"It's the poison. It will take several weeks for you to regain your strength." Karelia helped Eliinka remove her dress. She paused and touched the uppermost scar on Eliinka's back and winced. She shook her head at the faded scar on the front of Eliinka's shoulder. "You have so many scars."

Eliinka spoke to distract herself from her fears. From her loss. "The ones on my back, the scars from the whipping, were ordered by the governor because I struck a man to save our lives."

"The scar on your chest?"

"I stopped an assassination attempt on Jereni."

"Jereni?" Karelia asked as she pulled the nightdress over Eliinka's head and helped pull an arm through the sleeve. She held Eliinka stable, keeping her from falling.

"My queen, the Queen of Viru."

"Yet you were born in Pelto?"

"Yes, here in RitVa. My father was Kallela." Eliinka grabbed Karelia's wrist. "You must know. Jereni saw you. She told me to trust you. Her mother was of Eleman Puusta. Queen Jereni is of our faith."

"That's impossible. No one in Viru is—"

"She is," Eliinka interrupted. She tried to not think of her mangled hand, of the threat of war. "First, we signed a contract, but the contract has been sealed with our blood—" Eliinka showed Karelia her inner arm, "—sealed by the ritual of Vala. She's now my literal sister. At times she is impetuous and rash, but she is good."

"She did this to you?" Karelia ran a finger down the scar. "On purpose? I don't understand."

"I can't move my hand." Eliinka tried to wiggle her fingers.

Karelia prodded Eliinka's hand. "Can you feel anything?"

"No."

"What about here?" Karelia worked her fingers around Eliinka's wrist and lower arm.

"No! No, I can't." Eliinka wanted to scream, to smash her arm, to do something to make her hand feel.

When Eliinka's guards returned, Karelia did not look up, but continued to prod and massage the hand.

"So you have no pain?"

"Not in my hand."

Karelia moved to the base of the bed and grasped Eliinka's closest foot. She put pressure, first in one spot, then in another and another, on the sole of Eliinka's feet and her toes.

Eliinka watched, curious. How did touching her feet affect her hand?

Next Karelia rubbed Eliinka's temples with small circles. "You must relax." She placed her fingers at several points on Eliinka's face.

A warm energy entered her skin.

Karelia used her fingernails to pinpoint selected points on Eliinka's ears. She returned to the feet and repeated her previous pressure techniques.

All of a sudden Eliinka jerked.

"Your hand can feel," Karelia stated while Eliinka knowingly grimaced. "I'll give you a syrup to remove the pain, and then you must rest."

Eliinka sat up, wondering if she preferred the pain to not feeling her hand at all and drank a thick, tasteless liquid from a cup that Karelia held to her mouth.

After she finished the last drop, Karelia asked, "How do you feel now?"

"Weak. There is a sharp burning in my hand. The room is spinning." The syrup was making her dizzy.

"Lie down. That will help."

The room fell beneath her and the ceiling shifted to the side. Eliinka put her good hand on the bed to keep her balance. "Karelia, will I be able to use my fingers again?"

Karelia gripped Eliinka's shoulders and forced her to lie down. She touched each of Eliinka's right fingers in turn. "I hope so. Do the markings on your hands and forearms have meaning?"

"Yes, great meaning. Jereni . . . " Eliinka gasped. "I said I would attend the meeting. I can't miss it!"

"It's the middle of the night. You must rest. The syrup will help you sleep."

"No. No . . . you didn't. Oh, you did. You added a sleep root. Please, I can't sleep through this meeting." Eliinka tried to sit up.

Karelia placed one forearm across Eliinka's chest to hold her down and pulled a blanket over her.

"Please wake me in the morning," Eliinka pleaded. "You must! I need to meet with Pelto's parliament again." She tried to fight off the sleep. She didn't care about the pain as long as it didn't stop her.

"Rest now. I'll wake you and see how you are in the morning. But I must also sleep." Karelia wrapped Eliinka's hand. She touched her forehead. Again, deep energy entered Eliinka's body with a vibrant, flowing sensation. After several minutes Karelia reclined nearby on a cushioned bench.

Karelia shook Eliinka's shoulder. "The sun rises. Do you always sleep with men watching you?" She motioned to the guards

The light entered the window at the low angle of winter sunrise. Eliinka blinked. "Only when I'm in Pelto."

Her hand! Her fingers! The throbbing. What was she going to do?

"Karelia, you now know me. I opened myself to you. Yet I only know your name."

"That's part of your healing process. Yet with this healing, I'm forever entangled by Viru, who casts her web on all who glance her way."

Karelia unwound the bandage. "Move your fingers."

Eliinka could not even make a tiny movement.

"No! My music! My harp!" Eliinka shrieked as she grabbed her right fingers with her left hand and forced them to move. It felt like nails slamming into her flesh. Why? Why had she fought to live? Life wouldn't be worth living now, not without Zerin and now without her harp.

"Stop." Karelia grabbed Eliinka's left hand. "We'll increase your control of your fingers in time. Healing takes time and effort. With my care your hand will heal."

"I'll never be able play again." Eliinka stifled a sob. She wanted to look at her hand, but as she lifted it, Karelia grabbed it and held it down, out of her sight.

"Your hand is damaged, but you were able to wiggle your fingers a little today. You'll be able to move them again." Karelia bandaged Eliinka's hand with a clean, white cloth.

Eliinka sat up, and hunching her shoulders, curled her body over her knees. A deep haunted pain, a pain much deeper than her flesh, festered, and tears beaded in each tear duct. With her left hand she reached for and held tight to Karelia's hand as if holding onto hope itself. "I must go to the meeting this morning! My voice must be heard."

"Can you stand?"

Eliinka ordered her guards to leave the room. She hung her legs over the side of the bed and placed her feet on the floor. Even though the room tipped, she let go of the bed and faked a steadiness she didn't have. She did not dare ask Karelia if she was well enough to attend the meeting. She knew what the answer would be.

"I need help dressing. I'm sorry to ask, but could you help me?" Eliinka took two cautious steps.

After Eliinka was ready for the day, Karelia asked "Would you like more pain medicine?"

"I can hide it no better from you than I can from Jereni." Eliinka lifted her bandaged right hand and turned her palm back and forth. "If it makes me drowsy—no. If it makes me dizzy—no. If it blurs my thoughts—no. And if it puts me to sleep—definitely no."

Karelia chuckled.

Eliinka opened her bag and set her crown on her head.

"I've never seen a crown before." Karelia crossed her arms and leaned against the bed. "It adds color to your eyes. It brings out the gold specks."

"Thanks." Eliinka's hand ached. She clenched her teeth, tightening her jaw.

"You are too stubborn."

Eliinka hobbled to her dress from the previous night and removed the hidden knife. A darting sunray struck the blade, and she placed it into the hidden pocket of her dress.

"You wear a knife?"

"It wasn't useful last night," Eliinka pointed out. She gave Karelia a warm smile. "I can never thank you enough. You must be hungry. Please join me for my morning meal."

Eliinka staggered toward the door. Karelia turned up one side of her smile and linked her arm through Eliinka's left arm and walked her to the kitchen. She no longer showed any hesitation, only acceptance.

What had Karelia seen in her last night? What had Eliinka said to her last night? She did not remember much.

The guards bowed to Eliinka. Next, a guard helped her sit. Another guard pulled out a chair for Karelia, and they set eggs, warm bread, and juice before them.

Karelia ran a finger across her top lip and stared at Eliinka. "How should I address you?"

Eliinka choked on her food. "Call me Eliinka? Just think of this," Eliinka pointed to the crown, "as another piece of jewelry." She stumbled through her morning meal, eating with only one hand.

Karelia ate without comment, even though the Pelten food was prepared in the Virun way, with more spices. After taking her last bite, she leaned back in her chair, juice glass in hand. "Eliinka, you can't go to the meeting. I won't allow it. You can hardly walk. Timo won't allow it either. He should be here any moment. He said he'd come see you on his way there."

"I'll ride my horse."

Karelia tipped her head to the side. "You should stay here, but I doubt you would rest. But your horse must walk, only walk, and walk slowly, and you must have guards at your sides in case you lose your balance and fall."

"Thank you. I'll assign two guards to watch over you and accompany you wherever you choose to go."

Karelia pushed away from the table and her chair scraped loudly on the floor. She exhaled a large flood of air. "I don't need guards, I don't want guards."

"I want you alive. Those who tried to kill me won't be pleased that you saved my life." Eliinka reached out and squeezed Karelia's hand. "Thank you for your healing touch. Please take my men with you if you leave the villa this morning. They'll be discreet. You won't notice them. I'll return at midday."

"What will Kivi say?" Karelia murmured.

Chapter Forty-Seven

~ SENSE HER DETERMINATION ~

The Parliament Room stilled as Eliinka stepped through the door, gripping her guard's arm.

"Lady Eliinka," said Governor Tuli, "we are so sorry about the attack last night."

"Shocking," Kettu said. The anger that had appeared in his eyes smoothed.

"Perhaps not everyone is sorry," Eliinka responded. Everything blurred at the edges of her vision, and she tightened her grip on her guard. She would not collapse. Not here. "Can we come to an agreement?"

"We need more time," Governor Tuli said.

"You always need more time." Eliinka frowned. Would her efforts be a waste?

"We can surely agree on something," Karis, Mikali's friend said. "We could allow for limited trade. We'll only deal with Mikali."

"Mikali is a traitor, marrying that woman," called a man from the left. "We should have no contact with Viruns."

"But trade would bring us wealth," Councilor Gervald said. He dropped his voice, speaking only to the governor, but Eliinka heard his next words. "And information."

As the men discussed a possible trade agreement, she glanced at Kettu. He leaned back in his chair and drew his hand across this throat. A subtle movement. But clear. She had thought she was too hurt to feel fear . . .

"Would you rather not make a simple agreement?" Eliinka asked. "Do you wish me to deliver a message to Queen Jereni? Or should I tell her that Pelto does not want peace? Ever." As she spoke, she wondered whether it was really wise to make a peace of sorts with Pelto, but she was here and would give her best efforts. After this morning she would leave and never again return.

Eliinka expected to walk away, accepting that the differences were too great. Even having a discussion was progress. Better than war.

But she didn't walk away empty-handed. She was surprised. In less than an hour, an agreement was made and signed. It was a simple treaty. Neither land would attack the other. Pelto's parliament would discuss the possibility of holding future negotiations with Viru that could lead to a more extensive treaty. In addition, limited trade would be permitted, but only with Mikali. Both Karis and Kettu had ensured that this clause was included.

A light snow fell in wisps and swirls, coating Eliinka. She swayed, struggling to sit upright as her horse clopped across the cobblestone. When she arrived back at the villa, Karelia rushed out. Her dark brown hair, twisted up on her head, was damp from bathing. Though Eliinka protested, saying she could dismount by herself, Kivi lifted Eliinka from her horse.

Eliinka avoided Karelia's knowing shake of her head as she tried to take a step, and Kivi caught her before she fell to the ground. Karelia folded her arms, frowning. Kivi scooped Eliinka up, carried her into her room, and laid her on the bed.

"Look! I have the treaty." Eliinka's left fingers curled around a rolled parchment.

Karelia's mouth stretched taut. She placed her hand on Eliinka's forehead and ran her fingers down Eliinka's neck to where she felt for her heartbeat.

"I want to return to Viru now. I'll be safe there." Eliinka handed the treaty to her head guard.

"Eliinka, you exerted yourself too much. You must rest." Karelia draped a blanket over her. She cradled the injured hand and after removing the bandage, bent each finger one at a time.

Eliinka took a breath and another and another as her whole body stiffened. She couldn't show any pain or Karelia would insist she not leave. "I'm not very dizzy. I'll begin my journey this afternoon."

"Dizzy? While lying down? That's not good. You can't travel. You can't even support yourself on a horse."

"After a short rest, I'll leave. Today! It's critical that the actual document is placed in Queen Jereni's hands." Eliinka ordered her guards to prepare for the journey.

Karelia shook her head. She continued to probe Eliinka's screaming hand. "You're too weak to travel. I can't let you die on the back of your horse or at a remote campfire. The poison still affects your entire body."

Kivi and Timo hovered too close.

Eliinka wanted more air and space; she wanted out of the room, out of the villa, but told herself to be patient. "Karelia, please help me sleep and when I wake, we'll see how strong I am and if I can travel today."

As soon as Karelia finished mixing the syrup, Eliinka took the cup, tipped the contents into her mouth, and swallowed.

"Take a deep breath and relax." Karelia pressed Eliinka's forehead with her middle three fingers, sliding them to just above Eliinka's temples.

Eliinka relaxed and closed her eyes, knowing that sleep would soon come. More drops, cold and sharp, entered the raw flesh in her right hand.

"Timo, Eliinka doesn't have the strength to travel," Karelia said.

"She should stay until she heals," Timo said.

"No. I need to return to Viru," Eliinka insisted. Her whole body tensed.

"Relax, Eliinka," Karelia said. "You won't be ready in even a week. It will take that long for the poison to work its way out of your system, and it will take even longer, perhaps a month, for you to regain your strength." Karelia talked while bandaging her hand. "Now go to sleep."

Eliinka closed her eyes and breathed deeply. She needed to sleep if she wanted to heal.

A few minutes later they began to talk again, in quiet whispers.

"Nothing will delay her," Kivi said.

"How can she travel?" Karelia snapped. She lowered her voice. "You had to lift her off her horse and carry her. She needs to heal if she wants a chance to play her harp again."

"She doesn't believe that it's possible to play again." Timo stroked Eliinka's brow. "And she's not sure she wants to live, but she wants to return to Queen Jereni."

Eliinka wished they would leave the room and let her rest, but she kept taking long, deep breaths, pretending to be asleep. What would Karelia say about Eliinka's chances to fully heal, to play the harp again? It took effort to listen, to stay awake, especially since the sleeping medicine was beginning to take effect.

"She played last night at the banquet," Kivi said. "Her music is inde-scribable. It was so beautiful . . . I requested to be seated at her side. I touched her hand, and I sensed her determination. Her harp is embedded in her soul." Kivi spun the rings on Eliinka's left hand and brushed each finger. He was bold to touch her hand while he thought she was sleeping, but if she pulled away, he would know she was awake, so she kept her hand limp.

"She isn't scared of death." Karelia removed Eliinka's crown from her head and tucked the blanket around her. "That will make her more com-fortable. She doesn't like wearing the crown anyway."

"Kivi!" Karelia yanked his hand away from where he still caressed Eliinka's. "Would she allow you to touch her that way if she were awake? Remember she's from Viru."

Timo laughed. "Eliinka has more of Pelto in her than she will admit. She allowed Kivi to hold her hand at the dinner, in front of everyone. They don't touch in that way in Viru." Timo paused, then said, "I wonder how my daughter is doing."

"Your daughter?" Kivi asked.

"My daughter, Toivo, has been living under Eliinka's care in Jalolinna to learn the language and Virun culture." Timo sounded thoughtful, ques-tioning. "Let's go to the kitchen and eat our midday meal."

Throbbing drummed in Eliinka's right hand. It felt like shards of ice nee-dles pierced it. She opened her eyes and clenched her jaw, fighting the pain away with pure willpower. She would not ask for more of that drink.

Karelia, sitting in a chair at Eliinka's right, had collapsed in exhaus-tion onto the edge of Eliinka's bed. She shifted in a troubled, uncomfort-able sleep.

A guard added wood to the fire, and the last light of day succumbed to the first dark of night. The sun set early this time of year. Eliinka had slept all afternoon, longer than she wanted. It was too late to leave today.

Karelia breathed heavily, and in her sleep lifted her head, laying it down, this time on her right cheek, her face now in the direction of Eliinka. Her long, dark eyelashes fluttered as though she experienced an unsettling dream. Her pronounced cheekbones, slightly long nose and dark-pink lips created a picture that would draw most men's attention. Her dark brown hair had fallen out of its clips and fell in intense waves to the middle of her back.

Street lamps cast their muted glow through the dark window, and a light snow fell, amplifying their light. Eliinka slid out of bed, careful to not disturb Karelia. After she murmured a quiet command, her guards left the room. She did not need them in here with her.

Eliinka took three small steps, settled in a chair in front of the warming fire, and unwound the white bandage. She had not seen her right hand since she had seen both ends of the arrow shaft piercing its center.

It was time.

She closed her eyes as the last wind of white fell from her flesh and extended her hand in front of her, palm to the fire. After a deep breath, wondering if she truly wanted to see her hand, she opened her eyes. She clamped her jaw shut, holding in her scream.

The wound was centered in the blue diamond.

Eliinka dropped her injured hand to her lap, flipping it over to see her palm. Beginning with her smallest finger, she squeezed the lowest joint, and glided her firm, pinching touch down each finger, to the nail. She forced each finger to bend, pulling her lips between her teeth to suppress her gasps.

There was no way she would ever be able to play her harp again! Why had she chosen to live?

Her stomach rumbled, reminding Eliinka that she had missed the midday meal. She doubted she would be able to walk to the kitchen on her own. She leaned back in the chair. No bread or other food sat on the table in front of the fire. Perhaps they assumed Karelia would be serving her. She should have asked her guards to bring her food before sending them out earlier. But she wouldn't call them, not for this.

Yet she did have food with her, the round of nightmilk cheese. Eliinka slowly stood and held onto the chair, another chair, and the bed as she walked to her bag where she pulled out a large package. She slowly returned with it to the chair in front of the fire. She reached into her dress for her knife.

Gone.

Karelia! She was the only one here that knew of her knife.

Eliinka scanned the room and gave a slight laugh when she saw her crown and knife sitting on the side table. With faltering steps she struggled to the table, picked up her knife, and sat again in front of the fire. She sliced downward on the cheese and it tipped over. It was not possible to cut the nightmilk cheese with one hand, not when this unsteady, so she leaned her head against the back of the chair and let out a deep sigh, lightening her grip on the knife handle. Eliinka could not remember the last time she had gone a day without nightmilk. Although her stomach complained—and not just from missing the midday meal—and her mind screamed, she would wait for Karelia to wake.

Eliinka thought over the past day and remembered Karelia's words: She must live so Pelto could live. Karelia had looked past her prejudice and found the compassion to heal Eliinka, a foreign stranger. Though she couldn't wait to return to Viru, a piece of her longed to stay in Pelto. It would always be the land of her birth, the place where Zerin rested. Part of Pelto would always be in her heart. Unless someone managed to kill her before she returned, she would keep hoping that the two lands could reach a true, lasting peace.

The logs slowly burned down until one broke and fell onto the hearth. The flames crackled. Karelia woke with a sudden jerk.

"I hope you enjoyed your much needed sleep."

Karelia pushed her body up from the empty bed, rubbing her eyes, sweeping the sleepiness away.

"Would you cut my cheese, Karelia? I tried, but . . . " With a practiced flip, Eliinka reversed the knife in her left hand and handed it to Karelia, who accepted it without hesitation. She examined the blade, and Eliinka said, "It's clean. I've only used it on food."

Still not saying a word, Karelia cut a paper-thin slice of nightmilk cheese and handed it to Eliinka.

She chewed slowly, savoring the deep earthy flavor, reaching through her memories. Jereni's words came back. "Life is more than music." Was she correct? Could she live without ever playing her token harp again?

"Where are your guards?" Karelia cut another sliver from the cheese.

"One is just outside the door; another is standing outside, under the window. There are other guards that walk the perimeter. They've been extra vigilant after the attack." Eliinka ate another piece of cheese. "Your hair is down. It's very beautiful."

"I only let it down when I'm inside." Karelia placed the knife on the table, next to the cheese. "You removed the bandage," she said, picking up Eliinka's injured hand and moving her fingers back and forth.

"That hurts."

"Pain is part of healing." Karelia stopped moving Eliinka's fingers, but did not release her grip. "You may have more of the syrup if you wish."

Eliinka shook her head. "I want to be awake to eat my evening meal. Later this evening, right before I go to sleep, I'll drink more. There's a white powder for pain that we use in Viru. It takes the edge away and gives fewer side effects. I prefer it. I'll send you a large supply to use in your healing. But first, I must return. Go ahead. You believe this will help."

While Karelia manipulated Eliinka's fingers, Eliinka breathed deeply and imagined her music, playing each note, each phrase, each melody, and harmony.

"How do you control your pain so well?" Karelia put more gold droplets into the flesh. "You acted like I wasn't touching your hand."

"I play my music in my mind." Eliinka's voice shook slightly. "Karelia, I still wish to depart soon—tomorrow morning. What do you think? Please say I can travel. I should return to Queen Jereni as soon as possible and deliver the treaty into her hands."

Eliinka dragged the fingers of her bandaged right hand from the circle on her left forearm to trace the diamond on her left hand. "The man responsible for the arrow was angry to see me today."

Eliinka motioned Karelia closer. "Today Kettu drew his finger across his throat when I glanced at him. No one else saw it, and there is no way I can prove he threatened me or that he is responsible for this." She lifted her hand. "He can't kill me if I'm in Viru. I need to return to protect the peace between the two lands. I must return to protect Pelto. Today, if possible. My murder would anger Jereni, and she would declare war."

Karelia's forehead wrinkled. "Don't worry. Your guards will protect you." But her body tensed, unable to hide her concern. She pointed to Eliinka's forearms. "Queen Jereni gave you those lines. You started, but never finished telling me the meaning."

Eliinka didn't remember Karelia asking about her arms, but she didn't remember much from the previous night. "These lines are a symbol of the interweaving of my life and Queen Jereni's life, forever. Queen Jereni is the blue diamond."

"Our lives are also intertwined," Karelia said.

"That's right. You saved my life."

Karelia knelt in front of Eliinka. She pointed to the left wrist and undamaged hand. "May I?" Eliinka nodded, and Karelia ran her fingers along the blue lines, tracing each individual strand as if she searched below the skin. She turned Eliinka's arm over to the white scar.

Suddenly, Karelia stood. She glared at the fire, pressing her fingertips into each other, flexing them taut. Gray gases rose from the flames, the wood disappearing into a mist. Suddenly the fingers of her right hand clenched. She turned to face Eliinka and wiped a tear from her cheek. "I know you want to leave today, but you should wait at least a week to travel."

Eliinka stopped breathing.

Even with her guards, she wasn't safe here. Even if she couldn't play her token harp, she still wanted to return and have it nearby. If needed, she would order her guards to carry her back. She needed to leave! Now!

"I can't wait. Not that long. I—"

"But you would be able to ride tomorrow—if you have help. I've decided. I'll come with you—I'll sit behind you on your horse. It's important for you to return soon. It will take me at least a month to heal your hand so you can play the harp again."

"Thank you, Karelia. You'd do that for me?" Eliinka rose too quickly from her chair, but regained her balance before she fell. There was a chance she might play again!

Eliinka caught Karelia in the embrace of Viru and kissed her on both cheeks. "Thank you! Can Kivi pack for you? You won't need much. I'll supply you with new clothing and anything you need during your stay." She released a stiff Karelia from her embrace. "Do you truly believe you can restore my hand?"

"Your hand will be able to regain most of its dexterity. But your speed for touching the harp strings might not be as rapid."

Eliinka pulled out her travel harp and ran her left hand over the strings, picking an occasional note with her left pointer finger.

"It will take time," Karelia said, "and much effort from both of us."

Snowflakes landed in Eliinka's hair. Karelia stood at her side, wearing a new fur-lined cloak and new, knee-high, fur-lined boots, both supplied by Eliinka.

"Thank you so much for bringing Karelia to heal me." Eliinka reached out and shook Kivi's hand, but pulled back when his eyes lit up. She did not mean to encourage him. "She's the reason I'm alive."

"Must you leave this morning?" Timo asked.

"Promise me you'll come next month." Eliinka gave Timo a hug. "Toivo will be so happy to see you. You'll be amazed at all she's learned."

"I'll come as soon as I can, Eliinka."

Kivi was arguing with Karelia on the far side of the yard.

"I'm proud of your bravery," Timo said.

"I did not fully succeed at making a complete peace. Jereni may never fulfill her dream of visiting Pelto."

"Yet you achieved much. What should have been impossible, you have done. Your deeds are like those in the legends, like in the old books." Timo scratched his temple. "Safe travels, Lady Eliinka." He bowed low.

Kivi rushed up to them. "I'm coming with you." His smile spread over his entire face. He rested his hand on Eliinka's shoulder. "I'll catch you on the road before the midday meal."

"Queen Jereni will be delighted to meet another member of parliament."

Kivi kissed Eliinka's cheek.

This was awkward. No man had ever kissed her, except Zerin. Eliinka turned away to her horse, sure her face had turned red. She shouldn't allow his kisses; he wasn't who she wanted. She wanted Zerin back.

Still, she allowed Kivi to lift her into the saddle. Karelia mounted behind Eliinka, reached her hands around to the front, grasping the reins. "Queen Jereni needs you to arrive safely, so we will rest as often as needed. Let me know as soon as you feel sick or dizzy."

Chapter Forty-Eight

"Do you always travel this fast?" Karelia asked. They sat in the muted, predawn light, in the relative comfort of the tent. The snow had stopped falling, and a brazier sat near them, emanating heat and the sweet scent of rich wood.

"Usually we ride faster. I'm slowing us down," Eliinka answered, wishing she were already back in Jalolinna.

Karelia massaged and manipulated Eliinka's fingers and hand, like she did every morning and evening. She also sliced the cheese every night with Eliinka's knife, in her perfect, paper-thin slices. Once, she smelled it and wrinkled her nose, but she never asked for a taste.

"It will take us two additional days at this speed."

The previous afternoon, Karelia had stared at the roiling ice in the river, but had not said a word when they reached the crossing. She had not flinched when they had removed their boots and forded the river, laden with ice chunks. Karelia avoided talking about herself, so Eliinka knew essentially nothing about her, but Eliinka knew she needed to know more for her report to Jereni.

There was one way. Eliinka told herself it would be a sincere gesture, and as she searched inside her feelings and thoughts, knew that she was not deceiving herself.

"Karelia, will you be my friend, forever?" Substituting her left hand instead of her right, Eliinka extended her hand in the Pelten ritual of friendship, palm up, thumb and fifth finger stretched wide. She needed friends in Pelto as well as Viru.

"You offer the unbreakable vow of friendship." Karelia stared at Eliinka's hand. "You don't even know me."

"But you know me. Karelia, even if you don't accept at this time, my hand is always extended to you, and I promise that I will forever be your devoted friend."

For a moment their eyes met, Karelia's contemplative. But the sound of pounding hooves, which grew louder and louder until it sounded like the tent was going to be trampled, interrupted. Karelia set down Eliinka's injured hand and opened the tent door to the heavy breathing of horses that had run too far and too hard. "It's Timo and one of your guards," Karelia said. She pulled Eliinka's boots onto her feet for her, placed Eliinka's cloak over her shoulders, and helped her stand.

"Thank you, Karelia." Frustrated, Eliinka gripped Karelia's arm with her left hand. Her strength was returning much slower than she had anticipated, slower than her recovery from other injuries, and this journey did not help. She actually was weaker today.

"I must speak with Eliinka! Now!" Timo's voice rose above the camp.

Karelia helped Eliinka through the door of the tent, supporting her as they walked.

"I came as fast as I could," Timo said. "I must speak with you."

"I thought you weren't coming for a month."

Timo bowed to Eliinka, his face stretched tight like a bow. "Allow me to speak to you. Alone." He hooked Eliinka's elbow and holding tight, half walked, half carried her outside the camp. The cold nipped at her face, neck, and hands.

Timo stopped. He held Eliinka up by her shoulders. "I didn't get here in time. What have you done?"

"What? What have I done?"

"You don't know? You have acted innocently?"

"What are you saying? What did I do? Timo, I've no strength to do anything."

Timo let go. He frowned.

Eliinka grabbed for his cloak as she fell.

He caught her and lowered her to the snow-covered ground.

"Timo, I can't even stand on my own. I should've stayed longer in RitVa." Eliinka pulled her cloak tighter around her shoulders as she held back her tears. She couldn't take the medicine that made her sleep and also travel. Yet when she didn't take the medicine, pain stacked on top of pain until she could barely ride.

"You really don't know. Haven't you heard the tale, the folklore of the crossing?"

"What crossing?"

"The river crossing."

Eliinka shook her head.

Timo sat on the crunchy snow and grabbed Eliinka's good hand. "Queen Jereni would have told you if it were true. She would have warned you."

"Warned me of what?"

"I doubted its truth. I still doubt, but after you left, I searched for an old book, for a story I have heard told. I found it. I read the tale of the crossing."

Eliinka's breath formed a little cloud in the frigid air.

"I wondered when Toivo did not want to come home, and even more when I heard that Rakel had returned to Viru."

"Timo, what tale?"

"It tells of those who cross into Viru with a person of royal blood. Somehow, their hearts are changed and they are forever connected to Viru. They can leave, but must always return."

Eliinka's voice squeaked like an old hinge. "This can't be true, can it?" Her volume increased. "And you sent Toivo with me, having heard of this tale? And Karelia and Kivi crossed with me. If it is true—what have I done?"

"There is more. The story says that the change in the heart becomes permanent if they eat or drink a special item. It doesn't say what it is, but there is a special food reserved only for the royal family. Surely Queen Jereni would never feed it to Toivo, if this food exists."

The cold from the ground rushed upward through Eliinka's clothing, into her bones. She tried to pull her hand away from Timo's, but he held tight. Back at the campsite, Karelia stood under a tree, watching from a polite distance, waiting.

"Please forgive me. I shared this food, a very special cheese, with Toivo on our journey. Our travels were very challenging. I didn't know."

Timo dropped Eliinka's hand.

Her heart sunk.

He took a couple steps into the trees and peered into the whitened forest. He scraped his hand up and down the rough bark of the nearest tree and pulled off a strip, rubbing it between his fingers until it shredded into pieces, which he let fall to the ground.

"Maybe the stories aren't true." Eliinka scooped up a handful of snow. Crushed snowflakes slipped through her fingertips. Her voice curled upward like the smoke of a small, dying campfire. "Maybe it's just folklore, another of the many stories about Viru."

Timo stared into the woods. "All folklore, all myth, all legend, all stories began from a truth somewhere, sometime."

Eliinka crumpled like a lost child. She pushed away from the ground with her good arm and lifted her head. Timo bent down, brushed the snow from her face and hair and lifted her limp body. "It is done. We must return to Pelto. We will cross the Urho River. You will take me over the crossing. You will connect me to Viru."

"No! I can't. I refuse to take anyone across again."

Timo carried Eliinka back into the camp, and immediately he lifted her into the saddle of his still-foaming horse. "Tell your men that we'll return within an hour."

"This isn't necessary, Timo."

"Please. For me. For Toivo."

Karelia supported Eliinka, holding her by the waist. Bitter air froze inside Eliinka's lungs and nose. *Can I even ride as far as the river?* she thought.

The head guard approached her side, his hand on his sword.

"It is fine," Eliinka snapped at him. "I'll return shortly. Build up the fire."

He bowed and gave a command. Two guards added several large logs to the small morning fire.

Timo removed the boots from Eliinka's feet and handed them to Karelia. She squeezed Eliinka's good hand.

The cold air sliced at Eliinka's bare skin the way the tale had sliced into her heart. Her lips quivered. "Karelia, I'll be fine. Everything will be fine, I hope."

Timo swung his leg up over his horse and landed behind Eliinka. He urged the horse into a gallop toward Pelto. Two guards leaped onto their horses and followed.

They forded the river as stripes of pink sunrise exploded into a brilliant blue. The icy liquid bit at Eliinka's feet and calves. The water nipped her knees. Timo lifted Eliinka from his horse and set her for a brief moment on the earth of Pelto. The snow burned her nearly numb feet.

He lifted her again to his horse and they crossed the river, back into Viru. When they reached the Virun shore, Timo dismounted and dried her bare skin. He placed a blanket on her lap and wrapped it around her feet and lower legs.

Eliinka shivered, not only from the cold, but from the knowledge of what she had just knowingly done. The tale—was it true?

They galloped back to camp, not stopping until they were on top of the roaring fire. Timo carried Eliinka from his horse and placed her onto a waiting fur, positioning her so her now blue feet and frozen legs faced the flames. Though she was shivering, Eliinka couldn't sense the cold anymore; instead, she felt an odd warmth. Kivi placed several blankets behind her back, helped her recline, and sat at her side.

Karelia draped a heavy fur blanket over Eliinka. She scowled at Timo. "Her lips are blue. She is too cold. It's your fault if she has frostbite." She handed Eliinka a mug of warm liquid the color of light blue.

Eliinka's good fingers were stiff. Because she could not grasp the mug, Karelia lifted it to Eliinka's lips and encouraged her to sip. Eliinka did not dare ask what she drank. Her arms, legs, and lips all shook uncontrollably.

"I should learn to speak Virjalo," Timo said, "since I will be visiting Viru often."

"I'll teach you . . ." Eliinka's halting words were even difficult for her to understand through her chattering teeth.

Karelia tucked Eliinka's hands under the blanket as she glared at the men. Her eyes were like two small flames at the end of a dark tunnel. She checked Eliinka's pulse. "Even her neck is as ice. Eliinka is now unable to travel today. You are hampering her recovery. Kivi, bring fresh coals for our brazier. She'll rest in the tent. It's warmer there."

Eliinka flashed Timo a tilted smile while Karelia bent over, grasped Eliinka's good hand, and helped her stand. Timo carried her into the entrance of the tent.

In the depths of the tent, her arms wrapped around her bent knees, Eliinka felt as if she dangled in the hollow of a giant cavern. She did not like the aftertaste of the flavorless syrup that Karelia had insisted she drink the moment they had entered the tent earlier in the day. It always knocked her into a deep sleep for several hours after it landed heavily in her stomach. And she was sure Karelia would insist that she take it again before bed tonight. Even though the sleep and rest helped, she was tired of lying down. She was tired of sleeping. She was tired of the exhausted, weak feeling she could not shake. Also, she dreaded the thought of going out into the cold again.

Karelia sat with crossed legs and folded arms, her face closed and unreadable. Her hair was loose, falling down her back, just combed and damp. She must have bathed while Eliinka slept.

Eliinka turned to her bag to sort through everything. She set the cheese aside, inhaling the earthy sweet smell. She'd eat a slice soon. Next she placed the travel harp on her lap and plucked a short tune with her left hand, wishing it were her token harp instead. "I can't thank you enough, Karelia."

"I hope Queen Jereni is pleased." Karelia's lips narrowed. "I hope your safe return will keep her from attacking Pelto."

Eliinka pulled more items from her travel bag: a leather knife pouch, the fabric-lined box that held the crown, and the vials of suklaa. "These are for Queen Jereni. We want to make more healing balm. I traded several lengths of fabric for them." She pulled out the remaining fabric. "Our weavers are very talented." She handed the length of cloth to Karelia who unfolded her arms to run her fingers over the fine weave. Eliinka pulled out a purse of coins, which rang as they struck each other; a cylindrical leather case that protected the treaty; the flute; and the leather bag that held the stones.

Memories soared through Eliinka's veins as she held the flute. "Maybe if I play the flute, the people who live here in the wilderness will come tonight and play for us."

Karelia lifted her eyebrows.

"I can't describe the sound of a hundred flutes blowing through the trees." Eliinka shifted her position. The stones spilled from their bag onto her bedding. Awkwardly, she picked up the shimmering stones with her left hand and started to drop them back into the bag.

"Stop." Karelia's voice sounded excited. "Where did you get those?" She spoke with the slight tension of a low harp string. The thinness of her mouth had returned to its normal oval shape.

"The people who live in this region gave them to me with the flute. But I don't know what they are."

Karelia leaned closer to the translucent stones. "I've only read about these stones. They're called hlithklettr. And you have four! They are more than rare. I've never heard of anyone that has even seen one. Everyone I've heard speak of them refers to hlithklettr as archaic, non-existent stones, only found in legends and folklore—" Karelia curled up the corners of her mouth, "—somewhat like your cheese."

"Karelia, I need to tell you about my cheese."

"The manuscripts speak of hlithklettr as real." Karelia slid even closer to Eliinka, and she stared at them, her golden eyes larger than normal.

Eliinka held out her open hand, the hlithklettr glimmering. "But they don't do anything. They're just pretty, like gems."

"Have you ever heard of them?"

"No."

"Believe me. They're much more than pretty. For instance, one will light this tent."

Eliinka set three hlithklettr down and held the other one in her hand. Ignoring the complaints of her fingers, she cupped her hands around it and peered through a crack into the hollow her hands made. "It doesn't glow."

"Have you ever looked at them after the sun sets?"

Eliinka shook her head "no."

"That's when they'll emit light. The tales say they'll give light for whatever size hall they're placed in."

"That's useful." Eliinka wondered if the stones would really do so, but didn't express her doubts.

"The tales also say they can strengthen the owner."

Eliinka picked up the other three stones and held all four in her left palm.

"Karelia." Eliinka saw so many thoughts dashing though Karelia's expression that it seemed impossible she could process them all. "Give me your hand." Karelia stretched out her hand, and Eliinka placed two of the hlithklettr into her shocked palm. "I'll keep one for me and one for Queen Jereni. The other two are yours. When you find out how they work, you can teach us."

Karelia looked through a stone toward the tent wall, in the direction of the shielded setting sun. She gave Eliinka a real smile. "Thank you. Maybe these will help heal your hand."

Eliinka carefully replaced the other two stones into the pouch, wondering, doubting.

"Few have heard of the power of the crossing." Karelia caught Eliinka's left wrist and slid to where their knees touched. She tightened her grip. "But you should know this, as a princess of Viru. You were never taught?"

"Today is the first I've heard of it. I don't know whether to believe Timo's words. Wait." Eliinka stared at Karelia. "How did you hear? Do you believe in the crossing?"

"Timo, he believes."

"If it's true, if the legends are true, I'm so sorry. I wouldn't have allowed you to come if I'd known." A chilly breeze blew through a tent seam.

Karelia released Eliinka's wrist and rested her fingers on the back of Eliinka's hand, on the blue diamond. "I had read that some people received markings. It seems all the tales are true." She rubbed both hlithklettr between her fingers. "I'm sorry it hurts, but it's time to exercise your fingers again."

Chapter Forty-Nine

~ FEARLESS PRINCESS OF THE LEGENDS ~

An icy breeze blew up under Eliinka's cloak and she shivered. Tendrils of morning fog curled around the bare trees, and they continued downhill on the narrow trail that wound between tall, angular rocks. The Syrjassa Mountains in Viru were rugged and wild, and they now had to ride single file. Several guards rode in front of her and the rest rode behind. All of them were anxious to return to Jalolinna. Yesterday they had not traveled, and she had rested. In two or three nights she hoped to sleep in her own bed.

A branch cracked loud at her left and Eliinka jerked toward the sound. Suddenly, two men yanked hard on the bridle, one on each side, and Eliinka's horse came to a halt. Cold steel pricked Eliinka just below her left jaw in the flesh of her upper neck.

She froze.

The large Pelten man glared at her.

We are in Viru. This is an act of war, Eliinka thought angrily.

A voice in broken, heavily accented Virjalo yelled, "No one move or the woman dies." Karelia leaned forward. Her thighs compressed inward on Eliinka's hips.

Eliinka's men halted their horses.

They were fools to attack. It was especially brazen to do so after she had entered Viru. If she played this well, she and all her men would survive. It would be harder with her injured hand, but that gave her the advantage. They wouldn't suspect she would fight back.

"Princess." A mid-sized man spat out the words as if a bug had flown into his mouth. He was dressed in the upper class clothes of an aristocrat and spoke in Pelten. "Forty men have you surrounded. Surrender the treaty. We'll take you and this traitor who sits behind you to ensure your queen will comply with our demands. If you cooperate with us, we'll spare your men."

"If you'll spare my men," Eliinka said. Only my men, he was inferring. She leaned backward, away from the sword, bumping her head into Karelia's. "I'll get the treaty from my saddlebag. Karelia, help me down." The man pulled his sword a hand length back.

As Karelia stiffly dismounted, Eliinka flashed a hand signal to the guards closest to her. "We'll move to that tree," Eliinka whispered through closed lips as Karelia lifted her from the horse.

The man lowered the sword slightly, still pointing it toward Eliinka.

She lifted the flap, removed the flute, and rummaged through the compartments in her saddlebag. Suddenly, as she shoved Karelia away, Eliinka pulled her knife from its hidden skirt pocket, and with her left hand released it in a smooth throw. It sliced an upward arc through the air.

The man jerked backward, the knife embedded in his severed breathing passage. He dropped the sword, and his hands went to the knife in his throat.

"Now!" Eliinka yelled in Virjalo. She grabbed a leather pouch from the saddlebag.

Karelia dragged Eliinka to the more protected location of a tree. Eliinka fumbled with the pouch. As soon as she had it open, she yanked out a throwing knife with her left hand and dropped the pouch to the ground. The other man holding the bridle rounded the front of her horse. Her knife hit him square in the chest.

He grabbed for the horse's saddle, but fell down under the hooves.

"Karelia, grab a stick, rocks, anything you can use as a weapon." With her uninjured hand, Eliinka held the flute to her lips and played a long single note, a shrill cry of desperation, a call for help.

Karelia stumbled backward. Her back hit the tree, and she froze. Eliinka ignored her stare and put the flute again to her lips. She repeated the wailing call.

The dense brush and winding trail made it hard to see far. Sword clanged against sword. Men yelled. The guards that had been riding immediately in front and behind Eliinka were off their horses, each fighting several men.

"Can we win? They are so many," Karelia said through her clasped teeth.

"We must!" Her twenty guards against forty men? Eliinka spread the remaining throwing knives from the pouch onto the crusted snow and sat back on her heels, ready.

One of the attackers broke through and came at a run toward Eliinka. She threw a knife with her practiced left hand, and he went down. One of her guards swung his sword at the fallen attacker, ensuring he would not rise again.

Again, Eliinka put her flute to her lips, and as she blew, several Flute People bounded in front of her. They formed a protective circle around Eliinka, their staffs and knives ready. Over a hundred people that lived in the wilderness flowed through the rocks and shrubs and joined in the combat.

"We have the advantage now, Karelia. The battle will be over soon."

Karelia faced the tree. Her shoulders shook and her choppy breathing broke up her words. "Eliinka, Kivi only carried a knife." She gulped in air between half sobs and sank to her knees, covering her face with her hands.

"We can only wait and hope for the best," Eliinka said.

The sounds of battle slowed, and Huoli pushed past the Flute People.

"It is over." Huoli bowed to Eliinka.

Kivi ran up to Karelia and hugged her. "Thank goodness you're safe."

"Your arm? What happened?" Karelia asked as she stretched out his arm. Blood dripped from the back of his forearm. A cut stretched from his elbow to his wrist.

"Got nicked by a sword. Not much more than a scratch." Kivi turned to Eliinka. "Princess? Do you need any help?"

"I'm fine."

Am I really fine? Eliinka wondered. More men had died at her hands. She never wanted to be in a position where she needed to fight for her life again.

"Karelia should bandage your arm, Kivi."

"Huoli, bring our wounded here, if they can be moved." Eliinka gave her orders in rapid Virjalo. "Karelia will care for them. Count the dead of the enemy. Their leader said he had forty men. Hunt down any who escaped."

"I'm fine," Kivi said. "Others need help first." He dashed away with Huoli.

"You speak Virjalo extremely well." Karelia handed the pouch to Eliinka. A bitter tone, a jagged voice interjected her sobs. "Why did Queen Jereni place you in such peril for a peace that may never take hold, which many people don't want? We could've died." Her head sagged.

"I'll tell you about Queen Jereni. Her mother was a woman from Pelto, kidnapped by the prince of Viru when she was about our age. Prince Juusi so appreciated her beauty and bravery that he took her as his wife.

Because of her mother, Queen Jereni has always dreamed of peace with Pelto. Queen Jereni married Mikali, a Pelten man. She wishes for all to freely travel between Pelto and Viru. Queen Jereni deeply loves Pelto."

"Peace is a dream. A dream few want." Karelia dropped her head. Her jaw trembled as if she were stopping herself from crying.

"Calm down." Eliinka gripped Karelia's shoulder. "Prepare your healing supplies. You must be ready for the wounded."

When Karelia retrieved her bag from the horse, she had to step around the fallen attacker. She turned a sick gray-green, but straightened her shoulders and removed Eliinka's jeweled dagger from the man's throat. She wiped it clean on the reddening snow, poured water on the blade, and returned it to Eliinka.

"You killed three men." Her detached voice hung in the air between them.

"Don't count." Eliinka leaned against the tree. She took a deep breath and said, "It's hard for me to deal with my feelings of guilt."

Karelia stepped backward. "You imply this is not the first time."

"No, it isn't." Eliinka stabbed her knife into the tree and seized Karelia's shoulders. Her voice fell flat. "The others were also either in defense of my life or Queen Jereni's life. You saw the scar of one of those encounters. I almost died that night."

Karelia's whole body shook under Eliinka's hand.

"These men would have abused us—and they would have killed us if we went with them. Never trust a man who holds a sword to your throat. I only did what was necessary."

Karelia nodded. Her face flooded a washed-over gray-white. She dashed behind the tree and Eliinka heard heaving sounds. In a minute, she slowly emerged, keeping her face down as she sat on the tree roots and placed her elbows on her knees. She stared at the ground.

Eliinka removed her knife from the tree and cleaned it again. When satisfied, she slipped it back into its sheath in her hidden pocket. She sat at Karelia's side, her useless right hand relaxed. "It's understandable to mourn for the death of anyone."

Silence stretched between them.

Finally, Karelia whispered, "You are the fearless princess of the legends."

The past two years passed through Eliinka's thoughts: Her lonely life in that small room in Pelto. That time after her parents had died where she had struggled to make enough money to buy food, the time when she did not belong anywhere. Coming to Viru, where everything was different and she only had her music to cling to. Falling in love with Zerin, their time together, and now . . . though her role wasn't what she wanted, what Karelia said about how she had become like the princess of the legends was true.

"That is what I've become."

With her left hand, Eliinka again extended the Pelten hand of friendship. "Do not refuse me. Please. Karelia, please be my friend."

Eliinka kept her hand in the air, waiting. Karelia stared at it, then closed her eyes like she was thinking.

Finally Karelia opened her eyes and grasped Eliinka's hand. They interlocked their thumbs and small fingers as their three middle fingers touched each other's wrist. Their voices blended in unison. "Forever."

Chapter Fifty
~ THE ANCIENT WORD ~

I*wish I could play the token harp*, Eliinka thought as she gripped the reins with her left hand, waiting. But how could she without the use of her right hand? Only an hour earlier, she had urged her horse into a trot when the palace, stretching high above the city, came within her sight. Now she sat on his back in the center of the courtyard, listening to the other horses' hooves clip across the stones, unable to dismount. She was more drained by the short ride than she had anticipated.

Kivi bounded off his horse. Even though Eliinka waved him off, he lifted Eliinka and set her on the ground.

Karelia appeared at Eliinka's other side, shaking her head. "Because you chose to ride alone, you now need help to walk."

"I can walk on my own," Eliinka said as opened the saddlebag and pulled out the parchment.

"No," Karelia said. "You don't have the strength."

"Eliinka!" Jereni ran across the courtyard. She wrapped her arms around Eliinka—her pregnancy made the hug awkward. "You've returned! Your hand, it's injured."

"I have the treaty!"

Jereni released Eliinka. All in the courtyard rose from their bows. When Jereni took a step back, leaving Eliinka unbalanced, Karelia grabbed onto her.

"Eliinka, introduce me to your companions," Jereni said in her perfect Pelten.

"Queen Jereni, I would like to present Karelia to you." Eliinka motioned to Karelia.

"Welcome, Karelia." Jereni greeted her with a smile.

"And this is Kivi, Karelia's brother. He's a parliament member."

"Welcome, Kivi. May you enjoy your time with us."

Timo stepped forward and bowed.

"Councilor Timo! What a surprise. Toivo will be overjoyed to see you."

Eliinka motioned toward Milla, who stood at a distance. "Milla will show you to your rooms."

"And a servant will bring you to my study in two hours." Jereni nodded. "Yes, two hours should be enough time to refresh."

Karelia still held onto Eliinka's elbow.

"I'll be fine, Karelia," Eliinka said.

Jereni took Eliinka by her arm and helped her walk up the steps to the large doors. They slowly walked to Eliinka's room. Jereni's maid was already inside, pouring hot water into the bath. She bowed as she left.

"It is simple and short, but it's an agreement," Eliinka said as she handed Jereni the treaty. Exhausted, she wanted to collapse in her bed.

"Thank you." After Jereni skimmed the words, she set the parchment aside on the table. "Your hand?"

"It's healing. It's a long story," Eliinka sputtered.

"Give me a short summary right now."

"Before I talked with parliament, I was shot by an arrow," Eliinka explained. "Their sympathy may have helped facilitate the treaty. On our way back, after we had entered Viru, we were attacked by a group of renegade Peltens. I called and the Flute People came and assisted us. There were several injuries, but not one of your men died." Eliinka paused and swallowed the emptiness that caught in her throat. "We took no captives." They had left the handful of injured to fend for themselves.

"It appears we have more to talk about. But first, do you wish to bathe? You can give me your formal report tomorrow."

After Eliinka removed her dust-covered travel dress, she stepped behind the screen into the brass tub and sank into the water, relaxing as she basked in the comfortable warmth. Finally, she was warm. And for the first time since leaving Pelto, she could thoroughly bathe. This was much better than a bucket in the tent.

First, she washed the dust off, holding her right hand above the water to keep it dry. She struggled to wash and dry her hair with one hand. She did not hurry, and did not step out of the bath, until after the water had cooled. After drying off, she chose a dress from her cupboard, one of her more formal dresses. Jereni sat, waiting, in front of the fire, flipping through pages of a book.

As Eliinka awkwardly combed her hair with her left hand, she could no longer wait to ask the question that haunted her. "Timo told me a story,

one of the folktales of Viru. The folklore or tale of the crossing. Is it true?"
She sat next to Jereni, not sure if she wanted to hear her answer.

"It's often hard to discern what is true and what is not. How does one
determine truth?" Jereni took the comb from Eliinka's hand.

Eliinka closed her eyes and breathed out the dreaded question. "Do
you believe in the power, in the effect of the crossing?"

"Yes."

Eliinka's eyes sprang open. "Jereni, what have I done? Timo believes
in it and so does Karelia. And I shared the nightmilk cheese with Toivo
during our journey here. I didn't know."

"I could tell she had eaten it. I would have offered nightmilk to her if
you had not." Jereni continued to comb Eliinka's hair.

"But there is more. Timo met us just inside Viru and insisted that
I return to Pelto and cross again, with him. We crossed together on his
horse."

Jereni did not speak until she finished combing Eliinka's hair. "Toivo
will also come to the study today. Sit and rest until it's time to go."

Eliinka stumbled as she walked to her chair, as if her floor was uneven.
Jereni caught her. "Why do you struggle to walk?"

"The arrow that entered my hand was poisoned so I balanced between
life and death."

"Who—"

"Karelia saved my life and made our treaty possible," Eliinka interrupted. "She's healing me. She says it will take at least a week, maybe a
month or more, for me to recover."

"Obviously you took risks you should not have taken, but in doing
so, you opened the door to my dream of peace with Pelto. Thank you.
Eliinka, understand this. The treaty is preparing the ground and planting
the sapling of peace."

Jereni cracked open the door to the hall and spoke through the slit.
When she returned, she sat again and asked, "What do you know of
Karelia?"

"Almost nothing except that she is of Eleman Puusta." Eliinka
shrugged. "She doesn't say much about herself. I extended the Pelten hand
of friendship."

Jereni leaned forward. "Did she accept?"

"Not at first. But later I insisted and she accepted."

Worry lines streaked out from the corners of Jereni's eyes. "Show me
your hand."

As Eliinka loosened her bandage, her door opened. Karelia stopped inside the entrance, wearing the unreadable face that Eliinka had seen so many times. With her hair down and wearing a deep-red Virun dress, she could pass for any of the noblewomen in the palace.

"Karelia, come here," Jereni said in Pelten.

She stepped forward, stood in front of their chairs, and bowed.

Jereni narrowed her eyes. She raised her voice, and in Virjalo demanded, "Karelia, you know a sign, you gave me the sign of 'we must talk' in the courtyard, yet your name is not known to me. Explain yourself."

"She doesn't understand you."

Jereni ignored Eliinka.

After a small nod to Eliinka, Karelia crossed her wrists, palms up, and bowed her head to Jereni. She spoke in perfect, unaccented Virjalo. "I have disobeyed my instructions by coming here and will accept my punishment." She raised her chin. "The circumstances were unusual, and Eliinka insisted that she must return home. She could not travel without me. Fourteen years ago, when I was a child, I vowed my loyalty and my heart to the Kingdom of Viru and your father, King Juusi."

Eliinka inhaled, holding in her questions and thoughts.

"You pledged your heart to Viru." Jereni leaned back in her chair. "And you accepted the hand of friendship from Eliinka! It does not displease me, but it uniquely binds us together. What is your town?"

Karelia lowered her hands to her sides. "I am from KesKi, in the north."

"So Ilu chose you."

"Ilu, my nanny, taught me Virjalo and the ways of Viru. No one knows of this—not Kivi, not my mother. She was preparing me for an important task, she said, but then she suddenly died four years ago."

Jereni interjected, "Yes, before you were taught everything, before we had your name, and before you were made my subject. Yet Ilu chose well. You have already done more for Viru than most my agents do in a lifetime."

Karelia knelt. "Every year Ilu had me reaffirm my vows." She again extended her arms, crossed, palms up to Jereni. "Queen Jereni, I promise upon my very life to serve you, and the Kingdom of Viru, with all the efforts of my heart, mind, and body until my death."

Eliinka gasped.

Karelia's eyes shifted to Eliinka for a moment, but then her attention returned to Jereni. "What do you wish me to do?"

"At present, your main objective is to heal Eliinka. You made a good decision to accompany her. But you cannot return to KesKi. Another has filled Ilu's position. Now tell me about Eliinka's injury and why you chose to accompany her."

She removed the bandage from Eliinka's hand. Jereni touched the area around the wound. Her lips tightened. She flipped Eliinka's hand front to back, examining both sides.

"She should've stayed in Pelto to heal," Karelia said as she took Eliinka's hand. While she spoke, she moved Eliinka's fingers. "But we came. I didn't want her to die on the way. She needed my help. Now she needs to exercise her fingers. I help her manipulate them several times a day." Karelia rewrapped the hand. "I think Eliinka will be able to play the harp again. In time."

"Eliinka, how is your heart?" Jereni asked.

"I am alive." Eliinka tossed Jereni a half smile. "That is something."

"Your music will return. It must return."

"It might," Eliinka said.

Jereni turned to Karelia. "In saving Eliinka's life, you have saved the peace between Pelto and Viru. That pleases me and will please my husband, Mikali."

"Peace is a fragile thing, Queen Jereni. It is a cause worthy of great sacrifice," Karelia said. "I hope Pelto and Viru will someday achieve a real peace."

"Thank you," Jereni said, "for all you have done. For the sacrifices you have made. You will be rewarded as a sign of my appreciation. You and Kivi are invited to join me in my study this evening. At this time, it is best for you to pose as my honored guest and only speak in Pelten."

When Eliinka and Jereni entered the study, Mikali greeted Eliinka with a kiss on her cheek and placed his hand on Jereni's abdomen, patting their unborn child. He draped his other arm around Jereni's shoulder.

The room was as Eliinka remembered it, warm and inviting. A pleasant breeze, bringing with it the sweet scent of the lehti flower, entered through the open windows. Several lamps brightened the room and small flames flickered in the fireplace, the light tinkling on the strings of the token harp.

Rakel rose from a chair, approached Eliinka, and awkwardly bowed low. It appeared that her baby would be born soon. "Lady Eliinka, it is good to have you home with us."

It would take time, but Eliinka wanted to heal completely. "Rakel— no need to bow to me, and please, call me only by my name. I'd like to reclaim our friendship." Eliinka kissed Rakel on each cheek. "Come to my room tomorrow morning. We'll share a meal."

As Timo, Kivi, and Karelia entered, Jereni motioned them forward. Timo approached first, and Jereni took his hand. "Councilor Timo. Toivo will arrive soon."

"Karelia, welcome to my study." Jereni embraced and kissed Karelia on both cheeks with the Virun greeting. She nodded to Kivi.

Jereni's maid entered the room carrying a tray of goblets and a tall narrow pitcher. She set them on the low, central table. After returning with another tray of food, she filled the goblets with juice.

"Come, sit with us." Jereni took goblets for Mikali and herself and they sat. She leaned her head against Mikali's shoulder.

Eliinka settled into her chair, the one she had shared with Zerin. When Kivi sat next to her, she shifted away. His flirting was not appropriate. He didn't understand Viru. He would never understand her either.

The door swung open and Toivo ran to her father. They held each other tight until Toivo saw Eliinka.

"Eliinka!" Toivo rushed over, and, bouncing up and down, said, "It's so good to see you. You brought me my father."

"Your father wanted to visit you. Is everything well?"

"Yes." Toivo smiled big as she settled on the table in front of Eliinka. She knew that Toivo would soon tell her about everything that had happened while she'd been gone.

"Karelia and Kivi also returned with me." Eliinka motioned to her right. "Karelia saved my life. Her brother, Kivi, is a member of the Pelten parliament."

"You share your chair with him," Toivo said, smiling even larger. "Pelten men are more forward."

Kivi laughed and winked at Toivo, leaned closer to Eliinka, and put an arm around her shoulders, pulling her close.

This was too much! Eliinka jumped from her seat. For him to express friendliness in Pelto by touching her hand was very different than taking such privileges here. She had thought the study the most comfortable place in the world, but it wasn't tonight.

Eliinka plopped into the chair next to her token harp. This window in the study had a perfect view of the mountains between here and Pelto. She dropped her head into her hands. Pelto could never again be her home. The treaty wasn't strong enough, and it wasn't in people's hearts. She would never have another chance to visit Zerin's grave. Was it possible to soothe her heartache? She crossed her arms, wondering how she could play the harp with her injured hand. It would sound flawed.

"Eliinka, you have not yet found peace." Jereni flashed Kivi a warning glare.

Jereni stood, and after picking up the harp, sat in the chair nearest Eliinka. "Listen." She plucked one string after another as she went up the scale, each string echoing clearly. Pure music flowed as she picked out a one-handed melody. Arpeggios rolled beneath, adding depth to the song Jereni created.

"This might place you on a path toward hope." Jereni placed the harp into Eliinka's arms. "This harp is yours."

"You can't return it."

"Traditions can be broken. There are a few traditions that will be changed for my children, such as the one that brought you here. Any law can be changed by me." Jereni rested a hand on Eliinka's shoulder. "Think of the harp as a gift."

Eliinka had not thought it possible. She clasped her own harp and ripples of excitement spread into her fingers. After a moment, she reached up and touched the necklace.

"No. Keep it." A quaver entered Jereni's voice. "Will you move out of my palace?"

Eliinka winced. That thought hurt. "No. You are my sister, forever."

"Forever," Jereni echoed. Her shoulders and face visibly relaxed.

"Is it the time to tell Toivo?" Eliinka asked.

"It is." Jereni's voice jumped up several pitches.

After all, Eliinka thought, Jereni had found everything she wanted.

"Timo, Toivo, come look." Jereni led Toivo to the wall of portraits. She stood in front of her mother. "This is a portrait of my mother. She taught me about Pelto and passed to me her love for her native land."

"She looks like my grandmother," Toivo exclaimed.

"Your grandmother, Kulta," Jereni said. "Yes, my mother does. That is because Koru, my mother, is your grandmother's younger sister. My father brought her here from Pelto. I wanted to be sure of our relationship before telling you. Your mother is my cousin." Jereni hugged Toivo and held her tight. "Timo, Toivo, you can now be introduced as part of my family."

Jereni pulled Eliinka to her feet and embraced Eliinka, who still gripped her harp. "Thank you. You brought me my family. My mother would be pleased. She chose my name, and I now understand her hopes. Jereni is the ancient word for peace."

Timo gasped. "Koru is your mother? Queen Jereni, your mother and Eliinka's were best friends. Koru disappeared when she was traveling to Hlin's summer cottage."

"My mother mentioned Hlin to me at times. She is why my mother insisted I learn the harp." Jereni stared at Eliinka. "You never talk about your mother."

"My mother gave me her harp. She taught me to play." Eliinka flipped her harp upside down. The faded name, Hlin, was lightly scratched into the wood.

Jereni examined the bottom. "So this harp was your mother's?"

"Yes." Eliinka settled herself on the low table in front of the warm fire and held her harp close. Her left hand moved deftly across the strings, playing the lullaby, both the melody and part of the harmony, while her right forefinger lightly touched an occasional string so she could create overtones, and she used her gift lightly as she encouraged peace and relaxation. She imagined the future notes she would play on its strings when she was healed.

Upon finishing the tune, Eliinka stood, clutching her harp to her chest.

"I've never heard the lullaby played more beautifully," Jereni said.

Eliinka could still feel the music growing inside her and a warmth of healing. This was where she belonged.

"Jereni, I felt like I'd given part of myself away when I gave my harp as my token. I didn't trust you, not at first."

"Trust takes time." Jereni nodded. "So does friendship and love. Eliinka, you are my true friend."

Eliinka hugged Jereni. "I didn't think I'd ever love Viru, but I do, now and always. I am home."

~ FINIS ~

Acknowledgments

Enormous thanks to my husband and children. Our adventures of living internationally are life-changing and the catalyst for my becoming a writer.

This book would not exist without Katherine Cowley and Rose Green, brilliant writers who read many versions of the manuscript. I'm blessed to count them as friends.

Thank you to Kathi Appelt and Martine Leavitt who believed. Also, a big thank you to my early readers: Robin Prehn, Debi Faulkner, Karen Johnson, Rebecca Davis, Beth Nelson, Melinda Morley, Shea Hall, Kirsty Stewart, Elena Jube, Tracy Abell, and to my late-draft readers: Elayne Petterson, Hannah Moderow, Meredith Davis, Rukhsana Khan, and Kim Hurst. Their feedback was instrumental in this book's development. Others who helped me in various ways include Uma Krishnaswami and Tami Lewis Brown. Thank you to the wonderful community at Vermont College of Fine Arts. Also, much appreciation to BreAnne Johnson for reading the last draft.

The Republic of Finland, the amazing country where I lived when I initially wrote *Crossings*, holds a special place in my heart. I think of Finland as the birthplace of my writing.

Crossings is a book about friendship, although I didn't realize that until recently. Thank you especially to Nancy Palmer, Karen Stephenson, and Deeanna Price, true friends. Also, I'm grateful for all the friends I've made over the years who have enriched my life. This book is dedicated to all of my friends, each one of you.

Finally, I want to express gratitude to my mother, who taught me to read and love books.

About the Author

Sarah Blake Johnson has stepped in quicksand in Brazil, walked on the frozen Baltic Ocean in Finland, cooked dinner in a geyser in Iceland, learned to play an ancient instrument in China, explored abandoned castle ruins in Germany, worked as an economist in Nigeria, and scuba dived in the Red Sea in Egypt, all countries where she has lived.

She has an MFA in writing for children and young adults from Vermont College of Fine Arts and a bachelors in business management from Brigham Young University. When she isn't writing or spending time with her family, she can be found roaming with her camera.

Scan to visit

www.sarahblakejohnson.com